MARCO'S PENDULUM

First published in the UK in 2006 by Usborne Publishing Ltd.,
Usborne House, 83-85 Saffron Hill, London EC1N 8RT, England.
www.usborne.com

Cover photography: Glastonbury Tor © Greenhalf
Photography/CORBIS. Clouds © Digital Vision.

The name Usborne and the devices ♀ ⊕ are Trade Marks of Usborne
Publishing Ltd.

This is a work of fiction. The characters, incidents, and dialogues
are products of the author's imagination and are not to be construed
as real. Any resemblance to actual events or persons, living or dead,
is entirely coincidental.

A CIP catalogue record for this book is available from the British
Library.

JF AMJJASOND/06
ISBN 0 7460 6760 7
Printed in Great Britain.

MARCO'S PENDULUM

THOM MADLEY

USBORNE

Marco

Josh was Marco's mate and also his psychiatrist.

When he heard about the situation, he rocked back on the heels of his trainers, and then he clutched his chest like he was having a major heart attack.

Which wasn't how psychiatrists were supposed to behave. They were supposed to nod seriously, make notes, that kind of thing. Possibly Josh was just realizing this, because he recovered his composure and went to sit down behind his desk.

"Hold on...let me get this right." Josh opened his laptop. "You're telling me you've never seen them? *Ever?*"

"Well not these particular ones, no," Marco said.

"Like, *not once*, in your entire *life*?"

Marco sighed. "So this is unusual, right?"

"Unusual? *Unusual?*" Josh sank into his executive chair, shaking his head. "To have a whole pair of grandparents – a *complete set* – who are still alive, but you've never seen them? Ever?"

"Well, it's just that— "

"Okay." Josh raised his hands for silence. "Let me spell this out for you. Number one – presents. Do you realize how many presents you must've missed out on? Think about it. Count the birthdays, count the Christmases, *do the arithmetic.* You are one deprived person, Marco. Your situation is like out of the Third World."

Marco doubted this. His understanding was that, in the famine-stricken countries of the Third World, about four generations of the same family would be living in one small house. So, for your whole life, you'd probably be eating and sleeping with *all* your grandparents, in the same room.

Right now, they were in Josh's bedroom, which had this very executive feel – low, curved desk with, as well as the laptop, a lamp you could move electronically to any angle. All this was because Josh's bedroom also served as his consulting room.

"I'm being serious," Josh said. "To realize how bad your situation is, you have to understand the psychology of grandparents."

Marco sighed again. In Josh's view, everything came down to psychology: if you knew why people did what they did, you'd know what they were going to do next. So you'd always be ahead of them.

Josh's dad was a leading psychiatrist. Josh said that when he grew up he was going to be an even more leading psychiatrist because...well, obviously, because he'd already started. His dad had been, like, thirty or something before *he'd* started. Josh, however...by the time he was sixteen, he would know the inside of people's minds as well as he knew his own en suite bathroom.

Or, at least, he'd know the inside of *Marco's* mind, as Marco suspected he was Josh's only client.

"Okay." Using a dial on his desk, Josh angled the lamp on Marco. "What you have to understand about grandparents is that both sets like to think that they are the *major* grandparents – like, the ones who really count. So, if one set buys you a present, the others have to buy you a *bigger* present, to prove that *they* are the major grandparents. You getting it so far?"

Marco looked away from the light. The TV and the main computer were in a separate alcove because Josh's parents didn't like him to sleep in the same space as all that electronic radiation, in case it damaged his enormous brain.

"Now," Josh said, "once you understand this – as I did from an early age – you can start cashing in big time, playing one lot off against the other: 'Oh, look, Gran, this is what Granny Goldman bought me. Isn't it truly excellent?' And her eyes go all glazed and hunted-looking, and then she's straight off down the shops with her credit cards, before they close.

And, of course, if your parents get divorced, it's even better."

"Divorced?" Marco stiffened.

"Because now, you're looking at *serious* presents. This is because the two sets of grandparents always hate each other even more than the parents who've got divorced. And both sets think they have to make it up to you because they're the only evidence of stability in your life. Geddit?"

This was getting much too close to home. Marco needed to head Josh away.

"So, like...what if your *grandparents* get divorced?"

"Well, that's even more excellent," Josh said. "It means they *each* buy you a mega present, because they're each trying to outdo the other in the battle for your affections."

"All right then, what if your grandparents get divorced, and then they both get married again?"

Josh's eyes went all glazed and possibly hunted-looking, too. Excellent.

"And just suppose," Marco said, "that their new partners have already got ten grandchildren from previous relationships, and they're so broke from paying their lawyers that they can't afford much anyway?"

"That..." Josh folded his arms and looked stubborn. "...that could be outside the bounds of known psychology."

"That's *life*," Marco said bitterly.

Sometimes you could almost feel sorry for Josh, to whom money and possessions were everything. Every present he got, he was straight on the Net to make sure it was top-of-the-range and state-of-the-art and to find out how much it cost.

When you asked him about this, he just shrugged and said, *Doesn't everyone do that?*

"Anyway," Josh said, "in your case, none of this will ever happen. Your grandparents can get away with giving you any old crap, knowing they have no competition. It's tragic."

"Whatever," Marco said.

"However..." Josh pointed to the bed. "Sit down. I want to know all about this." He moused-up something on his laptop. "So the missing grandparents...these are your dad's parents, or your mother's?"

"Mother's."

"Uh huh." Josh tapped out a note. "Presumably you've seen your paternal grandparents?"

"Obviously. They only live in Islington."

"So where do your mother's parents live?"

"Miles and miles away. Like, hundreds of miles, probably."

"Tuscany?" Josh said. "Samoa?"

"Um..."

Josh started to smile, then looked evil. "You *delusional dweeb*! You don't even mean abroad, do you?"

Marco had that swollen feeling where you knew you were going red.

"Smmsst," he mumbled.

"Sorry?"

"Somerset."

There was a silence, broken only by the tap-tap of Josh putting the word into his organizer. When he looked up, his face was aglow with this kind of gleeful contempt.

"So that would be, like, Somerset in the West Country? That's – hold on, let me work this out – that's a whole *three hours' drive away*. Well. No wonder you've never seen them. They'd have to get up *really* early to come to London and make it home the same afternoon. Like...wooh...10 a.m."

"Okay," Marco said. He'd had enough. "What happened... I think there was a row, going back to before I was born. Maybe before my mum was even married to my dad. So like I don't actually think she's spoken to her mum and dad in years. So *I've* never had any contact with them either."

"Hah! A *family rift*."

They'd learned about rift valleys in geography, but Marco didn't think that this was where Josh was coming from.

"Family rifts," Josh said. "This is a well-known syndrome."

"Oh, a *syndrome*. Right."

With a little help from his dad, Josh could find a *syndrome* for everything. It was one of those words that meant whatever he wanted it to mean, and it got on your nerves after a while.

"Family rifts," Josh said, "are the most difficult kind. Where one side of the family hates the other, this can last whole lifetimes. Or whole generations. Which is when it turns into a feud, and then you're in real trouble. It's because inside families you've got, like, masses of *emotional baggage*. So your mother totally hates her parents, right?"

"I didn't say that."

"What then? Remember, you don't have secrets from your psychiatrist."

"Well, it...it's just that my mum's parents...my mum thinks...she thinks they're weird."

"Weird how?"

"I don't know. It's just what she says."

All the times, over the years, that Marco had asked his mum about her mum and dad, she'd been too busy to talk about it, or she'd just say, *We don't get on. They're weird.*

"Now that's interesting," Josh said. "Grandparents, in my experience, are seldom weird. Dull, certainly. Nosy...vaguely annoying...full of boring stories about the old days and how bad it was for them when they were kids. But weird, this is actually fairly uncommon, with grandparents, until they get really, *really* old."

"You're just saying that."

"No, I'm not, mate. Grandparents are blindingly predictable. They even all look the same."

"You're just saying that because you know I've got to go and stay with them, and I can't get out of it. You're just trying to make me anxious."

"Anxious?" Josh shut his laptop and leaned back in his leather chair. "Just because your parents are breaking up, and it means you've got to spend the entire summer in the West Country where they're all hicks and rednecks with yokelly voices...just because you've got to go and stay, *for the whole summer*, with some totally mad old people you have never met in your entire life before, *ever*, and who are so completely sick and weird that even your mother can't put it into words, which means they're probably totally *psychotic*..."

Josh pressed something that made the chair rise with this gassy noise, so that he was looking down on Marco, over his shining desk, with a totally evil grin on his fat face.

"...what on earth have you got to be *anxious* about?" Josh said.

Part One

In the wall

There was a monk.

It was. *It was.* Oh God.

She'd been trying to tell herself it was just damp patches or something, but she could see it now. Or, at least, she could *make* herself see it, and that was worse – now she knew *how* to see it. Any time.

What you did was turn your head on the pillow and half-close your eyes, so that they weren't focused on anything in particular, just the misty greyness of the wall. Normally, your eyes were either open or shut, so you didn't see things this way. But it happened automatically when you were just waking up and your eyelids felt like they'd been glued down, and if your head just happened to be turned the right way...

...then you would see him.

Him.

He'd be just a blur at first but he would slowly become more defined – those deep, quiet eyes, black smudges in the white face, watching you from far back in the folds of his cowl.

Oh please...

Rosa rolled over in bed, away from him, closing her eyes and bending the pillow over her head to block out everything.

Knowing, all the same, that she'd have to do it again – turn over and half-close her eyes so that the room went dark and the colours faded. Doing it in the hope that this time he *wouldn't* be there. Doing it time and time again, until it became compulsive. Well, she knew how *that* worked: every morning, she'd have to look at the monk four times before she was allowed to get up. And then it would be eight times. And then twelve times, and then...

Oh God.

Rosa screwed her eyes tight shut, and these squares appeared like tiny TV screens, images she'd trapped. The little, square window in her bedroom had been full of pale light for hours and hours, it seemed like. It must be nearly time to get up, and she did *want* to get up.

And yet she didn't. That is, she didn't want to get up *here*. She'd never lived in the middle of a town before, and it had been cool at first, looking out of your bedroom window and seeing shops down there.

Which would have been all right if they'd been ordinary shops, selling food and sweets and DVDs and clothes and perfume and jewellery and things.

But they *weren't* ordinary shops, and although some of them did sell clothes they weren't ordinary clothes either.

Some were more like robes. A bit scary.

And the jewellery, if you could call it that, would be, like, flat stones with strange markings on them and faces. And the perfume you could smell when you went into some of the shops was strange and musky and *not ordinary.*

This was not an ordinary town. It was a dead old town. When her dad had taken her to see the Abbey, there'd been a sign that said the Abbey itself was *so ancient that only legend can record its origin.*

To Rosa, *ancient* had somehow come to mean *dark.*

Which was odd, because this town wasn't actually dark at all. It had buildings and stonework the colour of lightly-tanned skin, and the roofs were covered with bright red tiles. It was much lighter than the grey northern town where Rosa had been brought up.

But it was more ancient, and so it was dark.

Dad knew something about that. Dad looked dark, too, these days. Grim.

Like the sky. The sky over this town was always a gloomy grey. They'd been living here for nearly a week and, although it was summer and quite warm, there hadn't been one sunny day.

Not that you'd notice the sun much, anyway, inside this

dingy flat. With its small rooms and its small windows, the narrow stairs and the nightly sound of people being drunk out in the street, this flat was a totally, *totally* crap place.

How could somewhere this crap be *home*?

Except to a ghostly monk in the wall.

Rosa started to sweat. She wanted a shower. But how was she going to get to the bathroom without looking at the wall?

She pulled the pillow tighter over her head. This was a dead awful place. And when the holidays were over she'd have to go to a dead awful school full of strange kids who spoke with curly, drawly accents.

And then she'd come home, and it would be dark and she'd have to go to bed in this minging little room with the monk in the wall. Who would still be there when it went dark. And even though she couldn't see him in the dark, *he* could see *her*. He'd be watching her all night, standing in the wall.

Rosa caught her breath before it could come out as a sob.

She could hear her dad moving around downstairs. Her dad, who didn't like this town either. Once, when they didn't know Rosa was listening from behind the door, he'd said to Mum that this town was evil.

So why, if he hated it so much, had they *come* here? *Why?*

Dad didn't know about the monk in the wall, and Rosa knew there was just no way she could ever tell him.

Maybe Mum, though, when they were on their own. Just *maybe* Mum...

Dumped

"**O**f *course* they're not weird," Marco's dad said.

"*Mum* says they're weird. Mum says—"

"Mum says a lot of things." Dad's lips went tight, and he almost threw Marco's bag into the back of the Volvo, and Marco was worried because his laptop was in that bag, and while it wasn't as expensive as Josh's laptop it was still a pretty crucial piece of kit. It was how they'd keep in touch.

It was a dull morning in July. The blocks of flats were stacked all around, like cardboard packing cases at Sainsbury's, and what you could see of the river was flat and still and dark grey, like tarmac.

And Marco had this sense of being double-crossed.

At least, he was certain, now, that his dad was double-crossing his mum. And this, in Marco's experience, would always rebound on *him*.

He glanced back over the seat at the red bag containing his laptop, a stack of games and DVDs. And Marvin, the little blue stuffed rabbit. Josh would probably have a special psychological term for kids who carried around a stuffed rabbit at the age of thirteen, even if it was zipped up in a bag with Manchester United on it, but Marvin and Josh had mutual history.

So what you need to do before you go is find out exactly why your mother hates her folks so much, Josh had said. *Is it maybe because they didn't like your dad and didn't want her to marry him? Or is it something really heavy? This could be fascinating.*

Fascinating. Sure. Seriously fascinating for Josh and Josh's dad, the senior psychiatrist. But Josh didn't have to go and spend the whole summer with grandparents he'd never seen in his whole life before.

And who were weird.

As they came off the M25 onto the M4, Dad sighed.

"Sorry, mate."

He meant he was sorry about Mum. Dad seemed to say he was sorry every time Mum was mentioned. But the time for being sorry was *well* over. Mum and Dad as an item – that was like the Norman Conquest, the Wars of the Roses, Atomic Kitten. History.

They weren't actually divorced yet, just having a *trial separation.*

Huh.

Marco hated the way they were so polite to one another, and distant and cold. It was terrible to have to watch and made him feel really lonely.

There was one particular night, about a month ago, when Dad had come to the house and, after a lot of polite stuff between him and Mum, Marco had gone to bed. But, by the time he'd doubled-back and had his ear to the door, Mum had been going off like a whole box of fireworks.

"No, *you'll* have to have him. I'm telling you, I've *got* to go, I can't put it off. It's my career. Look, it'll take four weeks, that's all – maybe six, to include editing. So *you* can take some responsibility for a change!"

Dad had mumbled something about Mum's parents that Marco couldn't quite make out, but that had *really* set Mum off.

"*Them?* Are you *insane?* Listen, I've managed to keep him out of that madhouse for nearly twelve years, and I'm not ruining everything now, not for the sake of you and your precious girlfriend."

At this point, Marco had heard Dad stamping towards the door and had raced back to his bedroom in a state of mild shock.

Dad had a girlfriend?

Next day, Mum had sat Marco down and told him she had

to go to America for a month or so, to make a documentary for the BBC. She'd said Marco would be staying with Dad at Dad's new flat. She hadn't said anything about the precious girlfriend. Or the grandparents.

It was his dad who'd first mentioned them. This was on the afternoon of the second day of the school summer holidays, when they'd watched his mum drive off to the airport. As Mum's BMW was shrinking into the distance, Dad had kind of coughed.

"Look, matey...okay...there's been a change of plan. Something's come up at the office, and it means I'm going to be a whole lot busier than I was expecting. So we've arranged for you to go and stay with your grandparents, down in Somerset."

Just like that! Not a word about it until Mum was out of the way.

"But—"

"Hey..." Dad grabbed hold of Marco's shoulders and beamed at him. "Listen, I just can't tell you how much I envy you."

"Huh?"

"All those green fields and rolling hills. Your grandparents...they've even got their own *fields*! It's going to be, you know, absolutely great. Wow! I only wish *I* was going to be staying there, too, instead of being cooped up in this boring old city."

"But I've never—"

"You'll have a *fantastic* time. The way you're into history? Marco, I have to tell you, that whole area is just *oozing* history

– ancient buildings, a medieval abbey. Come on, you love all that stuff, don't you? And, hey, they're dying to meet you!"

Marco was bewildered. How did his dad know they were dying to meet him? If his mum didn't speak to her own parents, how come his dad did? They weren't *his* parents. How long had he been going behind Mum's back? What kind of deal was going down here?

It was like...he was being *dumped*.

He glared at his dad. "Does Mum know I'm going?"

Marco's dad coughed again. "Of course she knows."

Oh yeah, sure. Right from the start, Marco had realized that this was probably something Dad had fixed up on his own, to get the kid off his hands. Probably so he could spend more time with his *precious girlfriend*. Whom Marco had never met. The world was full of people Marco had never met, and some of them were weird.

"Actually, Mum *doesn't* know," Dad had admitted. "I'm taking you into my confidence here, okay? You've got to keep this a secret."

"A secret."

"An *important* secret," Dad said.

Which was why Marco had only told Josh. And then wished he hadn't. Okay, all that stuff Josh had come out with about his grandparents being psychotic axe-murderers, that was just...

...like, it was just...

Get me out of this!

* * *

"You remember what I said about keeping it a secret?" Dad said. "You have, haven't you? I mean you haven't told anyone?"

Marco said nothing.

Dad looked straight ahead as they followed the signs that said: *Bristol and The West.* He was wearing a shirt with thin black stripes, and a tie. His jacket was carefully hung up in the back of the car. Dad was a lawyer, but not the interesting kind. Not the kind who got to appear in court defending people accused of murder; Dad just dealt with companies and boring stuff.

"Perhaps I need to explain a few things," Dad said.

"Oh."

Mum had once told Marco that when Dad said he was going to explain something, it didn't necessarily mean he was going to tell you the truth. This was because he was a lawyer, Mum said, but she was clearly hacked off with Dad at the time.

Right, then. Marco decided this was as good a time as any to force the issue.

"So, like, does this mean you're going to tell me exactly why Mum hates her parents?"

"What?" The car jerked as Dad's foot slipped off the accelerator.

"Like, why we've never been to visit them? Why they've never been to visit *us*? Like, why I'm going to stay with people my mum hates worse than chocolate cream eggs and Channel Five?"

"Good heavens." Dad shuffled in his seat. "Marco, it's not that she *hates* them, it's just that they're...different. Yes, that's the word – different."

"Different." This could take a while. "Meaning what?"

"Just that they have different ideas about how things should be done. How life should be lived. Nothing *wrong* with that. Most people like to do things differently from their parents...sort of break away. And, of course, Mum always wanted to work for the BBC, and she couldn't do that without moving to Bristol or London."

"Did they have a big row about it?"

"They just accepted they were very different kinds of people, and that was it. And that's why...er...that's why, when your mum rings you on your mobile, from America, it might be as well to say you're still in London."

Marco blinked. "You want me to *lie*?"

"Of course not. Just don't tell her everything. If she asks about me, just go on about me being busy all the time and tell her about the stupid things Josh has said."

"You mean so she'll think I'm still hanging out with Josh, therefore I'm still in town, right?"

"Exactly. It's for the best, Marco. She's a long way away, and she's got a very demanding job, and we don't want to worry her, do we?"

"This is what you lawyers call being economical with the truth, isn't it?" Marco said.

"Oh look, here's a service area," Dad said. "Why don't we have an early lunch? I thought we could spend the afternoon checking out Somerset before we go to your, um, grandparents'. Just the two of us. Guys' day out."

"Why?"

"To show you what a...what a cool place it is. Let you get a feel for the area."

"Won't they...I mean, won't my grandparents show me around?"

"Well, yes. Kind of. It's just..."

"What?"

"I don't think they have a car," Dad said.

"*Everybody* has a *car*."

"Well, yes, everybody...that is, everybody—" Dad parked the car opposite the burger bar.

"You were going to say 'everybody normal', weren't you?" Marco said.

In the burger bar, they both had cheeseburgers.

"Good?" Dad asked, when Marco had finished his.

"It was okay."

"Because, er...because you probably won't get another burger for quite a while."

"Huh?"

"I think I'm right in saying your grandparents don't eat burgers. They don't eat, er, normal food."

"What do they eat – *children*?"

"Ha ha," Dad went. "Ha, ha, ha, ha, ha."

Only, his eyes weren't going *ha ha.* Not at all.

The Shadows of Dark Things

"What kind of monk?" Rosa's mum asked. "And how do you *know* it's a monk?"

Telling her hadn't been easy. It sounded totally daft when you came out with it. Rosa had been arguing with herself all morning about whether to say something. Looking for signs to decide the issue, like *If the sun comes out, I have to tell her.*

It had been such a gloomy morning that this had seemed unlikely. They hadn't seen Dad – he'd gone across to the church to follow the vicar around and learn where the wine and the wafers and things were kept, because it was going to be his turn to take a service this Sunday. So Rosa and Mum had been on their own, rearranging furniture to try and make this place less like an overcrowded second-hand shop.

It was while Mum was washing up after lunch that it had happened – for the first time this week. Weak rays of sunlight fanned across the draining board.

So that decided it: something horrible would happen to Rosa or, even worse, to Mum, if she didn't tell her.

"One with...with a thing over his head," Rosa said.

"Cowl."

"Yeah. So you can't really see his eyes, but you know he's looking at you from under there."

"Right," Mum said, and Rosa could have sworn she smiled to herself as she stacked a dish on the drainer. It was the blue drainer they'd brought from home. It was the only blue thing in the kitchen, and it didn't look happy here. The drainer, like all the cups and saucers, and the knives and forks and the toaster – and Rosa – just wanted to go home.

But their old house wasn't home any more. They'd sold it. They couldn't go back to it, because it belonged to someone else now. *This* was home.

Nooooooooooooo!

"Did you sleep all right?" Mum asked.

Rosa shrugged.

"You'll soon get used to it. I've never lived in the middle of a town before, either."

"Mum, it's not even a proper house!"

"It's a flat. Lots of people live in flats."

"Not over the top of somebody's filthy old shop," Rosa said.

Then she wished she hadn't mentioned the shop. Because of the monk, she'd managed to go to the toilet, have a wash, get dressed and eat breakfast without once thinking about the old shop.

She looked down into her cup of tea. "Mum, are we really poor?"

"Of course we're not poor." Mum came over and stroked Rosa's hair. "You keep asking that, but we're not."

"Hmm," Rosa said. She'd asked her dad, too, and he'd said nobody was poor if they had God on their side.

Yeah. Big deal.

"And we'll have a proper house, quite soon," Mum said. "In a quieter road with not much traffic. We're just staying here until your dad gets settled in as curate, and we'll have more money when I start work at The George and Pilgrims tomorrow. We're not rich, and good houses are more expensive around here, but we'll be all right. We'll find something."

Rosa didn't see why, if his big mate God was everywhere, her dad couldn't be a curate back home in the North, but she didn't say anything. She tried to drink her tea, but her lips were kind of trembling on the rim of the mug.

"This monk," Mum said thoughtfully. "Would *I* be able to see him, do you think?"

Rosa thought for a long time before answering.

By then, she discovered she was crying.

"I don't know," she whispered. She felt ashamed.

Mum came and sat down and looked at Rosa and then pursed her lips and thought to herself for a few moments. This was something Mum often did, like she was wondering if you were old enough for her to discuss what was on her mind.

Then she said, "You remember that shop we went into a couple of days ago. Where we bought the crystal ornament to send to your gran?"

Rosa nodded. She hated most of the shops here, but she'd liked that one. It was all glittery, like a magic cave, with chunks of glistening, twinkling rock for sale. The big ones had been really expensive, so they'd had to buy a very small one for Gran. It had come in a white box, with a gold label that said, *The Crystal Grotto of Glastonbury: stones that heal.*

"You remember the man in charge of the shop asked if we were on holiday," Mum said, "so I had to explain about your dad's new job."

Rosa sniffed. She'd kind of liked the man, too. He'd kept putting on mysterious smiles, like he was full of secrets, and he'd had on this purple smock thing that looked soft and fuzzy, like the linings of jewel boxes.

"Oh," Rosa said. "I think I know what you're going to say."

The man had told them he felt this was really *his place.* He said he'd always wanted to rent a shop on High Street, because nearly all the shops and houses here backed on to the ruins of Glastonbury Abbey and some of the back walls had actually been built out of stones from the Abbey walls. So this shop was really part of the Abbey, and that was what gave the shop its awesome atmosphere.

Rosa remembered wondering if their own building, which was only a short way up the street, had also been built out of the old Abbey stones. This idea had even made her feel a bit better about the place...until they got home and it was just as gloomy as ever and not the least bit glittery.

"I know what you're going to say."

"Go on, then," Mum said

"That guy said he felt at home here because he was sure that, in a previous life, he'd been a monk at the Abbey, before it was destroyed by Henry VIII. Right?"

Mum nodded. "And when we came out, I said that was fine if it helped him feel at home."

"And I said I wished there was something to help *me* feel at home."

Both of them knew Dad would have said the man was talking rubbish, as nobody had ever had a previous life. You only had one, and then, as long as you'd been a fairly good person, you went to heaven. So this man was just fooling himself. Dad said this town was full of people fooling themselves.

"You kept asking about the Abbey all that night," Mum said. "And we said we'd take you to look at it on Saturday. And we did."

"Yes."

There had been no abbey there at all really, just ruins.

Rosa looked over Mum's shoulder at the kitchen window. Down below, there was a very small, overgrown garden with two spindly trees in it and a high wall. Dad said that when the trees lost their leaves in the autumn you'd be able to see into the Abbey grounds from this window.

"Did you have dreams about what the man said in the shop?" Mum asked. "About the stones of the Abbey going into the walls of the older buildings in High Street?"

"Not that I can remember," Rosa said. "See, I knew you'd think it was that."

"Think what?" Mum asked. She knew exactly what, of course, but Mum always liked *you* to say it.

"You think I must've scared myself thinking about the ghosts of the old monks hovering around the ruins. And that, like, if the stones from the Abbey had gone into these walls, that maybe...maybe one of the monks had kind of...come with them."

Mum shrugged. "It was just a thought."

"And because his spirit was in the piece of stone, his shape had somehow formed in the plaster..."

"You've always had a wonderful imagination, Rosie."

"That is totally daft," Rosa said.

"I'm glad you think so."

"Insane," Rosa said. "Bonkers."

"And even if it *was* true, which it isn't..."

"...because Dad says there's no such thing as spirits, apart from the Holy Spirit, which is different?"

"Yes," Mum said, although Rosa knew she didn't always go along with everything Dad said. "But even if it was true, Rosie, the point about monks is that, while they might have looked a bit sinister in those long robes that made it look like they were floating around with no feet..."

"Aw, Mum, look—"

"That was just to keep their legs warm in the stone cloisters in the wintertime."

Rosa shook her head slowly and then raised her eyebrows.

"You know, Mum," she said, "sometimes you talk to me like I'm about five years old."

Mum smiled her most brilliant smile.

"Hey," she said, "in our nightmares, we're *all* five years old."

"What's that mean?"

"I don't really know." Mum stood up. "Let's go and buy some bread before all the crusty cobs have gone."

"Okay."

"And then we'll call in at the DIY shop and see if they've got any of that white emulsion paint left that they were selling off cheap because the cans were dented. And when we come back, we'll paint your bedroom wall. What do you think?"

"Right." Rosa found a grin. "Cool."

They might not have much money, but when Mum realized there was something that was really *really* bothering you, she'd always do her best to put things right.

And usually it worked.

The problem was that to get out of the flat you had to go past the door to the old shop.

The shop was closed down now, which was so much worse than if it had been open.

It was directly underneath the flat. It had a front door to the street, but there was also a side door, which led into the passage at the bottom of the stairs leading down from their flat.

And while the front window had black blinds down over it, so you couldn't see in from the street, the door in the dim and musty hallway, at the bottom of the stairs, had a pane of glass in it and no blinds.

If the doors upstairs were open, light would come down the stairs and the window in the shop door would just be full of cloudy reflections, like a switched-off TV.

But when – like this morning – the upstairs flat had to be locked up and the hallway was dark, you could see through the glass pane into the old, abandoned shop. You could see dangling bulbs and cobwebs and the shadows of dark things. It was a place that was always dark, day and night, a place where there were no colours.

The door was locked, of course. She'd made herself try it once and had been dead relieved that it was locked. Every time she went past, she told herself she was definitely *not* going to look through that window into the place of endless darkness.

And yet she did. Every time.

She had to. If she didn't look through the glass, the shadows in the old shop would start to move...and then, behind her, as she went past, she would hear a key turning in a lock and then the hollow creak of the door beginning to open.

"Rosa?"

Mum was standing by the front door, shaking her head.

"Sorry." Rosa had bent down, pretending the lace on one of her trainers had come undone.

"Rosa, I *promise* we'll be gone by the end of the summer."

Rosa froze. "Gone?"

"Found somewhere else to live," Mum said. "Somewhere... normal."

"You mean..." Rosa stood up and turned her back on the pane of darkness. "You mean in another town?"

Mum smiled a funny kind of smile. Well, not funny at all, really. It was too dark in here to be sure, but Rosa thought there were actual tears in her eyes.

The Hill

Marco was starting to feel seriously messed around.

The plan for the *guys' day out* had crashed big time when Dad's mobile had gone off, just as they were leaving the burger bar.

Dad had snapped it open and he'd been like, *Who? When did this happen? Typical! Can't leave you people to handle anything, can I?*

After that, it was over three hours – *three hours,* could you believe that? – before they'd hit the road again. All that time they'd spent in the motorway service area, with Dad either calling people on his mobile or sitting tapping his fingers on the dash while he waited for somebody to call *him*.

Sorry, matey, he'd said every now and then, *it's what I do.*

Yeah. Whatever. Marco had tramped around the motorway service area and found it was...well, it was a motorway service area. Couple of computer game machines, pretty obvious stuff.

Now they'd finally left the motorway behind and they were well into the countryside. There were long hills and woods and church towers and steeples, and roads that snaked between the hills so that the sun kept disappearing and then bobbing up again, going orange now and turning the landscape the colours of toast under a grill.

Eventually, the hills gave way to green fields with the odd river trickling through them. The air was hazy, as if the ground had been steaming.

"These are the Somerset wetlands," Dad said. "I believe all this used to be under the sea."

"When?"

"Oh, I don't know. Centuries and centuries ago, I expect."

Marco looked around. It *did* look as if it had been under water. In fact, you half-expected to see boats that had run aground. For almost as far you could see, the land was totally flat, except for...

"What's that, Dad?"

"What?"

"That funny hill."

"Which one?"

"What do you mean, *which one*? How many funny hills can *you* see?"

The one Marco could see was completely on its own. Normally, hills were clustered among other hills, but this one just rose up suddenly, like it had been...*put there*. Or, like, computer-generated. In the late-afternoon light, it was grey-brown and misty. It was like a rounded Egyptian pyramid, or a pear with a stalk rising from the point.

It was so out of place you just couldn't stop looking at it.

"Ah," Dad said. "That one. Yes. That must be, um, the Tor."

"What's that on top of it?"

"On top?"

"On top of the funny hill, Dad."

"Ah. I think that's probably, ah...a church. Well, not a whole church, just the tower. That's all that's left, I believe."

"It's weird."

"Oh, it's just a hill," Dad said casually. "Just a hill. *Such* a pity we didn't have time to go to Weston-super-Mare, on the coast, we could've had—"

"Why would anyone build a church on top of a hill, Dad?"

"I have no idea, Marco." Dad sounded a touch impatient now.

"I mean they wouldn't do that now, would they? Disabled people wouldn't be able to get their wheelchairs up."

"I expect that's why it isn't used any more," Dad said through his teeth.

But Marco was into this now. The strange hill dominated the whole landscape, and he had this feeling that he'd seen it before somewhere. The way you sometimes thought you'd remembered seeing something in a dream...only you hadn't really, you'd probably just seen a picture, or something on TV, and forgotten about it.

A thought came to him. He watched his dad driving, eyes fixed steadily on the road ahead.

"I don't suppose, Dad, that this would be, like, in the general area of where we're going?"

"What?"

"This hill?"

"Er..." Dad's eyes began to swivel. "Well, probably not far away. I mean, I'm guessing. It's years since I was here. Years and years. And years. Yes."

"What's it called?" Marco said. "The hill."

"I told you. The Tor. I think."

Now the weird hill had disappeared, and the landscape was more bumpy, and there were more trees and then more buildings – indications that they were coming to a village or maybe a town. And then a sign appeared.

The sign said:

GLASTONBURY

Ancient Isle of Avalon.

Marco stared at Dad.

"Huh?" he said.

"Problem?" Dad said.

"But this...this is *Glastonbury*."

"Didn't I say?"

"*This* is where they live? But this is like—"

"Where the rock festival's held, yes," Dad said, like this was some minor detail. "The Glastonbury Festival."

Marco blinked. "But that...that's like the biggest music festival, probably, in the entire world! *Dad*...why didn't you *tell* me?"

"Didn't want you getting overexcited, matey." Dad tossed the map into the back. "Because, you see, they held it last month. It's all over now."

"Well, I know *that* – it was on TV."

And now he remembered where he'd seen the weird hill. It was always there in the distance when the bands were onstage at Glastonbury and the coloured lights were strobing and flashing.

"And, it's only *called* the Glastonbury Festival," Dad said. "It's actually held on farmland a couple of miles away. And don't expect to see The Darkness or Franz Ferdinand around the town. They just come for the festival and then they vanish again for another year, and Glastonbury goes back to sleep."

"You didn't tell me it was an island, either," Marco said.

"The Isle of Avalon?" Dad laughed, as he pulled out into the traffic. "That's a bit of a joke, actually. Avalon just means apples, I think – there have always been lots of apple orchards around here. And, apparently, Glastonbury used to be an island, centuries ago, when the sea used to come right up to it. But now, of course, the sea's about twenty miles away. So you see, that's a bit of a con."

"A con."

"There's a lot of that sort of thing in Glastonbury. It's, er...well, you'll see."

"See what?" Didn't you just hate it when there was stuff other people knew and you didn't? "Dad..."

"What?"

"Are you being, like, economical with the truth again?"

"I do very much wish," Dad said, "that your mother had never taught you that insulting phrase."

"Well, are you?"

Dad abruptly pulled the car into the side of the road. A lorry driver behind hooted in annoyance and then accelerated past. Dad applied the handbrake, switched off the engine and turned to face Marco.

"Okay," Dad said. "You're not a child any more. You're old enough to form your own opinions. So I'm going to spell it out for you. I'm going to tell you the situation."

Marco sank back in his seat. He hadn't been expecting this.

"You mean about...?"

"About your mum, and why she, ah, doesn't get on with your, ah, grandparents."

"Oh."

Dad loosened his tie and wiped a blob or two of sweat from his chin.

"You see, there are some towns that are...not like other towns. And they attract a certain type of people. People who are..."

"Different?" Marco said.

"Bonkers," Dad said. "That's probably the best word."

"What?"

"What it comes down to...there are some people who live

in Glastonbury who have funny ideas about the town. They think it's a...a *special* place, where strange things are supposed to happen. In fact, they get totally obsessed by it, so that the town – the idea of just *being here* – has come to dominate their lives in a way that seems ridiculous to sophisticated urban types like you and me."

Marco looked out of the side window and couldn't see anything strange. There were buildings on both sides now, and a garage. And, although he could see a long green hill, he could also see what looked like factories, with the sun burnishing their metal roofs and reflecting off their skylights. He saw a few ordinary-looking suburban shops and a newsagent's poster that said: *TOWN SPLIT OVER AVALON WORLD*.

The Isle of Apples was a nice name, but so far this seemed to be a town like any other town: boring.

"Why do they think it's special?" he said.

Dad took in a long breath through his nose. "I expect your grandparents will tell you about that. Sooner or later. The thing is, they believe in all this stuff, and your mother...doesn't believe in any of it. And she didn't want you to be exposed to what...what *they* believe in."

"What about you? Do you believe in it...whatever it is?"

Dad laughed. "Of *course* not. But, you see, I don't let it *worry* me the way your mother does. I accept that some people are a bit..."

Dad started the car.

"A bit what?" Marco said.

"Well..." Dad glanced in his rear-view mirror and drove off. "You know..."

"Bonkers."

"I didn't say that," Dad said.

"Yes, you did. You can't go back on it now."

"All right, I did, but—"

"My grandparents are bonkers." Marco kept his voice flat. "Not weird, just bonkers."

"Well...you know...in a *harmless* kind of way."

"Harmless."

"Oh, *Marco*..."

"Let me get this right. You are dumping me with some people who are, like—" Marco had a vision of Josh's fat, evil grin. *So completely sick and weird that even your mother can't put it into words.*

"Anyway," Dad said. "It'll be an experience for you. A lot different from the city. And that's, you know, that's *good*. But, hey, if you're at all worried about what's going on, why don't you...keep a kind of diary?"

"A diary?"

"A personal record of all the, ah, things that are happening. Type it all into your laptop, and then e-mail it to me."

"That wouldn't be a *personal* diary, then, would it?"

"Well, no, but it would be, ah...my way of keeping an eye on you. And it would give you a point of contact. Like if...something odd was happening."

"You think something odd might happen?"

"I don't think anything, matey. But if it *did*...then you

could tell me about it, couldn't you? And I could, ah... advise you."

Marco felt his eyes narrowing. Was this his dad's attempt to convince himself that he was still fulfilling his proper parental role while actually having a good time with his girlfriend, with his kid well out of the picture?

"So what you do, matey, what you do *is*...you sit down every night – up in your bedroom where it's quiet – and you tell me what's going on. Unload all your problems. A sort of...father-and-son e-mail consultation process. Give me something to look forward to when I come in from the office. Let me know you're all right."

"What if I'm not all right?"

Dad beamed. "Then I'll come and collect you, of course. Like a shot."

"Tell you what, Dad..." Marco found he'd tightened his seat belt so far he could hardly breathe. "...why don't we save all that e-mail expense and you just, like, turn the car around now?"

Due to the seat belt, his voice had come out all tight and strangled. Dad just laughed and drove on. Was this the same Dad who, just a few hours ago had said scornfully, *Weird? Of course they're not weird*?

Marco wrenched the seat belt even tighter to hold in a deep sense of personal betrayal.

Totally mad old people! Josh shrilled in his head.

Completely sick and weird!

Probably totally psychotic!

Dad grinned and patted Marco on the knee and drove into the centre of Glastonbury, where – like it had been devised especially to welcome them – something seriously bizarre was already beginning to happen.

Droopy

Rosa and her mum had spent most of the afternoon in town. After they bought the paint, Mum said she had some other things to do, although Rosa suspected she just didn't want to go back to their dingy flat.

The sun had stayed out, and the air in High Street was warm but kind of dull and somehow yellow, as if you were looking at the world through a Lucozade bottle. Rosa felt strange, like she was floating in it and nobody could see her.

And, probably, nobody could. Or bothered to. They all must have thought they were *far* more exotic than a dull girl from the North. All these people in their odd clothes – like the guy wearing a pink top hat, and one woman, who was probably as old as Mum, with so many rings in her bottom lip it looked like a coiled spring, and you could imagine it springing out and bits of lip flying everywhere and...*yuk*.

Mum saw her wince. "What are you thinking about now?"

Rosa shrugged. She was fed up with being told she had too much imagination.

They had tea in a café that was called The Cosmic Carrot and did vegetarian food and nothing else. Rosa had a vegetarian pasty, which didn't taste so very different from an ordinary Cornish pasty. The waitress who took their order had green and purple hair and wore an apron with MEAT IS MURDER printed on it. When she came back with the food, she was carrying a tray, so the only word you could see was MURDER. Rosa didn't like that; she was afraid it was a *sign*.

When they came out, they walked up towards the church with the tall tower, where Dad was going to work. There was a war memorial in front, with a tall stone cross and steps up to it. Around it, a band was playing. Well...if you could call it a band and if you could call it playing. Someone was banging on the kind of drums you hit with your hands, and someone else was blowing down something that looked like an exhaust pipe off a lorry and was just going *whump, whump* without any kind of tune to it. They all looked a bit miserable.

Pointless, really, Rosa thought. It was like a lot of people on the street were playing some kind of dressing-up game, and...well, they were *adults*.

"It's like someone's making a film here," Rosa said.

Mum looked at her, curious.

"Like *Lord of the Rings* or something," Rosa said. "It's like all these people are...what do you call the ones who aren't really actors? The ones who are just there for the background."

"Extras?"

That was it. It was like all these people were extras, just hanging around waiting for someone to shout 'action'. Except that, in the heavy air, most of them looked too droopy for any kind of real action.

She saw a man walking up the street wearing a long, brown robe-type thing like a priest, but not a priest like Dad, this one was halfway to being a...

...a monk.

Rosa felt a shiver in her insides and was glad when Mum took her into the estate agents' to pay the rent on the flat. At least everyone in here wore ordinary suits and ties.

"Settling in, Mrs. Wilcox?"

A thin man with a thin moustache and gelled hair had come out of an office at the back.

"We're fine, thank you, Mr. Coombes." Mum handed the man some money. "We're very grateful you could find somewhere for us."

"Connections." Mr. Coombes tapped his nose. "Of course, if the owner decides to sell his shop, the flat will go with it and we'll have to try and find you somewhere else."

"Perhaps we'll have found a proper house by then." Mum was looking at all the photos of houses for sale on the walls.

"It's just that they're all...well, more expensive than we'd expected."

"Yes, the area's becoming a lot more sought after, despite all the rabble on the streets. And..." Mr. Coombes lowered his voice. "Word to the wise, Mrs. Wilcox...I wouldn't wait *too* long because soon...quite soon...prices are going to rise quite steeply. Mark my words."

"Oh dear," Mum said. "We'll have to live in a tent."

"Or perhaps your husband will be promoted to vicar, and then the Church will give you a house," Mr. Coombes said brightly.

Mum smiled. "I think that could be quite a while. He's only recently been ordained."

"Oh, really? What did he do before he, er, answered God's Call?"

"He was a policeman," Mum said.

"Really." Mr. Coombes's face went serious. "Well, Mrs. Wilcox, I'm afraid there are quite a few people in this town who'd be rather glad if he was *still* a policeman. There aren't anywhere near enough police on these streets to cope with all the problems we have now – the drugs and the drunkenness and the break-ins. Still, I expect your husband will keep an eye on things. Once a copper, eh?"

"Yes, I..." Mum looked a bit worried. "I expect he will."

"And how do *you* like it here?" Mr. Coombes bent down. "Rose, isn't it?"

"Rosa," Rosa said, and left it at that. No way did she want to tell this man how she liked it here. There was the polite answer and there was the truth, and Dad said you should always, always, *always* tell the truth.

"Got any friends here yet, Rosa?"

"Er...not really." And telling the truth about what she thought of this town wouldn't exactly make her any.

"Can't have that," said Mr. Coombes, and he looked around. "Jasper!"

Oh no... Rosa's heart seriously sank. She'd become aware of a boy of about her own age, maybe a bit older, leaning against one of the display stands, unwrapping a stick of chewing gum.

"This is my son, Jasper," Mr. Coombes said. "Jasper, this is Rosa. Her father's the new curate at St John's."

"Cool," Jasper said in a voice that suggested that this was not the word in his head, unless, in this town, somehow *cool* had come to mean *sad.* He was tallish and leanish and wearing a black and white baseball shirt with a big number six on the front.

"Why don't you show Rosa around?" Mr. Coombes said.

Oh no! Why couldn't they just get the paint and go home and paint the wall? It wouldn't be dry before bedtime, now. Rosa threw Mum a desperate look, but Mum was checking out Jasper, who didn't look any more enthusiastic than Rosa felt.

"Around?" Jasper said. Then he looked up at Mr. Coombes and suddenly smiled. "Yeah, okay. No worries, Dad."

Now he turned the smile on Rosa, like a flashlight.

Rosa blinked. Jasper's smile was a wide smile because he had a wide mouth, and his teeth were very white and even. And that flashlight effect – when he'd turned to her, the sun had actually come out and shone through the shop window, lighting up the display stands.

"So, Rosa," Jasper said, "you want to check out the fleshpots of Glasto, yeah?"

Fleshpots...

She didn't know what that meant. It sounded disgusting.

"Jasper likes to joke around," Mr. Coombes said to Mum.

"Well," Mum said. "That would be very kind. When we're new in a place, we do tend to spend a bit too much time on our own. Don't we, Rosie?"

Rosa was thinking, *Get me out of this,* but it was too late.

Invisible Magic Power

O ut on High Street something was happening.

For a start, the band on the steps outside the church had begun to get bigger and louder.

Rosa saw that quite a crowd was gathering in the forecourt, people sprawled around the war memorial, which was in the shape of a tall cross with squiggly patterns on its stem. She saw that two blokes with tattoos, serious body piercing and guitars had joined the band. Then a fat guy in a nightie with zigzag patterns sat down with a penny whistle.

Which meant that the one playing the exhaust pipe now had to blow much harder to make it heard, and his cheeks were puffed out like he had an orange stuffed in each side.

"What *is* that thing?" Rosa asked Jasper.

"It's a didgeridoo," Jasper said. "Aborigines play them in Australia. And idiots in Glasto."

"Idiots?"

"They're like kids," Jasper said. "If you don't want to grow up, you come to live here."

"*I'd* like to grow up," Rosa said. "Sort of."

"Then you probably need to get the hell out," Jasper said.

"That's why I want to grow up – I *want* to get—"

Rosa clammed up. What was she *doing*, shooting her mouth off to a stranger?

Jasper looked at her, gave her his big wide grin. He had these tight, dark curls and kind of smoky eyes. She thought he was probably about fifteen. He probably had girlfriends. She didn't think, somehow, that she was quite *ready* for Jasper.

"Hey, you talk like somebody off *Heartbeat*," he said. "Not that I watch that crap, of course. Is that where you're from?"

"No," Rosa said. "That's Yorkshire. We're from Lancashire."

"Is there much difference?"

"Yes," Rosa said.

He talked a bit posh. Rosa guessed he went to one of those private schools – Mum said estate agents like Mr. Coombes made a lot of money.

"Look, if you haven't grasped the situation here yet,"

Jasper said, "you've got two different types of people in this town. And mostly...mostly they hate each other."

"Oh."

"There are those who were born here – the *local* people – to whom this is just an ordinary country town, a bit run-down, not enough decent shops. I mean where you're from, I expect they've got big towns with big shops, with escalators and stuff."

"Well...yeah. Some."

"Well, if you want *that* level of service here – like if you want any really decent clothes – you've got to go to Bristol or Bath. Because half of our shops just sell..."

Jasper turned to the shop behind them which had a purple sign that said, KERIDWEN'S KAULDRON. It had closed for the day, but the window was full of...

"...total junk," Jasper said. "Stupid crystals and pot goddesses and incense-burners and Tarot cards and books about how to find your hidden self."

Rosa peered into the window of KERIDWEN'S KAULDRON and nodded. It did look a bit like junk.

But *scary* junk. The crystal shop was okay, sort of velvety and glittery, but there were some shops you just didn't want to look into at all – even when they were open, with lights on. You didn't want to, but you did. You *had* to. You had to put yourself through these things.

"And the thing about *these* shops, right, is that they were all set up by the *other* group of people," Jasper said. "That's the newcomers, yeah? Well, some of them are not *that* new any more, they've been here years and years. They were like the original hippies – you've probably seen them in old films and stuff?"

Rosa nodded. She'd seen them on TV. Men with really long hair and beads and old military uniforms and the barefooted women in long dresses you could see through.

"Well, this is where they all came," Jasper said. "And they're still here. And they started it all – they started the first Glastonbury Festival, and that's still going on, of course, and it just gets bigger. And so more and more of these younger, so-called *alternative* people started coming into town. And it just never stops. They're nearly all weirdos, the newcomers."

"Why do they keep coming? Because of the festival?"

"No, that's just another symptom. This town's got a reputation, you see. It's suppose to be..." Jasper wrinkled his nose in contempt. "*...a place of power.*"

"Power?" Rosa was picturing an electricity power station and long lines of pylons.

"An invisible, magic power," Jasper said, "that travels along ley lines, and all the ley lines meet at the Tor."

Rosa had heard about these ley lines, although she wasn't sure exactly what they were. But she didn't want to show her ignorance to Jasper, so she just nodded.

"So that's their *magic place*, the Tor," Jasper said. "Where they go to worship *the old gods*. And do you know what?" He arched his body towards Rosa, spreading out his hands. "They're completely barking! It's all a stupid fantasy. They're just big kids! I mean, will you look at *that*!"

Jasper pointed at what was clearly a classic example of an old hippy, strolling down the hill towards the church. He was short and a bit tubby, and had long white hair and a big white moustache. He wore these ridiculous yellow flared jeans and a bright green waistcoat over a red T-shirt with the words GRATEFUL DEAD on it. He had a little pot belly that stretched out the word *DEAD*.

Rosa made herself look at the word DEAD the way she'd had to look at MURDER on the waitress's apron. Just to *deal with it*, in case it was a *sign*.

"Yo! Woolly!" said one of the guitarists, who was stripped to the waist and had a red and blue tree tattooed on his chest and his nose chained to one ear.

"Hi, Orf," the little white-haired guy said.

The tattoo guy held out his guitar. "Gissa toon, Woolly."

"Not in the mood, man. We gotter get serious, look. I keep tellin' you, things is bad."

"Hey, you hear that?" the tattoo guy said to his mates. "Woolly's not in the mood. Ho freaking ho!"

And then a whole bunch of them, men and women, mostly young enough to be the old guy's children, started this chant.

"*Wooll-y...Wooll-y...Wooll-y!*"

They all had three-tone hair and rings everywhere and big holes in their jeans, and a few of them had chains around their necks with those Egyptian cross-things and metal pentacles.

Woolly reluctantly accepted the guitar and slipped the strap over his shoulder.

"I gotter make this quick, okay?" he said. "What's it gonner be?"

"*Eight Miles High,*" Orf shouted.

Woolly shook his head. "Too complicated. I'll give you *Wasn't Born to Follow.*"

He put one foot on the lowest step of the war memorial and played a few chords, and the other musicians joined in, and then Woolly began to sing in a voice like his nose was all blocked up, something about cascading fountains and arguing with your lodger.

Some of the others started to join in, and when it was over they all stamped and clapped and cheered and hooted and shouted, "*More, more!*"

Rosa noticed a couple of obvious tourists taking pictures of Woolly, but most people wearing ordinary clothes just walked past as if they'd seen it all before.

"All right, one more, and then we gets serious," Woolly said. "*Avalon Blues,* okay?"

Fists went up in the air as Woolly hit the bass string and set up this heavy-duty riff, and then he started to sing in a growly voice.

"*Woke up dis mornin', found ma crystals lost their glow.*"

Everybody cheered.

"*Yeah, ah woke up dis mornin', found ma crystals lost their glow.*"

The didgeridoo man gave a couple of *whumm*s that were out of tune but on the beat, just about. Woolly beamed.

"*And even ma best pendulum...was spinnin' kinda slow.*"

And it went on like this, with Woolly singing about how bad things were, but you couldn't take it too seriously because his face, with its huge droopy moustache, looked so comical.

When the song was over, they all went, *"More, more,"* but Woolly gave the guitar back to Orf, the tattoo guy, and held up both his hands.

"No!" he shouted. "We got to cool it, now! We gotter get serious!"

Somebody booed.

"Listen, I mean it," Woolly protested. "Holy Joseph! Life ain't just about lyin' around an' havin' fun, is it?"

People started going, "Yes," and "Course it is."

"See," Jasper said. "They're just like children."

Something occurred to Rosa. "I thought you said all the weirdos were people who'd moved in. This Woolly, he's got an accent just like the local people. Or have I got that wrong?"

"No," Jasper said grimly. "He's the exception. He's a local person who defected."

"What?"

"Went over to the other side. Went weird. A long time ago."

"Oh."

"He's a traitor," Jasper said.

Rosa looked at him to see if this was a joke, but Jasper wasn't laughing.

"All right, then," Woolly said. "If you cats ain't gonner listen to me, maybe you'll take notice of someone much more important."

The weirdos went quiet, then. Rosa looked around to see

if there was anybody who looked important. All she saw was a black Volvo estate car parked at the kerb behind them.

Woolly had climbed to the top step and stretched himself up as tall as he could get, which wasn't very.

Shadows were starting to fill the street so, while the bottom half of Woolly was in shadow, his face was turned bronze, like a statue, by the red sun.

"Maybe," he cried, "you'll listen to *the voice of the goddess.*"

Darkening Sky

"I thought you said it was all over," Marco said.

Although most of the shops seemed to have closed, the traffic was only crawling through the town centre because of some roadworks further on.

"What are you on about?" Dad said.

"The Glastonbury Festival. If it's all over, what's *that*?"

Because there was clearly a mini festival going on *right in the middle of the town*, featuring some kind of World Music band, with bongos and a didgeridoo.

"Oh that's nothing," Dad said irritably, "that's—"

And then he suddenly pulled the car across the road into a

parking space in front of some shops, and his tone changed, went smooth and even again.

" — actually a very good example of what I was telling you about. The kind of everyday lunacy you find here. Why don't we check it out? I suppose at least it'll give you an idea of the sort of thing that goes on in this town."

It was totally unlike Dad to do anything this spontaneous. So Marco was quite surprised, a couple of minutes later, to find them both standing opposite this church with a tall tower ending in spikes and pinnacles that caught the orange sun and looked like they were alight.

The air was warm and close and had a kind of heavy, sweet smell. The street was mostly in shadow, now, but the sky was on fire.

And as soon as he left the car he felt...*different*. Maybe it was the new brown-tinted shades he was wearing that turned everything deeper red, but the town – a fairly ordinary mixture of old and new buildings – felt...odd.

The church was set back from the road, and there was a paved area in front of it with a memorial in the shape of a long Celtic cross, and all the people were spread out around it, displaying body piercing on an industrial scale and a walking art gallery of tattoos.

In other words, the kind of people you'd see around London, like at the Notting Hill Carnival. Only there didn't seem to be a carnival on here.

And from what Dad had been saying it was *always* like this.

"They all *live* here?" Marco said.

"Some of them. The rest will just have come over for the day from their squats in Bristol or wherever they're camping illegally in old vans. Glastonbury's a magnet for misfits."

Actually, in his shirt and tie, it was Dad who looked like a misfit here. Marco looked down at his T-shirt and jeans, wondering if *he* stood out like that, too.

Meanwhile, across the road, a weird little guy with a big white moustache, who looked like a garden gnome, was standing under the big cross, looking a bit miffed.

"All right, then," he said. "If you cats ain't gonner listen to me, maybe you'll take notice of someone much more important... Maybe you'll listen to *the voice of the goddess*."

Huh? Marco blinked behind his dark glasses.

Suddenly it was quiet, and people starting turning round, as if *the goddess* was coming.

But nobody new had arrived except...

Well, except *them*.

Marco thought they must all be looking at him.

And some people *were* looking at him...or at least at Dad who, with his sharp haircut and his expensive shirt, was more obviously a stranger.

But, of course, Dad wasn't bothered about being stared at. He wasn't stopping here, after all. Oh no, Dad was going to drive away from it all.

Having dumped his son in the middle of it.

Suddenly, Marco felt totally exposed...and like totally...

...*panicked.*

The shadows seemed to have swallowed him. Shadows

seemed to be swallowing his whole life. Everything was coming apart, not least his mum and dad. He didn't know anybody down here, and he was being abandoned among a bunch of complete loonies who were waiting for the *voice of the goddess.*

Marco lost it.

He glared hard at Dad, started flashing him an emergency signal – a big-eyed look that was screaming, *Don't you dare leave me here!*

Dad looked down at Marco, gave him a kind of wry grin.

Marco flashed back stark fear.

Dad gave him a manly punch on the shoulder that said, *You can handle this, son.*

Marco shot back a vicious *You have no right to do this to me!* look.

At this point, Dad's expression changed to that old favourite: *Sometimes we all have to adapt to situations we don't particularly like. It's part of growing up, I'm afraid.*

They always threw that one in. And Marco was just in the middle of working out an expression that would convey the message, *You have betrayed me...your only son...and I won't ever forget it...*

...when something began to happen.

A woman was climbing the steps near the cross. Despite the sultry weather, she had on a dark cloak, and her hair was long and tangly.

She looked kind of witchy, but she was no goddess.

The little guy with the snowy facial hair helped the woman to the top step, by the big stone cross. She folded her hands, holding the folds of the cloak together at her waist. She looked down, as if she was praying.

Marco discovered he'd crossed the road and was standing on the edge of the kerb, just a few yards from the action. In the street behind him, the traffic had faded.

Suddenly the woman looked up, and he saw – well, he *thought* he saw – that her face was pale and blurred, and her eyes had slotted up into her head leaving only a kind of whiteness where they'd been.

Marco found he was standing next to a bloke in denims who had two biggish white and brown dogs sitting either side of him. "*...arco!*" he heard from behind him, across the street, like an echo. "What are you doing?"

And then, up on the steps, the woman was speaking. Her voice was soft, almost whispery, but somehow you could hear every word coming out, in rhythm, like she was reading poetry.

"*I have been dreaming...of Gwyn ap Neeth and his Hounds of Hell. I saw them rushing through the darkening sky, with eyes of fire and fangs bared...*"

There was a hush. The band had put down their instruments. Except for the man with the didgeridoo, who was holding it upright and had both arms wrapped around it. One of the dogs with the man in denims made a small noise at the back of its throat.

"...fangs bared for the kill."

The dog whimpered. The red sun made the pinnacles on the church tower look like sharp, bloody spears, and Marco – although he didn't understand any of this – felt himself slipping down into a feeling he'd had before...like he was sliding under water.

Nothing you could do to stop this. It happened sometimes when you awoke in the morning after a vivid dream – one of those dreams where you couldn't quite remember what had happened, but you remembered the strange colours and the haunting atmosphere.

And, somehow, those colours and that atmosphere would stay with you for hours after you got up – sometimes all day. Wherever you went, you couldn't lose it, and the whole day would be painted in different colours, and everything would seem kind of luminous. Which was a bit worrying because it made you feel that the world wasn't the *same* world. All the time, you'd feel as if you were walking round in a dream – one of those dreams where you knew you were dreaming.

It was like being outside yourself, watching yourself do really ordinary things like lacing up your trainers or taking the top off your boiled egg. And it was like you'd never been aware before of how *odd* these ordinary things were.

Marco shut his eyes and opened them again and shook his head to try and feel normal again, but it was no good. Something had altered, exactly the way it did in dreams. The colour of the sun had deepened, and it was like everything was – this was ridiculous – bathed in luminous blood.

"*And with the coming of the Hounds of Hell...*" The woman's voice was like a sigh. "*I saw...death.*"

Quite a few people gasped.

"*I saw a foul darkness gathering around us all. I saw the candles flickering out. I saw the sword Excalibur arise from the depths...but its blade was blunt and blackened with age and could not protect us...*"

Someone moaned.

"No!" a woman in the crowd shouted out. "We don't want to hear this. Please...my children are here..."

But the woman in the cloak went on like she hadn't heard the protests. Her voice rose into this kind of harsh, fractured wail, like a seagull or something.

"*And the Grail...*"

Marco felt cold and tingly as she threw up her arms, pale and thin and bony, and the cloak slipped away and fell in a heap at her feet, revealing a flimsy white dress. He saw that she was quite old. And that she looked weak, now, and drained.

"*The lovely, shining Grail...*" She was in tears. "*...became black...black and blistered before my eyes!*"

Next thing – and this was truly eerie – both of the white and brown dogs had raised their muzzles, and they were howling into the sunset. Marco had never heard a dog do this before, except on TV. The sound was hollow and seemed to make its own space, with the air growing still around it.

And then someone screamed, as something appeared on the steps that was big and black and hard against the sunset.

God's Bouncer

"**Y**ou *scum!*" It was a hard, male voice that Rosa recognized right away. "You filthy scum!"

Oh no...

She backed away, up against the window of KERIDWEN'S CAULDRON and felt slightly sick.

He was wearing his long black cassock. Rosa had never liked that; she always thought it looked daft – a big man, with a big black beard, in a frock.

He didn't look daft now, though. He looked a bit scary, up on the steps, next to the cross, towering over the elderly woman in the cloak and bawling at her.

"How dare you? How *dare* you conduct your sick, evil rituals outside the house of God?"

He must have slipped out of the church and probably nobody had noticed him joining the crowd.

"Look, mate... Let's be cool, eh?"

A hand touched Rosa's dad's arm, and he swung round and knocked it away. It was Orf, the guy with the tree tattooed on his chest. His other hand was around the neck of his guitar, and Dad must have thought he was going to use it as a club or something.

Because he snatched the guitar away.

"You leave that alone!" Orf screamed.

Rosa's dad was a lot taller than Orf and looked down at him like he was considering beating him up.

"Show me your street-music licence, sonny."

"What?"

"You show me your licence to play music in the street...and I'll show you a flock of flying pigs."

Everybody booed.

"Don't you have nothing better to do?" Orf said. "Like... a service to take, or some'ing?"

"Aye, I do, lad." Dad put his face right up to Orf's. "And I want to be able to hear myself pray, instead of your pathetic apology for music. So you and your mates've got exactly two minutes to get away from my church door before I get the police to *carry* you away, in a big van."

"Aw, *man*..." Orf looked pained. "...the pigs are cool with this. They know we don't do no harm to nobody. And like, the vicar never give us no hassle, either."

"Well times have changed, and *I'm* here now, to *help* the vicar." Dad grinned coldly through his beard. "And this is the House of God. You got that? *The House of God.* And you might want to think of *me* as God's bouncer. And I can assure you and your scruffy, work-shy pals that I've spent years bouncing lads a lot bigger and a lot harder than you...so anybody wants to take me on, I'm up for it."

"We're not into violence, man," Orf said. "We're into peace."

"And that's your idea of peace, is it? Bawling out your old hippy songs and then trying to scare people with *pagan rituals.*"

"It's not illegal, man," Orf said. "Anybody can believe what they want."

"Not in front of my church they can't. Go away! *Now!* Or I'll have the lot of you for causing an affray."

"You talk a bit like a copper yourself." The little man with the droopy white moustache and the red T-shirt with GRATEFUL DEAD on it had climbed up next to Dad. "Who exactly are you, man?"

Dad rounded on him.

"David Wilcox is my name. The *Reverend* David Wilcox. I'm the new curate here. But don't get that wrong – it doesn't mean I'm a wimp. And *you* –" He jabbed a thumb at Woolly. "– are old enough to know better than cause a public nuisance."

Rosa became aware of Jasper grinning at her. "Hey! That's your old man!"

Rosa blushed and walked across the road, hoping her dad might see her and...well, calm down or something. Jasper followed her.

"...might not be a wimp, man," Woolly was saying to Dad, "but that don't mean you gotter go round trying to prove it all the time. Where's your sense of spirituality?"

"*Spirituality?* Don't you come lecturing *me* about spirituality, you little... *Look* at you! Look at *all* of you, with your tatty clothes and your heathen jewellery and your pathetic magic crystals...pretending you're plugged into some mythical earth force. Well, *I'll* tell you what *you're* plugged into—"

"Aw, man..."

"*Evil!*" Dad roared. "And you can't even see it. You're turning this town into a sick, pagan playground, and you've been getting away with it for too long. Well, where I come from we don't put up with it."

"What a plonker," a boy said to Rosa.

Rosa spun round. The boy was wearing sunglasses. He was shaking his head in kind of disbelief.

"I mean, what's *that* doing for the Church's image? This gorilla coming out and threatening people for just, like, singing? And then he's frightening old ladies. It's him ought to be taken away in a van."

Woolly and Rosa's dad were still arguing, Dad jabbing a finger at Woolly's chest.

"He's my father," Rosa said.

"Oh." The boy looked up at the sky with a kind of *How*

was I to know? expression. "Ah. Right. Well. Of course, I do this all the time. I won the student of the year award at my charm school for, like, tact and diplomacy."

The way Jasper was looking at the boy in the sunglasses, Rosa imagined they probably knew one another.

Turned out they didn't. Jasper scrutinized the boy closely now, and he was...hostile. Everybody was so *hostile*.

"Bit of advice, friend," Jasper said to the boy. "Tourists who stick their noses into Glasto affairs? They tend to get them flattened. You need to know that."

Rosa moved away from both of them. She just wanted to go home, even to that disgusting, dingy flat.

The boy looked at Jasper through his dark glasses.

"Blimey," he said. "No wonder my mum's been trying to keep me out of this place."

Marco's dad pushed Marco into the car and slammed the door on him. Then he strode round to his side and got in and started the engine. He looked furious.

"But I didn't start *anything*," Marco said. "It was *him*. He was just, like...he just hit me...*bam*... I mean, *look!*"

He bent his head forward and pointed to his lip, but Dad wasn't looking; he was already steering the Volvo out into the road, and there was a police car coming the other way, causing the crowd around the cross to start breaking up. Now the big vicar guy was standing on his own with his arms folded, looking like he wanted to fight somebody.

Actually, *he* was the one who'd started it. No question. The vicar...curate...whatever.

"I *know* you, Marco," Dad said through his teeth. "If anyone...*anyone*...is calculated to come out with the wrong smart remark at exactly the wrong time, it's you."

"I didn't say *anything*! I just—"

"You could start a riot at a vicarage tea party."

"If it was *his* vicarage tea party, they wouldn't need—"

"Shut up," Dad said. "At least your grandfather didn't see you."

"Why, what would *he* have said?"

"He..." They came to the roadworks, and the temporary traffic lights had just changed to red. Dad hissed in annoyance and trod on the brakes. "Never mind."

The lights took for ever to change back to green. Dad sat tapping impatiently on the wheel. Marco kept quiet until they'd driven out of the town centre and into a lane that went uphill, with trees overhanging it, the setting sun dripping like marmalade through the branches. They went on, in low gear, until there was a gap in the trees and then...

"Hang on..." Marco pulled off his shades. "It's the *hill*!"

It was just suddenly bulging out on their right, and against the deep red sky it looked huge, and they were so close to it now that you could see that the finger of stone on the summit really was a proper church tower with battlements.

"Damn," Dad said. "We've come too far. It's all your fault, getting involved in that fracas. Now I've lost my bearings."

"You said they lived near the hill, the..."

"The Tor. But I can't remember which side. There's a whole network of lanes...damn, damn, damn... It's no good, we'll have to turn back."

He carried on until there was somewhere to reverse into, near a field gate, and turned round, which took for ever with the road being so narrow. When they were creeping back down towards the main road, Marco found himself thinking about the woman in the cloak and her dreams of darkness and doom and how kind of hypnotic that was. How, until that guy had hit him, he'd been feeling...

"Dad..."

"What?"

"Dad, do you ever get this feeling that like...you know...you're *here*...but, like, you're *more* than here?"

"What are you on about now?"

"Like, you can suddenly see everything really clearly, but it's also like you're watching it on TV. You can see the colours of everything you wouldn't normally notice, and the colours seem brighter and stronger and—"

Dad stamped on the brakes and the car shuddered to a stop and the engine stalled. Gripping the wheel, Dad swung round at Marco.

"If I *thought* you'd been taking drugs..."

"Huh?"

"Seeing strange colours, and it's like you're watching it on TV? Has someone been... Is it Josh?"

"No, honestly...I haven't taken anything! Ever. It was just

that this feeling came over me...down there in the street. It was like the air was... I'm not explaining it very well."

"Then perhaps," Dad said through his teeth, "it might be better if you didn't bother."

They came to the bottom of the lane, and Dad stopped the car and looked this way and that.

"It's *somewhere* round here..."

"Is it a big place? Like a farm?"

"Of course it isn't."

"You said they owned their own fields."

"They do. Well, a couple. They've got what's called a smallholding. That means not nearly enough land to be a farm, but bigger than a garden. They grow their own vegetables."

"Instead of going to the supermarket, they just pop out and pick something?"

"It's the principle," Marco's dad said. "For them, it's all about principles."

"Why don't you just ask somebody where it is? Haven't you got an address? Ask this bloke walking up... Oh, look, it's *him*...the gnome."

The old hippy was stomping up from the town, with his hands jammed in his pockets, and he looked even more like a gnome now, due to the little red woolly hat pulled down over his white hair. He was also wearing tiny, round dark glasses that were so dark they were almost black. He looked dangerous. The word DEAD was glowing on his stomach.

Dad said, "Oh."

"It's the guy who was down at the church, arguing with the vicar. Didn't you see him?"

"I... Yes. I'm afraid I did."

"Huh?"

Dad lowered his window, and the gnome saw him and wandered over. He peered at the car through his dark glasses.

Marco looked at Dad and then he looked at the little guy, who suddenly gave him a big, scary grin, revealing a row of teeth like a long-abandoned graveyard.

And Marco was like,

Huh??????

He turned to Dad.

"You're kidding," he whispered. "You have just *got* to be kidding."

Imagining Things

"I think we should have a little chat, don't you?" Rosa's dad said.

He couldn't help talking like this. There was still a lot of the policeman left in him. When he wanted to deal with something serious, he'd sound like he was arresting you.

"I want a lawyer before I say a word," said Rosa, who sometimes watched *The Bill*.

"This is important," Dad said.

"Sorry."

Rosa came and sat down. It was nearly dark. Or it was in the flat, anyway.

Her dad put on one of the lamps and joined her on the sofa. Usually, at night, he'd change into something more casual, but tonight he was still wearing his church shirt and his white dog collar. He leaned forward into the lamplight with his hands clasped together, and now he was a priest about to deliver a sermon.

Spare me...

"You saw what happened down there tonight."

Rosa nodded.

"That," Dad said, "is why we're here. Or, at least, why *I'm* here."

She'd heard him talking to Mum about this. How this town was full of people who were deluded and he'd been offered the job at this particular church because the Bishop thought he looked like a real down-to-earth northerner who might knock some sense into them. Apparently, Dad told Mum, they'd had one curate who had "gone native" and started smoking cannabis in church. If Dad had been here at the time, he'd have nicked him.

"I expect you heard that insane woman screaming about darkness and the hounds of hell."

Rosa nodded.

"It's *rubbish*, Rosa. It's disgusting nonsense. You see, a lot of old stories – legends – have woven themselves into the fabric of this town. Crazy stories, weird stories. Ridiculous nonsense!"

"Like that this was supposed to be the place where Christianity first started?" Rosa said.

"Er, no, that's true," Dad said quickly. "This was certainly one of the first places where Christians gathered in England."

"And that Jesus' uncle, Joseph of Arimathea, sailed here after Jesus had gone – when this was the Isle of Avalon – and stuck his staff in the ground, and it turned into a thorn bush and—"

"That *might* be true," Dad admitted. "Or it might just be a story."

Rosa hoped this one was actually true. One morning, she and Mum had walked up this hill, Wearyall Hill, where there was a thorn tree, on its own, that was supposed to be directly descended from the one that grew where Joseph of Arimathea had planted his staff. If he'd planted his staff in London or Los Angeles or somewhere, they'd have built a big monument with a statue of Joseph on top. But here, two thousand years later, there was still just this little tree, all bent in the wind, and that was nice, really.

Well, not *just* the tree. They *had* built the Abbey, which had apparently been one of the biggest and richest in the country. But, while the Abbey was in ruins now, the Glastonbury Thorn still flowered every year – usually around Christmas. That was a fact, apparently.

"I wasn't talking about the Christian stories," Dad said. "I meant the other kind."

"What other kind?"

"The, er...less pleasant kind. The stupid kind, put about by people who think Glastonbury was a..." Dad frowned. "...a place of power, long before Christianity...in the days when the

Druids were here and carried out human sacrifices and things like that. Some people are twisted enough to find blood rituals and human sacrifice more exciting than Christianity."

"You mean paganism?" Rosa said. "The old gods?"

"The old gods didn't exist," Dad said sternly. "People in those days simply didn't know any better. And a lot of people here still don't. They're dabblers in the occult, which is evil and dangerous. But that's my problem, not yours."

Dad stood up suddenly and drew the curtains as if he was shutting out all the evil, rising in clouds from the street. Below the window, someone was singing, out of tune, that ancient Oasis song about living for ever.

"So what's *my* problem?" Rosa said.

Dad sat down again in the soft lamplight.

"Your mum's spent most of the evening painting your bedroom wall."

"Oh," Rosa said. "Has she?"

Although she'd asked Mum *not* to tell Dad about the wall, it looked as though he'd managed to get it out of her. Probably couldn't cover up the smell of paint.

Mum was in the kitchen now, keeping out of it.

"You know, it's very easy, in this town, to start imagining things," Dad said.

"Oh."

"Because, as you've heard tonight, a lot of adults do it, too. Get carried away with their own fantasies. They don't realize they're exposing themselves to evil until it's too late."

"I...suppose she told you about the monk," Rosa said.

"Yes, she did. And about that fool in the crystal shop who thought he'd been a monk at the Abbey in a...a previous life."

"Right."

"Sadly," Dad said, "there are a lot of people in this town who seem to *need* something like this, to make them feel special."

"Why?"

"Because there's something missing in their lives."

"You mean God, right?"

Sometimes – well, most of the time, actually – she wished he was still a policeman, and not only because they seemed to have so much more money then.

"Well..." Dad screwed up his eyes, as if he was finding this hard to explain. "Well, *yes*. But not *just* God. I mean, perhaps they haven't got a job that makes them feel fulfilled and useful. Or any job at all. So they go in search of something. Something to make them feel special."

"I'd have thought that telling people you used to be a monk in a previous life would just make you feel a bit daft, actually," Rosa said.

"Anywhere else, *yes*. But not in this town. It's full of people who like to think they're in contact with strange forces – old gods, flying saucers, any old nonsense. And these people..." Dad bent forward to look into Rosa's eyes. "...are very seriously deluded."

"Oh."

"And all these shops full of crystal balls and pottery goddesses and fortune-telling cards are just pandering to their stupid obsessions. Oh, they might seem innocent enough to you..."

"No, they—"

"But they're *not*. They're often run by people who can't cope with reality any more than their customers. And if you get involved with them, they'll pull you into their delusions. Now, don't get me wrong – I'm not saying that the man in the crystal shop isn't a perfectly nice man. But some of them aren't. I was a copper, Rosa, I know about evil."

"So...what's this got to do with the bedroom wall?"

As if she didn't know.

"Rosa..." Dad took one of her hands, like Jesus about to heal her or something. "Do you know what I mean by contagious?"

Rosa sighed. "Dad, I'm thirteen years old. That's a *teenager*. Of *course*, I know."

"We all know that a disease can be contagious. But so can evil. And so can delusions."

"Oh, right." Rosa was getting annoyed now. "So you think that like, because that man told us about how he used to be a monk and we might have some of the Abbey stones in our wall, you think I *imagined* the shape of a monk on the plaster. That's what you think, is it?"

"Rosa, love," Dad said sadly, "your mum couldn't see any trace of a monk."

Rosa rocked back on the sofa like she'd been pushed hard. She felt her lips trembling.

"There was nothing at all there," Dad said, "except the usual smudges you find on walls in need of a fresh coat of paint."

"There *must* have been." Rosa was gripping her knees, rocking backwards and forwards. "She wasn't *looking* properly. And it was getting dark. It's always dark in..."

No. This was not possible! She *had* to have seen something. You couldn't miss that monk, you *couldn't.*

Dad was shaking his head slowly.

"I see." Rosa stopped herself rocking, made herself sit up straight. "So you think *I'm...* having delusions, whatever..."

"Rosa—"

"You think I'm *mad.* You think if I go on like this I'm going to be taken away to a mental hospital. You think—"

"What I *think*—"

Rosa stood up. "Well, thanks very much, Dad!"

"Rosa, sit down!"

Rosa sat down on the very edge of the sofa, as far away from her dad as she could get.

"What I think," he said gently, "is that you're feeling very insecure and vulnerable. And I realize it's all my fault. *You* didn't ask to come here, to the other end of the country. To this strange...this *very* strange town. I know life would have been much easier for you – and Mum, too – if I'd stayed in the police instead of taking quite a big pay-cut to do something I felt was important, not just for me but for the...for the human race."

Rosa scowled. You'd have thought he'd become the boss of the United Nations or Amnesty International or something, not just the vicar's assistant in a grotty little town full of loonies.

"I think you're just feeling a little lost," Dad said.

"Whatever," Rosa said.

"A bit lost and out-of-it at the moment. And that's only to be expected. But when you start school in September and make a few friends, everything will seem different."

"Can I go now?" Rosa said. "Can I go to bed? I'm dead tired."

"I'm sure you are." Dad stood up and helped her to her feet for no other reason than that he probably thought it was what Jesus would have done. "Goodnight and God bless."

He smiled down at her through the daft beard that he never had when he was a policeman. His eyes were full of understanding. Except he *didn't* understand.

And if he didn't understand his own daughter, maybe he didn't understand those people out in the street tonight. That frightening woman in the cloak who was the *voice of the goddess.*

And with the coming of the Hounds of Hell...I saw...death.

"Night, Dad," Rosa said miserably.

Merlin

When they all got out of the car, Marco's dad did one of his tight smiles.

"Right," he said. "Okay. Well...here we are."

Marco looked around. They didn't seem to be anywhere much.

They'd driven back up the tree-shaded road, and then the gnome had shouted, *Whoah!* from the back seat, tapping Dad on the shoulder and pointing to this tiny little gap in the hedge on the left that they hadn't even noticed the first time.

The sides of the Volvo had got scratched by twigs when they were squeezing through, and Dad had been frowning as they bumped along a track of dried mud with a streak of grass down the middle. Then the sun appeared ahead, like a huge red football rolling towards them, turning the grass pinky-orange. But the glow that Marco had felt earlier – the feeling of being *more than here* – had gone completely now, and he just felt tired, and kind of used-up.

Or maybe just *used*. That sense of being double-crossed again. He felt too knackered to work it out, but there was *something*.

Anyway, now they were parked in this clearing, where the mud was baked the colour of a pizza-base. It was on the edge of a small wood, but there was no sign of a house or anything.

"So," Dad said. "Here we are, then."

The gnome looked up at Dad, hands on his hips. "You ever come before, Angus? I can't quite recall..."

"Er...once. I think."

"Only, thing is, we thought you wasn't comin' over till tomorrow. Nancy's down at her aura-perception class, look. We'd've had a proper meal ready if we'd known."

Even Marco hadn't known. He glared resentfully at Dad, who just shrugged.

"Change in the schedules, I'm afraid, Woolly. Had to re-diarize at the eleventh hour."

"Pity that," the gnome said. "Nance reckoned the planetary formations was real auspicious for a historic meeting... *tomorrow.*"

"Well...sorry. Does that, ah, alter things?"

"Totally," the gnome said.

So far, he didn't seem to have noticed Marco. Maybe he was going to wait until *tomorrow* to notice Marco. Like when the *planetary formations* said it was okay to actually notice your actual grandson, who you were meeting for the first time.

The first time in thirteen years.

Which was, as it happened, your grandson's entire lifetime!

Marco kept staring at the gnome. Maybe if he stared hard enough he'd wake up in his own bed, and this would all have been a weird dream: like...his granddad turning out to be someone who looked like he'd just failed the audition for one of these Jurassic rock bands, and hanging out with a woman who spoke with the *voice of the goddess*...how ridiculous was that? Answer: it couldn't *get* more ridiculous.

Could it?

Oh my God... What if the goddess woman in the cloak was his grandmother?

"Well..." Dad opened up the boot of the Volvo.

JUST DO NOT SAY HERE WE ARE!

Dad lifted out Marco's big case.

"This is, ah...this is Marco, by the way," Dad said.

Marco blinked.

This is Marco by the way!

It just got worse and worse, didn't it? Bad enough that all that stuff about his grandparents being entirely weird was proving to be totally and completely true in every last little detail...now here was Dad introducing him to this gnome – who, according to his T-shirt was grateful to be dead – in this offhand way, like Marco was one of his less-important clients who just happened to have dropped in.

GET ME OUT OF HERE!

Okay...calm down. Think about it: Dad hadn't seen his father-in-law in many years but, somehow, he knew him well enough to arrange to bring Marco here, without saying a word to Mum. Totally behind Mum's back, in fact.

To organize this, Dad must have had secret talks with a guy who hung out with tattoo-freaks and weird old ladies who predicted *a foul darkness*.

"Marco, this is your Granddad Woolaston," Dad said.

Marco tried for a smile, which, right now, was like prising open a very stiff door.

The gnome smiled at Marco.

Actually, his granddad's teeth weren't as bad as they'd seemed through the windscreen; they were just misshapen. There was a gap at the front. The grown-up people Marco's parents knew didn't have gaps, they had crowns and bridgework. The gap made his smile seem kind of comical... that is, like out of an actual comic book.

Marco and the gnome shook hands. It felt like grasping one of the soft leathers Dad kept in the car to wipe the windscreen in winter.

"I'm Marco," Marco said, just to underline it.

"I can tell," Granddad Woolaston said.

He wasn't that much taller than Marco and quite a lot shorter than Marco's dad. Mum was small, though, and it was clear now where that came from.

But whereas Mum had big blue eyes that could sparkle with fun (and also with annoyance) her dad just had these little, round, very dark glasses. So there was no way at all of knowing what *he* felt about this situation.

"Come on then," he said, like he had nothing else to say to them.

He turned away, and bunches of assorted metal bangles slipped down both wrists as he picked up Marco's big case. Then he led the way between a couple of trees, and into the wood.

The sun had slipped down so far that everything was looking brown and faded, like in one of those really ancient photographs.

The three of them walked silently through the trees. Three generations – Marco, Marco's dad and the gnome who was Marco's granddad, none of them talking.

None of them saying a word! How awkward was *that*?

Dad, carrying the Man United bag containing the laptop and Marvin the rabbit, came alongside and looked down at Marco with a totally phoney encouraging smile that said, *Hey, don't worry.*

Don't worry.

Huh.

And then they emerged into something that was almost a garden.

Well, actually, it was more like a very small field, with a couple of wooden sheds, all black against the red light, and an ancient-looking wall on two sides and, in between, all knotted together, a bunch of big apple trees with branches like spider legs and little apples on them.

Between the apple trees, you could see a house or a cottage, which seemed pretty small and built out of dusty orange stone.

And behind it – well not, *right* behind it, it could be nearly half a mile away, but in the red light it looked very close and very strange, and almost spooky – was *the hill*.

It was there. It was real.

It was *more than real*.

Marco stopped. He'd gone all still inside.

The feeling of being *more than here* was coming back, and this time he didn't fight it, he let the glow settle around him.

And then something thumped him hard in the back.

Marco turned round in shock and stared into eyes like brown billiard balls.

He stared into a shaggy, hairy face and big, grey rubbery lips with whiskers sprouting out.

Above all this were ears that went on for ever.

The brown, shaggy face was kind of smiling in a knowing way. And then the head went down and butted Marco hard in the chest, flattening him against one of the wooden sheds, and one of the long ears nearly went up his nose.

"Aw, *Merlin*," Granddad Woolaston said.

The donkey just glanced at him and then turned back to Marco and lowered his head for another push.

Marco backed off a little, along the side of the shed.

"I'm afraid Marco hasn't had much to do with animals," Dad said, moving a safe distance away in case the donkey should turn round and attack him, leaving nasty marks on his business trousers.

Marco frowned. "I'm fine."

The main reason he hadn't had much to do with animals – probably the *only* reason – was that Mum and Dad had never let him have so much as a hamster.

He looked into Merlin's gleaming, globular eyes.

"I reckon he could get to like you," the gnome said.

Marco put out a hand and rubbed it experimentally along the side of the donkey's face. It felt like an old hearthrug. A hearthrug that had been draped over a rock.

"What he likes best is being tickled behind his ears," the gnome said.

Marco was about to try this when Dad dumped the Man U case with the laptop inside, and looked at his Rolex.

"Good God...is that the time? Look, ah...I need to be back in London. Got an important breakfast meeting tomorrow."

Granddad Woolaston glanced at Marco, then put down the big case and took off his dark glasses and laid them on top of it.

"Stay cool," he said. "No hassle, man."

Dad looked irritated and fingered his tie.

The little man threw up his arms and did a little twirl with his hands open, as if he was about to catch something from the sky, possibly the sun. Then he peered curiously up into Dad's face.

"You really don't see it, do you, Angus?" he said.

"See it?" Dad said.

Granddad Woolaston just shook his head.

Dad looked at Marco and raised an eyebrow, as if to say, *Now*, this *is what your mum means, when she says—*

"You don't *feel* it," Granddad Woolaston said.

"Feel it?"

Marco's granddad looked at Marco's dad, and Marco had to admit that they looked very odd together, his dad in the dark suit-trousers and the shirt and tie, and the little guy in the yellow flares and the red T-shirt and the ponytail and the beads and the bangles.

And you know what was really odd?

Suddenly, it was *Dad* who looked weird.

Marco's granddad came over and put an arm around Merlin's great shaggy, lumpy neck. They stood there together, with the muddy sunlight glinting from quite a big gold ring in Granddad Woolaston's left ear.

"Cup of tea, Angus? Glass of home-made cider?"

"Ah...no..." Dad said. "Thank you, but, ah...I'd better be off."

"Ar," Granddad Woolaston said. "Maybe you better had, or you ain't gonner be back in the smoke before midnight."

"Take care, matey." Dad gave Marco an affectionate punch on the shoulder. "Don't forget – call me, e-mail me. Okay?"

"Sure."

Dad gave Marco an *its going to be fine* look.

He opened the car door and got in, turning once to give Marco a final wave before driving off.

Marco felt strangely detached, like he was watching this from a long way away, or on TV.

When Dad's car had gone, Granddad Woolaston took his arm from around Merlin's neck and gave him a mild tap on the bum. Merlin wandered off, nonchalant, walking like Clint Eastwood in one of those old movies, and then nibbling some grass like he wasn't bothered one way or the other.

Marco noticed his granddad's feet were in sandals with a thong between the toes – what he thought were called Jesus creepers.

"Right, then," Granddad said.

The air seemed to go very still, and Marco was aware of the old guy looking hard at him. Then Granddad Woolaston's hand was going up, palm outwards, as if he was about to deliver a big, angry smack across Marco's face.

Somehow, Marco didn't flinch.

The hand stayed in the air for a moment.

"Yo, Marco," Granddad Woolaston said.

Wow... Marco's own hand came up instinctively, and the two hands met in a high five.

"Yo," Marco said. "Yo, er, Grand—"

"Woolly."

"Sorry?"

The old guy looked stern. "I ever hear you call me Granddad again, and you're straight up to Castle Cary and on the first train for Paddington. You got that?"

"Oh," Marco said. "Right, er..."

"Woolly."

"Woolly," Marco said.

Woolly's face lit up like a turnip at a Hallowe'en party.

"'Tis gonner be cool, Marco," he said.

Out of It

She'd been deep inside something that didn't exist, and now she could hardly get her breath.

When she woke up, she was cold and terrified.

It was impossible. Tourists could come into the town and never know it was there at all. It was hidden by shops and streets, and there wasn't much left anyway.

In the dream, however...

Rosa had been on her own in the centre of one of the green lawns which had been laid where the Abbey used to be, with the ruins scattered here and there like the edges of a jigsaw puzzle you'd barely started.

She'd become aware of a soft chanting, which had begun at ground level, a deep moaning, which had begun to rise and swell through the broken walls. As it grew louder, the stones had begun to glow softly, as if there were hidden light bulbs inside that were fading up.

The stones had also begun to...kind of squirm against one another. And then, as the chanting had been joined by a throbbing and a rumbling from underground, she saw that the stones were *growing*.

Rosa had spun wildly, realizing that something awesome was happening all around her and...

...and below her, too. The soil around the ruins had begun to crumble and crack, and shadows had appeared in the green lawns, as if the grass was sinking.

Rosa had wanted to run away, but her legs wouldn't move. The ground was trembling under her feet, and there was this huge, creaking, tearing sound, and shadows were rising. She was so scared she started shrinking into herself, as something enormous began to form.

She stood there with her arms wrapped around herself and watched the huge pillars growing like enormous trees out of the ruins, growing until they were higher than the surrounding walls and soaring over the shops and the cars and trucks and buses. And then they began pulsing out towards each other and...

...*thunk*...

...crunching together, becoming arches. A line of arches was forming, like a big ribcage in the sky, and the voices of the invisible monks were rising and falling and chiming like bells until they were were filling the whole town, and the arches were assembling a great skeleton of stone over all of Glastonbury and...

Oh!

With a throb of terror, Rosa had awoken, the chanting of the dead monks passing in and out through her head in waves.

And here she still was, lying here, wide awake, scared witless in the darkness of her shabby room. Knowing that the Abbey itself was very close – just over the wall at the end of their yard.

And perhaps it had grown out. Perhaps the great ghostly form arose at night to enclose the town. Perhaps if she looked out of the bedroom window, she'd see...

Rosa stiffened. The wall. If the walls of other houses and shops in this part of the street had been partly built with stones taken years and years ago from the ruins of the Abbey, it seemed very unlikely that this wall *hadn't* been.

So she really *was* inside the Abbey.

And the monk...

You couldn't just paint the monk away. He was part of the Abbey and he lived in the wall.

Rosa shut her eyes tight and kept them shut and heard her own breathing, hollow in the room, remembering how, before she'd fallen asleep, she'd been crying.

Weeping quietly with dismay and frustration at the way Mum had betrayed her so easily to Dad, who thought she was mad.

Dad – who was always talking about Jesus and miracles that

happened in the Bible, but didn't seem to believe that anything could happen *now* that you couldn't explain.

Mum hadn't said anything to *her* about not being able to see the monk – she'd just told Dad.

So this meant that *both* of them thought Rosa was mad.

Was she mad?

Did normal people have dreams like this?

Did normal people *know*, without any doubt, that if they turned on the light now, their monk would be back – in the new paint – dark and cowled, like a figure of smoke?

Rosa began to shake, and she pulled the duvet around her, keeping herself turned towards the curtained window, her back to the monk's wall, opening her eyes very slightly in case she somehow was facing the wrong way, facing the monk's wall.

She wasn't. But a tiny sliver of moonlight, where the curtains met, leaked into the room and made the curtains themselves seem like hanging robes.

Rosa shut her eyes again. She was imagining all this.

Please God, let me be imagining this.

Maybe it was what this town did to you. Dad had said it was full of people who wanted to believe in legends and crazy stories. Maybe the town was feeding them, and they were feeding their craziness back into the town and, like Dad had said, it was *contagious.*

Perhaps she was becoming *one of them,* and the craziness was creeping into her dreams and if she didn't do something about it she'd have a nervous breakdown and get taken away to a hospital with high walls where they kept injecting you with drugs just to keep you quiet.

Rosa began to cry softly again. She'd gone to sleep feeling more lonely than she could ever remember, because she knew that she'd never be able to tell even Mum about anything like this ever again. Not even *Mum*.

Life here had already seemed unbearable, but now...

Now Rosa heard a sound.

Not in the room, not just under the bed, this was *below* the room.

The breath clotted in her throat as she recalled how, in her dream, the cracks had formed in the soil before the great walls and the arches of the Abbey had come surging up like some prehistoric monster.

This wasn't *that* big a sound. Just a little noise. But a much bigger noise, really, because it wasn't in a dream, this rolling, bumping noise, like something had been knocked over and fallen to the floor. It was a real noise, where there shouldn't be a noise.

Rosa clutched the duvet to her chin in cold panic. Had somebody broken into the house?

But this wasn't a house, it was a flat, with nothing underneath it except...

Except the old shop.

The old, dark, derelict, locked-up, abandoned shop.

There was somebody in the old shop.

Real Night

For a long time, Marco couldn't bring himself to go to bed. He just moved from one window to the other, fascinated.

At home, his bedroom overlooked what his mum called the courtyard, which was really just a concrete square with tubs of flowers in it. Their building was almost completely surrounded by other blocks of flats, including the one where Josh lived – although, naturally, the apartment where Josh lived with his father and his father's partner was twice as big and overlooked the river, whereas all you could see from Marco's room was Josh's block and the courtyard.

At home, it was never really dark because there were lights

everywhere – lights in the apartments all around, security lights on the forecourt, and the millions and billions of lights all over the city that battered the night into apologizing for not being day.

But here, from upstairs in Woolly and Nancy's cottage, under an oak beam like a giant chocolate flake, you could see...

...*real night.*

With stars and stuff – constellations, where you could join the dots and make patterns. But the stars were the least of it. There were bigger mysteries a whole lot closer.

When Marco had finally made himself go to bed, he couldn't sleep. He could almost feel the weight of the huge beam overhead pressing down on him. It brought on his claustrophobia, which made him think of his psychiatrist – Josh. He'd send his first e-mail to Josh, not his dad. He'd send it from his laptop in the morning.

So I'm in this attic, right. It has two windows, one at each end. One overlooks some of the town, which is about a kilometre away, below us. The lights in the town are quite soft and low, and the night sky is like a real night sky, the colour of a box of Milk Tray...except in one corner where it's shimmering like it's been sprinkled with gold dust.

Gold dust? Nah, too soppy and poetic, Josh wasn't the poetic type.

Anyway, that wasn't important; it was to the other window that Marco kept returning. He just couldn't stop looking at the misty, powdery silhouette of the Tor that seemed to fill this whole piece of the night.

Or was that just because of what he knew about it now?

Okay. Glastonbury Tor, right? Tonight, just before I came to bed, Woolly took me to the window and told me a bit about Glastonbury Tor.

It's not very high, but it kind of dominates a huge area of Somerset, because its shape is so weird, like a pyramid. And apparently, it's world-famous, because...*get this*...

To a lot of people in Glastonbury, this is like a shrine of <u>ancient power</u>. According to Woolly, quite a few people reckon they've had <u>strange experiences</u> up there – you know, <u>seeing ghostly things</u>. They also say you can see UFOs from the Tor, because <u>extra-terrestrials also realize it's a place of serious power</u>.

And Josh would reply:

These are purely subjective experiences. Therefore delusional, possibly hallucinatory. Your grandfather is clinically insane.

Hmm. Maybe it was best to approach this from a historical perspective.

Way back, the Tor is supposed to have been a place where the Druids worshipped the old gods and carried out blood sacrifices and stuff. When Christianity started up here – and this was, like, one of the earliest places in Britain to get Christianity – they built a church on top. But most of it fell down and there's only the tower left now, like a huge standing stone, which Woolly says is a pagan symbol. And Woolly also says

Okay, stop right there. *Woolly*. At some stage, he'd have to explain to Josh about Woolly, and it wasn't going to be easy. If he actually *described* Woolly, Josh would just go into heart-attack mode again, rocking back on his heels and howling, "What did I say? What did I *tell you*?"

So if Josh – as Josh surely would – started asking questions about his grandparents, best just to send something like:

Can't understand what all the fuss was about. They're perfectly...normal.

Because sometimes it was easier to lie.

Especially when it came to describing your grandmother. *Nancy*.

Within just a couple of minutes of Woolly giving Marco the high five and telling him how cool it was going to be, Nancy had come back from her aura-perception class, whatever *that* was about.

And, oh yes, talking about Nancy called for some serious lies.

Grandma Woolaston likes to wear traditional clothes...

Wearing this long, flowing purple frock, she'd emerged

from between the two lines of apple trees like something out of one of those tapestries from the Middle Ages.

Except that Middle Ages women did not, as far as Marco knew, have masses of pink, green and gold hair with mad ringlets and braided bits and these kind of twigs sticking out.

Marco was also fairly sure medieval women hadn't worn nose studs...but he *could* be wrong about that.

This nose stud was seriously impressive. It glowed red like a huge electric wart, matching Nancy's wide, scarlet lips and setting off the heavy blue-green stuff, dusted with silver, around Nancy's eyes.

All this eye make-up had started to run big time when Nancy had wept. And Nancy had wept in torrents when she spotted Marco, leaping on him and hugging him like she'd just learned he had only a week to live.

"Oh, lovey!" Nancy had cried. "*Oh lovey!*" And then she'd held him at arm's length, staring at him through her tears. "You're so like Alison, you are. *So* like Alison!"

Alison. This was Mum.

Marco would have liked to tell Nancy how much Mum looked like *her.*

Except, like...no *way.* Mum wore dark suits and carried a briefcase. Mum would rather die than look like Nancy. Who also, by the way, had little gold rings in the skin at the corner of each eye. Maybe she also had one in her navel.

Marco's grandmother.

My gran, the serial body piercer!

When Nancy finally let him go, her face looked like she'd been mugged by Dark Age warriors covered in woad.

"Oh, lovey!" Nancy moaned, shaking her head, all the ringlets and twigs rattling.

If Woolly was merely strange, Nancy seemed seriously deranged.

So Marco mentally rewrote the whole of his proposed e-mail to Josh.

...and there's only the tower left on the Tor now, like a huge standing stone, which my grandfather says is a pagan symbol.

My grandfather, William Woolaston, is a well-known local amateur historian with a particular interest in neo... neolith... ancient monuments. He and my gran live in an old farmhouse in a very rural location.

In fact the cottage was so crooked and ancient you could imagine it had actually grown out of the ground like a mushroom, and Marco had seen bigger bus shelters.

...with lots of antiques and curios, many of a religious nature.

Stuck to the rough wall on one side of the front door was something Marco had recognized from *Buffy the Vampire Slayer* and other similar stuff on TV: a five-pointed metal star inside a circle. A pentagram.

A symbol of, um, witchcraft.

Well, he hadn't liked to ask. He'd just followed his

grandparents inside, where the problems Mum had with Nancy and Woolly became ever clearer.

At home, you see, Mum was into what she called "minimalist furnishing", which seemed to be about making your living room look like a dentist's waiting room. Lately, Mum had taken to calling it their "living *space*".

Whereas, in Woolly and Nancy's room, there was no space at all, and if living depended on breathing it was a miracle either of them was still around. They had to clear a pile of books off the table just to make room for Marco to eat, and Woolly had to put the books on the floor because all the shelves were overflowing and sticking out at funny angles, due to none of the walls being straight.

My grandparents are very interested in world music...

Propped up between the pictures and hanging from the huge oak beams were several acoustic guitars and some other string instruments with crooked necks and bulgy backs. There were also bongos and flat drums and other things you banged on. And the walls looked even less straight at the bottom on account of they were bulging with huge stereo speakers and hundreds of those old black vinyl records with giant covers that opened out to reveal pictures of five long-haired blokes in animal masks standing on some remote hillside, with nowhere to plug in their guitars. And higher up...

...and they also collect works of art.

...were these paintings with no frames, done in big splattery colours like they'd come straight out of the tube. It was fair to say the paintings had all been done by Nancy because it said *Nancy* in the corner of each in big splattery letters. And, like, what were the paintings *about*?

"Well..." Nancy had done a lot of thinking before answering Marco's question. "I guess they're about *splatters*, lovey. Now what you wanner eat?"

Marco had said he was really tired. Long journey, all that. Said he didn't normally eat at night. He was hearing his dad saying, *They don't eat normal food.*

Too late. The items on his plate had resembled some of the splatters in the paintings. Bit like fried vomit. But then there was a sort of chocolate cake and a can of Pepsi, so that was okay.

"So what do you normally do at night, Marco?" Woolly asked him, with a glance at all the albums. "Chill out to some sounds?"

"Er...watch TV?"

"Ah." Woolly looked at Nancy. "Bit of a problem there, then."

None at all? Not *one*? Not even an antique one with a wooden cabinet and a square screen? Couldn't they *afford* one?

Well, that didn't seem likely. After all, they had this huge stereo system with hundreds of albums that were like archaeology. *Captain Beefheart and His Magic Band*? For heaven's *sake*!

And, obviously, there was no computer here either, so it was a good job he'd brought his laptop and a bunch of games and DVDs.

Marco sank back on a pillow that smelled of herbs or something.

Through the open window, he could hear a snatching, ripping sound from below that he knew was Merlin the donkey moodily tearing out clumps of grass at the foot of an apple tree. He didn't think animals ate at night.

He must have fallen asleep. But it seemed like only seconds later that his eyes sprang open in response to a new noise outside that was like...

Errrgh...errrgh...errrgh...

"No!" he heard through the open window. "Not now, Merlin, you fool. You want the devils to know we're on to 'em?"

It was Woolly.

Marco slid out of bed.

Through the window, he could see a small moving light, a bit reddish. He guessed this was Woolly with his hand shading a torch beam.

Nothing else happened, and after a few minutes the light disappeared and he heard the back door slam.

He crept out onto the landing.

"...gone," he heard Woolly saying from the kitchen. "But there's another hole and fresh soil where they been diggin'."

"We should never've took this on," Nancy said. "We're too old for this."

"Speak for yourself, girl. I ain't too old to see these devils off."

"Don't go out again. Please. We don't want no violence. Not with Marco here. Oh, Woolly, we should never've let Angus bring him."

"Nancy, man, 'tis gonner be all right. I'll *handle* it."

"'Tis *not* gonner be all right, though, is it? What if something happens to him? Our only grandchild?"

"It's me they want out the way," Woolly said. "What could happen to *him*?"

"You want a list?" Nancy said.

The Promise

Rats.

It was probably just rats.

Rosa completely rolled herself up in the duvet, lying on her back with just her eyes over the top, staring into the fuzzy dark.

She should tell Dad. She should get up and go and knock on their bedroom door. *Dad, there...might be somebody in the old shop.*

But she'd have to get up to do that and walk past the monk.

Who would *be* there. It was impossible, after that dream, that the monk would not be back in the wall next to the bedroom door.

The room was ashy grey with moonlight, and if she turned over she knew she'd see the light gleaming off the newly-painted wall, and she knew that the monk would be there, and – oh God – his spindly, dead hands would probably be reaching out for her from the drooping sleeves of his rotting robe.

She went rigid in the duvet as the noise came again.

A bit different this time, a sliding, grating noise.

It was no good; she couldn't ignore it. She'd have to do something this time. Mum and Dad's bedroom was over the hallway, so they wouldn't have heard anything, even if they'd been awake. It was up to her.

So Rosa had to make a promise to herself and to God.

I'll put the light on.

If he's there, I won't move. I won't be able to move – you do understand that, don't you? If he's there I'll just...die or something.

If he's not there, I promise I'll get up and do something about the noise. Maybe tell Dad.

There was no going back now. She reached up for the light-pull over her bed, held the plastic knob-thing in her hand, breathing very fast. She had to do it now – she'd promised, and it was binding. If she broke her promise, something totally horrible would happen, like Mum would get cancer or something.

So she had no choice. She shut her eyes and pulled on the cord and opened her eyes, with a gasp, blinking in the sudden light, wrenching her head round to face the wall by the door, and the room was as bright as day, and the wall...

...the wall was all white.

No monk.

Rosa sobbed. An instant of terrible relief.

Which didn't last. She knew it wouldn't last. She couldn't totally believe it, you see. She never believed anything first time. She had to do this *three more times,* very deliberately, concentrating dead hard, before she could believe it. Four times altogether. Four was a compact, even number, a safe number. You could trust four.

Still staring at the wall, she switched off the light and then pulled the cord again.

No monk.

Again.

Nothing.

Again.

This time she left the light on and, still staring at the wall, because she didn't trust herself, she slid out of bed and dived into her slippers. Then she pulled a sweatshirt over her pyjamas, half-afraid that when her head came through the hole, after a moment of darkness, the monk would be smiling at her from deep inside his cowl.

He wasn't.

She felt almost faint with relief. And then she made herself turn away and look again, *four times,* before she could accept it was safe and let herself ease open the bedroom door, leaving it fully open behind her as she stepped out onto the grim brown lino on the landing.

The light from her room showed the way along the narrow

passage, which was kind of an elbow round the stairs, with doors to the bathroom and the big bedroom where her parents slept. The closed doors opposite, across the stairwell, were to the kitchen and the living room.

Rosa paused outside Mum and Dad's bedroom.

Dad, there's somebody in the old shop.

Her fist was raised ready to bang on the door. She'd have to bang four times, of course, to make sure—

Rosa froze.

What if there was nobody down there? What if Dad went down in his dressing gown and there was nobody there for him to shout at? Nothing. Just like there was no monk in the wall.

They already thought she was mad. This would be the final proof.

Her arm dropped to her side, her hand still clenched into a fist. She couldn't do it, could she? Dad was very big on getting a good night's sleep, and if he didn't he was usually in a terrible mood the following day, and she and Mum would have a hard time. Rosa was even doubting, now, that she'd heard a noise down there. But that didn't matter; she had to do *something* or she'd have broken her promise and something bad would happen.

Therefore *she* would have to go down. She didn't have a choice. If she didn't go down, if she went back to her room, she'd have gone back on her promise, and the monk would be there waiting for her, as a sign of...what was that hard-sounding word that Dad used in church?

Retribution.

It meant payback.

Payback for being a coward and not keeping your word.

Rosa stood at the top of the stairs, staring down into the darkness.

Only it wasn't *totally* dark down there. Faint street light was oozing in through the pane of grimy glass over the front door. Mercifully, you couldn't see the door to the old shop from up here, otherwise she'd have had to make herself look over the banister at it, four times, every night before going to bed, but you always knew it was there, and that was bad enough. There was something evil about that door, evil as sin.

Holding tight to the banister with both hands, Rosa edged down the stairs – one by one, so she wouldn't trip and make a noise.

Let it be rats. Please let it be rats. Furry, squeaky, scrabbling rats.

She counted the stairs as she went down. She knew there were thirteen, and that was unlucky, so she always either jumped over the bottom step, making it twelve or – which she did now, because she didn't want to make a noise – stepped on the bottom step twice, making it fourteen. Which wasn't the safest of even numbers, but it would do.

Now she was at the bottom.

She'd never been down here in the dark before. It was chilly and musty and it smelled of fly spray – when you couldn't see much, you were always more aware of the smells – and the light from over the big front door came down over her like thin, transparent plastic, and the dust tickled her nose and made her want to...

Don't let me sneeze!

She clamped a hand over her nose and ducked down behind the post at the foot of the stairs. Between the stairs and the front door was the door to the old shop. She would look at it four times, to make sure it was closed and then...

...what?

Could she bear to go up to it?

There was no sound. Total silence.

And yet the silence itself seemed like a noise. A hollow, yawning noise, as if she was not in some cramped little hallway but a vast place, the size of a ballroom. And then there was another noise, like a kind of sob, and she realized that it was her own breath coming out.

And then she looked at the door to the old shop and had to bite on her hand to stop herself screaming.

By day, the glass in the door was always dark.

Now it wasn't.

It kind of glowed. And the glow was shivering.

No! It must be the reflection of the light from the street. And it must be *her* that was shivering. Mustn't let her imagination take over. Mustn't...be afraid.

But she was, she was terrified. Only, she'd made a promise.

Sobbing inside, she stood up and forced herself to walk towards the door, telling herself that maybe, when the shop had been open, it had not been like one of the weirdo shops, but just an ordinary shop, like a grocer's or a chemist's or a hardware store or a small supermarket with signs like *Special Offer* and *Buy One, Get One Free*.

She went right up to the door. Put her nose up to the greasy glass, standing on tiptoe, supporting herself by holding onto the handle. See...there was nothing there, nothing at—

The handle turned in her hand and, with a wheezing sound, the door – the *locked* door – opened.

Rosa's breath slammed into the back of her throat as her body fell forward into the shop.

She stumbled and clutched at the handle, but it was too late. She was standing in the open doorway, with old, musty air all around her, cold as winter, and long, dark shadows that were like drab, rotting coats hanging on the walls.

Rosa stood there, couldn't move, choked up with a fear she couldn't explain, becoming aware of an awful smell. A foul smell of, like, when Mum had found some old butter once, at the back of a cupboard and it had gone off, gone – that word that sounded just like what it meant – *rancid*.

The smell was like old, rancid fat.

Rosa clamped a hand to her mouth, choking, as the shadows moved, like the coats were unhooking themselves from the pegs and slithering towards her.

And then, with a rippling shudder, she became aware of the origin of the glow.

It was a little ball of cold white light in the farthest corner of the room, but it wasn't lighting up anything. It was just *there*, floating in the blackness.

And Rosa finally gave in to the terror and screamed.

Part Two

"Unlike most things which scientists measure, men are not all alike. Some can see, hear, feel and experience things which others cannot."

TC LETHBRIDGE
Ghost and Divining Rod

The Blight

It was morning, and Marco had woken up with a headache.
Huh?

Sorry, but this didn't happen. He didn't *get* headaches.

Well, okay, once. That time, last winter, up in Josh's
executive bedroom, when Josh had produced these cans of
lager from his mini-fridge. It had seemed a cool and daring
thing to do at the time, and how was Marco to know what the
effects would be?

Like, how could he have realized it was going to take him
more than three quarters of an hour – falling, en route, into
several flower tubs and the ornamental water feature – to find

his way home across the courtyard to the block directly opposite? And how was *he* to know that, having made it across the courtyard and into the building, it would somehow take another half-hour to find the right flat?

He dimly recalled being dripping wet and continually pressing the wrong buttons in the lift, going up and down and up and down and feeling more and more sick.

He remembered about an hour of *being* sick in the lavatory, with Dad standing over him looking grim. And, he remembered *very* clearly spending most of the next day wishing he was dead.

Admittedly, it wasn't quite that bad this time. He didn't feel sick or anything, but his head was certainly thick and dull and full of pinpricks of pain, as if it had been packed solid with Brillo pads.

And when he could bear to open his eyes, everything looked drab and colourless. His room seemed smaller than it had last night – he felt squashed in, and he didn't like that; he was claustrophobic.

The walls looked more grey than white. The only bright spot was the painting (obviously one of Nancy's), on the wall opposite the bed, of a white-hot splatter of yellow, like a full-on sun that was so glaring it hurt your eyes.

But this was the only sun around this morning, even though it felt warm and stuffy in his little room. The oak beam over the sunken window seemed like it was holding up the whole weight of the sky, which was as grey and heavy as the inside of Marco's head.

The window...

He stumbled to the nearest window, with vague memories of standing there last night and feeling this excited kind of glow. What had happened to him last night? And where had it gone? Why was he feeling like this? Had Woolly and Nancy spiked his Pepsi? Were they big-time dopeheads? Had Nancy's chocolate cake contained cannabis? Was *that* why his mum had kept him away?

Marco moaned. Nothing at all glowed out there now. The town buildings looked dull and yellowy. Maybe the glow had just been a dream. What he remembered of it had certainly felt unreal. After all, he must have been really knackered last night. Maybe it had all just been wishful thinking. Josh would probably say his tortured mind had created a fantasy-Glastonbury to stop him going mad and chasing after Dad's car, screaming, *Wait, wait... Take me home, take me home!*

And yet...Marco ran across the room and peered through the other window. There was the Tor, although it didn't seem quite so close this morning, or quite so powerful. The church tower on top was...just a church tower. Quite stubby compared with the tower of the church in the town but, because of its prominent position on top of the hill, it made much more of a statement.

If anything could be said to be making a statement on a morning this grey and dreary.

* * *

"Aha!" Woolly beamed at him. "You know what you got, boy...you know what's wrong with you?"

Marco gave his granddad a moody look. If he knew *that*...

"You got an Avalon hangover. An overload! Happens occasionally to newcomers. And, don't knock it, dude...it's a good sign. Means you're tuned into the energy."

"Huh?"

"Course it ain't helped by the Blight. The ole Blight's come early this year."

Woolly was trying to make some room on the living-room table, which appeared to have filled up again overnight with books and CDs and all kinds of junk. Nancy was in the kitchen preparing breakfast. Not that Marco felt much like anything to eat. Maybe a slice of toast, with marmalade. Okay, maybe a *couple* of slices.

"What's the Blight?"

He looked up at Woolly, whose hair was loose, hanging down each side of his face like a white waterfall. He wore a T-shirt that had once been orange. Without his dark glasses on, you could see his eyes were bright blue like Mum's, but all crinkly, as if Woolly had spent a lot of his life laughing. Which, with the best will in the world, you probably couldn't say of Mum.

"Ah...well...usually we don't get the Blight till the middle of August, look," Woolly said. "'Tis when the atmosphere goes real close and heavy and it seems like you can't hardly breathe. And tempers get terrible frayed, and fights break out in the pubs, and the town goes all Us and Them, kind of thing."

"How d'you mean?" Marco said.

"Well..." Woolly put his head on one side. "Us – that's the locals, folks born and bred locally."

"Which is you, right?"

"Well, that *is* me, yeah. But also..." Woolly tilted his head to the other side. "I'm also one of *Them*, look. *Them* is the mystical cats – the Avalon pilgrims."

"Pilgrims?"

"It's what I call the folks from outside what comes to live here on account of the legends and the magic. Most local folks – the Glasties – they pretend they don't believe a word of any of it. They goes around moaning about the town bein' overrun by loony shops selling magical candles and crystal balls and incense sticks and all that tackle. *They* wants more butchers and hairdressers and Marks and Spencers and leisure centres. Oh yes, things gets real bad sometimes between the locals and the pilgrims."

"But if nobody wants these pilgrims, why do they keep coming?"

"Because of the *magic!*" Woolly's arms came up, like some magic had just shot through him. "Because of the *legends* – of which we got more than almost any place in the entire world, and that's a proven fact. So way back in the 1960s and 70s, they all came pouring in, *to feel the magic.*"

"Legends?" Marco's head was throbbing. Some of the stuff Woolly had talked about last night, about the Tor, was coming back.

"All down to the Holy Grail, look. You wanner know the whole story?"

"Um..."

"'Cause if you gets in with the pilgrims," Woolly said, looking him in the eyes, "you're on the slippery slope. You oughter know that."

"Now you stop that teasing, Woolly Woolaston!" Nancy had come in from the kitchen with a plate of hot toast. "He don't need to know any of this stuff, do you lovey?"

"Stop what?" Woolly said, looking innocent.

"Filling him up with...*you know*. He's not been here two minutes and you're off!"

"Nancy, if the boy's gonner spend the summer here, he needs to know how the land lies."

"Might be better if he don't." Nancy said, fixing Woolly with this dark, warning look.

And Marco remembered something else from late last night – the voices of Nancy and Woolly in the kitchen, and Nancy whispering, *And what if something happens to him? Our only grandchild?*

She looked less deranged this morning. Her hair was like a haystack, and the ruby-red nose stud was in place, but she hadn't got her lurid make-up on yet. She was wearing a dressing gown with pink dragons on it.

Woolly looked at Marco, like he couldn't decide about something. Marco wondered why Woolly called some people "pilgrims".

"So which was Mum?" he asked, as brightly as he could. "Was Mum...*Us* or *Them*?"

Woolly looked at Nancy and Nancy looked at Woolly, as

if he'd started something he shouldn't have. Marco felt a bit embarrassed for both of them, but he was curious now. There was something going on here which Woolly wasn't quite sure that Marco should know about, but Nancy was definitely sure that he *shouldn't*.

Which, of course, meant he had to find out.

Woolly looked down at the cooling toast.

"Neither," he said eventually. "Alison never cared who believed what and who hated who in this town. She just wanted out."

"And she never came back?"

"No. At least, not after..."

Marco waited. Woolly concentrated on spreading half a slice of toast with Marmite.

"After what?" Marco said.

"So what would you like to do today, Marco?" Nancy said cheerfully.

"Yeah, what about a tour of the sights?" Woolly suggested, taking a bite of toast.

What about telling me why my mum hasn't been back here for at least thirteen years? Marco thought, his head throbbing so hard he was surprised they couldn't hear it.

"I...um, I need to send some e-mails," he mumbled.

And then mega-disaster struck.

Up in his room, he pulled the laptop out of his Man U bag along with Marvin the rabbit, figuring Marvin would sit well in this room because Nancy had painted rabbits all over a chest of drawers – blue, red and yellow rabbits with lopsided grins frolicking under an orange sky. Looked like the cover of one of Woolly's old vinyl albums.

Marco plugged in the laptop at the power point next to his bed and set it to boot up, thinking maybe he could also put *Glastonbury, Avalon* and *magic* into Google, see what came up about the Tor and the pilgrims.

Only the laptop didn't boot up. Even the pilot light didn't come on.

What?

Marco unplugged the lead from both the power point and the computer and then plugged them both back in firmly and switched on again.

Nothing. The laptop was dead.

"No...*please...*"

He kept stabbing at the on-off button. This *couldn't happen.* He *needed* this laptop. It was a major part of his *entire support-mechanism.* It was his lifeline. Without it, he couldn't e-mail Josh, or Dad. But mainly Josh, who seemed to rely on his daily electronic input.

He was stuffed. Stranded. Alone with the loonies and the pilgrims, with no one out there to talk to about it. He looked at Marvin, and Marvin looked gloomily back from the chest of drawers. Marvin had only one expression: gloomy.

There was a tap on the door and Woolly's voice came from the landing, hesitant.

"Problems?"

Marco stood up and sniffed back his...frustration. He opened the door.

"How's the headache?" Woolly said.

"Worse," Marco said.

"Sorry to hear that. Can I come in?"

"Sure."

Woolly came in carefully, trying not to stand on all the stuff Marco had taken out of his bag and spread on the floor – the computer games and the DVD of *Harry Potter and The Chamber of Secrets* – and sat on the bed, pinching his chin meditatively.

"See, what it is, Marco...some folks come to Glasto, have a walk around the Abbey, do a bit of shopping and don't feel a thing. Folks like your dad. I ain't *knockin'* your dad, you understand. He just don't feel some things. Maybe that's lucky for him. Be a bit hard to function as a big city lawyer if you was always feeling stuff, wouldn't it?"

Marco stared down. If there was so much energy in this town, how come none of it was passing through his laptop?

"On the other hand," Woolly said, "I could tell straight off, something was happening to *you*. I could see it, the way you were moving round, and so could ole Merlin. Donkeys are very wise, and they sees it all. Remember how he come straight up to you?"

"He butted me in the back."

"*Exactly*. He don't do that to everybody. He could tell you was – and I don't use this word lightly, dude – an Avalonian."

"Huh?"

"I oversimplified it a bit just now. There *is* two kinds of people here, but it's not Them and Us, it's more important than that. There's the Glasties – that's the folk that lives in the town just like 'tis any other town – and there's the Avalonians. And they're the ones what are tuned into a deeper vibe. They're the ones that comes here and finds their inner selves – their souls, kind of thing – was here before them. Don't tell me you didn't feel something entering your soul last night, Marco, 'cause if you did I wouldn't believe you."

"Well...yeah," Marco said. "But it wasn't as if it was something that hadn't happened before."

Woolly's eyes widened. "*Really?*"

"It was just like...you know, being in a dream. Only you're still awake. I don't really like it."

"Better than a hangover, though, eh?"

"It's just a headache, Woolly."

"Ah," Woolly said.

"Oh come on, it's just a headache!"

Woolly slowly shook his head. "No, dude, what it is, look, is your body coming back down. You was up there last night – don't say you wasn't – and now you've come down with a bump and it's left you with a hangover. That's how powerful the vibe is in this town. Least it is for the *Avalonians*. Sometimes it skips over a generation, look."

"What does?"

"The vibe. So, while your ma couldn't get away fast enough, there's some part of you that knows it *belongs here*."

"Which is more than you can say for this computer," Marco said.

Woolly leaned down to have a look. "What's the problem?"

Marco kept staring at the screen and prodding at the mouse. But it was useless. The mouse just clicked emptily, and the screen stayed grey and vacant.

"It's kna—" Marco gritted his teeth. "It won't work."

"That happens around here, I'm afraid, boss." Woolly looked doleful and pulled at his droopy moustache. "Things goes off. Just stop working." Woolly shrugged. "It can get a bit inconvenient, naturally, but it's one of the things you just gotter get used to if you lives in Glasto. Electrical things gets affected."

Marco felt his eyes rolling. This was getting ridiculous. The most likely reason there was something wrong with the laptop was the way his dad had been throwing the bag around yesterday. *That* was the problem – absolutely nothing to do with the vibes in Glastonbury. The problem with Woolly and his mates, the pilgrims or the Avalonians or whatever, was they were completely half-baked in a way that Josh could probably explain. Maybe they didn't have enough to do. What did Woolly do, for instance? Marco didn't know if he was retired, or what.

Anyway, none of it mattered. He was seriously hacked-off. No TV and even the stupid laptop was dead. *This place...* Marco stabbed at the mouse in anguish, thinking, *This whole place is totally and utterly crap!*

"Sorry, dude," Woolly said. "Still, sometimes there's an

upside to it, look. Sometimes, things what have never worked proper anywhere else, you bring them here and they *starts* working."

"So what I need," Marco said bitterly, "is some clapped-out old computer that hasn't run a program since like the last millennium?"

"Yeah, well, maybe the energy don't work so well with computers." Woolly picked up the DVD, which Marco was never going to be able to watch as long as he was staying here. "What's this one about, then?"

What? Marco looked hard at Woolly. Was the old guy serious?

Woolly blinked innocently. "I've probably *heard* of it somewhere. It do look a bit familiar, 'specially the kid in the glasses."

"Okay." Marco sighed. "The kid in the glasses has secret powers, right? And he goes to wizard school to learn how to use them."

"Oh," Woolly said. "So you've already watched it, then."

"Well, of *course* I've—"

"Wizard school, eh?"

"The idea is that the school exists in this kind of...parallel dimension."

"Ar." Woolly put down the DVD and nodded. "You ever fancy that yourself? Going to wizard school kind of thing? We got a couple of schools like that around the town. They don't take kids, though."

Marco figured the old guy was seriously winding him up

this time. He explained – with more patience than Woolly deserved, frankly – how the kid in the DVD was only accepted at the special wizard school because he was *already* a wizard. One of the Chosen.

Woolly sniffed. "Sounds a bit elitist."

"Huh?"

"Like, only for 'special' kids. Why can't *anybody* be a wizard?"

"It's complicated," Marco said.

"I never said it wasn't, but that don't mean—"

"Anyway, what am I going to *do,* Woolly? I'm totally stuffed here. I can't even access my e-mails."

It would be another four, maybe even six weeks before Dad came to take him home. *Six weeks.* Marco turned to the window and stared out at the Tor, feeling hostile, like it was the Tor that had blasted his laptop.

Don't go there. Mum's voice.

"So, like, what *am* I going to do?"

"Ah." Woolly put his head on one side, his white hair resting on the shoulder of his yellow velvet waistcoat. "Now there's a question."

Marco waited, hoping Woolly might finally remember some mate of his in the town who was a genuine computer whizz. But Woolly just felt around in his waistcoat pocket, eventually fishing out a piece of blue twine. He pulled on the twine. Something toppled out of the pocket, and Woolly caught it in his hand.

Marco briefly closed his eyes. Not a conjuring trick...*please.*

Woolly opened his hand. The end of the blue twine was threaded through a metal clasp at the top of a pale stone about the size of a door key. Woolly let the stone drop to the end of its string, about twenty centimetres, and then he held it up. What small amount of light there was in the room seemed to be collecting in the stone.

"Right then," Woolly said. "What are you going to do, now you're here? That's our question, is it?"

The hanging stone began slowly to move, swinging from side to side – Marco watching it and wondering if Woolly was about to try and hypnotize him or something. Then the stone started to move in a different way, going round in circles, swinging out, and spinning faster and faster like a tiny version of one of those fairground rides that made you feel sick, although you never admitted it.

Marco didn't know what to make of this. He looked up at Woolly, this old man in trainers and frayed jeans and a yellow waistcoat over a T-shirt that was so old the name of the band had worn off the front.

"Er...what are you doing, exactly, Woolly?"

They both watched the stone revolve. It seemed to be flashing and shimmering with warm, starry colours. Staring at the stone, Marco realized his headache had gone.

"I'm waiting for an answer," Woolly said.

"Okay." Marco gave in. "What *is* that thing?"

"It's a pendulum."

"Like in a clock?"

"No," Woolly said. "Not like in a clock."

"What does it do?"

Woolly smiled, and his whole face lit up like a lamp.

"Wrong question. What you oughter be asking is, *What don't it do?*"

"I don't understand."

"Oh, you *do* understand," Woolly said. "Deep inside you understands everything." He stood up. "I reckon we oughter take a walk."

"Where to?"

Marco heard Nancy shouting from downstairs. "Woolly, if you're filling up that boy's head with... Woolly!"

"Where to?" Marco said.

"Woolly Woolaston, you come down here this minute!" Nancy screeched.

"To the magical heart of it all." Woolly tapped his nose.

Then he pointed out of the window towards the Tor.

Land of the Dead

As soon after breakfast as she could, Rosa had got out of there...got out of the flat, gone racing down the stairs, for once not even looking at the door of that...that *disgusting*...

She was so upset, so sick, so...mad.

Now she stood in the street, under the thick, soupy sky, breathing hard and looking desperately around her. There was about an hour every morning when you might get the idea that this was actually quite a normal town: people going to work – some men even wearing suits – provisions arriving at the *normal* shops, deliveries of milk and mail, that kind of ordinary morning stuff.

Simple, commonplace, unexceptional. Normal, normal, normal.

Oh *sure*.

It had been just awful in there, over breakfast. Eating was agony. She'd been so cold and stiff inside that her tummy felt like it was lined with lead, like a church roof.

Dad hadn't even spoken to her. His face had been like some religious statue. When he'd finally gone off to the church, Mum had said, "I'm sorry you had a bad dream, but..."

And then she'd begun to clear away the breakfast things before Rosa could say, No it wasn't! It *wasn't* a dream! It wasn't, it wasn't, it *wasn't*!

Still, she didn't remember how she'd got out of the shop. Only all the lights being on and Dad, furious, pulling her to her feet in the hallway, with his hair all sticking up, and Mum halfway down the stairs, holding her dressing gown to her throat, crying, "Dave, please...make *allowances*!"

Make allowances for Rosa being mentally ill was what she'd meant.

Oh, it was clear enough what they were both thinking. Last night, Dad had made a big thing of shaking the shop door and then stood back and made Rosa shake it, too, looking like he wanted to shake *her*.

"Locked. You'll agree that it's locked!"

"It is *now*," Rosa had sobbed. "But it was open, I swear it was open...and there was a noise...and a light..."

Dad had made an exasperated noise through his teeth and turned away. Just thinking about it had made Rosa realize she was all hunched up – like rigid – at the memory. She could feel a deep well of tears behind her eyes, but she was beyond crying now; she was in despair. *Something had been waiting for her in the old dark shop.*

She stood on the edge of the pavement, staring down the hill towards the market cross and the ancient inn, The George and Pilgrims, where Mum was going to work on the reception desk. Christian pilgrims had always come to Glastonbury, Dad had said, but now it was mostly pagans attracted by *the evil* here. He was always going on about the evil in the town, but he couldn't see the *real* evil under their own flat. *He* thought evil was something that only existed in people's minds and the things they did – the sort of evil he'd had to deal with as a policeman. *I left the police to become a priest,* he'd told her once, *because I wanted to help people instead of just putting them away.*

And now he was probably thinking about putting his own daughter away. You could tell they'd been talking about her, him and Mum, by the way they'd exchanged silent glances over breakfast.

"How's it going, Rosa?"

Rosa spun round. Jasper Coombes was leaning against a lamp-post, chewing gum, looking cool. Jasper with his tight, dark curls and his smoky eyes. She'd forgotten all about Jasper.

"Something wrong, Rosa?" Jasper said.

"Why should there be something wrong?"

Jasper just smiled. Rosa blushed. She probably looked

awful. She probably had rings under her eyes and tear stains on her cheeks.

"That shop under our flat – whose is it?"

She hadn't meant to ask that; it had just come out. Well, he'd know, wouldn't he? His dad was the agent who collected the rent for the owner.

And she realized she was desperate to tell somebody about last night and about the monk and everything – somebody who wouldn't think she was mad.

"Why do you ask?" Jasper said.

Rosa shrugged. "Just interested. Just wondered who owned it."

"Some guy," Jasper said. "And he rented it to some other guy. Shops change hands all the time in this town."

"What did it sell?"

"What do any of them sell?" Jasper said. "Rubbish nobody wants unless they're half crazy. You want to come to a party tonight?"

"What?"

"We're having a party. We thought you might want to come."

"Who?"

"Some friends of mine. It's a very select party. Guaranteed no freaks."

"I've...got a lot to do," Rosa said.

"Yeah?" Jasper said. "I'll see you around, then."

Rosa was embarrassed. She just couldn't go to a party full of strangers.

A man came past in a kind of pink frock. Jasper didn't look at him, just strolled off. Rosa walked miserably up the street. She saw the man from the Crystal Grotto getting out his keys to unlock the door of his shop.

And then found she was running towards him.

"But what is it, *really*, Woolly?" Marco stared up at the Tor. It seemed huge now. "I mean it's not just an ordinary hill, is it?"

"The Tor's the key to everything," Woolly said. "It's the main reason all the pilgrims come flocking to Glasto."

He and Marco had walked over the fields and come out in the narrow road he and Dad had driven up last night. The trees on either side were heavy with leaves and, even though there was no sun, the air smelled of summer the way it never did in London.

According to Woolly, it was crucially important to come to the Tor on foot.

"Think of it as a pilgrimage," he said mysteriously.

They were standing by a wooden gate, now, looking over to a field out of which the hill just suddenly swelled up, like a huge green tea cosy, and you could see the church tower on its summit. The tower looked strong and dark, with battlements. There were luminous, sandy-coloured clouds above it.

"We're lucky," Woolly said. "There's usually quite a few tourists here by now. There'll probably be a few people up there, but it won't be too bad."

"Pilgrims?"

"All sorts. It's a tourist attraction, and everybody feels they gotter climb it once. And you *definitely* can't be a true Avalonian till you been up the Tor. Come on."

Woolly nodded at the stile and Marco climbed over, and they walked across the field. Buttercups were out everywhere, and the dullness of the day somehow made them shine in the grass, and Woolly seemed to be shining, too. He had his dark glasses on, and his T-shirt was orange and his face was brown.

"Woolly, how come there's just a church tower on top, but no church?"

"Ah." Woolly smiled. "That's an interesting question. Goes back to the question of who's really in charge of the Tor."

Woolly explained that, although nobody knew this for certain, the traditional theory was that, in pagan times, there'd been a great circle of stones on top of the Tor – like Stonehenge. But when the Christian Church took over, the stones were taken away and a church was built on top, dedicated to St Michael.

"You know who *he* was, dude?"

"One of the top angels, right? An archangel."

Woolly nodded. "And also – and this is the key point – he was the one in charge of holding back the ole gods, the Forces of Darkness."

"Er...right."

"But the ole gods were real powerful here. It was believed the Tor was hollow, look, and this was where the King of the Underworld held court."

Woolly looked up at the top of the hill with a kind of reverence.

"This was the actual entrance to the Celtic Land of the Dead," he said. "And some folks believes it still is."

"Erm...excuse me...have you got a minute?"

The man turned round in the shop doorway and smiled vaguely at her. He was plump and had ginger hair with a fringe at the front. Rosa wasn't tall enough to see whether he had one of those little circles shaven on top of his head, like monks had. But if he had, she didn't think she'd be surprised.

"Ah...*I* know who *you* are." The man was wearing his purple velvet smock, with a silver chain around his neck. "You came in with your mother. You're the new vicar's daughter, right?"

"Curate," Rosa said. "He wants to be a vicar, one day, but he's only a curate at the moment."

"I see. What can I do for you?"

"I just... Can I talk to you? There's something I need to know," Rosa said. "It's about what you told us about the stones from the Abbey being in the wall. And how you used to be a monk."

"Oh," he said, "well, I can't prove anything, you know. It's just a feeling I've got."

He jangled his keys nervously. Rosa didn't move.

"Look," he said, "if you're doing a school project or something, I don't think—"

"Things have been happening to me," Rosa said. "And Mum and Dad think it's because of what you said."

"Oh, hell." He blinked. "Sorry... Look, just let me go in and put some lights on, okay?"

When he finally let her into the shop, the crystals were glittering wildly out of cushiony nooks of black velvet, the displays brought alive by concealed lighting. He'd also switched on a couple of extra lights in the ceiling, so it was a lot brighter in here than it had been the other day.

"I hate it when something like this happens," he said. "I never want to scare anybody. That's not what it's all about."

"It wasn't you who scared me," Rosa said.

"Look, have you talked to your father about this...whatever it is that's bothering you?"

"He wouldn't believe me. My mum and him, they think I've gone crazy. They think I'm imagining things."

"But your father's a clergyman."

"It's not *the same*," Rosa said. "Just because you believe in God doesn't mean you believe in...other things."

She turned away, brushing her sleeve quickly over her eyes.

"Look..." He sighed and went behind a counter. "Where exactly do you live?"

"Just...just along the street. In the flat over the shop that's closed? With the black blind down? And I..."

She stood staring at him for a moment; she could feel her bottom lip quivering.

And then it all just came out, faster and faster, like being sick. And, just like being sick, once it had started she couldn't stop it.

"...I kept seeing a monk on the wall, only nobody else could see it, only me, and so they think I'm out of my mind and mentally ill...and then last night there was a noise in the old shop and I went down and there's a door in the hall where you used to be able to go into the shop but it's locked up now, but last night it wasn't locked, it was open and I went in, although I didn't want to go in, but something seemed to *want* me to, and there was *something in there,* in the dark, except it wasn't dark, there was this little white light like a candle, only there didn't seem to be anybody holding it and the smell in there was totally disgusting and it was evil...totally sick and evil just like I knew it was going to be and I...and they think I'm mentally ill and—"

She broke off, blinking, then looking around at all the crystals. What was she doing here, blurting all this out to a total stranger?

The man looked down at the counter. Rosa could see he was biting his upper lip.

"I suppose we'd better talk about this, hadn't we?" he said.

He didn't look happy.

Too Much Magic

They'd reached the foot of the great hill, this huge bulge in the earth. It kept changing. Close up, it looked like it had circular ridges around it, a bit like a misshapen beehive, and it was easy to believe it could be hollow.

"The King of the Dead was called Gwyn, and he used to ride out with his pack of hounds, through the night sky, rounding up souls," Woolly said.

In his head, Marco saw the witchy woman Woolly had introduced as the voice of the goddess, and she was going, *"I have been dreaming...of Gwyn ap Neeth and his Hounds of Hell. I saw them rushing through the darkening sky, with eyes of fire and fangs bared.*"

"Gwyn ap Neeth, right?" Marco said.

"Spot on! It's spelled A-P N-U-D-D. It's Welsh – that's the old Celtic language. That's what they spoke when the Druids did their rituals on the Tor."

"Blood sacrifices?" Marco said.

"So some folks says. They thought they had to honour the Lord of the Dead. See those ridges that rings the hill – that's said to be a ritual maze going round and round the Tor, where the Druids had their processions."

"Spooky." Marco stood on a grassy hump, with his back to the Tor. "So the Christians built a church on top of the entrance to the Land of the Dead?"

Woolly nodded. "They wanted to stamp out the ole superstitions and prove that their religion was on top. But it didn't last, look. About a thousand years ago, there was this earthquake, and the whole church fell down, except for the tower – which from a distance, as you'll have noticed, looks like a standing stone. And a standing stone...well, like I said last night, that's a symbol of paganism."

"So this is now, like, a *pagan* church."

"In a way." Woolly stood among the buttercups, nodding. "But I prefer to see it as a bit of a compromise between the old religion and the new. Like, something here's saying, okay, you can keep the main bit of your church, but however people want to worship up here, that's up to them, look. And if you want a church service up here, you can have one, but it's gotter be in the open air, so you don't forget where you are. Course there's some as says the dark rituals never stopped – that they was carried on for centuries in an underground maze – a secret labyrinth under the town and the Abbey and the—"

Woolly stopped, looking beyond Marco, at the hill. He was facing the light, but Marco was sure he'd gone paler.

There was the sound of a slow, rhythmic handclap.

Marco spun round. A man stood there.

He was tall and thin and, seen against the light, seemed like a silhouette, all black. But where had he come from? There was only the hill behind. It was almost like he'd come out of the hill.

The man kept on clapping, in a lazy rhythm. It sounded contemptuous, somehow, but he seemed to be smiling.

"Nicely put, Mr. Woolaston," he said. "All drivel, but it was nicely put."

Woolly said nothing, but Marco noticed he was breathing harder.

"So what brings you to my domain?" the man asked.

His black shirt was open to his chest, and there was something on a chain around his neck. It looked like some kind of cross.

Woolly stood very still. He was about a head shorter than this man and – Marco wasn't much good at estimating people's ages – probably about twenty years older.

"It ain't your domain," Woolly said. "And if you're looking to wind me up, you picked the wrong day, man."

"Who's the child?" the man asked.

He walked over, making this slithery sound because of the leather trousers he was wearing. Now Marco saw his full face. It was long and bony, and he had a hooked nose. His head was completely bald, but dark with stubble.

And he wasn't actually smiling; he just had one of those faces that made it look as if he was amused by you and didn't care what you thought about that because you were nothing to him anyway.

He certainly didn't care what Marco thought of him. He'd called him a child.

And there was no going back from *that*.

"I can't see no child," Woolly said. He turned to Marco, "You seen a child anywhere, dude?"

Good old Woolly. Marco was about to say something when the man walked right up to Woolly.

"You thought any more about our offer, Mr. Woolaston?"

Woolly didn't back off, but he didn't look very comfortable with this guy right in his face.

"Sure," he said.

"And?"

There was a silence. Marco looked at the man, then at Woolly and sensed something dark and heavy in the air between them.

"Well..." Woolly put his head on one shoulder. "I thought about it for around fifteen seconds. Then I decided I'd probably got better things to think about." He looked up into the man's face. "Like which hand to scratch my bum with."

Big silence. Marco looked at Woolly with serious admiration.

"And you know what, man?" Woolly said. "This ain't never gonner be your domain. Not as long as I'm alive."

A sliver of sun came through and made thin, trickly veins in the clouds, like the filament in a very weak light bulb. The grass on the side of the Tor seemed to darken, as though a long shadow had been cast across it – or so it seemed to Marco.

"Oh dear," the man said. "*That* doesn't leave us with much of an alternative, does it?"

He smiled and walked past Woolly towards the stile.

Marco watched him go and wondered if he'd heard right.

A gravel footpath had been made up the side of the Tor. Woolly said this was because so many people were scrambling up the hard way that the soil had become eroded. The Tor would probably look like an apple core by now, if that footpath hadn't been made.

So this was where the man had come from, Marco decided. Down the path. Not out of the hill.

Marco followed Woolly up the path, knowing his granddad had been seriously shaken by the encounter with the man, but was doing his best not to show it.

"Who *was* he, Woolly?"

It wasn't long before the top of the hill came in sight. The church tower looked huge now.

"The ole tower's been rebuilt, of course, over the years," Woolly said, panting. "It looks solid enough, but 'tis hollow inside, look, like a chimney. You'll see."

"Who was *that guy*?"

"Look at that view," Woolly said. "You ever see anything like that?"

"Yeah, it's very nice, but—"

Woolly pointed at the grass, for Marco to sit down. Marco sat down a few metres from the foot of the tower, and...

Wow. Despite the dull sky, the view *was* amazing. You could see most of the town, which looked quite small and ordinary, with red-brick housing estates and the shiny roofs of factories.

But somehow you could also see the *shape* of things – the shape of the land itself on which this jumble of buildings had been erected. You could follow the slope of the Tor down over a lower hill and through the pink river of bricks and mortar to a long hill, on the other side of the town, that came up like the humped back of a big fish breaking surface. Woolly pointed to it.

"That's Wearyall Hill, look, where Joe 'Mathea stuck his staff in, and it sprouted and grew into a thorn bush."

"Who?"

"Joseph of Arimathea." Woolly sat down next to Marco. "He was the uncle of Jesus Christ, and he was a rich merchant – big international trader, kind o' thing – and it was said he used to come here, all the way from the Middle East, in his ships. According to one story, he even had Jesus himself with him once, when Jesus was a young lad."

"Jesus came here?"

"Why not? It's possible. You never heard that hymn, 'Jerusalem'? *And did those feet in ancient time walk upon*

England's mountains green? Well, that was Jesus' feet, right? And them mountains green was these same hills what you can see around here."

"They're not exactly mountains, though, are they?" Marco said.

"Well, mountains was just a word that fitted better. Anyway, mountains ain't green, they're all grey and rocky. Take it from me, this is the place. And after Jesus got crucified and rose again and all that stuff, ole Joe 'Mathea, he come back with something real special."

"What?"

"The *Grail*, dude. The Holy Grail. The cup that Jesus had used for the wine at the last supper. It was the holiest relic of them all and, after Jesus had gone, ole Joe, he brought it here, and he's supposed to have hid it away, or buried it, just down there – you see that hill what comes off the side of the Tor down there. That's Chalice Hill, and that's where he's supposed to have stashed it. There's a spring down there called Chalice Well, where the water runs red, like it's got blood in it from the crucifixion. It's iron, really, but never mind."

Marco looked up at Woolly.

"So has nobody ever found it? The cup? I mean, it's not a *very* big area to search, is it?"

"Nope." Woolly shook his head. "The great King Arthur and his Knights of the Round Table, they was round here lookin' for it. But the ole Grail ain't the sort of thing you can find with a metal detector. It's kind of magical, and folks only ever sees it in visions."

"Right," Marco said. "Erm...there seems to be a lot of magic in this town."

Woolly smiled. "That's right. Too *much* magic, some reckon. That's why it ain't an easy place to live, whether you believes in it or not."

Marco thought about his dad, who'd said he didn't believe any of it. Neither did Marco's mum, which was why she'd left and never come back.

And he remembered what Woolly had said earlier this morning, up in his room: *Don't tell me you didn't feel something entering your soul last night, Marco, 'cause if you did I wouldn't believe you.*

"Point I'm making," Woolly said, "is that some places got it and some places don't. And this place – this town, this hill – must've got it big time, whatever it is, 'cause they all felt the need to come here, didn't they? From the pagan Druids to ole Joe 'Mathea with the Holy Grail. For reasons none of us is ever gonner know, this is likely the most magical place in the whole country. The Isle of Avalon."

Woolly looked down the side of the Tor, and Marco followed his gaze...and suddenly the grass below him seemed to be shimmering in much stronger colours. The buttercups looked like tiny lights shining up from the ground. And even though there was no sun, Marco felt he could see the deep shadow thrown by the church tower behind him.

And he knew he was slipping back into that weird dreamy state that had come over him last night...and left him with a terrible head this morning.

He scrambled to his feet.

"Woolly..."

"You all right, boy?"

"What's happening to me?"

"*Glasto*'s happening to you. Holy Joseph, dude! You're a natural Avalonian, and you've come home."

Marco saw that the glittering stone on the string – his pendulum – was dangling from Woolly's fingers, and it was spinning frantically, the way a dog's tail went when it was pleased to see you. Woolly regarded him solemnly, as if he wasn't aware of the stone or what it was doing.

"I reckon this could be decision time."

"What?"

Woolly looked down at his trainers, then at Marco.

"Long time ago...twenty-odd years back, me and Nancy come up here. With your mother."

"Oh."

"She was a few years older than you at the time, but still at school. And I knew it was now or never, kind of thing."

Marco looked around him. On his right, he was sure he could see the sea glittering on the horizon. But he couldn't see his mum up here, no way.

"See, there's a family tradition to hand on," Woolly said. "I had it from my dad, and he had it from his mother. And I needed to know whether Alison was up for it or not. Before she went away to university."

"Tradition?" Marco said.

"Dowsing. With the rods and the pendulum. Some people

call it *divining*. And they usually means water-divining, on account of that's what it's mainly used for. Us cats that can do it, we're always in big demand with farmers who needs to find a water supply for their animals, look."

"You can do water-divining?"

Marco had certainly heard of this, although he didn't know much about it.

"It's a real ancient thing," Woolly said. "Goes way back. You never hear of the feller in the Bible, taps his stick on a rock and all this water comes gushing out to prevent the Children of Israel dying of thirst on the way to the Promised Land?"

"I don't think there's much call for it in London, though," Marco said. "So, is that what you do for a job?"

"Partly. I've had a few regular jobs as well – postman, taxi-driver, landscape gardener. But those are things you just *do*. A dowser is something you *are*. And there's more to it than just finding water, look. You can divine almost anything – metals, stone...lost things...lost people...ancient secrets."

"But Mum..."

"Didn't go for it. She could *do* it, no question of that. But she turned away."

"Because she wanted to go to London and work for the BBC?"

"That was likely part of it. But I reckon there was something else. I reckon she had an experience of what it's like to be a dowser in Glastonbury, and it...could be something affected her badly. Could be one day she'll tell you, but she never told me and Nancy, and when she left she never came back."

"Was there a big row?"

Marco was thinking about what Josh had said about family rifts and family feuds. Maybe it was really important for him to be here now, to make things up. Maybe Dad had realized this, and that was why he'd gone behind Mum's back while she was out of the country.

"Erm, we did have a bust-up some years later," Woolly said. "But I'd rather she told you about that than me. Last thing I wanner do, look, is come between you and your ma."

Marco started to wonder about the "experience" Woolly thought Mum had had. Was this something...psychic, or what? He looked up at Woolly, who seemed to know what he was thinking.

"Some weird things can happen to you in Glasto. And if you decide to develop your natural talents, life ain't always a cool trip. You ends up following a certain path, and you're faced with big hassles and decisions you wouldn't have had to make otherwise. Like with that feller we ran into just now."

Woolly's face darkened, and Marco felt as if the shadow of the man had just stepped between them.

"Who was he, Woolly?"

"Oh...he's just a feller."

"Hmm." Marco suspected this was like saying Premiership football was just a game.

"Just a feller who wants us to sell him our house," Woolly said.

"Why?"

"'Cause it's in the way. He's in with a bunch of blokes who

already own a lot more land nearby, and they wants to build a huge hotel and leisure centre there. A lot of folk think it's a great idea, but a few of us knows better. And the track up to our house...that's the perfect place, as he sees it, to have an access road from the town. They can't knock the cottage down, 'cause it's a listed historic building, but they can turn it into a bit of a gatehouse and information centre. But they gotter get us out first, look. And we ain't goin' nowhere. Not for the likes of them."

Marco remembered how menacing the man had seemed, and how Woolly had stood up to him.

"You said that he wouldn't get the land as long as you were alive, and he said..."

"He's a bad man, Marco," Woolly said. "And he's part of a bunch of people threatening to...well...to destroy the magic of Glastonbury. It's as simple and terrible as that."

Marco's mind took him back to the previous evening and the woman standing under the tall cross outside the church, throwing up her thin arms from under her cloak and crying out, *I saw a foul darkness gathering around us all. I saw the candles flickering out. I saw the sword Excalibur arise from the depths...but its blade was blunt and blackened with age and could not protect us...*

"This town's always taken a stand against evil," Woolly said. "And there's always been pilgrims to help. Back in the Second World War, when the Nazis were planning to invade Britain, a group of mystics from all over the country focused their willpower on the Tor. The idea being that their combined mental force and the ancient power of Avalon would erect psychic barriers against Adolf Hitler and the enemies of Britain."

"Did it work?"

"Well...we won the War, didn't we?"

"Hmm," Marco said.

"Course, Nancy said I shouldn't tell you all this stuff, bein' as how you're only here for a bit of a holiday. But I knew, soon as I seen you, that you was gonner be the heir to our family tradition. And that's why I brought you up here."

Woolly held out the pendulum in the palm of his hand.

"See how it feels, dude. See what happens."

The Stench of Tallow

The man in the crystal shop looked really uncomfortable, like he wished he'd never met Rosa.

"Look," he said, "perhaps I'm not the best person to..." He shrugged and smiled, kind of bashfully. "I'm, er...I'm Edmund, by the way. Teddy."

"Rosa."

She carried on telling him about the monk in the wall that nobody else seemed to be able to see. And also about the noises and lights and the smell in the shop.

"Rosa, look..." Teddy squeezed his hands together. "How can I put this? Sometimes things *do* happen in some of the buildings around the town. It's nothing to worry about...not usually. This is a really holy place. After all, the Abbey was where it all started in England – Christianity. You know?"

"Is that actually true?"

"Absolutely," Teddy said. "You know the story of the Holy Grail, don't you?"

"My dad mentioned it, but I don't really—"

"Well, if people believed that the Holy Grail was brought here – and even Jesus himself came, as a boy – it was obvious there must be something special about Glastonbury. And so first a church was built – possibly the first church in England – and then this huge abbey. And it *was* huge...and very rich."

"So how come it fell down?"

Teddy smiled. "Because when you're very rich, people get very envious. Especially kings. Back in the sixteenth century, when King Henry VIII decided *he* was going to run the Church of England instead of the Pope, he just couldn't wait to get his hands on Glastonbury Abbey and all its treasures. And if treasure wasn't handed over immediately, Henry turned nasty."

Teddy leaned his elbows on the counter and looked up towards the ceiling, with his eyes half-closed, as if he was somehow actually remembering all this.

"What happened, you see, in the year 1539, some of the king's heavies came down here to search the Abbey."

"Did they have a warrant?" Rosa asked. As the daughter of an ex-policeman, she liked to get these things right.

"Warrants weren't exactly difficult to come by in those days, Rosa, especially if you worked for the king. Anyway, these men said they'd discovered a gold chalice, which they claimed the abbot – Abbot Whiting – had been hiding."

"I suppose they just planted it to stitch him up."

"Yes, I think you're right. They probably *did* plant it. And they also said they'd found some papers that Abbot Whiting had written that were disrespectful to the king. So he was accused of treason – which was very bad."

"What did they do to him?"

"They did something pretty horrible, Rosa," Teddy said. "So if you're already having nightmares..."

"It's okay, I know what Henry VIII did to some of his wives," Rosa said, thinking of the beheading block at dawn.

Teddy looked very sad. "It was even worse than that, I'm afraid. A lot worse. And I'm inclined to think it accounts for some of the problems here – why some of the old monks still aren't at peace, you know?"

Teddy fell silent, his hands moving around some of his own treasures on the counter – sparkling blue pointed crystals set in rock, soaring like mini cathedrals.

"Go on," Rosa said, "You can't stop now."

"I wish I'd never started. It makes me very upset."

"Because you were one of them in a past life? One of the monks?"

Teddy sighed. "Problem with me is I've got a big mouth."

"So have strange things happened to *you*?"

She desperately wanted not to be alone. Not to be the only person who was...

...*haunted.*

"You don't give up, do you?" Teddy said. "Yes, a few things have happened. Sometimes I've had dreams about walking in the Abbey grounds, and I'm always dressed as a monk. And the Abbey's not all in ruins, like it is now, it's huge and grand, like it used to be."

"With big...arches?"

"Huge arches, yes."

"Only, I dreamed of that last night," Rosa said.

Teddy looked up from the crystals, startled. "*You* did?"

"There were these big arches that, like, sprouted over the whole town like they were alive."

"Yes," he said. "*Yes...*"

"And then I woke up, and it had gone very cold. And then there was the noise from down in the shop, and then... Well, I've told you about the candle and the really disgusting smell."

"I think what you smelled," Teddy said, "was the stench of tallow. It was what the cheaper, everyday candles were made of in the old days, rather than wax. It was animal fat, so it smelled...unpleasant."

"It was totally horrible," Rosa said.

All the crystals in the shop had gone blurry, like neon lights through a car windscreen in the rain, and she realized she must be crying because she was so grateful that someone believed her. But she was also horrified to think that what she might have been smelling was a candle from...from *back then.*

"Please, don't..." Teddy looked upset. "Rosa, you're not the first person something like this has happened to lately.

159

The monks...well, some of us think the old, long-dead monks, who are the guardians of Glastonbury...we think something that's going on here is upsetting them."

"You mean...*my* monk...?"

"...is warning you of something. Are you a...shall we say, a psychic sort of person, Rosa?"

"I don't know what you mean." She stared at Teddy in dismay. "Don't you see...I don't *want* him. I don't want to see him ever again. He scares me. I want to get rid of him! I hate it. Can't you help me?"

"I..." Teddy shook his head helplessly. "I don't know. I think you should ask your father for help...as a priest."

"I can't." Rosa gazed into one of the big crystals and saw her own face, all in fragments. "He already thinks I'm going crazy." She looked up at Teddy. "What did King Henry's men do to the abbot? You can't make me any more scared than I already am."

Teddy sighed. "They put him on a hurdle. Do you know what that is?"

"Something horses jump over?"

"Sort of. In this area it's made of branches woven together, a bit like a section of larchlap fencing. So they put poor Abbot Whiting on this hurdle and they dragged him all through the town. And then they dragged him up to the top of the Tor."

"Why did they take him there?"

"Why indeed?" Teddy said. "You'd have thought if they wanted to humiliate him, make him look small in front of all the townsfolk, they'd just have hanged him right there in the middle of the town. But I think they wanted to do more than that...much more."

Teddy was silent for a while, staring into the crystals.

"The abbot was a good man, Rosa. Not all priests are good men, but he...no one could deserve *this*. I can never go to the top of that hill now without thinking about it. You see, the Tor was a very special place long before there was an abbey here. The Tor is the living shrine of the Old Religion. The Druids worshipped there. So what I think they were doing, you see, Rosa...they were giving the soul of the poor abbot to...to the old, dark gods—"

"I don't understand," Rosa said.

"There's so much conflicting power in this town, you see. The Abbey's a shrine to Christianity, and the Tor is the home of..."

"Evil?"

"I didn't say that," Teddy said quickly. "Paganism isn't evil in itself. And a lot of people think the Tor's a wonderful place. But sometimes, there's still an awful tension between the two forces, and you get periods when it affects the whole atmosphere of the town."

Rosa swallowed and straightened her shoulders.

"Are you going to tell me what they did to him?"

"He was..." Teddy closed his eyes. "This gentle, frail old man was hanged, drawn and quartered. That means they hanged him until he was nearly dead and then they took him down and...cut him open and...pulled out his insides."

"While he was *still alive*?"

"So we're told. It was probably the most appalling thing you could do to anyone in the king's name. Then...finally, when he died, they cut his body into four quarters and each one was taken away in a different direction. And they stuck his head on the Abbey gateway. And then they drove all the monks away and tore down the Abbey, and some of the stonework was plundered and used to build houses."

"And shops?" Rosa said.

"Yes. Used to build what are now shops. Sometimes..." Teddy looked up at the beams in the ceiling, and Rosa thought there were tears in his eyes. "Sometimes, when I imagine it, I can actually see it. See it happening before my eyes, as though I'm reliving it. As though I was there." He rubbed his eyes. "It's probably stupid. This place gets to you."

"It won't... You won't let it get to *me*, will you?"

If anything, she felt worse than when she'd first come into the shop. She'd never be able to look up at the Tor again without thinking of what had happened to Abbot Whiting.

"Look," Teddy said. "Why don't you ask your father to say some prayers in your room? Ask him to bless the room. He ought to do that for you, and it might work. It might stop things getting..."

Teddy stopped.

"Getting what?" Rosa demanded. "Getting worse?"

"I didn't say that. Please don't—"

Rosa started to cry. "Teddy, he doesn't believe me, don't you see? Please, you've got to help me. You're the only person

162

who believes me. Please come and tell my mum and dad I'm not insane. *Please...*"

"No!" Teddy backed away. He looked horrified. "I can't..." He slumped over the counter with his head in his hands. "I *can't.*"

"Well, I'm not going back there tonight," Rosa said. "I'll run away. I'd rather sleep in a shop doorway, I'd—"

"All right!" Teddy put up his hands. "I'll...I'll tell you something you can do to...to ward it off. But you mustn't tell anyone. You must never tell anyone I told you this. Do you understand?"

Rosa felt her whole body start to tingle. She nodded. Teddy came round the counter, mumbling to himself, "I shouldn't be doing this."

"Who says?"

He shook his head, and it was not what you'd call comforting to see a grown man looking as frightened as this.

The Fifth Waveband

Woolly's pendulum was hanging limply from its string between Marco's fingers, as if the air was weighing it down. Marco followed Woolly around the tower and then Woolly pointed to a patch of woodland about half a mile away.

"That's where they're figuring to do it, look. There's an ole farm they've bought, with about seventy acres, and they've applied to the Mendip Council for permission to build this huge place there – a big hotel and an exhibition centre, with all sorts of stuff going on for tourists. And high-tech rides for the kids. They're gonner call it Avalon World."

"Like Disney World?"

"Ar," Woolly said. "A bit like that." He sniffed. "I suppose, at your age, you'd think that wouldn't be a bad thing."

Hmm. Josh had been to Disney World when he was younger. It was all right, he'd said, although it didn't provide the kind of intellectual stimulus he now required from a holiday. But that was Josh. Marco suspected he'd quite enjoy Disney World himself, if anybody wanted to take him.

He looked up at Woolly.

"So, like, this Avalon World – why don't *you* think it would be a good thing?"

"Because..." Woolly lifted his hands like he was carrying something really heavy. "Because it wouldn't be *real*. Just like the castles at Disney World ain't real castles. It's all gonner be totally phoney. Like, for instance, they reckons you'd be able to go into this Avalon World and put on some kind of fancy headset and experience the world of Joe 'Mathea and King Arthur all around you and you'd be able to find the Holy Grail. Like a virtual experience in cyberspace kind of thing."

"Wow," Marco said.

"See, there you go." Woolly let his arms drop. "You ain't gettin' the point, dude. It won't *be* the Grail, it'll be some phoney computerized simulation thing. It won't be *real*. And it'll be exactly the same for everybody who can afford it. There'll be nothing *spiritual* about it."

Marco wasn't sure he understood.

"Look," Woolly said, "let me put it this way: when people comes to Glasto, they gotter use their imagination a bit to get into the magic. The town's a bit modern here and there, and it's full of cars and the Abbey's in ruins, so you got to *search* for the magic, right?"

"Well..."

"But the thing is...it's the *searching* what's important. It starts something going..." Woolly patted his chest. "...inside you. And when *that* starts to happen...then it's like, really heavy, man. That's a *real* mind-blowing experience."

Marco must have looked a bit dubious about this because Woolly looked sad and his moustache was drooping. Marco tried to think of something encouraging.

"But, like, having this entertainment complex here...that won't really *destroy* the magic, will it?"

Woolly looked even sadder.

"First thing it'll do, look – all the little magical shops in the town, run by the Avalon pilgrims, will go out of business, on account of Avalon World will have bigger, glossier shops and a big car park. And who's gonner visit what's left of the Abbey, when they can all go up to Avalon World and experience the Abbey the way it used to be?"

"So you're saying Avalon World will become like...more important than the town?"

"Exactly," Woolly said. "And that's what's going wrong with everything in the world today. It's all becoming phoney. What's phoney is becoming more important than what's real."

"Yeah..." Marco thought about this. He thought about the woman in the cloak waving her arms about like it was the end of the world. If all she was getting uptight about was an expensive new entertainment centre outside the town...

"I mean, that's not really *evil* or anything, is it?"

"Ah..." Woolly jumped back onto a little hump in the grass. "*That* depends who's behind it, don't it? And what they're prepared to do to get their way. Maybe they got *reasons* for wanting to destroy the magic of Glasto."

Marco thought of the man who seemed to think it wouldn't be such a bad thing if Woolly was dead. He felt a small tug on his wrist and looked down.

And saw that the pendulum was starting to move. It was going round in slow circles on the end of the string he still held between his fingers. Anticlockwise.

Marco looked up at Woolly. Woolly's eyes gleamed.

"It's moving," Marco said. "On its own."

"Ar."

"What's it doing?"

"It's answering your question," Woolly said.

"What?"

"'Tis goin' round widdershins."

"Huh?"

"It means anticlockwise. It don't always work this way, but usually *anti*clockwise means negative. Going backwards. Not good."

"I don't understand."

"You asked a question," Woolly said. "You were wondering if it was good. And the pendulum's givin' you the answer."

"It's saying it *is* evil?"

As Marco spoke, the pendulum speeded up. Still going anticlockwise.

Woolly grinned.

"What's happening?" Marco stayed very still and looked at Woolly, a little scared. "Are you making it happen?"

"Course I ain't. It's you. Or rather, it's the inner part of you that you ain't normally aware of. See, far down inside you – inside all of us – is a deep well of knowledge you don't know you got. And the pendulum...that's just a tool for bypassing your normal thinking processes, to tap into the depths."

"That's spooky."

Woolly smiled. "That must mean *you're* spooky. And that this whole place is spooky."

"It *is* spooky."

"Only if you don't know what you're dealing with," Woolly said. "But see, if you was plugged into a headset or whatever, at Avalon World, all your senses'd be bunged up and you wouldn't be able to receive answers from deep inside. Just like if the Tor was made out of concrete or something, it wouldn't have no real magic at all, no matter how they painted it and wired it up with lights and stuff. That's technology, that ain't magic."

It was exciting, though. Marco thought of all the films and DVDs he'd seen with fantastic special effects. And which Woolly, apparently, *hadn't* seen, so how could he know how cool it all was?

He looked down at the pendulum, which had stopped swinging, and he could hear a voice from deep inside, and it was Josh's.

I can't believe this. You haven't been there one day yet, and already you're becoming a victim of Impressionable Kid Syndrome. *You are one sick person, Marco.*

Woolly had wandered over to the tower, where a huge arm of stone projected up almost to the battlements.

"Wanner give this a try, dude?"

"Give what a try?"

"This is a buttress, to stop the whole thing falling over," Woolly said. "And I've found it also operates like a standing stone."

Marco must've looked blank.

"Like the standing stones put up in the Stone Age and the Bronze Age," Woolly said. "It was always thought prehistoric folks used to worship the ole gods in stone circles, and that's likely true enough. But us dowsers, we've found that standing stones are usually planted on places of power. Places where the earth-energy gathers. This making sense?"

"Er..."

"It's a big thing, dude. To really understand it, you gotter realize that the Earth itself is alive – a living being – and it's got kind of a nervous system. Imagine great natural cables spreading electricity all over the planet. Most folks ain't even aware of it. The electricity in the Earth – the nerves of the Earth – connects with our nerves and tells us things. Lets us into a few of the Earth's secrets. And because these stones was placed on what you might call power points, the energy flows up and down the stone, see?"

Marco tried to concentrate, but he wasn't sure he was taking it all in. Was it some kind of science, or was it just bull?

"Now stone circles – like Stonehenge – were built on the places where the power was strongest. And some experts reckon there used to be a stone circle up here on the Tor, right? And that maybe the properties of the stone circle – the magic, if you wanner call it that – was taken on by this stone tower."

Woolly went up to the corner buttress and laid his hands on the flat stonework, about on a level with his chest. After a couple of seconds, he took them away and shook them briefly, as if they were tingling, before standing back.

"Now, you."

Marco moved tentatively up to the stone, trying not to think of the sneer on Josh's face if he could see this.

In spite of the warmth of the day, the stone was cold when he laid his hands on it.

It felt like...well, like stone, actually.

"Up a bit," Woolly said.

Marco raised his hands to just above his own head-height, as if he was holding up the wall.

"That's it. You got it."

"What do I do now?"

"You wait."

Marco pressed his palms into the stone, concentrating hard, to please Woolly. *Just* to please Woolly, because all this seemed very much like a load of old...

"What *are* you doing, dude?"

"I don't know, do I?" Marco said patiently. "On account of I've never actually done it before."

"You're concentrating."

"Yeah, I'm doing my *best* to concentrate, but..."

"Well don't."

"Huh?"

"Don't concentrate."

"What am I supposed to *do* then?"

"*Not* concentrate. Just relax and hang in there. No, no, don't go droopy...stay firm, but not tense. *That's* more like it."

"I feel like a plonker."

"Occupational hazard, dude. Don't think about it. Go with the flow."

"Flow? What fl— *Oh!*"

Marco found himself sitting on the grass, with the tower rearing over him. The tower seemed to be rocking.

Dizziness.

"Ho, ho!" Woolly was jumping up and down. "Hee, hee! *Yesssss!*"

Marco got up. There was a mild pins-and-needles sensation in his hands and up his arms.

"Must've tripped."

"Oh, ar, you *tripped* all right," Woolly said gleefully.

"Woolly—"

"Try it one more time, see if it happens again."

"This is ridiculous."

"Okay." Woolly nodded. "Fair enough. We'll go back down the town and get a bite to eat."

"No, okay. I'll do it again."

"Only if you want to."

Marco sighed and brushed himself down and went back to the wall and placed his hands on the cool stonework.

This time, he was ready for it.

It was a kind of jolt. Not like an electric shock, but he did feel his balance start to slip. Like a TV picture freezing for just a fraction of a second and then starting up again, with everything out of sync.

He didn't fall this time, though. He went and stood in front of Woolly with his hands behind his back.

"Okay, what was it?"

"What was it?" Woolly beamed in delight. "*That*...that was the reaction of a natural dowser to what we call *the fifth waveband.*"

Marco was determined not to ask. He just waited.

"The earth-force," Woolly said, "usually goes up a stone in a spiral, creating seven bands of energy on the stone. And the fifth one is the one that has an effect on us. Well, the seventh, too, but you wouldn't be able to reach that."

"Like an electric shock?"

"More or less. In fact, that's what it is. It's a form of electromagnetism that collects in the stone. Not enough to be dangerous, or I wouldn't've let you go near it. And most folk wouldn't even feel it first time like you did – let alone get knocked off their pins."

"I just lost my balance."

"That's what it does. It's like being drunk."

Marco thought this whole town seemed a bit like being drunk, but he didn't say anything.

"What I wanted," Woolly said, "was for you to feel what a dowsing-response was like before we really got going with the rods or the pendulum. I wanted you to know it wasn't a load of ole rubbish. You satisfied on that point now?"

"I don't know. It's all kind of...weird."

"That's the word, dude. Ain't it wonderful? Don't it make you feel truly alive and part of the world? Like being plugged into the electricity of the planet."

"I don't know. I think I'm going to have one more go, okay?"

"Well, don't OD on it. It's like anything – moderation's best."

"Just once more." He had somehow to convince himself that this wasn't a case of *Impressionable Kid Syndrome*.

Marco walked over to the tower. There was a piercing crack of brightness in the sky, directly over the battlements. It must be close to midday and the sun was trying to push through the cloud bank.

He placed his hands on the stone, knowing instinctively this time where to put them, as if the stone had been marked with hand-shaped dotted lines. He found it easier, too, not to think about anything in particular, aware only of the warmth of the sun, through his T-shirt, on his back.

He closed his eyes for a moment and felt his breathing alter. In fact, he became very aware of his breathing just happening, very evenly, as if it was nothing at all to do with him. It was so strange and pleasant that he just went along with it, went with the flow.

A long way below him, he could see the humped summit of the Tor, like a helicopter landing pad, with the green land falling away on all sides. Kind of spinning, far below him, he saw the huge grey-brown stone that was the tower, and far, *far* below, he saw a boy in a green T-shirt and jeans, with his hands on the stone, and then he saw a man with a white ponytail and a droopy moustache, his feet apart and his hands on his hips watching the boy.

He saw the curve of the Earth, felt it tilting in his hands.

He felt light as air.

He *was* air.

"Oh my G—"

Got to Go

Woolly grabbed a corner table in a café called The Cosmic Carrot and ordered veggie hot dogs with all the trimmings.

"You're hungry, right, dude?"

Marco sat down at the bright green wooden table with lemon yellow place mats that said MEAT IS MURDER in big green letters. The colours sang out at him – no *really*; he could almost hear the colours. He was in that intense dream-state again, aware of every little thing he was doing.

And he didn't remember when he'd felt more starving.

"Yeah," Woolly said. "It does that to you. Or so I'm told."

He stared at Marco across the luminous table, his eyes bright and shocked – just like they'd looked when Marco had opened his own eyes at the foot of the tower on the Tor.

"The real scary thing...the thing is, dude, it's never actually happened to me. *Never.*"

"Huh?" Marco couldn't figure what the fuss was about; he felt totally chilled out. Just really, *really* hungry.

"I been dowsing for over thirty years," Woolly said, "but I ain't never had...an OOBE."

"OOBE?" Marco wondered if this was some kind of rash.

"Out-of-body experience," Woolly explained.

Marco stared at him. "You don't *really* think that's what it was?"

"'Tis not all that uncommon. Not in this town. See the lady over there?"

He nodded at a woman in a long grey frock just coming into the café and stepping lightly towards the counter. She had long black hair, with a headband in the form of a snake circling her forehead. It was the woman in the cloak who said she'd dreamed of the Hounds of Hell in the dark sky. *Oh dear.*

"*She* has them all the time." Woolly thought for a moment then he half rose. "Eleri! You got a minute?"

The woman drifted over. She had big dark eyes, a small silver nose ring and white lipstick, though frankly she looked a bit too old for that kind of stuff.

"Gotter be fate, you walking in like this," Woolly said. "Eleri, this is Marco. He's, er, he's..."

"Your grandson?" Eleri didn't smile. "How do you do?"

"Holy Joseph!" Woolly said. "How did you know that?"

Eleri motioned in the air with her hands, like that was a really trivial matter and it was pointless going into it. Woolly shrugged.

"Eleri, Marco only came here yesterday, for the first time..."

A pulse of real surprise went through Marco's head. Only yesterday? It felt like he'd been here for ever.

"Did he really?" Although she looked like some ancient Egyptian queen, Eleri's low, musical accent suggested she might be Welsh or something.

She kept glancing at him and those glances, he thought, were not entirely friendly.

"So," she said, "what is the problem?"

Nobody had said anything about a problem. She seemed to be the kind of person who saw problems that no one else could see.

Woolly explained how, when he'd realized Marco could be a natural dowser, in the family tradition, he'd decided to take him up the Tor.

"That was bold of you." Eleri looked unhappy.

"Too bold, as it turns out," Woolly said bitterly. "I figured the best thing, look, would be to see if he could pick up the fifth wavelength from the west buttress. Well, I should've realized..."

"Ninety per cent of people could lean on that buttress from now until midnight and come away with nothing but cold hands," Eleri said.

Woolly turned to Marco. "Tell her what happened. Tell her everything. Don't leave nothing out."

So Marco did, feeling a bit stupid. Yesterday he'd left London, today he'd left his body. How likely did *that* sound? When he got to the bit about the change in his breathing, Eleri's head went up.

"Stop there!" she snapped. "You say you felt a degree of separation at this point?"

"Separation?"

"What was *different* about your breathing? Think about it."

"Well, it was just..." Marco imagined himself back on the Tor, but not too hard, in case...well, you never knew *what* might happen. "It was like I'd never really realized I was breathing before, if you see what I mean. Like you spend the whole of your life breathing non-stop, but you never think about yourself doing it, do you? Only this time, it was like I realized breathing was this really powerful thing. And I could feel it happening and hear it...almost like *somebody else* was doing it."

"Hah!"

Eleri brought both hands down on the table. She must have had about fifteen rings on her fingers. She looked at Woolly.

"The real thing, then?" Woolly said. He didn't sound at all happy about this.

Eleri turned back to Marco. "What happened then?"

Marco felt embarrassed because he couldn't exactly explain how he came to be looking down on the Tor and the tower and Woolly and himself. He'd just been feeling really, really relaxed and content and then he was just *doing it*. And the second he realized he was, like, *up there,* he'd totally panicked – terrified he was going to fall to his death.

"And then?" Eleri leaned towards him in a cloud of this herby-smelling perfume.

"Well, there was just...you know how when your ears block up and you go deaf. And then your hearing suddenly comes back – with this kind of small pop."

"And that's when you were back in your body?"

Marco nodded. He just wished the hot dogs would come.

Of course, he knew exactly what Josh would say. Josh would say it was a total delusion. Marco had been taken out of his normal environment and put down in a place where there was a whole tourist industry built on bizarre legends. Where some people actually believed that *JC Himself* had taken a stroll over the hills in ancient times and that his uncle came back and hid the Holy Grail.

Josh would just not believe how Marco could be taken in by a place full of deluded people. Like Woolly, who thought he could find things out by dangling a stone on a string from his fingers. And like this Eleri, whose opinions Woolly seemed to think were really important, even though she looked like the mad queen in a pantomime.

Who was she? The fact that he even slightly wanted to find out must be a sign that he was being swallowed up by the place and the legends and the loonies.

He needed to get his act together before it was too late.

"All right." Eleri leaned back in her chair as a waitress with about a dozen lip rings arrived with the food. *Yes!*

Eleri waved at her imperiously. "Keep them warm for a few minutes, would you? We don't want distractions."

The waitress rolled her eyes and carried the hot dogs back behind the counter, the starving Marco wanting to follow her on his knees.

"You have a decision to make, Woolly," Eleri said.

Marco sighed. It was one of those days when everybody seemed to have to make a decision. *He'd* made one up on the Tor, and look what had happened! For just a few seconds, he'd become as deluded as the rest of them.

"The days are darkening over Avalon," Eleri said. "*You* know what I mean."

And now she was off again with the doomy stuff. Could take hours. Marco stared at the counter where his hot dogs and all the trimmings had vanished.

Woolly looked grim. He coughed. "We, er...we saw him this morning. Like a long streak of...darkness."

"Where?" Eleri demanded.

"Coming down from the Tor, like he owns it already. Like him and his London money owns the whole town."

Eleri frowned. "You know that the Mendip Council Planning Committee are coming down to view the Avalon World site tomorrow...along with the Tourist Board officials, the MP and everybody who is anybody?"

Woolly blinked. "*Tomorrow?*"

"It will be the final inspection before a decision is made on whether the plan goes ahead. They've been keeping it quiet so we don't have time to arrange much of a protest."

"Prob'ly a done deal already," Woolly said in disgust. "Cromwell and his rich mates've likely bribed everybody. Wouldn't be the first time our beloved mayor has took a bung."

"It certainly does not look good," Eleri admitted. "Last night, in my dreams, I had a vision of the barge again – the black barge gliding towards Avalon, carrying three hooded women, weeping over the body of Arthur, mortally wounded. It was a dream of death, Woolly."

"Oh," Woolly said.

"This will be a *black summer*!" Eleri suddenly reared up from her seat. "All those living here who are *sensitive* will be tested – perhaps beyond endurance, in some cases."

"Don't say that, Eleri," Woolly said.

"I *must* say it..." She leaned towards him, and Woolly went pale. "And *you*...must decide whether you want your grandson to be exposed to it."

"Ah." Woolly sighed and leaned back. "You got to the core of my dilemma there, Eleri, man. All the evidence is the boy's got it in his blood. A natural Avalonian. Belongs here, and one day he's gonner realize his destiny. I figured he was...you know...*sent*. Only thing is, is he still too young?"

Eleri said nothing, just looked grim.

"Hang on a minute." Marco sat up. This was getting ridiculous. "I *was* sent. I was sent by my dad because, like, he and my mum are going down the tubes, marriage-wise, and he doesn't want me to see his girlfriend."

"True enough," Woolly said.

"So, like, are you saying I might've been sent for...some other reason?"

Eleri and Woolly looked at each other. Marco knew that if his mum was here she'd be dragging him out so fast that by the time he reached the door there'd be no rubber left on his trainers.

Woolly sighed deeply.

"You're right. Eleri. I been a total idiot. It's too dangerous. I never should've taken him up the Tor. I never should've shown him the pendulum. I'll get on the phone to his dad and get him on the train from Castle Cary, soon as—"

"What?" Marco was on his feet. They wanted him to leave? He'd been here less than a day and already they wanted him out?

"Castle Cary's our nearest train station," Woolly said. "You'll be okay, it's—"

"Like...*bog off*! I'm not going back. What do you think I am?"

"We think – we *know* – that you are *sensitive*," Eleri said. "Which can be a curse."

Marco shook his head. She'd only met him a few minutes ago. She didn't know anything about him. She was a total loony.

"Marco..." Woolly looked up at him. "This ain't a game, you know. When you gets a place that's as powerfully sacred as Glastonbury, it attracts the pilgrims, but it also attracts, you know..."

"Evil," Eleri said.

"Ar. And there's things I could tell you, but Eleri's right –
it needs to stop here. When evil comes, it looks for an easy way
in, and it homes in on – pardon me, dude, I don't mean no
offence by this – the innocents. The children. And a child
who's *sensitive*..."

"So, you think – like the bald guy on the Tor – you think
I'm just a *child*, right?"

"Look," Woolly said, "whatever natural abilities I got, with
the ole dowsing, it's starting to look like you got it worse.
What I'm trying to say – if anything was to happen to you,
imagine how I'd feel."

What if something happens to him? Nancy had said last
night. *Our only grandchild?*

"And imagine how your ma would feel after all these years
of keeping you away from...from it."

"But—"

"I can't do it, dude." Woolly looked near to tears. "You just
got to go."

"Right!" Marco stood up, outraged. "Then I'll go *now*!"

And before either Woolly or Eleri could say a word – and
before they could see the tears in *his* eyes – he'd pushed back
his chair and he was out of there.

Smart Mouth

He ran down the street and kept running. He felt like he could have kept on running for ever and not used up half his energy.

Maybe Woolly was even now on the phone to his dad, telling him to come and take his kid away.

Why did that seem so terrible? Last night he'd have been over the moon if Dad had just turned the car round and headed back to the motorway.

Marco slowed to a trot. He needed to talk to someone about this. One day – not even twenty-four hours here – and he was all turned inside out. He'd been hanging out with weird old people and it was like he'd been bewitched or something. He needed to talk to someone outside of all this. Like Josh.

That was what he'd do. He'd ring Josh.

He turned into a side street, pulling out his mobile. Nancy had frowned when she'd seen he had a mobile. She'd said they turned your brain into electric spinach. But surely that was no worse than what the Tor could do to you?

He found Josh's number in the memory and called it up, walking along the street and into another street, where it was quieter.

"*This is Joshua Goldman. I am not presently at my desk but, should you require a consultation, please leave me a short message which I can submit to voice-analysis.*"

"It's me," Marco said. "Stuff the voice-analysis, just call me back, okay?"

He dropped the mobile into the zip pocket above his left knee, which was probably far enough from his brain to be harmless. If it eventually turned his knee to electric spinach...well, he'd worry about that when it happened.

What am I thinking?

He leaned back against a lamp-post. He'd be normal again once he was back in London. Once he'd got away from—

Noooooooooooooooooooooo!

It was no good. The very last thing he wanted was to get away from here. Face it: this day, with a weird old person, in a loony town, had been possibly the most exciting day of his *entire life.*

Okay, maybe all this stuff about darkening days and dreams

of death...maybe that was a serious overreaction to this plan for Disney World Glasto. And the idea that the thin, bald guy would kill Woolly just to get hold of his house was totally ridiculous. And maybe the spinning pendulum and that feeling of leaving your body and rising up and looking down on yourself *was* just a hallucination.

Whatever, it was an awesomely *interesting* hallucination. Coming here was like he'd been plugged into something and had started to light up.

Now, however, on the advice of some loopy old woman who thought he might be *too sensitive*, his newly discovered grandfather wanted to send him home to boring London and a session of in-depth psyching-out by Joshua Goldman with his computers, his wall-size TV and his stupid, pompous answering machine.

Marco reached down and unzipped the pocket over his left knee and took out his mobile to switch it off. He decided he didn't, after all, want to talk to Josh and collect an earful of psychopoop.

It was at this moment that a foot inside what looked like a top-of-the-range Nike made contact with his hand and the mobile spun away and dropped, with a plasticky splat, on the pavement.

A voice said, "Oops."

And Marco looked up into a contemptuous gaze he'd faced before – just before a fist had come out of nowhere, and he'd spun away but still caught half a punch in the mouth before Dad had appeared and dragged him back to the car.

Marco bent to pick up his phone, but the boy with tight, dark curls kicked it away.

"Oops," he said again.

Marco stood up. He still felt full of energy, but he had to admit the boy was several inches taller and – unlike most people on the streets of Glasto – looked like he worked out. This was also a very quiet street that seemed to go nowhere but into a deserted yard. The buildings either side looked like lock-up garages, deserted.

Even Glastonbury, it appeared, had places that were distinctly short on magic.

"So what's *your* problem?" Marco said. "The vicar's daughter dump you?"

"I don't *have* any problems," the boy said. "But you have. You've got a smart mouth, and I don't like kids with smart mouths."

"Makes you feel inferior, right?" Marco said, then wished he'd just shut up and run.

Because it was worse than he'd thought. Three more boys were walking up, hands in pockets, spreading out across the width of the alley. So now there was nowhere to run.

"We know who you are, now," the first boy said. "You're little Woolaston's grandson."

"What if I am?"

"Woolaston's a traitor. He was born and bred in this town and his family's been here for generations...and he betrayed his roots. He went over to *them*."

"Them?" Marco said. "You mean the pilgrims?"

The boy sneered. "You're as stupid as him, aren't you? They're just drug-sodden old hippies, and they've turned this town into a joke. All their stupid shops and their meditation groups and dancing around on the Tor at dawn and pretending they can see UFOs and stuff. *Pilgrims.* Don't make me laugh."

The other three had formed a half circle around Marco. This could *not* be happening.

"If you go into other towns, you don't see all the streets full of weirdo creeps, do you?" The boy went up close to Marco. "Or maybe *you* think they're fun."

"They're more fun than you," Marco said.

The boy planted a big trainer on one of Marco's. Put his weight on Marco's toes. "Get his phone," he said to the others.

A stocky kid with red hair and skin like a relief-map of the Andes picked up the mobile and handed it to the taller boy. "There you go, Jasper."

"Ta," Jasper said. "Oh look, it's a cheap plastic one."

"You leave that alone!" Marco blurted through the pain, as Jasper held up the phone and switched it on.

The phone let out a squeak.

"You got a message," Jasper said.

Marco made a grab for the phone, but two of the other kids came behind him and bent his arms up behind his back. Marco started to pant and struggle, but it was hopeless. Maybe he should shout for help. Problem was, with so many people in this town playing music and doing mystical chants and stuff, who was going to notice a cry for help?

Jasper listened to the message. "It's some jerk called Josh. He says he knew you wouldn't be able to last a whole day without having to talk to somebody who's not totally psychotic."

"Wow," Marco said. "That's amazing. How could he possibly have known I was going to run into you?"

He couldn't help it. He'd always been like this. If a suitable remark occurred to him, he'd just have to come out with it. And the result was nearly always the same.

Jasper hit him in the stomach.

Marco went, "*Oof,*" all the breath knocked out of him. He choked and would have doubled up with the pain if the other two hadn't been holding him upright.

Jasper smiled. "You got anything else to say, smart mouth?"

This time, Marco couldn't think of anything remotely clever.

"All right," Jasper said. "You tell Woolaston he's holding up the Project. He's been offered a good price for his hovel. He should get out while he can."

"It's not a—"

Jasper hit him again. "Don't speak when *I'm* speaking."

This time they let Marco go and he went down on his knees, coughing.

Jasper said, "You'd better remind Woolaston he's an old man and he's living in a lonely place. Bad things can happen in a lonely place."

Jasper dropped Marco's phone and trod on it. Ground his heel on it, until the plastic splintered and the insides came out.

"In a lonely place, things can get broken," Jasper said.

OCD

Rosa was looking for somewhere quiet to *do* it.

Or to practise doing it, until she got it right. That was what Teddy had advised. *It's a very ancient thing,* he'd said, *and the method is important. You need to be able to do it at a moment's notice, and if something's scaring you and you fumble it, it...well, that might be worse than if you hadn't started.*

She tried the Chalice Well gardens, but there were people in there, sitting in the lotus position, meditating near the pool of red water that was supposed to be symbolic of the blood of Jesus, although Dad was very sceptical about that. Anyway, it was no use with all those people around. And she didn't want to go back and practise it in her bedroom – it had to be absolutely perfect before she did it there. Or she might let something in.

Rosa shuddered. She crossed the town and wound up in the car park behind The George and Pilgrims. The tower of Dad's new church soared above one of its walls, and there was a shady corner with no cars in it and nobody about.

So she started to do it there.

Teddy had said you should use your right hand, and the first, sweeping movement should be like you were drawing a big sword from a scabbard on your belt.

Up with the arm and then down again, and then up in a diagonal and then straight across and...

No, that came out wrong.

Rosa tried again, imagining she was drawing the shape in fire or something, as if she was using one of those things that they fought with in the old *Star Wars* films – like beams of solid light.

She felt a bit daft now, throwing her arms around in a car park, but she knew she wouldn't feel at all daft tonight, when a pattern in the air was the only thing between her and something old and terrifying. She had just a few hours to practise, practise, practise, until this was second nature.

Because she knew in her heart that if she did it wrong tonight, it would be the worse thing ever. If she did it wrong, she would be opening herself up to dark forces that would overshadow their whole household, and they'd never get away, ever. They'd be trapped in the clammy flat with the grimy lino and the evil influence of the empty shop underneath.

And if she couldn't get it right now...

The air itself seem to resist the movement of her arm, as if she was in a tank of water. She let her arm fall. She was nearly crying in frustration.

She tried again, and this time her arm went all crooked and the movements got all tangled. It had seemed so straightforward when Teddy was doing it in the shop and she was copying what he did. Now it was as if something *out there* was trying to stop her, working against her, making the air congeal like...fat...tallow.

Ugh...

Right. Stop. The thing to do was walk across the car park and come back and go directly into it.

She should do this four times – go across the car park and come back *four times.* And then go into the movement and pray she got it right.

Rosa walked across the car park and then walked back to the shady corner. And a second time. And a third time. Using the same number of steps each time.

Now the fourth. Knowing that, if she failed to get it right after this, she'd have to do it *sixteen* times – four times four. Because if she didn't, they'd be forced to live for years and years in the disgusting flat over the disgusting old shop... live there until Dad died and then Mum died and then Rosa would be left on her own for more years and years until she, too, grew old, shrivelling into a faded spinster with only dead monks to talk to. *Oh God, oh God, oh God, oh God...*

"What are you doing?"

The boy was standing against the wall, with the church tower behind him. Somehow, while she was walking back across the car park for the fourth and final time (unless she got it wrong again and had to do it sixteen times) he'd put himself in exactly the spot, in the shade of the high wall, where she had to be to *do it.*

"Nothing," Rosa said.

And she really hated saying that. It was the miserable word you used when you'd been caught with your fingers in the biscuit tin. When you were in a situation where you could not possibly give a reasonable explanation, because what you were doing was not reasonable.

"You've got OCD, haven't you?" the boy said.

He was about Rosa's age and quite ordinary-looking – except for his dark blue eyes, in which the light seemed to be dancing. Ah...that was it: she hadn't seen his eyes before. He'd been wearing dark glasses last night when he'd said her dad was a gorilla who ought to be taken away in a van.

"What?" Rosa said.

"OCD!"

"What are you talking about?"

"Obsessive Compulsive Disorder," the boy said. "It's where you can't leave your bedroom without checking half a dozen times that you've switched your computer off. Or where you have to keep doing stupid things over and over or touching things time and time again or something horrible will happen. It starts off in quite a small way – like not treading on

193

the cracks in the pavement and if you tread on one by accident you have to go back and walk that stretch of pavement again. It's very common."

"You're an expert, are you?" Rosa knew she was starting to blush and hated herself for it.

"Not exactly," the boy said, "but I've got a mate who is. His dad's a psychiatrist."

Rosa flinched.

"It's okay," the boy said. "It's really common. You just have to make sure it doesn't get total control of you and, you know, mess up your whole life."

"Get lost," Rosa said. "You're talking rubbish."

"No, I'm not. You were standing here, kind of waving your arms about, right?"

The boy started to wave *his* arms about and then winced and held his tummy for a moment. She saw that his otherwise new-looking cargo trousers had dirt on the knees and one leg was torn.

"And then you walked away," he said, "and then you came back and then you walked away again and then you—"

"Leave me alone!"

"I'm just trying to help. Because, like...I kind of had it, too. It was like with the cracks in the pavement, only with me it was the other way round – I *had* to walk on the cracks. Like, I'd go totally out of my way to find a crack, even though it was always causing serious grief. Like I'd be tripping up old ladies and getting tangled up in dog leads, just to get to a particularly good crack on the other side of the pavement."

"That's stupid," Rosa said.

But she knew it wasn't. Oh God, she knew. She wanted to just turn and run away, in the hope she'd never see him again, but she hadn't finished her crucial four attempts at getting *it* right and that meant... *Oh God.*

"So anyway," the boy said, "one day, I happened to do it in front of this mate, Josh, and he's like, *Hey, wow, you've got OCD, you've got OCD!* Because whenever he spots somebody with a syndrome or something, it just makes his day, totally. So I had to admit it. I mean, I had to admit it to *myself*, really, because you don't even think about it, do you, normally? You just keep on doing it. But I couldn't...I mean, you know, it was an absolute textbook case of Obsessive Compulsive Disorder."

"That's nothing to do with me," Rosa said stubbornly.

He nodded. "You're in denial, then."

"Just bog off and leave me alone!"

"That's the first reaction – go into denial. But when you think about it you'll realize that's what you've got, and if you don't beat it now, well...the prognosis is not good. It's going to completely take you over. It'll eat away at your life and pretty soon you won't *have* a life, you'll just be like this twitching bundle of nervous impulses."

"You're mad," Rosa said. "And anyway, it's none of your business what I do."

"You're right." He nodded. "It's nothing to do with me. And frankly, my first inclination was to leave you to get worse and worse until the men in white coats came for you..."

"Shut up!"

"...on account of you being a friend of this total bastard, Jasper, who totally hates my granddad. And your dad *also* totally hates my granddad. And, as I'm about to get thrown out of town for the crime of being too sensitive, I won't have to watch you twitching and rolling your eyes, and even the pilgrims avoiding you in the street... Okay! Okay!" He put up his hands and backed off. "I'm going."

"Good."

Rosa turned away and looked across the ranks of parked cars, blinking back the tears that were boiling up behind her eyes. Out of the corner of an eye, she saw him shrug and walk away and then, when he must be well out of sight, she let the tears roll and, in desperation, she flung out her right arm, like she was drawing a sword from a scabbard and then she flourished the imaginary sword and slammed it down then up on a diagonal and again and across and back in another diagonal.

She'd done it.

She'd got it right.

"You just drew a five-pointed star in the air," the boy said from right behind her. "What's that about, then?"

Growing Up

It was hard going, with this girl, it truly was, and it cost him a big chunk of the twenty quid his dad had slipped him before they left home.

Plus, he had to tell her stuff he was a bit ashamed of before he finally got a reaction.

"They *smashed your phone*?" This Rosa almost howled.

"Shhhh."

Luckily, there was nobody left in The Cosmic Carrot that Marco recognized – no Woolly, no Eleri, no pilgrims of note, just a few obvious tourists.

"They had something to prove," he said.

He'd just finished his third veggie hot dog splattered with mustard, and he felt halfway human again. Rosa had accepted a cup of decaf and a slice of carrot cake, apparently the house speciality. He'd quite liked the feeling it gave him, walking into a restaurant (of sorts) with a companion of the opposite sex and placing an order. Kind of cool.

Rosa seemed a little wary, which he supposed was only to be expected. She clearly had problems. Several times, she'd started to tell him something and had then gone all vague and changed the subject. But you didn't have to be psychic to know there was something she desperately wanted to unload.

She looked hesitant. "When...when Jasper hit you last night..."

"He obviously wanted to prove something to *you*," Marco said.

"Like what?"

"Like that when it comes to Woolly and the pilgrims, he and your old man are on the same side."

"He's *not* an old man. Not compared with your—"

"He's my granddad. Granddads are *supposed* to be old."

"Sorry. All I was going to say was, I'd only just met Jasper Coombes. So, him hitting you was nothing to do with me. His...his father's an estate agent and he collects the rent on our flat."

"And did *he* teach you how to do that...whatever it was?"

"Inscribing the pentagram," Rosa said solemnly. "It's an ancient thing you do to protect yourself from...from things that come in the night. It's a powerful symbol."

Woooh. Marco pushed his plate away. He remembered the metal pentagram next to the door at Woolly and Nancy's cottage. This was getting heavy.

"Things that come in the night, huh? We're not talking about bedbugs, are we?"

Rosa looked down at the MEAT IS MURDER place mat, her lips clamped tight.

"Sorry," Marco said.

"Do you have to try and say something clever *every* time."

"Most times," he admitted. "So *did* Jasper teach you how to...inscribe the pentagram?"

"No."

"Did your dad?"

"*God* no!"

"Then—"

"I can't tell you," Rosa said. "I promised."

Marco shrugged. "Fair enough."

Rosa fiddled with her fork, and then put it on her plate. And then picked it up again and put it on a different part of her plate. She saw Marco watching her and scowled.

"I wasn't—"

"Yes you were. And you've got to do it two more times, haven't you, before you feel safe?"

Rosa breathed in hard and pushed her hands down by the side of her chair and sat there, all stiff, staring down at the crumbs on her plate.

"Sorry," Marco said. "I won't mention it again, okay?"

Rosa didn't look up. "So why do they all hate your granddad?"

"Because he won't sell his house to some big business outfit that wants to tarmac his garden for an access road to something they want to build called Avalon World, which is going to be—"

"I've heard of that."

"Woolly says it's going to be phoney and a waste of space, as well as destroying the countryside and putting a bunch of shops out of business." Marco looked around The Cosmic Carrot, where every wall was painted a different colour. "Probably this place, too, if they're having a café there, which they're bound to have. If not two."

"Jasper hates all the weird people," Rosa said. "He says they're like children who don't want to grow up, and they're holding the town back from having decent shops and everything."

"If his dad's an estate agent, he's probably got that from *him*," Marco said. "And his dad's probably got a finger in the pie at Avalon World."

"And *my* dad thinks that, as well as not growing up, they're evil," Rosa said.

"Hmm," Marco said. "That depends on what you mean by not growing up."

He thought about this. *Growing up* meant no longer believing in Father Christmas and the tooth fairy and anything that wasn't to do with the Government and Getting an Education and a Good Job. *Growing up,* in the Glasto sense, obviously meant getting rid of all the messy little shops with hand-painted signs and magic crystals for sale and a general air of topsy-turvy chaos and replacing them with a new out-of-town high-tech complex, where you could plug yourself tidily into a virtual experience and discover a virtual Holy Grail.

Suddenly, he was seeing what Woolly meant – that would be totally soulless...and totally worthless.

He turned narrowed eyes on Rosa.

"Your dad said the pilgrims were all pagan scum."

He wondered, for the first time, if Woolly was a pagan. If Woolly and Nancy took all their clothes off and danced around on the Tor to worship the old gods. Just imagining that made him smile.

"My dad used to be a policeman," Rosa said. "He thinks that's why he got the curate's job in Glastonbury – to take a hard line with the pagans. Dad isn't scared of anybody."

"So with a big gorill...with a dad who isn't scared of anybody...what have *you* got to be worried about."

"I can't tell you about that," Rosa said.

"I might be able to help."

"I don't think so." Rosa was looking hard at her fork like she was fighting some primitive impulse to pick it up and put it down again. This was a major case of OCD, no question. "And I don't know whether I can trust you not to tell anybody."

"As I probably won't be here tomorrow, I won't have much chance to tell anybody anyway," Marco said bitterly.

Rosa looked up. "Where are you going?"

"I told you, they're sending me home."

"Why?"

"Because...this is going to sound stupid, right?"

"Everything here sounds stupid."

"All right..."

Marco told her about the pendulum and the dowsing. How Woolly had told him he was a natural and must have inherited the family tradition. Then he told her what had happened to him this morning on the Tor, which Woolly had said was an out-of-body experience. And how Eleri, the mad old woman in the cloak, who went round predicting doom and horror, had told Woolly that Glasto probably wasn't safe for somebody like Marco. Who, apparently, was too sensitive for his own good.

"Work *that* one out," Marco said.

Rosa was silent for a long time.

"All I know," she said at last, "is that some people are very scared of something."

"You mean people apart from you?"

She looked away. "I mean grown-up people."

"But not your dad."

"No. Somebody else."

"The same somebody who showed you how to inscribe the pentagram, right?"

Rosa met his eyes and then defiantly picked up her fork and placed it very carefully right down the middle of her plate.

Marco said nothing. Just sat there, thinking he had nowhere to go now except back to Woolly's, if he could find his way, and then...wait for Dad to collect him, he supposed.

It was all so crazy.

Just as he was getting a feel for this place. Just as he was understanding a few things. Just as he'd met someone who clearly needed help.

"Better be off then, I suppose," he said.

"Wait." Rosa picked up her plate and put it to one side where she wouldn't be tempted to mess with it.

"Huh?"

"Underneath our flat," Rosa said, "there's this old shop..."

"Uh huh."

"And on my bedroom wall there's...there's..."

The Cross and the Pentagram

"**I**t's quite deliberate," Rosa's dad said as they sat down to tea. "They're targeting the church."

"I'm afraid they just look like layabouts to me," Mum said.

She spooned ice cream into the blue dessert dishes on the table so it would have time to become nice and soft, the way she knew Rosa liked it. Rosa tried to smile gratefully.

"Oh no," Dad said. "If you look at them closely, you'll see they're all wearing obvious pagan symbols around their necks. Those five-pointed stars, for instance..."

Rosa knocked her teacup over and Dad gave her a sharp glance.

"Sorry...sorry." Rosa looked down into her lap.

"This town's always been a battleground between Christianity and paganism, light and darkness." Dad thumped the table with his fist. "And the pagans like to hang around outside the church because they think they can intimidate us."

"I don't think I've ever actually known you to be intimidated, Dave," Mum said quietly.

"Aye, well..." Dad's beard was suddenly sliced by this huge grin. "The clergy's been too soft for too long. When I see these toerags hanging round the church, I will admit to having an unchristian urge to slam them up against the wall...but then I realize I don't have any handcuffs any more."

Dad laughed. Rosa didn't.

"Still," he said, "at least I know who their leader is now."

Mum and Rosa both looked at him.

"He's not very impressive," Dad said, "but then evil seldom is. I'd never really noticed him before, but suddenly he seems to be everywhere, with that terrible old bat in the cloak."

"What does he look like?" Rosa asked.

"Just a little man with white hair and beads and bangles. Looked like just another old hippy at first, but when he tried to lecture *me* about spirituality, I knew there was more to him."

"But, Dad, that guy's—"

"What?"

"Nothing," Rosa said miserably. "I mean, he just doesn't look very dangerous, that's all. That's if...I mean, if that's the one I think you're talking about."

"Ah, Rosa..." Dad patted her hand. "When you've had as much experience of dealing with villains as I have, you learn how to spot them in seconds."

Was he joking? Dad might think *she* was mad, but Rosa couldn't help wondering if *he* wasn't losing it a bit.

She looked down at her empty plate, while Mum cut sandwiches. After that coffee and carrot cake, Rosa didn't feel at all hungry.

Why don't you ask your father to say some prayers in your room? Teddy had said. *Ask him to bless the room. He ought to do that for you...*

Oh, sure...

At least Marco had seemed to believe her. But look whose grandson he was. If Dad knew she'd been talking to him, he'd go completely berserk. He'd probably leap up and send her to her room.

Which was the *last* place she wanted to be. She hated her room now, more than anywhere else in the flat – and *that* was saying something.

"Still," Dad said, "I'm sure the situation will improve when this new hotel and tourist centre gets built, and all these so-called New Age and pagan shops get so few customers that they'll just go out of business. All right, the most profitable ones will probably move out there, but at least they'll be outside the town...and away from my church."

Rosa thought of something. "Does that mean Teddy at the crystal shop will go out of business?"

"That idiot?" Dad sniffed. "I certainly hope so."

And then his face went solemn and he bowed his head over the table.

"Let us say grace," he said.

He said grace every night. *For what we are about to receive...*

Tonight Rosa clasped her hands together much tighter than usual and wondered whose side she was on.

In the end, Marco had no problem at all finding his way back to the cottage. He just walked to the top of the town and then across the road and straight to Well House Lane, which led to the Tor.

And then, before he knew it, he was walking up the track that led to Woolly and Nancy's. Didn't even have to think about it. It was like he'd lived here for years. All his life, in fact.

Or longer.

Don't go there, Mum's voice hissed in his head.

It was just that the grass looked so luminously green under the muddy sky. And the Tor...the Tor was soaring over the cottage in a way he'd never seen before, looking so familiar now but, at the same time, so strange – glowing somehow, as if it was getting light from somewhere other than the sky. As if it was lit up from inside.

And he felt...he felt that the Tor had recognized him as he walked up the track...that the Tor *knew* him. That something had happened between them this morning, and he would never be the same again. Which was kind of comforting and disturbing at the same time.

You delusional dweeb! Josh snarled in his head. *You go on like this and it'll take months of therapy to get you functioning normally again!*

The thing was, in Glasto, your idea of what was normal had to be a bit flexible or you'd go completely crazy.

But now they were sending him back to London and to Josh, and the thought of leaving Glastonbury and the Tor – and even The Cosmic Carrot – was like having all your birthday presents wrapped up again and taken away and your birthday cake, with all its candles, put back in the tin and replaced with a cold baked potato.

Besides, he had to do something to help Rosa.

He realized, of course, that Josh would say she was suffering from advanced paranoia and that the monk she'd seen on her wall and the candle burning in the disused shop were just psychological projections of her own insecurity (it was amazing how much of Josh's jargon he must have absorbed), but his own experiences, during just one day in Glasto, had told him it wasn't going to be that simple. And he was pretty sure that Woolly would know people who could tell Rosa exactly what was happening to her.

But when he arrived at the cottage, Nancy was there on her own.

"Marco, where've you *been*?" There was a horrible grinding noise in the stereo speakers as she pulled the primeval record-arm off a piece of historic vinyl.

Marco decided this wasn't the best time to explain. As Nancy made space on the kitchen table for tea, he said, "I suppose he's told you about him and Eleri trying to send me home."

"Oh, lovey." Nancy looked genuinely upset. "It's for your own good, look."

"You sound like my dad."

Marco was glad to see her flinch at that. He took a good long look at his grandmother, who was wearing a kimono-type garment with purple dragons on it and had her hair pushed up into a big yellow mushroom. She was even harder to figure out than Woolly. Sometimes she seemed all over the place, totally away with the fairies. But he couldn't help suspecting this was an act. She was, after all, his mum's mother.

He said bluntly, "Are you and Woolly pagans?"

Nancy went a bit stiff. "Pagans?"

"Like, do you worship the old gods?"

"Oh dear," Nancy said. "Who told you that?"

"Somebody said all the pilgrims are pagans."

"Well, I..." Nancy put her head on one side, with all the jangling this involved. "I dunno what to tell you. Some of them worship the Goddess. I suppose that's a *bit* pagan."

"Goddess? Which goddess?"

"She's known by different names," Nancy said, "but I suppose you could call her Mother Earth. And if you means, do me and Woolly strip naked in the moonlight and perform weird rituals round a fire, well, that's—"

"You've got one of those pentagrams – a pentacle, or whatever – by your door."

"Ah." Nancy looked a bit put-out. "So you know what that means, then."

"Gran...Nancy...everybody who ever watched *Buffy the Vampire Slayer* knows what it means."

"However," Nancy said, "you'll likely have noticed that on the *other* side of the door we got a cross. See, religion's always been a bit like that in Glasto – a bit mix 'n' match. Christianity down in the town, with the Abbey and the Holy Thorn. And witchcraft and paganism up on the Tor. And look where *we* are – right smack in between the two."

"You mean you worship the old gods *and* Jesus?"

"Well, we don't actually *worship* the ole powers – we just recognizes that they're there. Be daft not to in a place like this. And I do like to see a bit of good in everything. Jesus was good because he gave us a moral code – he showed us how to do the right thing by one another. But paganism's also got its good side because it's a nature religion and shows us how to connect with the Earth. See?"

"Riiiight," Marco said warily, trying to feel his way into this idea.

"It's about feeling the elements, look. The wind and the rain. Feeling the shape of the hills. To know we're a part of it all. Woolly always says Jesus was a good bloke, no question, but he'd feel a bit lost without...*all this.*"

Marco thought about the dreamlike sensations he'd been having since he arrived here. Was that what Woolly meant? And this morning, at the Tor...*over* the Tor. Was that a *pagan* experience?

"Course there's good pagans and bad pagans," Nancy said. "And the good ones don't do human sacrifice, or *any* kind of blood sacrifice any more. And, of course, there's good Christians and maybe not-so-good ones. And the good ones don't go round persecuting people just 'cause they got a different view of things. It's all about tolerance. And peace and love. If you stands for peace and love, it don't bother me what you worships in your spare time."

"So these guys who want to build Avalon World..."

"Wilde-Hunt?"

"What?"

"That's what the company's called," Nancy said, "Wilde-Hunt. A firm called Wilde and Co. that builds amusement parks joined forces with a developer called Hunt."

"So are *they*, like, pagans, or what?"

"Them? They got only one god, Marco." Nancy looked stern. "And that's money. And that's almost the darkest god of all."

"Almost?"

"Well, most likely the *very* darkest god is Satan, 'cause he's the Antichrist."

"But don't the pagans worship Satan? Isn't he one of the old, dark gods?"

"Certainly not!" Nancy said sharply. "Some pagans worships a horned god, but he's got nothing at all to do with Satan. Some Christians and the pagans, especially in Glasto, got quite a lot in common, as it happens. But the Satan-worshippers, all they care about is...well...unholy pleasures I don't like to talk about. And money, of course."

"Money. So are you saying that the Avalon World people...?"

Nancy looked uncomfortable. "You're too smart for your own good, you are. The truth is, we don't like to say too much on account of Wilde-Hunt got clever lawyers who'd sue us for libel. But some of us got our suspicions, I can tell you that much."

"That they're Satan-worshippers? Actual satanists?"

"I don't know, Marco. They're just businessmen who probably don't think much about anything outside of how much profit they can make. But some of the people they got working with them..." Nancy bit her lip, looking fearful. There was a pile of heavy books on the table, and she folded her arms and pressed them down on it. "Woolly said you met Roger Cromwell today."

"That was the guy we saw on the Tor? The thin, bald guy?"

"He's their special adviser on the Glastonbury legends – the Holy Grail and King Arthur and all that stuff. He had a shop here for a few years, but the things he was selling..." Nancy shuddered. "'Twas horrible."

"What things?"

"I used to cross the road rather than walk past that shop, look. It got so's you could feel the...feel the evil coming from it."

"So like this shop..." Marco was thinking fast. He was thinking about the girl, Rosa. "...is it closed now?"

"Been closed near enough a year. In the end, Woolly and a few other people in town, they went to the feller who owned the building, said they was worried about the vibes it was spreading. They went to the Chamber of Trade, too – the committee that represents all the shopkeepers. Well, it was the first time they'd *ever* had complaints from the pilgrims – normally it's the straight shopkeepers, the Glasties, complainin' *about* the pilgrims."

"What happened?"

"When his lease was up on the shop, the owner wouldn't let Roger Cromwell renew it So he had to go. Listen, don't you go near that shop, Marco. It's a bad place. What Roger Cromwell was doing there left a real bad vibe. Two different shopkeepers rented it after he went, and neither of them stayed longer than a month."

"What happened?"

"Their businesses failed. They lost money. Accidents happened – there was a fire once. Plus, they got bad feelings. Saw bad things."

"What things?"

"Strange figures," Nancy said. "Things that maybe wasn't there. You get me talking about this, neither one of us is gonner be able to sleep tonight."

"You mean Cromwell..."

"Like I say, he left some evil behind." Nancy leaned all her weight on the pile of books. "And now he hates Woolly and the pilgrims for driving him out, and he'll do anything to hurt them. Anything he can."

"And he's working with this Wilde-Hunt firm?"

"To set up this huge out-of-town development and destroy all the little shops. Only with Cromwell, it's personal..."

Marco began to see why she was so worried. "So what can they do to you if you refuse to sell them your land?"

"Now don't you go botherin' your head about that," Nancy said. "When it's all over you can come back and have a proper holiday. When things are...better."

But he could tell she was far from sure things would ever be better. She straightened up, and the pile of books wobbled. Right at the bottom of the pile, Marco saw the white edge of an envelope sticking out. It disappeared when Nancy hurriedly straightened all the books in the pile. She turned away for a moment, and when she turned back to Marco, she was smiling, but he could tell that underneath all the colourful make-up she'd gone very pale.

"What is it?" he said. "What's happened?"

"Marco, lovey—"

"I can help. I'm not going. If you put me on the train, I'll just get off and find my way back. I'll hide in the woods. I'll sleep in Merlin's stable. I'll sleep out on the Tor with the pilgrims. But I'm not going. I *totally refuse to leave.*"

He knew this probably sounded childish, but it was the way he felt.

"Don't be silly," Nancy said. She sniffed. "I'll...I'll go and freshen up and then make us some tea."

When she'd gone, he looked at the pile of books on the table and then began slowly to dismantle it, until the plain white envelope underneath was fully exposed.

Marco bit his lip. It was like Nancy had put all the books on top deliberately to crush the envelope.

He picked it up. It was unsealed. There was a sheet of plain white writing paper inside. He glanced at the door then slid out the paper and unfolded it.

The short message was written in thick black fibre-tip near the middle of the paper, just above the fold.

Be sensible, Woolaston. Sell the house or you won't have nothing left to sell. You been warned old man.

Begone!!!

And now it was going dark. An almost-full moon was rising in a sky from which the thick cloud banks had been cleared away, like big sofas pushed into the corner of a vast living room.

And Woolly still hadn't come back.

Although they had electricity, Nancy lit a brass oil lamp and placed it in the window. She was looking very worried now.

"Why don't I walk down to the town and see if I can find him?" Marco said, thinking this would be a good opportunity to convince Woolly that it didn't make any sense for him to leave Glasto. "After all, it's my fault—"

"No!" Nancy turned from the window. "You mustn't leave this house...not after dark. He'll be all right."

Marco didn't say anything. He'd replaced the envelope under the books and said nothing about it. He was rubbing his tummy where Jasper had hit him. It was still sore. Suppose Woolly had been ambushed the way he had this afternoon by Jasper Coombes and his mates...

Woolaston's a traitor. He betrayed his roots.

But this wasn't Jasper. This wasn't kids. Woolly had real, grown-up enemies.

"Likely he'll have got pulled into a meeting at the Assembly Rooms," Nancy said. "They're having a lot of meetings at the moment, look."

"The pilgrims?"

"Woolly and Eleri are trying to make them all decide on a plan of action," Nancy said. "But unfortunately most of them just go, 'Hey, man, no hassle, it'll all be cool.' Which is their way of avoiding the issue."

The phone rang.

"That'll be him," Nancy said. "Thank God."

But it wasn't Woolly. It was Marco's dad. For Marco. Nancy held out the phone to him, looking glum.

"Been waiting for your e-mails," Dad said crisply, like he was talking to a client.

"Ah. Bit of a problem there, Dad."

"Tried to call you on your mobile, too."

"Bit of a problem there, as well. Well, first the laptop wouldn't work. Maybe it got bashed when you threw the bag in the car."

"Marco, I did *not*—"

"And the mobile, it's er, it's kind of gone missing. I'm still trying to sort all my things out. I expect it'll turn up."

"That's not good enough, is it, Marco?" Dad said sternly. "That's the kind of thing *they*'d say. 'Oh, it's broken, never mind.' That's a typical Glastonbury attitude."

"How do you know?"

"Well, I...it's what I've heard. Anyway, you go to a computer dealer first thing and have that laptop fixed. Give me their number and I'll deal with the charges. Okay?"

"Sure."

"Everything all right, matey?"

"Fine."

"Woolly's behaving himself, is he? Nancy sounded a little... anxious."

"He's fine."

"Listen..." Dad lowered his voice. "I know it's hard for you to talk with your grandparents in the room..."

"No, it—"

"But if anything's bothering you, I want to know about it, okay? I'm here for you, don't forget that. And I'm here for them, too. Woolly and Nancy. They're family, after all."

"Then how come you never even mentioned them in, like, thirteen years?"

"Ah. Well. The thing is, they're not getting any younger, and I hadn't realized what an isolated place that was. Seems to me they'd be far better in a nice little house in the town than out there in the hills."

"Where would they keep the donkey?"

"Anyway...you've got to keep me up to speed. Everything that happens, I want to know about it. Remember, I'm responsible for you. And I'm *here* for you. Okay?"

"Sure. But, like, what do you think could happen, anyway?"

"Marco…" Dad was silent for a moment. "One thing you need to understand about Granddad Woolaston is that, like a lot of people of his generation, he tends to feel everybody's got it in for him...when, in fact, they only want to help."

"You mean he's paranoid?" Marco thought about the letter. That was real enough. Unless, of course, Woolly had written it himself. But why would he do that? "You don't think somebody really *has* got it in for him, then?"

"Ha ha. Good heavens, no. Look, matey, got to go, urgent business meeting. Get that laptop fixed tomorrow, eh? Byeee."

Marco stared into the dead phone. His dad had an urgent business meeting at night? An urgent appointment with the girlfriend, more like.

One thing you need to understand about your dad, Mum had said, *is that he's a lawyer. It's a bit like the prime minister. What he tells you is what it suits his agenda for you to know. Even if it's not strictly true.*

It had taken Marco a while to work this out. He hadn't told Josh.

"You better get off to bed, Marco," Nancy said, "or you'll be looking like me and Woolly."

"What *about* Woolly?"

Suddenly Nancy did look quite old and forlorn and kind of fragile, like a faded doll in an antique shop. And Marco thought of Jasper Coombes, as he trod on the mobile, saying, *In a lonely place, things can get broken.*

Rosa lay in the harsh white light of the nearly full moon thinking, *do it...*

And then, *I can't...*

She'd been really tired when she went to bed – she'd made sure of this. After spending most of the day walking all over the town, she'd insisted she was far too wide awake and restless to go to bed, and she kept following her dad around the flat, asking him questions about evil pagans and what they did – and then she said she couldn't go to bed after all that because she'd only have nightmares about evil pagans.

The truth was that she wanted to feel so completely knocked-out that she'd go straight to sleep and absolutely nothing would wake her until the morning.

That way, she wouldn't have to do it and risk getting it wrong and have some awful bad luck come down on all of them.

Mum and Dad had kept looking at each other, Mum frowning at Dad as if to say, *This is all your fault.* And then Dad had sat Rosa down at the kitchen table, and Mum had made them all milky drinks, and Dad had said he was really sorry for going on about the pagans. He said they were just stupid, misguided people and *most* of them were still young enough to grow out of it and look back and realize how stupid they'd been. There was absolutely nothing to worry about, Dad said, because God looked after all good Christians.

And because *he* was an ordained minister – Dad had smiled and squeezed her hand – Rosa could expect Special Protection.

So there was nothing to worry about. Nothing at all.

After which, Rosa finally *did* go to bed and *did* go straight to sleep in the boxy little room at the end of the landing, with her head turned away from the wall and towards the window overlooking the street. Noticing, just before she closed her eyes, that she'd forgotten to draw the curtains. But knowing that if she got up now to do it she'd only make herself fully awake again and that was the last thing she wanted.

It must have been after midnight when she'd awoken with the nearly full moon in her eyes.

Awoken with a snap. Instantly, totally awake.

Instantly bathed in moonlight and fear.

And she knew she was not alone. The atmosphere in the room was thick with the silence of something that shouldn't be there. That shouldn't be in this world. And she knew that if she turned over to face the wall by the door, the cold moonlight would be glimmering dully in his far-back eyes as he came fading up, out of the plaster, his robe falling into dark mist and his hands rising up out of his rotting sleeves and—

You have to do it!

Because, if she could make the monk go away, all the rest would surely stop. If this old dead monk was still traumatized by what some long-ago king had done to the abbot, well that was just too bad. And it wasn't her problem. It *wasn't*. She had to make him leave her alone.

Rosa tensed her whole body, clenching her fists, the nails biting into the palms of her hands...and she wanted this, she needed the pain. At her old school there was a girl called Charlie who used to stick sharp things into her arms and leave horrible scars, and Rosa had found this shocking and revolting, but tonight she understood why Charlie had done it, why Charlie had needed to hurt herself. Because pain was real. *Nobody* could tell you that pain wasn't real. Nobody could pat you on the head and tell you, as you sat there all bloody and sobbing, that you were imagining it.

Panting hard, she kept her eyes frozen on the big moon through the window, as she slid out of bed on that side. This time, she was going to keep the bed between her and that wall. And she wasn't going to turn around until the very last second...until she was already *doing it*...drawing the imaginary sword from its imaginary scabbard and inscribing the pentagram in the air.

Now she was standing up by the window, watching the moonlight shimmering on the roofs of the shops across the street.

Knowing she was no longer alone in the room.

Feeling him behind her and knowing she was going to have to look at him.

She couldn't. Not yet.

She was shaking with total cold terror, now, squeezing her eyes tight shut, as she reached with her right arm to her left side, just above a pyjama pocket. Imagining herself gripping the handle of the great sword.

Please...please let me get it right.

Rosa spun.

Her arm came up so hard it nearly pulled her off her feet and, behind her closed eyelids, she saw the moonlight flashing from the blade of the great sword as she held it aloft and let it fall diagonally and then *up* again and *across* and —

As the sword fell for the final time, she cried out, like Teddy had told her...

"Begone!!!"

And her eyes sprang open and...

Oh God...

....he was there, in his robes.

Rosa just screamed and screamed until she thought her throat would burst.

Child of Satan

There was a tapping on the bedroom door.

"Wuh?"

Marco prised his eyes open. Through his window, he saw thin streaks of orangey red, like hot wires, in the sky. It seemed like he'd only just gone to bed, but could that be... dawn?

"Wake up," a voice said gruffly from outside the door.

"Woolly?"

Woolly was back. Woolly was okay. He wasn't lying beaten up in some back alley. That was brilliant.

Or was it?

"Get dressed," Woolly said. His voice was different... serious.

Marco clutched at the duvet. In his head, he saw a railway station, with a London train waiting. He saw his bags on the platform.

No. He wasn't. He wasn't going to get up.

"I'm not going! Woolly, I'm not going home. You can't send me home. I don't want to go."

"The Rolling Stones had it right, I'm afraid, dude," Woolly said sadly from outside the door. "You can't always get what you want."

"I'm part of the tradition! I've got the family tradition to inherit. *You* said that."

Woolly didn't reply.

Marco tightened the duvet around his neck. "Don't send me away..."

Even *he* thought he sounded pathetic, his voice all small and trembly.

"Get up, boy," Woolly said roughly. "I'll see you in the orchard in five minutes."

"Wh...what time is it?"

"Just gone four-thirty," Woolly said. "Don't waste no more time."

Rosa sat in the living room, in her dressing gown. On a hard dining chair, like she was an accused person in court.

Her mum and dad sat at either end of the sofa opposite her. Rosa stared between them at the picture of Wells Cathedral on

225

the wall. It was a very ornate cathedral, full of stone carvings, and she thought she knew every one by now.

Every light in the room was switched on – wall lights, ceiling light and a table lamp. The light was harsh and hurt her eyes.

But she didn't say anything.

She was keeping her mouth tight closed. She knew there was nothing she could say that would make her father, the Reverend David Wilcox, any less angry.

Sergeant Wilcox wouldn't have been bothered. But the *Reverend* Wilcox was looking at his daughter – his only child – the way Sergeant Wilcox might have looked at a serial shoplifter. Or worse. Maybe much worse.

Keep quiet, that was the only thing she could do. Say nothing – with or without a lawyer.

"As you can see, I haven't been to bed..." The Reverend Wilcox had his arms folded and the strong lights were showing a few grey whiskers in his big black beard. "...and I don't care if we sit here until morning."

Mum said, "Dave, this isn't an interview room."

"You go back to bed if you want, Shirley. Rosa and I will stay here until she decides to talk to me."

Mum just shook her head and looked miserable. It felt like they'd been sitting here for five hours already.

And Rosa knew that Dad didn't *really* want to talk to her. Not in the way that *she* wanted to talk. Not in a way that would make him understand why she was so afraid and what she was afraid *of*...because he just didn't want to understand, did he? He just wanted someone he could nick for what he'd decided was a really serious offence. He wanted a name. And there was no way she was going to give him one.

Dad was wearing his long cassock. He normally took it off at night. Maybe he'd kept it on because he thought there was evil in his own home. Evil as well as madness. Dad prowling around the rooms in his clergy uniform. He probably thought it made him look imposing, like some big authority figure. God's bouncer.

Unfortunately, as he'd stood very still against the moonlit wall in her bedroom, watching her inscribe the pentagram, what it had made him look like was...a monk.

With the distant lights of Glastonbury town making a golden halo over the orchard wall, Marco crept among the apple trees.

The air was already surprisingly warm. Two owls were *woo-wooo*oing at each other in the wood.

And the *old feeling*, the lurking dream-state, was snaking through Marco, up his spine, until it was flickering in his head. This time, he didn't question it; he just let it happen. It made him feel less worried.

Like he was cushioned by the night.

Woolly was waiting, standing still as a tree stump. He was wearing a tatty old fleece over his T-shirt. He wasn't smiling. His moustache looked stiff and mottled in the half-light, like a bent piece of pipe.

Marco said, "Woolly, I'm sorry I ran away. I'm sorry you had to go looking for me. I was just...I just couldn't stand the thought of having to—"

"You stay out here a minute," Woolly said.

"Where are you going?"

"I'll be in the shed. I'll call you when I'm ready."

And he walked off into the shadows.

Marco hadn't been in Woolly's shed, which stood back to back with the stable. He could hear Woolly moving around inside, and then a warm light flared and flickered, and Woolly called out, "Okay, you can come in now."

As Marco stepped inside the shed, he heard a noise like *hick, hick, hick*...and found himself eyeball to eyeball with the hairy head of the donkey. In the bleary white light from a hurricane lamp hanging from the ceiling, Merlin looked suddenly terrifying, like he was preparing to attack. His eyes were gleaming and bulging and his mouth was open, revealing a huge, pale tongue. He was sucking in air, going *errrgh... errrgh...errrgh*...and then... *haaaaaaaaaaaaaaaaaaaaaaaaaaaaw!*

The shed-shaking mega-bellow nearly blasted Marco back into the orchard.

"Ah," Woolly said. "Ole Merlin does like to guard this place. Better than a burglar alarm, eh?"

"Wow..." Marco clutched his chest like Josh did when he was faking a heart attack. "Where I live, that wouldn't even be legal."

He wondered what Woolly kept in here that needed guarding. The shed seemed much bigger than it had outside, but then he saw that it actually joined up with the stable, with Merlin on the other side of a wooden partition.

"Little feller keeps me company while I'm working," Woolly said.

"Working?"

Marco saw a workbench with tools on it – files and pliers and chisels – and what looked like a small lathe, which suggested there was electricity in here – so why had Woolly lit an oil lamp?

Woolly saw him looking at the lamp.

"Oh, we got electric in here. We got spotlights and all that stuff. But that's not right for a special occasion like this. Too harsh, look."

Special occasion?

The dream-state came down around Marco like a curtain of light.

"Are you going to send me home?" he said.

Woolly stepped to one side, and Marco saw a wooden bar running the width of the shed, just above his head height, close to the glowing bulge of the hurricane lamp. Many shiny, glittering things were dangling from it, like coloured balls from a Christmas tree.

Woolly sighed. "I think you *are* home," he said.

Marco didn't dare to smile. He hardly dared to breathe.

He saw that the glittering things hanging from the wooden bar weren't Christmas decorations; some were conical and some were tubular and each hung from a thin chain, and they were all vibrating, as if the light itself was a gentle wind.

"Needs a special time and a special atmosphere," Woolly said, "when a dowser chooses his first pendulum."

* * *

"You know something," Rosa's dad said, in a friendlier voice, "I really don't think you knew what you were doing, did you?"

Rosa said nothing.

"Which, of course, would make it *much* less of a sin," Dad said. "Not really *your* sin at all, in fact."

Rosa stared at a particularly intricate piece of carving on the wall of Wells Cathedral. She was feeling tired now and wanted to close her eyes against the harsh lights, but she mustn't.

"You were a victim," Dad said. "You were just doing what someone had told you to do. You couldn't possibly know that it was a terribly evil thing – an unholy, ungodly, pagan gesture that showed contempt for everything I stand for. *You* wouldn't do that to your dad. Would you?"

He must think she was stupid – or that she watched TV with her eyes closed and her ears turned off – that she didn't recognize the good cop/bad cop routine that detectives used to lull suspects into a sense of false security.

"She's tired, Dave," Mum said. "And she's upset."

"She's upset?" Dad forgot all about the good-cop routine and slammed his hand down on the arm of the sofa, his beard splitting into a snarl. "*She's* upset? How do you think *I* feel, discovering my only child performing a disgusting heathen ritual in my own home?"

"Dave, she didn't know. You just said that yourself—"

"Who was it?" Dad swung to face Rosa. "Who showed you how to do it?"

"Nobod—"

230

Rosa bit her tongue.

"Ah," Dad snarled. "So you *can* still talk. The devil hasn't got your tongue." He leaned towards her. "But he's got the rest of you, hasn't he?"

Mum sprang to her feet. "Dave, for goodness' sake—"

"No, Shirley... This is serious."

"It was the man in the crystal shop, wasn't it?" Dad said quietly.

"No!" Rosa went back so hard, the front legs of the dining chair lifted from the floor.

"Ha," Dad said. "You denied *that* very quickly, didn't you?"

"No!" Rosa screamed. "It wasn't. *It wasn't Teddy,* do you understand?"

Dad smiled.

"Teddy," he said softly, rolling the name around his mouth like a boiled sweet. "I think it's time *Teddy* and I had a little chat..."

"No...please..." Rosa leaped up and went behind her chair, gripping the knobs on the top, her hands shaking. "I'll never do anything like that again, I swear it! I'll come to church three times on Sundays, I'll pray to God, I'll... Please leave Teddy alone... It was me. I begged him to tell me what to do. He didn't... Dad, please...*please...*"

Dad stood up.

"Thank you, Rosa," he said. "You may go to your room now."

Emporium of the Night

"Now, walk towards me, slowly," Woolly said. "Hold your forearm parallel to the ground, look. Hold him steady. No, no...slow down!"

Marco thought of when his dad had taught him to ride a bike. The pendulum was swinging backwards and forwards on its chain as he walked.

"Right. Stop there."

Woolly held up a hand. Under his fleece, he was wearing a very old T-shirt on which you could only just make out the words COUNTRY JOE AND THE FISH. He had one of his own pendulums, a metal one like a builder's plumb line, with which he'd occasionally demonstrate a point.

It had taken Marco no time at all to choose his own pendulum from the collection in Woolly's shed. The one like an orange fruit drop had taken his eye straight away, and now it seemed even more incandescently brilliant – the same colour as the early sun, and it was somehow as if the pendulum *knew* that. He could almost feel it pulling on the end of its slender chain, like it was saying, *Okay, let's get on with it.*

Woolly had told him it was important to start work with a new pendulum at sunrise, when the earth-energies were strong around you.

Marco's hand tingled, then his arm, then his whole body. He felt suddenly full of *something.* He reckoned he must be feeling like King Arthur had felt when he pulled the sword from the stone, discovering a new energy that was going to become a major part of him.

He looked up at the Tor, wreathed in clouds like smoke rings. There *was* wizardry in the world – actual wizardry in the actual real world. And everything had been turned around. He should be on the way to the train station, but instead he was—

"You're swinging it, dude." Woolly was shaking his head. "You're too excited. You're tellin' it what to do. You gotter wait for it to tell *you.*"

"How does that happen?"

"I'll give you the science," Woolly said. "Everything's got its own force field right? Like an aura...an area of energy around it. An invisible cloud that tells you what it is. Reveals its essence, its true nature. *You* got one, I got one...that apple tree got one. And the pendulum – what it does is registers where a new force field takes over. Water's the easiest. Flowing water has a very powerful force field, and 'twas the most useful thing a dowser could find. So that was how dowsers made their living – tellin' people where to sink a well. But you can also dowse metals, and even feelings and... Aha! Look at *that*!"

Marco's pendulum was no longer swinging to and fro. It was making slow circles, clockwise.

"You wasn't thinkin' about it then, was you?" Woolly said.

Marco watched the pendulum. Until he'd looked, he hadn't even been aware that it was moving. It seemed to be doing it on its own. It wouldn't have taken much of a movement of his hand to make this happen, but he was pretty sure he hadn't done anything.

"What's that mean, Woolly?"

"I'll show you now, look."

Woolly swooped to the grass at Marco's feet. When he stood up again, he was holding out a curved piece of rusty metal.

"It's a horseshoe." Marco looked at him. "You knew it was there all the time, right?"

"But *you* didn't. Or – put it this way – you didn't *think* you did."

"The pendulum detected the horseshoe?"

"No, some part of *you* detected the horseshoe. You was entering into the force field of the horseshoe – iron. The pendulum just registered the fact, see? You can even go in search of different metals by *programming* the pendulum. Because gold vibrates at a different frequency to iron, you can detect gold – or silver, or copper or what you like – by altering the length of a pendulum's string. But that's a bit complicated for now."

"Why don't we learn about this in science?" Marco wondered.

Woolly snorted. "Because scientists can't explain it. And if they can't explain it, they reckons it don't exist. There's a lot of stuff like that. And places like Glasto exist to prove that the scientists don't know the half of it."

"And anybody can do this?"

"In theory. But it comes easier to some of us and we gets a stronger reaction. Your reaction will get stronger and stronger the more you does it."

Marco thought about this.

"Woolly…"

"Ar?"

"Like, you know yesterday, when you said you'd asked the pendulum what I was going to do while I was here, and it started spinning very fast. And then, on the Tor, you said it was giving *me* an answer."

Woolly smiled. "You can ask simple questions – yes-or-no questions – and get a reaction. The pendulum will change direction. But you gotter make sure you ain't helpin' him. You gotter detach your mind from the process."

"But really you're just, like…you're just asking *yourself*, aren't you?"

"Ar. But it could be you're asking a part of yourself you didn't know existed. Call me an ole mystic cat, but I reckon what you're *really* asking is your *higher* self. The part of you that's connected to something bigger and deeper."

"Like a sixth sense?"

"No, the sixth sense is only the tool that connects you to the higher self...which connects to something *out there*. The point is, your higher self ain't gonner lie just to please your *lower* self. Course I don't expect you to believe that, dude. Not yet. Only personal experience with the pendulum is gonner make you really trust the little feller."

They did some more experiments. Once, Marco got a strong reaction, with the pendulum starting to twirl, and he looked all around in the grass: nothing there. But Woolly, his eyes sparkling, pointed to the garden tap on the other side of the orchard and revealed that Marco's pendulum was spinning exactly over where the water pipe went.

"Will it *always* work?"

"Long as you uses it *only* for good. Use it for bad, selfish stuff, it'll come back on you in ways you won't like. And don't ask stupid things you can think out for yourself. And don't get cocky. It don't like cocky." Woolly looked up at the sky and put on his dark glasses. "Come on, let's go, time's getting on, and we got things to do."

"So you're not..." He hardly dared to ask. "You're not sending me home?"

"No, boy," Woolly said. "We ain't sendin' you home. I pretty much knew I wasn't gonner do that the minute you stormed off out of the ole Cosmic Carrot. We had to know what you was made of. If you was real Avalonian material. Remember what I said about the magic not just bein' there on tap? How you had to search for it? You went off on your own to find some answers for yourself, I reckon."

Marco glared at him. "You mean I've just spent like the whole night...thinking you were going to kick me out, and it was all just...just like a *test*?"

"Don't get on your high horse. Won't be the last test you'll face. It ain't an easy place, Glasto. Too many folks makes that mistake – thinks they can just come here and let the vibes do the rest. Big mistake. *Big* mistake."

Marco felt limp with relief and – like when they'd come down off the Tor yesterday – desperate for food. He still wasn't sure what the deal was between Woolly and the doomy Eleri, but he guessed he'd find out. And at least he'd be *here* to find out. He was *staying*.

Woolly peered at him. "And *did* you find any answers?"

"Well, not really. I just found a load more questions."

"And would these be questions you could ask the pendulum? Yes-or-no type questions?"

"I don't think so," Marco said. "For instance...er...what's happening at Roger Cromwell's old shop?"

The impact of this was mega. Woolly jumped back like electricity was going through him, and he went hard up against the stable and nearly lost his footing on the dewy grass. Merlin stuck his big hairy head out of the door to check out the situation as Woolly straightened up.

"Who the hell told you 'bout that?" Woolly said.

The red sun made tiny glowing balls in the lenses of his dark glasses.

"Nancy," Marco said. "And...Rosa."

"Rosa?"

"She's the curate's daughter. The guy you had the row with – big bloke, black beard? They live in this flat above the old shop and she keeps having these...you know, she sees things. I mean she's a bit screwed up, she suffers from Obsessive Compulsive Disorder, but I'm pretty sure she wasn't making it up. She's in a bad way, Woolly."

Woolly's face was grim. "She's bound to be in a bad way if she lives over that shop."

"Why?"

"Sees things, does she?"

"She's scared to go to bed. And she heard this noise and she forced herself to go down, and the door of the shop was open, even though it was always locked, and there was this horrible, disgusting smell and she saw like this candle burning...in an empty shop?"

"Ar." Woolly nodded.

"And she started screaming, but when her dad came down it was all dark in there again and the door was locked. And nobody believed her."

Woolly paced a circle around one of the apple trees, nodding.

"So, like, what was in that shop, Woolly? What did it sell?"

Woolly looked up at the smoky Tor, as if the Celtic

Lord of the Dead, Gwyn ap Nudd, was on his way down with his Hounds of Hell, to seize their souls.

"That shop," Woolly said, "was the biggest black magic supplier in this country. You know what that means?"

Just for a second or two, Marco thought of boxes of chocolates. And then he said, "Satanism?"

And thought of what Nancy had said last night. *The Satan-worshippers, all they care about is...well...unholy pleasures I don't like to talk about. And money...*

"Mistake a lot of folks make," Woolly said, "is to think paganism and satanism's the same thing. But pagans worship nature, and while some of them might be a bit loopy, they're basically all about healing. While satanists...they just worship theirselves. They calls Satan the lord of this world, and followers of Satan behave as though there ain't nothing *else* but this world, so you can do what you likes to other folks and there won't be no payback."

"And they, like, worship the devil?"

"They're specifically anti-Christian, dude. Everything the Christian Church does, they turn it around – say prayers backwards, spill sacrificial blood on their altars. And burn black candles."

Marco stiffened. "You reckon that—"

"The shop was called The Emporium of the Night...and that was when it opened – in the hours of darkness. It used to sell black candles made with animal fats, and they stunk rotten. It also sold sacrificial knives and black robes and *grimoires* – books of black spells for doing harm to people, and satanic bibles and black prayer books. Seemed like a joke at first. By day, all the blinds was down, but at night, candles would be lit in the windows and folks would come through the shadows to buy their things."

"Satanists?"

"Whatever you wanner call 'em, they'd come. Some from Bristol and London, sometimes in black cars with smoked windows."

"All that way, just to buy black candles and stuff?"

Woolly looked down at his trainers, as if deciding whether this was really a good thing to be telling Marco. Then he looked up.

"Like I keep sayin', 'tis a powerful place, dude. And Roger Cromwell's a powerful man. Likes to say he's descended from Thomas Cromwell, who was Henry VIII's hatchet man, responsible for destroying the Abbey and executing the abbot back in 1539."

"But you got his shop closed down, right?"

"And he hates us for it. That's why he went in with Wilde-Hunt to set up Avalon World. So he could destroy the town the way Henry and Thomas Cromwell destroyed the Abbey. Wilde-Hunt, see—"

"Gwyn ap Nudd, the Lord of the Dead, didn't he…?"

"Led the wild hunt, the spectral hounds, through the sky to steal souls." Woolly looked through his dark glasses into the heart of the sunrise. "The name of that firm's no accident. There's a deep darkness there. And that's why they want this land. Not only because it's the best access to their site – over there, behind that bit of a hill. But because they believe something they're after is buried here."

Woolly turned away. Marco felt suddenly chilled and began to understand what his granddad meant by Glastonbury not being an easy place to live. But he'd made his decision to stay here and become part of whatever was going on, and he couldn't back out now.

"Come on," Woolly said. "We'll take a walk down the town. You and that pendulum needs to feel some *good* vibes."

"What is it?" Marco said. "*What's* buried here?"

"It's kind of..." Woolly hesitated. "...kind of a cup."

"You mean like..." Marco swallowed. This was all just so *huge* that he could hardly get the words out. "You mean like...the Holy Grail itself?"

He was imagining it: this softly glowing, white-gold ancient thing hovering in the air.

Woolly turned to face him.

"No," he said. "Quite the reverse, I'm afraid."

The reverse? Marco thought of what Woolly had said about how satanists turned everything Christian around, turned white into black.

"I'm talking 'bout the anti-Grail," Woolly said. "The Dark Chalice."

Only Legend Can Explain...

When Rosa looked out of her window, the early light was smearing the red roofs higher up the street. But the lower part was in shadow, and so was most of her sick, sad bedroom. The room itself seemed brown and shrunken and its air felt damp.

Rosa didn't want to get up. It was like she could taste the day and it was a bitter and soily taste and she was really dreading what this day would bring.

What her dad was going to do.

It was the man in the crystal shop, wasn't it?

When she did manage to get up, her head felt all cloudy and

her legs wanted to give way. When she stood up, she was so dizzy she had to sit down on the bed again. She sat with her back to the window and the sun, whose first rays cast a thin amber light on the wall where the shape of the monk had formed.

Not there. Perhaps the pentagram had scared him off – even though Dad had been in the way when she did it.

Dad. Big, black-bearded, God-fearing, righteous, angry Dad. What had *happened* to Dad? He never used to be like this before they came down to Glastonbury.

He'd almost accused her of becoming a child of Satan, but he couldn't see that something was getting into *him*, turning him into some kind of...

...monster?

I think it's time Teddy and I had a little chat...

Oh God...Teddy.

Somehow she had to warn him.

It was still not yet 6 a.m. and the centre of town was very quiet. Marco and Woolly had walked all the way down from the cottage, not saying much. But the sinister words *the Dark Chalice* had hung between them like a shifting shadow.

Now they walked up an alley and into a backstreet and then, a few minutes later, Marco looked around and found they were in somebody's front garden. Woolly had led him through an ordinary gate outside an ordinary house and up somebody's drive.

243

"What are we—?"

"Don't worry, we ain't trespassing. Mate of mine lives here. He lets me go this way whenever I needs to."

Woolly led Marco down the side of a house and through another gate into a back garden with thick hedges and a high stone wall at the end with a wooden door in it that came to a point, like a church window. Woolly lifted a latch on the door, and it swung open. He extended a hand to usher Marco through, and Marco went through and...

Wow. Marco could almost hear the popping in his ears as the old living-dream sensation took him over.

He'd once gone into an empty church on his own and found it scary, the way he'd opened the door and the atmosphere had been huge and yawning, these great stone pillars and the echoes of his footsteps. He didn't think this could happen *outside*.

But something shivery was happening in the pit of his stomach as he gazed out over the remains of the ancient Glastonbury Abbey.

It must have been vast, once. Bathed in this luminous orange mist, the ruins were spread over a green space that seemed bigger than the town around them. Trees and lawns and golden stone...walls and arches that were sheared off, broken and jagged, but still soaring.

Marco felt something like pins and needles in the air. He held onto some broken masonry, as if he was in danger of floating over it all like he'd done at the Tor. It was not so much like stepping back into history as stepping *out of time*.

He and Woolly drifted down into the ruins in the misty, sparkly dawn. Marco stood under the sliced-off sides of what seemed like two towering arches and wondered why Glastonbury Abbey was so different from all the churches and cathedrals he'd been dragged around – the ones still functioning, with high, carved ceilings and stained glass and pews.

Why did this place, although it was in ruins, somehow feel more...more *alive* than any of them?

He shook himself. He imagined Josh standing here with his hands on his hips, saying, *Yeah, but what does it do? What's the point of it? You could get a whole shopping precinct on this site.*

For a moment, he was shocked, because it wasn't Josh's voice he was hearing in his head, it was Dad's.

You really don't see it, do you, Angus? Woolly had said to Dad. And maybe it was good not to see it, not to be affected by places like this, or else nobody would ever build new shopping precincts, with shops that sold DVDs and computer games.

Marco pinched himself hard on the arm. He needed to pull himself together before he started morphing into some kind of "pilgrim", growing his hair, having his nose pierced, wearing T-shirts with the names of neolithic bands splattered all over them.

"You know what they says about this place?"

Woolly sat down on a wall of golden stone, his legs hanging over a kind of well. Marco came and sat next to him.

"*A sanctuary so ancient that only legend can explain its origin.* That's what it says in the reception area. Which…" Woolly coughed. "…which we'd probably have seen if we'd waited until ten o'clock and then paid to come in."

"We're not supposed to be here, are we?"

"But if we'd waited, we wouldn't've been here on our own. The effect wouldn't've been the same. See, ole Joe 'Mathea, he wasn't daft, and he must've realized there was something real powerful about the vibes here. The energy. It was a place that was waiting for the Holy Grail."

"Yeah, but that would, like, be pagan energy, wouldn't it?" Marco said. "Coming from the Tor, right?"

"Energy's energy, dude. Depends how you uses it. When they built this abbey – first of its kind, remember, in these islands – they boosted the mystic power of Avalon. They added *their* power to the power already here."

"But with all that power, how come it's in ruins?"

"Ah, that was ole Henry VIII, greedy fat git."

Woolly shook his head in disgust and told Marco how the king's men had stitched up the Abbot of Glastonbury on phoney charges and then executed him on the Tor, the place which the pagans believed was the domain of Gwyn ap Nudd, Lord of the Dead.

"So, the idea was that the abbot, the boss of the Christians, should die at the place where the old gods ruled, right?" Marco said.

"Heavy scene, dude. But – and this is a real important point – it wasn't *pagans* that did it. It was the king's men. And they did it out of greed for money and gold. They couldn't care less about any kind of religion, Christian or pagan."

"Which is...much worse, right?"

Woolly nodded. "That's the black hole. That's satanic."

Marco was beginning to get a feel of how you could use one kind of power to destroy another.

"That's always been the big conflict in this town," Woolly said. "Not so much between the Christians and the pagans, but between the power of the spirit and the power of the wallet. You get where I'm coming from?"

"I'm not sure."

"Course not *all* kings was nasty." Woolly smiled. His teeth looked like the Abbey ruins in miniature. He stood up. "Come on, get your pendulum. Some'ing I wanner try out."

His bangles rattling, he led the way down what might have been the central aisle of the Abbey church to a rectangular patch of earth with a stone border. It looked like a grave, but there was no gravestone, only a sign on a short pole, and Marco was about to go round the other side to see what it said, when Woolly called him back.

"Hold it, dude. Don't read that."

"Huh?"

"Let's see what you can find out with the ole pendulum first. You got him there?"

Marco opened his right hand. The polished orange stone lay on his palm, with the chain coiled around it.

"Get him going, dude."

Marco set the pendulum swinging. Not that he needed to;

it seemed to be keen to start moving on its own – backwards and forwards above the mown grass.

"Let him get used to it," Woolly said. "Let him work out where he is."

Woolly talked like the pendulum was a separate person, but Marco knew his granddad meant *him* – or the part of him that responded to hidden things.

Marco nodded at the patch of earth. "That's a grave?"

"It was where a tomb once stood. A very important tomb – if whoever they *said* was buried here really *was.*"

"Who?"

"Let's see what the pendulum has to say about that. Now, without looking at the sign – in fact I'm gonner stand in front of it so you *can't* look at it – you step onto the spot... That's it."

Marco stood in the grassy area enclosed by edging stones.

"Now," Woolly said. "Let's find out what year whoever's body was in that tomb was first discovered. Was it the sixteenth century...ask him...go on!"

Feeling slightly stupid, Marco looked at the pendulum dangling from his thumb and forefinger.

"Er...was whoever was in this tomb discovered in the sixteenth century?"

The pendulum continued swinging slowly.

"Go back into history," Woolly said, "century by century."

"Was it in the *fifteenth* century?" Marco asked.

Nothing.

Fourteenth? Nothing. *Thirteenth?* No reaction.

But hardly was the word *twelfth* out of his mouth than the pendulum stopped for a moment and then began to rock from side to side before settling into a clockwise movement.

Woolly beamed.

"Was that right, Woolly? The twelfth century?"

"What do *you* think? Okay, next question – how many bodies were in here? Start small."

"Okay." Marco stopped the pendulum, then set it swinging again. "Was there...one body buried here?"

The pendulum carried on swinging.

"Was there t— Oh!"

Woolly clapped his hands, bangles jingling.

"There you go. Two bodies!"

"There were two bodies *here*?"

"Now, some folks – professors and suchlike – will tell you there never was *any* bodies here...or if there was, they weren't who the monks said they was. Most historians and professors reckon the whole story was made up by the monks in the twelfth century to make the Abbey seem like a more important place. But, hell, dude, why would they need to do that? It was already the most important church building in the country."

"So who was it? Who was in the tomb?"

Woolly stepped away from the sign.

It said:

**SITE OF KING ARTHUR'S TOMB
IN THE YEAR 1191, THE BODIES OF
KING ARTHUR AND HIS QUEEN WERE**

SAID TO HAVE BEEN FOUND ON THE
SOUTH SIDE OF THE LADY CHAPEL.
ON THE 19TH APRIL, 1278, THEIR REMAINS
WERE REMOVED IN THE PRESENCE OF
KING EDWARD I AND QUEEN ELEANOR
TO A BLACK MARBLE TOMB ON THIS SITE.
THIS TOMB SURVIVED UNTIL THE
DISSOLUTION OF THE ABBEY IN 1539.

Marco looked up at Woolly.

"This is the *actual* King Arthur? With the Round Table and the sword Excalibur?"

"People have different ideas about who Arthur actually was," Woolly said. "Some say he was king, others reckons he was just a tribal chief – a warlord. There's stories about him all over the West of England and Wales, but all the best legends say he came here, on his last journey, to the Isle of Avalon."

Marco remembered the slightly spooky Eleri in the Cosmic Carrot.

Last night, in my dreams, I had a vision of the barge again – the black barge gliding towards Avalon, carrying three hooded women, weeping over the body of Arthur. It's a dream of death, Woolly.

"According to the story," Woolly said, "the monks dug on this particular spot and, seven feet down, they uncovered a stone cross, with a Latin inscription that translated as 'Here lies buried the renowned King Arthur in the Isle of Avalon.' So the monks kept on diggin', and they finds this coffin made out of an oak log, hollowed out, and inside was the bones of this real big feller with the marks on his skull of ten blows, maybe from a sword. All that remained of the woman was a few smaller bones and a lock of golden hair that just crumbled into dust."

"Queen Guinevere," Marco remembered.

"Course some of the so-called experts likes to rubbish the story. *They* reckons the monks got some ole bones together from some other graves and *pretended* they was King Arthur and Queen Guinevere. But it makes perfect sense to me that the greatest king that Britain ever had should be buried in the holiest earth in the country. Makes *poetic* sense."

"So, like...what happened to the tomb?"

"After the Abbey got trashed – nobody knows. Maybe we'll find out one day, maybe we won't. But don't forget the legend that King Arthur is not dead, only sleeping, and will rise again when his country needs him. And it was King Arthur who sent his knights in search of the Holy Grail...and they never found the actual chalice, but some of them saw it in visions all glowing and bathed in white and golden light."

Marco looked down at the pendulum curled up on its chain in his hand, asleep again. Just a little stone, but somehow it had – well *maybe* – put him in contact – *sort of* – with the great King Arthur.

When he looked up, he saw that the sun had already been swallowed by clouds. The golden dawn was over. He might as well ask.

"So, like...what exactly *is* the Dark Chalice?"

* * *

"I'm going to make an appointment for her," Rosa's dad said. "We can't let this go on."

Rosa had her ear to their bedroom door. It wasn't a very thick door and, even though they had their voices lowered, she could hear everything they were saying.

"Dave," Mum said. "Can't we wait a *bit* longer? It's been an awful wrench for her, moving from one end of the country to the other. Maybe she'll settle down."

"But she's *not* settling down, is she?" Dad said. "She's getting worse. It started with nervous habits, and then she began hallucinating, and now she's come under the influence of this lunatic with his despicable pagan rituals. If she doesn't see a child psychologist now, I guarantee we'll both live to regret it."

"But what if…? I mean, you know what it's like when a child gets into the system. What if they want to take her away?"

There was a silence. Then...

"Perhaps, for a short time," Dad said, "that might not be an altogether bad thing."

"Dave, how could you—"

Rosa sprang away from the door in panic, her eyes pooling.

Unholy Relic

"The Dark Chalice," Woolly said. "Well...I seen it once, and I hope never to see it again."

They were walking back through the ruins and into the trees.

"'Tis a long story. Goes back nearly as long as Joe 'Mathea and the Grail – or even longer, some folks reckons. Goes to the mysterious heart of the Isle of Avalon...a place of real power, as you've learned, look. A place that can change your life. You know what I mean by that now?"

Marco nodded. He wasn't sure where the power actually came from, but he'd felt it so many times now that he couldn't deny it was there. It made you tingle, and all the colours glowed. You felt part of something *brilliant*.

But there were two sides to everything, Woolly said. Especially in Glastonbury.

"Sometimes you feels real good – on top of everything, all lit up inside, the world opening out all around you. Other times..." Woolly took a long breath.

"What?" Marco said.

"Imagine the reverse of that. Imagine the world closing in, bringing darkness and a feeling of *no hope.* A cold terror that shrivels you up, makes you wanner...die inside."

"I..." Marco looked around, as if the town might even now be closing in on him. "I can't."

"Then imagine the Holy Grail," Woolly said. "Imagine this shimmering, glowing cup on a cloth of gold. And now imagine the reverse of *that.* What do you see?"

"I don't really..." Marco felt a kind of dread. "I mean, I can't..."

What he meant was he didn't want to.

Woolly looked up, through his dark glasses.

"Imagine something hard and cold and dead. Like old bone. Except it's not dead. It's got a dark life of its own. Gives off the kind of evil you always find, like a poisonous virus, wherever there's the potential for great goodness. *That*...is the Dark Chalice."

Marco still wasn't sure whether Woolly meant something real or something that only existed in people's heads. Josh would have a lot to say about *that* kind of chalice.

"But like...I mean, the Holy Grail, no one knows for sure whether *that* really exists, do they?"

"It exists at least as an idea, as an inspiration," Woolly said. "But the Dark Chalice...I'm afraid that *does* exist."

"Really?"

"Really. Like I say, I've seen it once."

"When?"

Woolly looked down at the ground.

"When I buried it," he said.

Woolly and Marco stopped under the trees, with the Abbey ruins soaring behind them. Marco had an idea that Woolly felt he could only talk about the Dark Chalice if he was near somewhere holy.

It was really *that* bad?

Suddenly, Woolly was sounding more serious than Marco had ever heard him.

"Like I explained, there's a lot of people who come to Glasto to try and use the magic for good things. Healing and stuff. To heal people physically and mentally and heal the Earth, too. But there's also the ones who want to use it to get rich and gratify their dark desires."

"Wilde-Hunt," Marco whispered.

"Correct. Some of the fellers behind Wilde-Hunt want to bring down the town the way Henry VIII and his mates brought down the Abbey. Some of it's business and some of it's personal – because they been joined by Roger Cromwell, who's got a big grudge against me and Eleri and a few of the pilgrims 'cause we got his shop shut down. And Cromwell reckons possessing the Dark Chalice is part of his destiny, seeing it was his ancestor – or so he claims – that was responsible for..." Woolly broke off and sighed. "All right, I'll tell you the whole story."

They sat down on the grass, and Woolly continued.

"See, dude, Thomas Cromwell came here because the abbot had been accused of hiding a particular gold chalice, so that the king's men couldn't get their hands on it. But this chalice had been *planted* in the Abbey, look, by a certain double-dealing monk. And it was said that, as his reward for betraying the abbot, he got to keep the actual chalice for hisself.

"The monk who sold out, he was a bad man, a corrupt man. Sold his soul to evil and, for him, there was no going back. He just got worse...and he started something very nasty. According to the legend, when they carved up the abbot, this monk collected some of the old feller's blood in the gold chalice, the way Joseph of Arimathea was said to have collected drops of Jesus' blood in the Holy Grail when He was crucified."

A serious shiver rippled through Marco. He was suddenly seeing this – the abbot, still alive, laid out on a chunky table. He heard a sword or maybe an axe go whizzing through the air, and a *thunk* as something meaty fell off. He saw the sick smile on the face of a man in brown robes holding a golden bowl, as the blood plopped into it...*glup, glub, glup.*

"And so the chalice became the anti-Grail," Woolly said, "and was handed down, a symbol of cruelty and greed. It was kept on a stone altar in a secret chamber where blood rituals were carried out. And, over the centuries, its dark power grew."

Woolly said the Dark Chalice would go missing for centuries, and then turn up again. It was said to have been in the possession of a certain wealthy local family, but nobody knew for sure.

"Somehow," Woolly said, "it always resurfaces to help anyone who wants to damage Glastonbury. Happened about eight or nine years ago, when there was a plan to build a new motorway real close to the Tor. They wanted to fence it off to keep the pilgrims out. And something that was thought to be the Dark Chalice turned up in an old well near the centre of town. Only it wasn't a gold chalice any more."

"What was it?"

"It was something horrible," Woolly said. "That was how they knew what it was."

"Like...what?"

"I don't like to talk about it. Luckily, a bunch of local people who knows about these secret things – the Watchers of Avalon – they managed to keep it out of the wrong hands. They were good people." Woolly looked down at his hands, in which his pendulum now lay. "My brother, he was one of the Watchers."

"You've got a *brother*?" Marco said. Wow, he could have a collection of totally unknown relatives in Glasto. A whole clan of Woolastons.

"I *had* a brother," Woolly said. "He's dead now. He...he wasn't much of a dowser, but he was a real expert on all the secret energies in the Earth – mysteries you'll learn about one day." He sighed. "They used to call him Woolly too."

There was a silence. It was clear there were some bits of history Woolly didn't want to go into.

"What did they do with it?" Marco asked. "The Dark Chalice."

"Well...there was an ole bus..."

Woolly said that some of the bad people who were determined to possess the chalice were hiding out amongst travelling folk who came to Glastonbury in an old black bus, which they parked in a farmer's field near the Tor, where it was later abandoned. Because of the secret ceremonies they'd carried out there, the field had become...tainted.

"How d'you mean?"

"The atmosphere all round there had turned bad. In a psychic way. The farmer who owned the land was afraid to go near in case he saw something...not of this world."

"Like what?"

"Like something evil," Woolly said. "Something that was left in the air. So, the Watchers of Avalon – Eleri was one of them too – decided to deal with all the evil at once. They put the Dark Chalice in this bus and they set fire to it, burned it to a shell with petrol. And they called on Jesus and also the Goddess to protect the spot. And yet...even when all the bits of bus was took away, there was a black pit in the middle of the field where the grass would never grow."

"Never?"

"Never. Not even the next summer. So one day the farmer

goes out with his spade, figurin' he'll dig the patch over and plant some seed. Says his prayers and crosses hisself, and he starts to dig over the patch...and then his spade strikes something...hard."

"Oh," Marco said.

"Ar. It was a bit blackened, but it was there. More or less intact. The Dark Chalice had survived the fire. Well, the ole boy, he was terrified. He buries it again, real quick, and, bein' a serious Christian, he can't stand the thought of it even havin' been on his land. Thinks it's gonner haunt him the rest of his days. So he just sells up. Sells his whole farm and moves out."

"He sold it to you?"

"Hell, dude," Woolly said, "where would Nance and me get the money to buy a farm? No, he sold it to...what turned out to be the worst folks he could've sold to."

"Not...Wilde-Hunt?"

"Exactly. Course, nobody knew about Avalon World then. That came later. Wilde-Hunt bought the land through their agent, that feller Coombes in High Street. They bought the whole farm...except for one bit. A few acres of land, right on the edge. Which Don Moulder, the farmer, secretly sold to me for just a few hundred pounds...on one condition."

Marco felt his eyes widening. He stared at the great arches of the ruined Abbey, turned sandy by the rising sun.

"I had to find a safe place on that land, to put the Dark Chalice. Had to get the ole pendulum on the job, find a place where we could dig a real deep hole, away from any underground streams that could carry the bad energy down into the town. And we put the...thing in the hole and covered it over."

"And did the grass grow?"

"It did, thank God. And now I couldn't even point you out the spot. Wouldn't be able to find it without the pendulum. And that was good. It needed to be forgotten."

Marco thought about the implications of this. "So these Wilde-Hunt guys – did they know the chalice had been taken away again?"

"Not at first. They thought they'd bought the land where the bus was burned. It was only later that the truth got leaked to Roger Cromwell, who by then had become so-called 'spiritual adviser' to Wilde-Hunt. And that was when they started trying to buy me out."

"Because Cromwell wanted the chalice?"

"Because he thinks he's *entitled* to it. Don't you see what this could mean, Marco?"

Marco wasn't quite sure he did see. He said nothing. Woolly clutched at the air, trying to find the right words.

"Avalon World...well, obviously that would be a bad thing for the old town...close down all the pilgrim-type shops. But, if Cromwell gets his way, it'll be a...*a shrine to the Dark Chalice*...and all it represents."

Marco tried to get his head round this.

"They've been looking for the chalice, haven't they? At night," he said.

Woolly eyed him. "Makes you say that?"

"I woke up, and you were out there with a torch, and when

you came in I heard you telling Nancy you'd found another hole."

"Ar." Woolly sighed. "'Tis true. Somebody's been in the dark and dug at least six holes – likely they been tryin' to dowse for the thing. But they won't find it. I went to a lot o' trouble to cover my tracks, look. There's things we dowsers can do to lay false energy trails, confuse things. Plus, Eleri, she managed to shrink its energy field – its aura – by means of a formula laid down by the great DF – Dion Fortune, the woman who ran the mystic scene here sixty or so years ago. She was determined to contain the power of the Dark Chalice, was DF. Magnificent woman. No, the only way they'll uncover that thing is to buy the land and turn it over with a digger. But they ain't gonner get the land, are they?"

Marco said, "Um, Woolly...what *is* the Dark Chalice, exactly. You said you'd seen it once."

"The day we buried it."

"And you said you hoped you'd never see it again."

"That's true, dude." Woolly got up and walked towards the gate. "'Tis not some'ing you forget."

"And you said it wasn't a gold chalice any more."

"Ar."

"So what is it? What's it look like?"

Woolly stopped in front of the closed gate. "You don't wanner know. I don't wanner give you nightmares."

* * *

When Woolly opened the garden gate, Marco saw a big man was standing there, waiting for them. He was probably about Woolly's age, and he was holding a newspaper. Like Woolly, he had a moustache, but his was short and stiff, and his hair was short, too.

"Ah, Woolly, me ole mucker. Thought it was you."

"Don't mind, do you, Stan? This here's my grandson, Marco."

"Never knew you had a grandson," said Stan, who looked far more like a granddad than Woolly. He wore a cardigan.

"It's a long story," Woolly said. "Not a problem, is there?"

"I told you, you can come through here whenever you want." Stan looked at Marco and winked. "I owe this feller, look – my wife's wedding ring once dropped off in the garden, and we couldn't find it anywhere. But Woolly was on to it in a couple of minutes, with his dowsing. Amazing."

"Routine stuff," Woolly said gruffly.

"Nothing routine about you, Woolly." Stan held up the paper. "Don't suppose you've seen this, yet, then."

It was the local paper, the Western Daily Press. The big front page headline said:

THREAT TO GLASTO SUPER-CENTRE PLAN.

Woolly blinked at it. "What's it say? I ain't got my glasses."

"Big meeting today. The council and all the nobs and the government bods are coming over this afternoon to visit the site earmarked for this Avalon World. But the Avalon World people are warning they might have to scrap the whole plan because some people won't sell them the land they need," Stan said. "They don't name names, but we all know who *some people* is, don't we?"

Woolly said nothing.

"Seems three farmers have agreed to sell land to Wilde-Hunt for a small fortune," Stan said. "So *they* won't be happy at all if the plan don't go ahead and they miss out on all that money...because of *you*. Paper's also got a comment from the Mayor of Glastonbury, who reckons that if it's dropped, it'll be a complete disaster from which the town may never recover."

Woolly exploded. "That bloody ole Griff Daniel! I'd like to know what they're paying *him* to say that."

"Lot of support for it locally, Woolly. A lot of rich people who could become even richer by having a stake in Avalon World. And now they know that there's only you standing in the way...well, that could make you real unpopular."

Woolly snorted. "Like I care. *You* know what this is, Stan, this is just a scam to put the arm on me. They got no intention of backing off, whatever *I* does. But if they wanner make it personal..." Woolly's shoulders went back and the words COUNTRY JOE expanded on his chest. "Fair enough. I'm up for that."

"In that case," Stan said, "you better gear yourself up for Round One."

"What you on about?"

"It's all happening, Woolly. On High Street. Right now."

"What?"

"Radio Somerset's doing a live item for their breakfast programme. They're all out there now – Griff Daniel, Mervyn Coombes...they're getting ready to debate the issue. You want to have your say, now's your chance."

Woolly jumped back. "Me?"

"Go for it, boy," Stan said.

"I...." Woolly started glancing this way and that, like he was looking for somewhere to run. "Stan, I can't talk on the radio. I ain't smooth enough, I ain't educated. I'm just a clapped-out old hippy...I'll say all the wrong things."

He started shrinking back into the bushes. Marco couldn't believe it. The other night, he'd watched Woolly stand up and sing and play the guitar right in the middle of the town and then give the idle pilgrims a lecture about how they should get their act together before it was too late. And now look at him...

"There's big, powerful people behind this scheme," Stan said. "You don't go out there and stand up for what you believe in, Woolly, they're gonner rubbish you behind your back. Turn the whole town against you. The whole county, in fact."

"That's ridiculous. Come on, Marco, let's get some toast at the Cosmic."

"Your life won't be worth living," Stan warned. "They'll make it so you won't dare show your face in this town again."

"I ain't..." Woolly was rubbing his hands together. "I ain't thinking about me, Stan."

In Marco's hand, the pendulum felt suddenly warm – like a transmitter telling him what was in Woolly's mind, and what he heard in his own mind was the cracked voice of Eleri, one of the Watchers of Avalon, as she stood under the cross in her flimsy dress, with her bony arms flung out.

The lovely, shining Grail...became black...black and blistered before my eyes!

Part Three

"I often wonder whether the life of Avalon will ever stir again
or whether we shall be no more than a tourist show..."
DION FORTUNE
Glastonbury: Avalon of the Heart

Traitor

Rosa got dressed quickly and went quietly downstairs, walking sideways past the door to the old shop because, if she caught a glimpse of it, she knew she'd have to go and stare four times into its filthy glass, and she didn't want to do that ever again.

At the front door, she reached up on tiptoe and undid the bolts and the catch, and light from the street washed in, along with the sound of traffic and voices.

And then there was another voice, behind her in the hall.

"Where are you going, Rosie?"

Mum stood there, all dressed, with make-up on, ready to go to work at The George and Pilgrims.

"Going for a walk," Rosa said.

"You haven't had your breakfast. I've got to go to work, so Dad's making it this morning. He'll be back in a minute, he's just gone to the church."

"Don't want any breakast," Rosa said.

Mum sighed. "I think we've been here before, haven't we? Breakfast, whether we want it or not, is the most important meal of the day."

"Why would you care?" Rosa said bleakly.

Regretting it at once, when she saw the look in Mum's eyes, but she couldn't bear to sit in the kitchen for breakfast with Dad, knowing what he was planning for her. She'd choke.

"Rosa—"

"I can't," Rosa shouted. "I *can't!*"

And before she could start crying again, she was out of the door and slotting her hand into the letter box to slam it shut behind her.

Wondering if she would ever come back here again.

"Yes, it's good morning from Glastonbury!" the radio reporter screeched into her microphone. "A town which, as you say, Gary, is today in the middle of a major row!"

The woman was blonde and wore a red suit with tight trousers. She had headphones on, and there was a radio van behind her, with wires and stuff trailing from it, so Marco figured this Gary she was talking to must be the presenter of the breakfast show, in a studio miles away.

It was still early, so only about twelve people had gathered around the woman in the car park behind the old pub, The George and Pilgrims. Marco recognized Eleri, looking worried as hell, with a black shawl pulled around her. He also saw the shaven-headed man he and Woolly had met on the Tor.

Roger Cromwell. The man who wanted to dig up the Dark Chalice. He was wearing one of those suits that were apparently seriously expensive but looked like they'd been bought from an Oxfam shop and then rolled up and trodden on.

The radio woman was holding a clipboard and talking in this bouncy kind of voice, which was how everybody talked on radio and TV but nobody ever did in real life. Leaning on what she seemed to think were important words, like a teacher at nursery school.

"*Avalon World*," she was saying, "is a *multi-million pound scheme* which could attract *hundreds of thousands of new tourists* to this area. The centre is planned for a site outside the town...and the idea is to *bring to life* the *wealth of history and legend* for which this area is *world-famous* – like, er, King Arthur and the Holy Grail."

"*Bring to life!*" Woolly muttered next to Marco. "Kill it stone dead, more like."

"And with me now," the woman said, "is the project's *special adviser*, Roger Cromwell. Roger, good morning."

"Yes, good morning, Kirsty." While she was talking, Roger

Cromwell had glided over to the microphone like he did this every day.

"Roger, tell us how all this *began*."

"Well, Kirsty, as you say, the history and the legends – the sheer charisma of this area – make it second to none, in my view, anywhere in the world." Roger Cromwell's long, bony face sloped into a smile as a couple of people cheered. "And this project began when a few of us realized that the immense tourist potential of Glastonbury was just not being fully exploited." He spread his hands. "And we started asking ourselves...why."

"Yes, *why*?" Kirsty said.

"Kirsty, you only have to look around. What you have here is an ordinary little country town with very few facilities for mass tourism and a lot of little shops selling coloured candles and crystal balls and, ah, similar products. And I suppose you could say it's quaint...but it's all so ramshackle...so small-time...so amateurish."

Next to Marco, Woolly started to growl like a small dog.

"And of course," Roger Cromwell said, "the town gets overcrowded in summer because of the festival, and the car parks get full..."

A guy who was also wearing headphones was guiding another man towards the microphone. This was an oldish bloke in a tweed suit. He had a red face and a spiky grey beard and he looked kind of grumpy.

"So what *we're* proposing," Roger Cromwell said, "is a state-of-the-art visitor-complex with bigger and better shops, audio-visual displays, quality live entertainment, restaurants with the kind of food *normal* people want to eat...and masses of room to park and enjoy it all. A centre that's really going to put Glastonbury on the map as a top tourist resort..."

Marco was dismayed. It did sound pretty impressive. It did sound like it could actually be fun. And even if his voice was like a dark tunnel, Roger Cromwell was all shiny and friendly now, and you couldn't see any reason not to believe him

"A *top tourist resort?* Is that what the town *really wants?*" Kirsty beckoned to the old bloke with the spiky beard. "Here's the mayor, Councillor Griff Daniel. Griff...is it what *you* want?"

"Absolutely, Kirsty!" The old guy leaned over and blasted into the microphone, so close that Kirsty had to pull it away. "'Tis what I been bangin' on about for years! When I was a boy, this was a nice town...and then it got took over by a bunch of screwballs and turned into nothin' but a joke! Well I say we wants our nice ole town back! And this is how it's gonner happen, thanks to Mr. Cromwell and the good people of Wilde-Hunt Developments, who we at the council – make no mistake – are eager to assist in any way we can!"

"Well..." Kirsty looked down at the microphone, which was probably covered with Griff's spit. "It, er...it sounds as if there's a lot of support for this scheme. But not everybody agrees, do they? Some people say it's going to destroy the *homespun magic* of Glastonbury and create a sort of...*Las Vegas* type of thing, outside the town?"

"Magic!" This Griff looked like he wanted to snatch the mike and stamp on it. "Pah!"

"And one person, I believe, Griff, is refusing to let the developers put an important road across his land – without which the project may not be able to go ahead."

"Yes!" the mayor snarled. "One man is threatening the whole scheme. One man who wants to keep this town in the Dark Ages! One *traitor!*"

Woolly said nothing, but Marco felt him quiver.

"Well," Kirsty said, "we did try to get this Mr., er, Woolaston on the programme, but apparently he left his house very early this morning and—"

"Ha!" the mayor said. "That's no surprise. He obviously knew you was coming, and he hadn't got the nerve to show up. 'Tis typical of him! And all his supporters, the scruffy, work-shy hippies with their pink hair and bits o' metal all over their faces, you won't find none of them neither, on account of the idle devils don't get up till about twelve o'clock!"

Marco looked at Woolly. His face had gone nearly as red as Griff Daniel's, and he was starting to breathe very hard. But he still didn't say anything, and nobody seemed to have noticed him. Then another voice – a thin, hesitant voice – came out of the crowd that was getting bigger all the time.

"Just...just one moment!"

Eleri had pushed through to the microphone. She was clutching her shawl around her throat. The mayor looked at her and sniffed, but Kirsty pushed the mike towards her.

"Are you one of Mr. Woolaston's supporters, Miss, er..."

"Cadwallader. Eleri Cadwallader."

"And what do you do?"

"I...I'm a clairvoyant," Eleri said in her up-and-down Welsh voice. "I see things."

"Pah!" said Griff Daniel.

"Super," Kirsty said. "So *what kind of future* do *you* see for the town?"

The Mayor did this sneery smile and stood back from Eleri with his arms folded, like he was really going to enjoy this.

"Well..." Eleri said. "I have seen a number of things..."

Marco's heart sank. He had a good idea what the listeners were going to think when Eleri started coming out with all that stuff about the Hounds of Hell roaring through the sky and the barge full of hooded women mourning the death of King Arthur. They'd think that if Avalon World was going to put loonies like this out of business it could only be a good thing.

"Last night, for instance..." Eleri closed her eyes tight. "I had a most *terrible* dream—"

"*No!*" Woolly howled.

Eleri stopped and opened her eyes. Every head turned and the whole crowd watched as Woolly walked slowly towards Kirsty and her microphone.

"It's me you wanner talk to," he said.

Rosa was aware that something was happening on the car park behind The George and Pilgrims and kept away from it. She just hoped she didn't run into Dad on High Street.

Most of all, she just hoped Dad had not gone to see Teddy.

At Teddy's shop, she saw there was a blind down over

the main window. Not a disgusting black blind like the one below their own flat, but a dark blue one with the name of the shop on it and a picture of a glowing crystal.

And something else was glowing.

At the bottom of the blind was a narrow line of light. Rosa thought at first it was a reflection of the sun in the glass, but this part of the street was still in shadow. Good. It meant he was here already, maybe working on something, rearranging his crystals.

Rosa glanced over each shoulder. A few cars were going past, following a slow truck, and a man outside a newspaper shop was putting out a rack of morning papers and a news bill stand that said, THREAT TO AVALON WORLD!

Rosa slid into Teddy's doorway and tapped on the door. She put her mouth up to the glass.

"Teddy?"

No reply.

"Teddy, it's me, Rosa. If you're there, please open the door. Something's happened."

Nothing. She tapped harder, with the knuckles of both hands.

This was when the door opened.

Rosa stepped back into the street.

For the second time, a door that was supposed to be locked had opened for her.

"Teddy?"

Rosa walked slowly back into the doorway and tentatively peeped inside the shop.

"Teddy," she said hesitantly. "Teddy, are you—"

She stood frozen in the doorway. The inside of the shop seemed to be reaching out for her like hands in dark velvet gloves. The display lights were on, and the big rock crystals were glittering from their purply alcoves, sparkling like handfuls of stars in a deep night sky.

Some of the crystals were on the floor – a cluster of small ones gathered together on the carpet near the counter.

The lights over the counter were not on, making this the dimmest part of the shop. On the black carpet, only the crystals were shining, picking up light from the display-alcoves and from other gemstones.

The crystals on the floor were small and milk-white and – Rosa's heart jumped like a big toad inside her chest – they were arranged in the shape of a face, its eyes glistening and winking at her.

She stood there, hearing an awful pumping sound.

It was the sound of her own heart and her breath, coming out in sobs.

Because there *was* a face on the floor, and a body attached to it, its outstretched legs making a dark V.

As her eyes adjusted to the shortage of light, Rosa became aware that the face was Teddy's. He was lying on his back, still and silent.

There were milky gems in each of his eyes and – Rosa found she had no breath left to scream – some more twinkling out between his lips like a spangle of grinning teeth.

Goodbye Sanity

As Woolly reached the microphone, people started booing him.

Well, not *people* exactly, it was mainly Jasper and his mates, leaning against the car-park wall and looking smug, and Marco really wanted to go over there and...and...

And what? There were four of them. They were all bigger than him. Of course, if Josh had been here, they could both wander over, dead cool, and...

...and demolish all four with advanced psychoanalysis?

Yeah, right. Marco didn't move. One of Jasper's crew gave him the finger. Marco looked away to where Woolly was clenching and unclenching his fists and looking seriously apprehensive.

"Okay," Kirsty said. "So, if I can just get this right, *you are* —"

"Woolly," Woolly said.

"Ah...yes. Okay... Now, um...Woolly...you've *made no secret of your feelings* about Avalon World, and you've turned down what I gather is *a large sum of money* to sell *a small strip of your land* for an access road to the site. I mean, *what's so wrong* with this project, in your opinion? Surely it would relieve traffic congestion in the town and give tourists what they want?"

"Oh, ar," Woolly said. "Sounds real cool, don't it? But what they *don't* tell you is what they *really* got in mind."

"And what's that – in your opinion?"

"How long you got, girl?"

"About two minutes, actually."

Woolly sighed. "See what this is about, it's just the latest stage in an ancient conflict between light and darkness that goes back years and years to when ole Joe 'Mathea brung the Holy Grail to the Isle of Avalon."

"But, Woolly, I think a lot of people would say that that's, you know, *just a legend.*"

Marco thought, *Yes, that was what people would say*. That was definitely what Josh would say. And suppose they were right? Suppose Woolly was, if not exactly sick and psychotic, just a bit misguided? A victim of *Impressionable Elderly Person Syndrome*.

"People would say the Holy Grail *doesn't really exist*," Kirsty said. "So why not have a computer-generated virtual Holy Grail experience at Avalon World?"

"Because it'll be *phoney*," Woolly said. "And it'll take folks away from what's real. And what's real is here in Glasto. And that's a force for good, not just for money. And, whatever anyone says, girl, it's brought some good people into town."

"Right on, man," someone said, and Marco turned and saw it was Orf, the guy with the tattoos and the facial ironmongery.

"See, you takes Orf," Woolly said. "All right, he do look a bit weird. He's got a tree tattooed on his chest and it looks like if you pulls that chain on his face, you'll flush his nose or some'ing. But Orf, he takes care of his sister that was deserted by her husband and her two kids, and he ain't such a bad bloke, even though they named him after a sheep disease."

"Yeah," Orf said. "Whatever. Everybody oughter listen to Woolly, 'cause, like, he's the main man, right?"

"However..." Kirsty winced, like she was getting some serious stick from the studio, in her headphones. "Mr. Woolaston...Woolly...if we can just get to *the point—*"

"The point is," Woolly said, "that folks like Orf is basically on the side of the Grail, while some respectable-looking folks in suits gets *their* energy from...from..." Marco saw Woolly's hands clench tight at his sides. "...from the Dark Chalice."

Kirsty looked mystified. "What on *earth* is that?"

"Wherever there's light, there's creeping shadows."

"Well, I'm sure that's true. However—"

"The anti-Grail," Woolly said, "has been a secret too long."

"Certainly a secret from me," Kirsty said, making a face like someone in the studio was screaming in her headphones, *Get this loony off the air,* now!

"The Dark Chalice is the symbol of hatred and cruelty and human greed," Woolly said. "Like the greed and cruelty of Henry VIII who destroyed the Abbey and killed an innocent ole man just to line his own pockets."

"That was, um, you know, a long time ago, Woolly."

"And now – although they ain't never gonner admit it – it's become the secret symbol of Wilde-Hunt...who want to take the money out of this town and into their own pockets and turn Glasto into just another boring place full of boring chain stores and burger joints. And that'd suit the mayor just fine, miserable ole git, he is. But you can take it from me that, no matter what it looks like, there's a deep, dark evil at the heart of—"

"Well, thank you, Woolly." Kirsty whisked the mike away. "Let's have a final word from Roger Cromwell."

"*Who...*" Woolly followed the mike like a kid after a lollipop. "Who – you ask the smarmy beggar about this! – reckons he's likely descended from *Thomas* Cromwell, hisself – that's the feller organized the destruction of Glasto Abbey for Henry VIII. You ask him about that, girl!"

But the mike was in front of Roger Cromwell now, and he just smiled at Woolly the way people smiled at some toddler who'd got soot all over his face through looking up the chimney for Santa Claus.

"Well, you've heard what we're up against, Kirsty," Roger

Cromwell said. "Sadly, some people in this town have very little grasp on reality, and I'm afraid—"

"And *I'm* afraid that's *all we've got time for*," Kirsty said. "Gary – back to you in the studio."

Kirsty rolled her eyes and blew out her lips in relief as she handed the mike to the guy in the headphones.

"Just get me out of here, Dylan," she muttered, "before I say goodbye to my sanity."

Marco saw Roger Cromwell smiling the smile of a winner, as the radio people packed up their gear. Griff Daniel, the mayor, had turned his back on Woolly and was patting Roger Cromwell on the back. And Jasper and his mates were grinning maliciously at Woolly, who was looking totally, *totally* hacked-off.

But even Woolly didn't look as sick and desperate as the girl who'd just come running into the car park.

Smoke

She was just staring at Marco like she was trying to remember who he was. She looked so completely out of it, he wondered if she could even remember who *she* was.

"Marco?" he said helpfully. "The Cosmic Carrot?"

"I've got to get out of here," Rosa said. Her eyes started flicking all over the place, like somebody was after her and they could be coming from any direction – jumping over the carpark wall, abseiling down the church tower.

Over her shoulder, however, all Marco could see were Woolly and Eleri and Orf in a dejected huddle.

"Is it the monk again?" he said. "The candle? *What?*"

"I don't know what to do." Rosa was shaking her head. "I tried to tell people, but they didn't..."

"About the monk?"

Ever since Woolly had told him about the evil monk who'd betrayed the abbot and been given what would become the Dark Chalice, Marco had been half wondering if this was Rosa's monk...the monk in the wall. Scary. *Very* scary.

"About *Teddy*," she said. "It's horrible. It was the most horrible thing I've ever seen. His eyes were glowing, only it wasn't his eyes, it was—"

"Who?"

"Teddy! In the crystals shop. Who showed me how to make the pentagram? Only, Dad got it out of me who it was, and he said he was...he said Teddy was, like, this evil pagan or something. And he was going to...he was going to talk to him. And now he's *dead.*"

"Your dad?"

"Teddy! He's *dead*! I started trying to tell people, but what if my *dad...*"

"Huh?" Marco spotted Jasper and his mates edging over, and he grabbed Rosa's arm and pulled her behind the radio van. "Let's talk about this somewhere else."

"Where?"

"Just go."

They ran across the car park to the main entrance and out into a side street and then back into the centre of town. The shops were opening now, and there were quite a lot of people about – shoppers, tourists, pilgrims, policemen...

"That's her!" someone shouted. "That's the girl who found him. I'm pretty sure that's her, constable."

"Run!" Rosa hissed. "This way."

And she dragged him across the road, just as a bus was coming. A car's brakes screeched, the driver leaning out of his side window, roaring, "You stupid little—"

"Someone stop that girl before she—!" Marco heard behind them, and the rest of it was mangled by the traffic, and now they were across the road and into this kind of alley with a sign over it that said, THE GLASTONBURY EXPERIENCE.

Marco had a good idea, by now, what kind of experience this was going to be. Sure enough, there were shops either side, with the usual coloured candles and goblets and fortune telling cards, and he came face to face with a big green statue of some kind of goddess who looked a bit like Eleri except for the bird poo on her head, and from the street behind them, he heard a loud male voice demanding, "Where's my daughter? Has anyone seen my daughter?"

"It's *him*!" Rosa gasped.

"Your dad?"

"He mustn't find me!"

They ran down to the bottom of the alley, and there was just a shop there and a wall.

"It's a dead end," Marco said. "We're stuffed."

He looked back over his shoulder, heard heavy footsteps converging on the alley. On their left was a white wall with a sign warning of an INITIATED TEACHER OF TIBETAN MANTRA. And a black door that was ajar. Rosa dragged Marco through it, and they crouched down behind the wall, panting.

"Okay, what's happened?" he whispered when he got his breath back. "What's *really* happened?"

"I told you, he's dead. I think..." He saw her eyes go blurred. "I think my dad did it."

"What?"

"Who else could it have been? My dad killed him. *My dad killed Teddy!*"

"That's crazy!"

"It so is *not!*" Rosa faced him, crouching with her feet apart and her hands clawed, moving them up and down in anguish. "You don't *know* him. He gets so completely uptight all the time these days. He probably went to talk to him and he...lost it."

They heard stomping footsteps, then the powerful, hard voice said, "Have you seen a young girl – long, dark hair, red sweatshirt with sequins on the front?"

"Not recently, mate," someone said.

"*No,*" Rosa breathed. "*Please...* If he finds me, he'll have me taken away by social workers."

"Let's try up those steps," the voice said.

They heard clumping up wooden steps and a door opening and then the big voice boomed out like it was on some kind of public address system.

"ROSA! IF YOU'RE IN THERE, COME OUT NOW!"

Once a cop, now a preacher; it figured. Marco peered around the wall, and a man who was standing next to the goddess statue turned round and just...saw him.

Oh no.

Marco froze.

Woolly and Eleri walked all round the car park in different directions and then met up by the back entrance of The George and Pilgrims.

Woolly clasped both hands to his head. "Why's he keep *doin'* this? As if I ain't got enough to worry about."

"I warned you," Eleri said. "He's too young to be involved in all this. You should have sent him home."

"Well, I didn't. I don't reject your advice without due thought, Eleri, but that boy, he's one of us. He's a natural Avalonian. Holy Joseph, he was here a minute ago! He was standing right there!"

Woolly held out his dowser's hands. He could feel a real heavy vibe in the town this morning, and an instability in the air, like it was shivering. And there were police everywhere. Woolly didn't like this one bit.

"There's some'ing goin' on here, Eleri. Some'ing's happened – all this fuzz on the streets. What *they* doin'? What's happening?"

"Have you tried the pendulum? To find the boy?"

"It doesn't work as well with a moving target," Woolly said bitterly. "Time you picks up his vibe, he's gone off somewhere else. The only people you can really count on finding by dowsin' is..." He broke off, stared at Eleri. "What's wrong?"

Her face had gone still and expressionless and terribly pale. She was standing there between the wall of The Pilgrims and a parked people carrier, and her little thin body was swaying slowly from side to side. When he tried to look into her eyes, he saw they'd rolled up, leaving just the whites. It was like she'd had an epileptic fit, but he knew it wasn't that.

He knew because he'd seen her like this before, twice.

And neither time had it boded good. Oh hell.

Woolly kept quiet and watched, real apprehensive. Watched her swaying in a space of her own, her hands twitching every now and then. He could hear raised voices from High Street, a police-car warbler, and he knew Eleri would not be hearing any of it.

And then, suddenly, her eyes were back, emerald-hard and emerald-bright.

Her voice came out on a long breath, like the wind through a tunnel.

"Smoke."

"What?"

"Go home, Woolly."

"Now?"

"Go home *at once.*"

"Has he...has *he* gone home? Do you get a feeling Marco's at home?"

"Smoke," Eleri said. "I can see your cottage. And I can see it through the smoke."

* * *

The guy was wearing an orange jacket and a hat with fake jewels all round it. He looked hard at Marco, and then he put his finger to his lips.

Marco didn't move.

Moving like a cat, the guy went across the Glastonbury Experience arcade to where a flight of wooden stairs led up to a balcony with what looked like more shops up there. He looked up, looked back at Marco and beckoned.

"Go for it, man. The big beardy bozo's out of sight."

"Huh?"

"*Go!*"

Marco grinned in relief. *Cool.* And he signalled to Rosa, and they ran, crouching, round the wall and back up the alley to High Street. Behind them, up on the balcony, Marco heard Rosa's dad still telling his daughter to come out *now* because he needed to talk to her.

But it wasn't safe outside, either. Across the main road, a small group of people was gathered in front of The George and Pilgrims, and Rosa went rigid.

"It's my mum. We can't go that way."

She started moving up the street in a jerky kind of way, staying close to the shops with her back to the road.

Problem *now* was that, further up, the whole of the pavement and part of the road was sealed off by tape, and a tent-thing had been rigged up outside a shop. Three uniformed policemen were directing people around it, and Marco watched a man in a white plastic suit come out to a dark blue van, and he went truly cold inside, and he thought, *oh my God, it's true.*

He stared at Rosa. She'd not been kidding. She was not deluded.

Then someone grabbed his arm; it was Rosa, pulling him into a doorway.

And she had a key in her hand that she fitted into the door.

"At least they won't look for us here," Rosa said. But she didn't sound happy, as the door swung open and she pushed Marco into a dim, musty hallway, his trainers sliding on lino.

He turned around as she pushed the door to behind them. "Where are we?"

"This – God forbid – is where I live." Rosa leaned back against the door. "I never thought I'd be glad to get back here."

Marco looked around. It certainly was gloomy. Not much light. He saw a flight of stairs with a threadbare carpet and a naked bulb, with flies on it, hanging from a flex. He didn't, on the whole, think he'd like to live here, either.

Between the front door and the stairs, there was another door in a small, shadowy alcove.

"Is that it? The shop?"

Rosa wouldn't look at it. There was silence in the hallway except for the slow buzzing of bluebottles.

Marco said, "This guy, this Teddy...did he tell you about the shop?" He pointed at the shadow-hung doorway. "I mean, this shop. Did he tell you what it used to be?"

Rosa blinked.

"Maybe he didn't want to scare you," Marco said. "But Woolly – my granddad – he told me what the shop...what it used to sell."

Rosa stood there looking down at the floor.

"So what *did* it used to be?"

Marco walked across to the door and peered through the glass. All you could see was greyness and cobwebs. He tried the handle.

The handle turned.

Marco leaned on the door, and it just swung open. Not even a creak.

"Wooooh!"

"Shut it!" Rosa hissed. "Shut it, and come away, for God's sake!"

"You said it was open that night, and then, when your dad tried it, it was locked."

"It was!"

"Well now it's open," Marco said. "And as I've never been inside a satanic supplies shop before..."

And without thinking too much about the implications, he entered The Emporium of the Night.

Phobia

Woolly smelled it before he saw anything.

He'd run all the way, in a panic – out of the town centre and up Chilkwell Street and into Well House Lane, uphill all the way, the Tor looming up on his right, its tower like a stiff finger, warning.

And then into the track to the cottage – and Woolly was knackered by now. His legs felt like jelly and his heart was throbbing, and he was about to drop into the grass at the side of the track when he smelled it.

It was a thin, sharp smell that did something to your throat that set you off coughing, and you couldn't stop.

Woolly *did* drop down to the grass, then, coughing his guts up, his eyes watering.

And then he saw the smoke. *Smoke!* Just as Eleri, the seer, had seen.

It was coming from the cottage.

No!

Feeling sick to his gut, he started crawling towards it, until he managed to pick himself up. Desperate to get there and yet dreading what he was going to see.

"I'm not coming in," Rosa said. "Do you understand me? Are you hearing this? I am *so* not coming in."

"It's just a room," Marco said. "It's almost empty."

Or, at least, *he* couldn't see anything, except for a counter with the shadow of an old-fashioned till on it. It was the sort of till that you saw in old movies, that when it opened went *ting* in a friendly kind of way.

Except in here, it was somehow threatening. In here, everything was totally silent; you couldn't even hear the traffic outside. It was like all the sound was blocked, or your ears were blocked, with wax or something.

Marco didn't like this feeling. But that was stupid. His ears weren't blocked, it was purely psychological, all down to *Impressionable Kid Syndrome*. Josh had a word for when you thought you were ill but it was actually all in your mind – psycho-something. (All these words were psycho-something, and they all meant the same thing: you were kidding yourself.)

But there was nothing here. It was...

"It is *not* empty," Rosa said categorically, like she'd plucked his thoughts out of the musty air.

"What do you mean?"

"I don't know. It just came at me. Like the first time, the other night, it was a bad smell, and this time it... I don't know. Just come out of there, okay? Are you listening to me? This is not a joke, Marco. I'm telling you. *Come out!*"

"Just give me a minute." Marco moved towards the only crack of light he could see, at the bottom of the big window. "Let's get the blind up."

"No!"

"But we can't see anything."

"Then just be glad you can't and get the hell out," Rosa said.

"Do you want to know the truth about this place, or not?"

"Are you going to come out?"

"No, I want to sort this out. *You* want to sort this out, don't you? You don't want to keep having nightmares and stuff?"

There was a silence. It was a thick kind of silence. Marco shook his head to try and clear his ears.

"All right," Rosa said, resigned. "I'll go upstairs and get a torch."

He heard her walking away, leaving him alone in the waxy quiet. Standing next to the window, he couldn't even see the door where she'd been. He moved across slowly to where he thought it was and – *smack* – went up hard against a solid wall.

It hurt. His nose felt bent, and *that* wasn't psycho...

...somatic.

Psychosomatic, that was Josh's word for when you weren't really ill, just imagining it.

But it didn't apply here. This was genuine pain, and the door...

The door had gone. Oh God. Oh no. The wax had congealed all around him, and *he was sealed up*!

Marco totally panicked, completely lost it. He'd always known he suffered from claustrophobia – which masses of people had, so it wasn't a real syndrome or anything, and you could avoid it by staying out of closed-in places. But this was an almost empty room. It was just that the atmosphere in here had a way of closing itself in, making you feel all tight and...

Terrified – and with *no reason* to be, he kept telling himself that, over and over again – he began to slide along the wall, frantically feeling all around him with his cold-sweaty hands. One ran through something that was sticky and bitty, and he realized it must be a bunch of cobwebs full of dead flies, mummified flies, and...

...yuk... He tightened his fist and heard all the dead flies cracking and crunching between his fingers and, cringing inside, he tried to scrape it off on the wall and...

...there was *no* wall. He staggered into space.

He'd found the doorway.

He sank to his knees in massive relief.

This was ridiculous. He'd never been so totally spooked in his life. His whole nervous system had short-circuited.

He gulped in a long, hard breath...and sucked in – *Oh God!* – another cobweb.

It was all over his lips. *Gross.*

He sat there in the dust, retching and spitting and shaking his head and wiping his mouth with the hand that wasn't inside a sticky glove of dead flies and knowing that something had *definitely* changed. Something had hardened up. Something had become real. This was a serious situation, there was no getting round that, and it was time to do some serious thinking.

He stood up, in the near-dark, staying close to the doorway.

Rosa had been right. The shop wasn't empty. There was something here that seemed to have learned about him very quickly. Learned about his weaknesses – like claustrophobia, the fear of being closed in – a fear that occurred so rarely he didn't even think of it as a fear.

But the shop knew about it. It had started coming on as soon as he'd gone in, but it was only when he was on his own that it had really struck.

He kept putting out a hand to make sure the door was still open.

When Rosa came back with one of those miniature Maglite torches, he could have hugged her.

"You, um...you might be, um, slightly right about this shop," he said.

"What happened?"

She stood in the doorway shining the little torch around the room. All it found was the empty counter with the obsolete cash register on it. No splashes of blood on the grey-plastered walls. No pictures of snarling gods with goat horns.

"There's nothing here," Marco said. "And yet..."

"There is," Rosa said. "You just can't see it."

"Can *you* see it?"

"I don't know. Sometimes I think I can see something out of the corner of my eye, and then I turn away and try and see it again...and again..."

"Four times?"

"Yeah," Rosa said miserably. "You were right about that. I have to do things four times, or...something bad will happen."

"How long have you been like this?"

"I don't know." Rosa let the torch dangle, the beam pointing at the wooden floor. "I don't know when I *wasn't* like that. And I know it's dead stupid, and I know I shouldn't give in to it, but it's not easy...it's like half your mind's always thinking about it. Well not actually *thinking*...if you *think* about it you *know* it's stupid."

"Like half your mind's operating on the level where it's watching out for everything you do and reminding you you've got to do it four times?"

"What?"

"It's what Josh would say. Josh would say something in your mind's become kind of self-programmed, like a computer, to react in a certain way. It's like you've got a virus in your hard disk. Of course, Josh isn't *always* right..."

"It doesn't happen all the time," Rosa said. "Sometimes I can go hours and I don't have to do it. But it's always there, at the back of everything. Sometimes I can really try hard and actually stop it for a while. But it always comes back."

"Some part of your mind doesn't want to get rid of it," Marco said.

"Why, though?"

"There's got to be a reason. But when you think of how much of your life you're actually wasting doing things four times. Like, if you *stopped* doing that, your life would be four times longer, wouldn't it? Or at least you'd be able to pack four times as much stuff into it."

"I never thought about it like that. That's...scary."

"You still think *this* place is scary?"

"Yeah," Rosa said. "I do."

"Me too," Marco admitted, pacing around. He stumbled. He'd trodden on something that rolled under his trainer and then spurted away. "Can I borrow the torch a minute?"

She handed it to him, still not coming into the shop, and he shone it along the dusty floorboards that had footmarks on them. Surely *he* couldn't have made all those footmarks.

He squatted down and found something, picked it up and—

"Oh!"

Dropped it.

"*Marco?*"

"It was like...disgusting. Like a hard turd, or something."

He shone the torch on it. Okay, it did look superficially like a turd, in that it was short and tubular and there was a bit of something coming out of one end, but...

He picked it up properly this time.

"Rosa..."

"What?"

"It's a black candle." He lifted it into the torch beam. "It's like hard wax, but a bit, you know, grungy. It's got knobbly bits in it. And it – you were right – it smells nasty. Like cold chip fat or something."

"Tallow," Rosa said.

"Huh?"

"It's the animal fat they used to make cheap candles out of in the Middle Ages. So, it was a real candle. I saw a real candle."

"Looks like it. But like...who lit it?"

"Suppose..." Rosa choked back the rest.

"Huh?" Marco was back down on his knees. He'd spotted something else. He put the candle down and shone the torch on a crack in the floorboard.

"Suppose it was my dad?" Rosa said desperately. "*He* lit the candle?"

"You're saying your dad's a satanist?"

"No. I mean, I don't know. I don't know *what* I mean! I don't—"

"That's weird," Marco said.

"It's sick!"

"No, I mean *this* is weird. There's a metal handle in the boards. It's like...I think it's a hatch...a trapdoor."

"Leave it alone. Come out."

Marco grasped the handle and pulled.

"What are you doing? Leave it—"

Marco sprang back as the trapdoor just shot straight up, *bang,* like it was oiled.

"No!" Rosa said shakily. "This is bad."

Marco shone the torch into the hole where the hatch had been.

"Steps. It's a cellar."

"Don't even *think* about going down," Rosa said. "Do you understand?"

The steps were stone. Marco shone the torch to the bottom. He saw cracked stone flags. That was all.

"There's nothing scary about a cellar. Most buildings this old have them, don't they? If I just—"

"I'm warning you—"

"Look," Marco said. "I don't want to go down, okay? I don't like this place any more than you do."

"Good."

"But we have to."

"No, we do not. We *so* do not have to go down there."

"All right, I'll go."

"*No.*"

Marco looked up and she was standing next to him.

"We'll both go," she said.

"But we're only going down once," Marco said. "Four times is out."

"You always have to push it, don't you? Just get this over. And careful you don't drop the torch."

Marco swung his legs into the hole.

"How many steps are there?" Rosa asked.

"Not many." He started to go down. "Ten?"

"Be careful. If you break something—"

"*Eeergh!*"

"What are you...?"

Marco had dropped the torch. He started to try and pull himself out, but he couldn't move.

"Something..." He tried to just say it but it came out as a scream. "Something's got my legs!"

Honour of the Woolastons

Woolly stood with his sleeve over his mouth and nose, and his eyes full of tears, only some of which were caused by the smoke.

Helplessly furious, he crunched over the greasy, grey wreckage.

But the fury couldn't soak up the pain, and he could feel his heart sinking inside him, until it was like a brick at the bottom of an old leather bag.

"Don't," Nancy said. "Come away. It might still be hot underneath."

"Ar," Woolly said. "Hot as hell." He tightened his fists.

"They ain't gonner get away with this, Nance. *By God,* they ain't..."

"I'm sorry, Woolly." Nancy burst into tears again, her pinky-yellow hair spraying all over the place. "I called the fire brigade, look, soon as I realized what was happening. Only I didn't realize soon enough. When I first seen the orange light, I thought it was the sun coming up, and I turned over in bed and I could hear Merlin bawlin' away, but he's always... *Oh, 'tis all my fault!"*

"Course it ain't your fault. You could've been roasted in your bed. It ain't nobody's fault...'cept the beggar who done it. And when I finds *him —* "

"Don't you even *think* about going after them! *We* can't take the likes of them on, can we?"

"Who says we can't?"

"Woolly, there's just the two of us, and we ain't got much money, and – look at us. And this is only the start. 'Twill be the house next...if we don't give them what they wants."

The wooden shed had gone completely and, behind it, a side wall of the stable didn't look too...stable. Nancy stepped over some charred beams the firemen had pulled out and dumped in a heap on the edge of the orchard.

"Fire brigade said it must've been the oil lamp as tipped over. They said 'tisn't sensible to use an oil lamp in a stable with straw."

"Oh ar?" Woolly came out of the charred timbers. "And what did folks use 'fore there was electric, then? *Oil lamp, my arse!* That lamp was well out when we left. If it *was* caused by the lamp, then somebody else lit it and pushed it over. Somebody as saw me and the boy leave. Somebody waiting in the woods."

"But you can't prove it, though, can you?"

Woolly closed his eyes. "No," he said quietly. "Don't suppose I can."

Dangling from his fingers was the only pendulum he'd been able to find in the ruins of his workshop. The others must be buried under the grey sludge, the ones that hadn't melted away. His collection of pendulums, his pride and joy...all destroyed. It had been a deliberate, calculated attack on the very heart of his world.

An attack on everything he was.

When he held up the pendulum – a nice bit of quartz, all blackened now – the chain snapped and the pendulum fell into the mess, and he couldn't bear to pick it up. He thought of the latest anonymous letter:

Sell the house or you won't have nothing left to sell.
You been warned.

Looking around the fields, he saw how isolated they were up here – not another house in sight – and he felt weary and defeated and wondered if he'd ever have the heart to dowse again. And whether the stand he was making was even worth it.

"What if we're wrong?" Nancy said. "What if Avalon World's a real good thing and we're just holding up progress, 'cause we're mad and the whole town knows it?"

"We ain't mad, girl," Woolly said and, as if to reassure him that he was all there, Merlin came up behind and prodded him with his hairy nose and his rubbery lips.

Woolly hugged the donkey's heavy great head and thanked God and the Goddess and all the mystic forces of Glasto that it had been a warm night in summer and Merlin had been out browsing the orchard and well away from his stable when the angry flamoo had shot through the shed roof. He was safe...this time.

"I remember waking up once and hearing him hee-hawing," Nancy said. "He must've seen somebody. But he often makes his noise around dawn, look, so I never thought."

"Thank God he kept away from them."

"Woolly, who were they? Who *exac'ly* did this? Was it Cromwell hisself?"

"Nah, wouldn't dirty his hands. He'd get somebody else. Maybe kids. At least Marco—" Woolly looked around, in a sudden panic. "Hang on...he did come back, didn't he?"

"Marco? He was with you!"

"Well, he *was*, but things got difficult in town, look. Crowds of people, and the local radio was there and then..."

"You lost Marco?" Fear boiled up in Nancy's eyes. "You went and lost him *again*?"

"Well, he was there one minute and then he'd gone. I looked everywhere, and then I figured he must've come back hisself, like he did last night. And I had to go on the radio, Nance, and then there was a bit of a row and..." Woolly brushed the grey ash from his hands. "'Tis a real bad scene. The whole Glasto vibe's been pushed off the frequency. I better go back and try and find him."

"We ain't fit to be grandparents," Nancy said and mopped her eyes with her sleeve. The sick silence was broken by the sound of a car engine out on the lane. Woolly looked back at the end wall of the stable, still smoking under the tight, sandy sky. And he wondered again if it wasn't *him* that was off the frequency, with his talk of vibes and stuff. A daft old hippy with no place in the modern world. And then he thought of the threatening letter.

Be sensible, Woolaston.

That did it. *No* chance. He shoved his hands deep down inside the hip pockets of his purple flared jeans. Nobody in this world was ever gonner accuse Woolly Woolaston of being sensible. Being sensible wasn't a family trait. They could get stuffed.

"Sir Galahad," he said, thoughtfully. "Didn't he go in search of the Holy Grail?"

"Woolly, that's a *legend.*" Nancy looked up as the car entered their track. "Besides, Sir Galahad was young and tall and good lookin' and knew how to handle hisself in a fight. And in *spite* of all that—"

"Honour of the Woolastons, that's what this is about," Woolly said.

"In spite of all that, he never made it, Sir Galahad. He died, didn't he? He never got the Grail, he just died. Oh dear, who's this?"

The car door slammed and someone strode through the orchard.

"Honour of the Woolastons is on the line," Woolly said. "And the Woolastons don't back down."

He pulled himself up to his full five feet four and sucked in his belly. If this was that bloody Cromwell...

But it wasn't. Holy Joseph, it was *Angus.*

Marco's dad.

And Marco was missing.

"Oh hell," Woolly said.

Enjoy the Rats

Marco lay on the stone flags at the bottom of the steps. From up in the shop, he could hear Rosa screaming, but he couldn't help.

He was on his back, and his head was up against what felt like some kind of underground barred window. He could hear water seeping on the other side of the bars. And he couldn't get up.

This was because Jasper Coombes's friend, the solid, red-haired kid with the relief-map face, was sitting on his legs.

Panic throbbed in his chest like a fist punching him. Being in a dark and hostile place was bad enough, but in a dark place where you *couldn't move...*

Two other boys stood in the shadows – and down here it was all shadows – shining big, rubber-covered flashlights. Neither of them had said anything. Maybe it was hard to talk through the SAS-style balaclavas they had over their faces.

"Why aren't *you* wearing a balaclava?" Marco said to the red-haired kid. "Is it because your face is already out of a nightmare?"

By way of a reply, the red-haired kid lifted his bum off Marco's legs and then came down on them again, like a jackhammer. This was agonizing, and the message was clear: down here, a smart mouth could easily get your legs snapped.

"Shane doesn't understand clever remarks," one of the balaclava boys said. "He's got learning difficulties."

"Which doesn't mean he's mentally handicapped," the other one said. "He just has a problem with learning. Basically, he doesn't agree with it."

Marco said nothing. His own slight problem was that making smart remarks was the only way he knew of not becoming really, really scared. What had happened had been fast and violent, and it still made no sense. Jasper Coombes and his mates had obviously followed him and Rosa, maybe all the way from The George and Pilgrims car park. But how had they got under the shop...and so quickly?

Whatever, after they'd hauled Marco down by the legs, they'd shoved him around in the darkness and then they'd forced him to lie down, with the red-haired kid sitting on his legs. And then Jasper Coombes, who hadn't been wearing a balaclava either, had gone up the stairs, to what used to be The Emporium of the Night.

From where Rosa's screams had become muffled, now, as if Jasper had slapped a hand over her mouth. Then Marco heard him go, "You bit me, you little cow! You *bit* me!"

And now Rosa came stumbling down the stone steps, like she'd been pushed hard, and Jasper was shouting down through the hole, "Watch her, okay? I'm gonna seal this off."

The balaclava boys were already moving in on Rosa, and she was like, "Don't touch me, you scumbags!"

"Then siddown and keep your mouth shut."

One of them pointed to the corner nearest Marco. Breathing hard, Rosa came and sat with her back against the stone walls and her arms around her knees. Marco couldn't see her face, but he knew she'd be wearing this cold, stubborn expression, which was what she seemed to resort to instead of smart remarks.

"Sorry, Rosa," he said.

"Shut it, hippy-trash," a balaclava said. "We won't tell you again."

Above them, the hatch slammed down and shuddered. Marco winced. Then there was a heavy, crunching, scraping noise from up there.

"What's he doing?" He was trying not to sound nervous in front of Rosa; it wasn't easy.

"He's moving the old counter over the hatch," a balaclava said. "So you can't get back that way."

"So like...where are we?"

The pressure eased on Marco's legs, and he knew what was coming, tried to roll out of the way, yelled out, "No! All right, I'll— *Errrrgh!*"

The red-haired kid had come down on his legs again, like a sack of coal. You could tell he really liked doing this.

Marco lay there, moaning, Rosa going, "Leave him *alone!*"

"Why should we?" One of the balaclava brothers put his torch under his chin. "We don't like him. He comes from a bad family."

He shone the white beam up at his grin, which you could see through a circular hole cut in the balaclava. It made this horror-film effect with stark light and shadows.

What it said was that these were the kind of guys that...well, that there wasn't anything they wouldn't do to you if they got the chance. Marco had met their kind at school, and they were always losers.

Always losers, right?

It was as well to keep reminding himself of that because, in the semi-darkness, with the weight on his legs, Marco felt his claustrophobia setting in big time. His breath was coming in short spurts.

The thing was...being scared of kids your own age, or a bit older, or even a bit younger...that was nothing to be ashamed of. It was strange the way most adults seemed to think that little children couldn't be completely, totally, psychotically evil. Adults could be really stupid sometimes. Given the chance, kids were always going to say they just didn't know any better, or they came from a bad home, or they'd been abused. Being a kid was a licence to just keep on...and on.

A new light had appeared, way back in the blackness.

"Cool."

Jasper's voice. He was swinging his flashlight from side to side.

This didn't make any sense. How had *Jasper* got down here, if he'd just blocked the hatch from above? Marco started to ask and then bit off the question, thinking of his bruised legs, but then Rosa asked it for him.

"How did you get down here?"

"Shop next door." Jasper strolled into the torchlight. "Friend of my old man owns it. All these shops have cellars and some of them join up. I just came down different steps."

"Ah, so that's how you—" Marco shut up as he felt the red-haired kid shift on top of him.

"Nah, let him talk, Shane," Jasper said. "Let's find out what he knows."

"That's how you got in to light the black candle the other night, right?" Marco said. "You came down from this other shop and you went up the hatch into the black magic shop. I don't see the point of that, lighting stinky candles in an empty shop."

"It's about messing with people's minds," Jasper said. "Rosa's dad's this big, stupid priest, and he's already unbalanced, the way he goes around ranting at everybody. And he hates your weird little granddad and *his* mates. So if he thinks his own daughter's turning into one of *them*, he's going to freak big time, isn't he?"

"You *total—*" Rosa said.

"No, hey, we really *like* your dad, Rosa. He's part of the plan to clean up this town. My dad got him the job."

"That's so not true!"

Jasper smiled. "The last curate at St John's, right, he had a ponytail and he was always cosying up to the hippies, so Griff Daniel, the mayor, and my dad complained to the bishop about him, and the bishop fixed it so they hired someone who thought the same as Griff about hippies. *That's* how your old man got the job."

"That's a lie!"

"It's how things work, Rosa."

"I still can't figure why you hate them so much," Marco said.

"You talking to me, hippy-spawn?"

"The pilgrims – Woolly and Eleri and Orf. Like why do you hate them? It's not like they do anybody any harm, is it?"

"*Everybody* hates them, you London moron! When you're born in a place where people who are supposed to be grown up are always blabbering on about leaving their bodies and what they did in their past lives...after a bit, it gets right up your nose and you just want to wipe them off the face of the earth."

"They're not doing *you* any harm..."

"They're fooling themselves and they've turned this town into a joke. Watch my lips, friend – *nobody's* had a past life and you *can't* leave your body. *Nobody* has secret powers."

"You mean like dowsing? Woolly's known all over town as a top dowser. He finds things for people."

Jasper grinned. "Not any more he won't."

"What? What have you—?" Marco struggled to get up, but the red-haired kid put a hand over his face and pushed him flat on his back, so his head connected with the iron bars behind him with a dull clang. Which hurt. A lot. And he was really worried now. He'd been thinking about what had happened to this poor guy Teddy, the crystals man. And now—

Woolly. What had they done to Woolly?

Marco couldn't hide it any more. He'd started to pant. The thing about evil kids was that they never, ever, knew when to stop.

Rosa was hugging her knees. "How long are you going to keep us down here?"

"I'm sorry?" Jasper laughed. "How *long*?" He turned to one of the balaclavas. "She says how long are we going to keep her down here?"

The balaclavas and the red-haired kid all laughed. Marco noticed it had gone darker. There were only two torches left on and one was pointed at Rosa and the other was in his own eyes, blinding. He shut them, but that was worse. The guys were all around him and he couldn't move.

"Rosa," Jasper said, "you made a very big mistake. You formed the wrong kind of friendship. Wise people stay clear of the Woolastons. They're traitors. I told you that, but you didn't listen."

"I don't know anything about the Woolastons," Rosa said.

"You've got in with the wrong people, not just the Woolastons, that crazy guy in the crystals shop too. You've become one of *them*, and that means you may never see daylight again."

"Don't be...stupid," Rosa said, and Marco just hoped he was the only one who heard the tremor under her voice.

"Hey..." Jasper tossed his torch from one hand to another. "She thinks we're kidding. Rosa, sweatheart...listen... You're not at school now. This is not a game. The teachers won't come to rescue you. Nobody will."

"This is down to that Roger Cromwell, isn't it?" Marco said.

"See?" Jasper stopped smiling. "You *do* know too much to be out on the streets."

"It was just a guess," Marco said lamely.

"Well, guess what's going to happen now," Jasper said. "All right, I'll tell you. We're leaving you down here with the rats for a while."

"I can't see any rats."

"Well, you won't while *we're* here. But when you're alone, with no lights..."

Jasper made creeping movements with his fingers.

"You would not *dare*," Rosa said.

"Don't worry, if you get thirsty, you can always lick the damp off the walls. Or there's an underground stream just the other side of that metal grille. But you won't want to go that way...that goes into the labyrinth."

Marco instinctively turned his head as far as he could. He made out a gap between the bars and the stone flags.

"It starts as a kind of drain," Jasper explained. "You squeeze through, and you're in a tunnel. I used to do it a lot. Part of it collapsed centuries ago, so only kids can get through these days."

Marco remembered Woolly talking on the Tor, just seconds before Roger Cromwell had appeared.

Course there's some as says the dark rituals never stopped – that they was carried on for centuries in an underground maze – a secret labyrinth under the town.

"There's a network of narrow tunnels," Jasper said. "The one people talk about is from The George and Pilgrims to the Abbey – they found a bit of it when they were digging up the road to lay water pipes or something. But that's just part of it. The labyrinth goes on for ever – under the Abbey to the Tor. It's a way out of here, but most kids are scared. After all, some of them didn't come out."

Jasper waited for this to take effect.

"That's just made up to scare us," Rosa said.

"Never scared me," Jasper said. "I love caves and stuff. I'm in this potholing club up at Cheddar – totally cool. I used to spend hours down here, working out which passage goes where. It's really interesting, if you don't mind a bit of wriggling and squeezing. In fact, now I think about it, that might be your only means of escape. We'll leave you your little torch. If you stay here, you can always use it to fight off the rats."

Marco began to sweat. He'd once seen something on TV about potholing – these guys with lamps on their helmets, deep underground, struggling through these tight little passages, where you had to suck in your stomach just so you wouldn't get wedged. And sometimes you did get wedged. And sometimes you were trapped for hours and whole days.

Or for ever. Just the thought of potholing made Marco shrivel up inside. Too right he was going to stay here with the rats.

"These kids that were lost in the labyrinth?" Jasper said. "It was me found some of the bones, actually. They must have been years and years old. The underground stream you can hear...the water had washed them clean. There were ribs and a femur – that's a big leg bone to you, Shane. Human. No skull, unfortunately, but Roger gave me fifty quid for what I brought up."

"Roger?" Rosa said.

"A friend of mine. Roger knew people who'd pay for human bones."

"You're making this up."

"I expect there's some still down there. You'll see them if you decide to go in."

"We're *not* going in," Rosa said.

"Up to you, girlie. You can just stay here. We might come back for you tomorrow."

"Why are you *doing* this?"

"Or we might not. You came down here on your own, after all. Nothing to do with us."

"What do you want?" Marco said unsteadily.

"Sorry, hippy-trash?"

"What do you want? What are you trying to make us do for you rather than, like...go into the drain?"

"Nothing," Jasper said. "What could *you* possibly do for *us*?" He tossed his torch to his other hand. "Okay, we've wasted enough of the afternoon on these losers. Time to go, guys."

The red-haired kid must've got up from Marco's legs, but they felt so numb now he hadn't noticed.

Jasper made this coy little goodbye motion with his hand.

"Nighty-night," he said.

There was the sound of a hatch being pulled open.

And then the torches went out one by one.

"Enjoy the rats," Jasper said. "There's supposed to be really big ones down here. It's all that human flesh they've eaten over the years."

Practical Parenting

"**I** communicated with him on the phone last night, and did not like what I heard," Angus said. "I'd asked him to e-mail me, and he made some excuse about his laptop not working. I didn't like the way he sounded."

"Oh ar?" Woolly said. "What way would that be, exac'ly?"

They were still standing on the edge of the orchard, where Woolly was stalling for time, in the hope that Marco would come back. The kid's dad just showing up like this...this was a heavy scene. It had thrown him.

"Sounded to me as if he'd been exposed to some of the local lunacy," Angus said. "I rather thought he'd be too intelligent for all that rubbish, but I suppose we do tend to expect rather too much of our children."

"And what's that supposed to mean?"

"He's a very impressionable lad, I tend to forget that. Anyway, I was so worried about him I thought I'd better get up early and drive over."

"That was a bit drastic, Angus."

"Simply a question of caring, practical parenting," Angus said.

The thing was, he didn't look, to Woolly, like a man who'd driven all the way from London. He looked fresh and...what was the word that meant kind of smooth and slick?

Suave.

Woolly had never trusted suave. Never trusted lawyers, either, come to that.

"So," Angus said. "Where is he? Where is my son?"

Woolly looked around, but all he saw was Nancy...and Merlin watching them from under an apple tree, chewing slowly and nodding his head, like he was interested to see how Woolly was going to get out of this one.

"Ah...well..." Woolly took a long breath. "He ain't exac'ly here just now. Not *exac'ly*."

He could see Nancy wringing her hands, and Angus saw it, too.

"What do you mean, he *isn't here*?"

"He's, er... He's explorin', kind o' thing," Woolly said. "Glasto bein' a place where you comes to...poke around... discover things...find out things about yourself. 'Tis quite amazing what that boy's discovered 'bout hisself in the past couple o' days, look."

"Which is precisely what worries me." Angus's lips twisted in a contemptuous kind of way.

Problem with Angus, he was a city-type through and through, and he didn't see what folks like Woolly and Marco saw or feel what they felt. He looked into the magnificence of the sunrise, calculated how much time he'd have to get to the office before the traffic built up, and never heard the birds sing. His suit was sharp, his tie was straight and his eyes were blank.

And there was something else that bothered Woolly... something that Angus *hadn't* said. The air was still full of the acrid smell of fire, and there were bits of burned-out shed all over the place, and Angus hadn't even mentioned it. Which, even allowing for him being a lawyer, was a bit odd.

"All right, where is he?" Angus said icily.

"Ar." Woolly coughed. "Well, he come down to town with me, look, and then he, er...he kind of wandered off..."

"He *wandered off*?"

"He'll be *back*. Course he will. He always comes back."

Angus lurched forward like he wanted to grab Woolly by the throat, but he was a lawyer. Lawyers didn't do hands-on.

"You mean he's done this before? You let him wander off... *on his own*...in a town full of complete lunatics?"

"You're sayin' we ain't fit to be grandparents?" Nancy said.

"I'm glad you realize that," Angus said. "It's quite clear you're becoming...shall we say *forgetful*?"

"What you on about now?"

"You've forgotten where you left your grandson and..." Angus smiled coldly. "...and you also seem to have forgotten you left something burning in your own workshop, with the result that it caught fire, with potentially disastrous consequences."

"You *what*?"

Woolly was so choked up he couldn't get the words out. Typical lawyer: Angus had seen the remains of the fire all right, and he'd been saving it up as evidence that Woolly and Nance were...

....losing their marbles!

Woolly looked into the metallic eyes of his son-in-law – his *son-in-law*, how did *that* ever happen? – and felt a slow shiver rippling through him.

"You were lucky you didn't burn the whole house down," Angus said. "If you ask me, not only are you unfit to look after a child, you really aren't fit to be up here on your own any more. Do you get any help? Social services? Meals on wheels?"

"You cheeky beggar!" Woolly gave in, at last, to outrage. "How old you think we *are*?"

"Possibly old before your time," Angus said smoothly. "Drugs do that, you know. They rot your brain."

"We don't *do* drugs, you—"

Angus smiled. "That's not what everyone will think when the police raid your house."

"What?"

"They might not find anything, but...no smoke without fire."

"Why would the cops raid us?"

"Oh...they might have received an anonymous tip-off."

"What are you trying to *do* to me?" Woolly howled.

"I'm trying to help you, Woolly. When one hasn't seen someone for years one tends to forget how time can take its toll. It's quite clear to me that you're living very much in the past, with your 1960s clothing and your old LP records and your unfortunate delusions. I accept I made a terrible mistake. I entrusted to you my..." Angus's voice quivered. "...my only child."

"He ain't a child!"

"No? What do *you* think he is? An *elf*? A *goblin*? As I recall, Nancy used to paint charming pictures of elves skipping down from the Tor. Didn't you give us one as a wedding present?"

"Well, we hadn't got much money in them days, look. Now, I don't know what your game is, boy, but I gotter tell you—"

"And *I've* got to tell *you*," Angus said, "that if my son isn't here in five minutes, I'm very much afraid I'm going to have to call the social services. I'm sorry, Woolly – you don't know how much it hurts me to do this to my own father-in-law, but it's for your own good and...and the safety of my only son. You've become a danger to yourself, I'm afraid, Woolly. Action needs to be taken to help you move to a... a place of safety."

Woolly's head was reeling and Nancy had gone pale and Merlin's jaws opened and you could see his tongue retracting as he made this *erp, erp, erp* noise before letting out his breath in one long, terrible, mournful...

haaaaaaaaaaaaaaaaaaaaaaaaaw!

"Don't worry," Angus said. "I'm sure the authorities will be able to find somewhere for your animal."

Better Dead

T here was darkness and there was *darkness.*

In normal darkness, after a few minutes, your eyes would start to adjust and you'd begin to make out the shapes of things. But this was total, absolute, one hundred per cent complete darkness. You started stretching your eyes open until they hurt, in the hope of something becoming visible, but it was like you'd gone blind and that was very scary. That was like the ultimate claustrophobic situation – *you were trapped inside yourself.*

Also, this darkness...it was full of movement.

Scratching and scampering.

"The rats," Marco said. "I don't want to worry you, but I think the rats have come out."

The scratching stopped. He heard a sigh.

"That's me, you cretin," Rosa said. "I'm looking for the torch."

"Oh. Right."

"And that's totally sexist."

"Huh?"

"To think that girls are automatically frightened to death of rats."

"You're not?"

"We used to have one at school, a rat. His name was Fluffy. He was dead cuddly."

"But that would have been a white rat," Marco said. "These are—"

"So you're racist as well as sexist? They're *all the same*."

"Mmmm, well..."

"Found it!"

The little Maglite came on, with its slim, piercing beam, and the first thing he saw was Rosa smiling, and her face was glowing with sweat. And he thought she looked really nice, but that was probably the relief.

"Let there be light," Rosa said.

"Er...right."

"It's the first thing God said when he was creating the world. And he was right, wasn't he? In the list of priorities, light's the big one."

"It's not a big priority for blind people," Marco said.

"So that actually makes you a *sightist*."

"Yeah, yeah, *touché.*" Rosa switched off the torch.

"What are you doing?"

"There's only a couple of little thin batteries in here. We don't want to waste them."

"No. That's true." Marco stood up...very carefully in case Shane had broken any bones.

His legs held him up, anyway. It was a start.

"However..." Rosa switched on the torch and stood up and moved over to the corner of the cellar, where the bars were blocking off the low tunnel. "Jasper was right. We could get under there."

"No. No, we probably couldn't," Marco said, nervous.

"Of course we could. And if it's a way out...I mean, every tunnel has to lead somewhere, doesn't it?"

"*No!*"

"Of course it does!"

"I mean...no, we shouldn't go there."

"Why?"

"Just...*no*. Okay?"

"There no such thing as *just no*. There's *no, because...*"

"Okay." Marco thought fast. "No, because that's what he wants us to do."

"Jasper?"

"Jasper is an evil person. I've met his type before. He's a bully and a megalomaniac."

"What?"

"Someone who's like drunk with power, you know? What

327

he wants...he wants us to go down there, and then we...
we drown or something. Or we get lost in the labyrinth and
nobody finds us until we're white bones washed clean by
the water."

"Or we find a way out."

"No...listen. There is no way out. He wants us to think
there might be, so we'll give it a try. Why do you think he left
the torch? They want us to die. They know that if we get out
of here we're not going to keep quiet. I mean, we're not going
to keep it a big secret who trapped us down here, are we?"

"They'd just say we were making it up."

"But better all round if they didn't have to," Marco said.
"Better if we were dead."

"That's not going to happen. I don't really know what this
is about, but they're not going to win." Rosa shone the torch
between the bars. "Look, you can't really tell where it goes
from here...there's a bend, and the water's obviously round
there. It'll be an underground stream. And streams...well, they
always come out somewhere, don't they? Usually."

"It could be deep. And when the torch battery gives out,
we won't know where we are. And that's how it happens.
How you drown."

"Well, I'll just go in on my own and have a bit of a look
around." Rosa kneeled down. "It's a bit low, but we could get
through dead easy on our hands and knees."

The thought of being down there in some narrow little
passage with walls pressing in on him made Marco clench up
inside, and he turned away and ran up the stone steps – the

second lot of stone steps at the far end – until he came to the wooden hatch.

Which he pushed and pushed at.

Pointless. It was totally solid. It was either locked or there was something heavy on top.

"I won't be a minute," Rosa said from below.

He could see the torch beam swaying as she lowered herself to the ground, to slide under the bars.

"No!" He stumbled down the steps. "You can't!"

She stood up. "Why not?"

"Because it's what they want. They want us to die in terror."

"You don't know that. Look, I'll be back in one minute."

"And because..." Inspiration came. "...because you're only doing it because, if you don't, you think something horrible's going to happen."

"Oh," Rosa said, getting up. "Is that a fact?"

"It's an OCD thing, right?"

Rosa sighed. "You cretin."

"We'll think of something else, okay? There must be some way we can smash through one of the hatches or—"

"You *total cretin!*"

"There must be another way out."

"Marco," Rosa said, obviously struggling to keep her voice firm, "it is so *not an OCD thing*, okay?"

"Then what is it?"

"What it is...it's because..." Rosa shone the torch at him and screamed out, "It's because I want to go to the toilet!"

She was ages.

And he was thinking, *What if she's fallen into the stream and her foot's trapped or something?*

What if I have to go in and rescue her?

This was a terrible situation. This was a situation where having a smart mouth counted for less than nothing. Not that there was anything smart to say about suffocating in an enclosed space in the dark.

And then she was back.

"Better?" Marco said.

"Shut up." She shone the torch at him. "Right. Do you want to get out of here or not?"

"I *have* to get out, don't I? I think they've done something to Woolly. When Jasper said something like his dowsing days were over? You heard him?"

"What's that about?"

"Dowsing? It's where you find things that are missing, or underground water or something, and get answers to questions by tapping into the, like, inner knowledge you didn't know you'd got. Something like that. Your dad wouldn't like it."

"I didn't like what they said about Mr. Coombes and those people getting my dad the job. Is that…I mean, is that possible?"

"They were probably lying, but there *is* something going on. There's obviously a bunch of people in the town – like the mayor – who'll do anything to get rid of the pilgrims. But it goes deeper than that. I think it goes back to when Henry VIII and his heavies had the abbot topped on the Tor."

"How?"

"I don't know. I just think it *does.* Everything in this town goes back to ancient times, doesn't it? Like, Woolly said about this guy Cromwell having the same name as the guy who was in charge of getting rid of the Abbey and the monks. And he hates them because they got his shop shut down. And then there's..."

He was going to talk about the Dark Chalice, which seemed to have become like a secret emblem for Cromwell and his mates and maybe for Jasper's gang, too. It had seemed just a little bit crazy before, but down here in the damp and the dimness...

"We have to follow the stream," Rosa said. "You know that, don't you?"

"No. Look—"

"You suffer from claustrophobia," Rosa said, not looking at him. "That's what it is, isn't it?"

"Well, I—"

"I don't know many of these phobias and mental conditions and things, but even I know about that one. You're terrified of being trapped in a tight space, right?"

Marco sighed deeply. "Yeah."

"It's nothing to be ashamed of. Lots of people have it. Like, um, Obsessive Compulsive Disorder?"

He'd been waiting for that. "Look, I wasn't like...making a joke out of it or anything."

"Yes, you were."

"Well, okay, maybe a bit."

"You try to make a joke out of everything. It's how you cope with stuff, isn't it?"

"Well...yeah. And it usually works."

"Couldn't your mate do anything about it? The claustrophobia?"

"Josh?"

"Yeah, the psychiatrist."

"Ah, well, I made a big mistake there," Marco confessed. "I once admitted to him that I suffered from claustrophobia and he said he'd be delighted to help, and he suggested I should get into this cupboard in his bedroom. Like, it was just about big enough to get into if you lay on your side and kind of hunched up. But when he closed the door there wasn't even room to move your arms. And then..."

"He locked you in, right?"

"He said I had to face up to it and..." Marco shuddered at the memory. "I couldn't move in there. I couldn't breathe. I thought was going to black out. All I could move was my head, so like I started beating it against the inside of the door."

"What a jerk," Rosa said. "And you as well, for falling for it. You forgot that he wasn't a psychiatrist at all, he was just a kid, and he couldn't resist scaring the crap out of you."

"Er...right," Marco said, just the memory of it making him feel limp and faint. "That was about it, really." He felt ashamed.

"It might be a *bit* easier," Rosa said, "if we were both kind of...in the cupboard."

"You mean...under the bars. In the labyrinth."

Marco felt his right hand start to shake. Rosa put one of her hands over it. Her hand was surprisingly warm.

He felt even more ashamed at finding this comforting. Like, what a wimp!

"So, er, what was it like?" he said. "In there."

"Narrow," Rosa said. "I'm not going to lie about this, okay? I'm not going to make it sound better than it is. I'm not going to do a Josh on you."

Marco shut his eyes.

"So...there are parts where you probably have to wade through the stream," Rosa said.

Marco started on a deep breath. Getting his feet wet was hardly a major drawback.

"And you can't stand upright," Rosa said. "That's the worst thing."

The deep breath congealed in Marco's throat.

"I can't...I don't think I can handle that," he said.

Rosa said nothing, but she didn't take her hand away.

Spy

For the first time, Woolly felt in real danger.

Glastonbury had always seemed like the one place you could be yourself, do your own thing...not be under any pressure to conform and get yourself a Renault Clio and a satellite dish.

Glasto was the place where you could live quietly and, just as quietly, make contact with *bigger things*...mysterious, other-wordly things that most folks didn't like to think about. Things that blokes like Angus would never understand...and so would always try to pooh-pooh.

But there was something here that didn't make sense at all:

Angus had known exactly what kind of lifestyle Woolly had – a lifestyle that had driven Alison away to the big city. And yet Angus had still gone out of his way to bring Marco here.

"I'm not gettin' this, Angus," Woolly said. "When you brung the boy the other night, you seen that nothin' 'bout us had changed, but you still left him, didn't you? And now you're back, with all your threats. Who's got at you? Who's been bendin' your ear?"

"I'm not going any further into this now," Angus said. "I've told you what I want, and that's it, as far as I'm concerned."

"And I've told you he ain't here. I can't just produce him if he ain't here, can I?"

"Then you can expect a visit from the police within the hour. *And* the social services. Good morning."

Angus turned his back on Woolly and started to walk back towards his car, his head held high – until he brushed against one of the apple trees, and a small green apple fell off at his feet.

Angus looked down and kicked the apple savagely away.

Nancy had thrown up her arms in anguish. "I don't understand. Why's he tryin' to get us in trouble? I don't understand what he's sayin'! What's he sayin', Woolly? What's he *sayin'*?"

"*I'll* tell you what he's saying," said another voice.

Angus spun round, as Eleri Cadwallader glided like a sunbeam out of the orchard.

In her long cloak and her Egyptian serpent headband, she looked at her most majestic and stern-faced, a real faerie queen with the apple tree branches bowed around her, all laden with green fruit. She slid past Angus and didn't even look at him.

"I warned you," she said to Woolly. "I warned you about letting the boy stay here. I had an instinct."

Woolly blinked. "I'm not getting this."

"What do you know of this man?" Eleri demanded.

"He's Marco's dad."

"Well, yes, I guessed that. But what *else* do you know of him?"

Angus had stopped, brushing apple leaves from his suit. "If you're trying to convince me you're a reformed character, Woolly," he said, "listening to this ridiculous woman is hardly going to help."

"It's certainly not going to help our friend here," Eleri said. "Ask him who he was with last night."

"In London?"

"He told you he was in London?"

"He said he drove over this morning."

"That's what he told you, is it?" Eleri said. "Well, *that's* interesting. Especially as I saw him here yesterday evening, getting into a car with Mr. Coombes, the estate agent...and Mr. Roger Cromwell."

Woolly whipped back, like the Glastonbury Thorn in a gale.

He saw Angus's eyes slide from side to side.

"So what *do* you know of him?" Eleri said.

"He...he's a lawyer." Woolly looked at Angus, with his neat hair and his gunmetal eyes. "A business lawyer."

"Aha," Eleri said. "In which case, I wonder if we can put a name to one of his clients?"

"You mean to say—"

"*Wilde-Hunt*, for instance!"

Nancy gasped.

Angus didn't look at any of them, just gazed past the cottage towards the Tor, which he probably didn't even notice.

"Perfectly respectable company," he said mildly. "My firm's been representing them for some time."

"You mean, you... *My God!*" The shock went through Woolly like he was dowsing for water and had just stepped over an underground reservoir. "You're actually Wilde-Hunt's lawyer?"

"In which case, it is entirely obvious why he brought the boy to stay with you, isn't it?" Eleri said. "You were the last person holding out against Wilde-Hunt's development plan. He wanted to find out all about you and your personal situation. To find out in which areas you were vulnerable and how you might best be persuaded. And so the boy – I'm afraid my instincts were correct – the boy was nothing more than *a spy*."

Woolly felt his knees beginning to give way.

"That's why you wanted Marco to e-mail you every night? You wanted to find out about us...from the inside?"

He felt cold. It couldn't be true. Not Marco – a natural-born dowser. An Avalonian.

Or so he'd thought.

Angus's eyes flickered, and a small sneer twisted its way into one side of his mouth.

"You didn't think he was actually *interested* in all your nonsense, did you, Woolly?" Angus said.

Woolly couldn't speak. The anonymous letters, the burning of his workshop...all this was nothing compared with the thought that Marco – *a natural-born dowser* – might have betrayed him.

"You shouldn't be surprised," Angus said. "He's a perfectly normal modern boy – a city boy. His best friend is the son of a notable psychiatrist, with absolutely no time for cranks."

"It's not true—"

"Don't delude yourself, matey," Angus said. "Just because your sad little life is built on foolish, primitive superstition, you can't expect a healthy, modern boy—"

"Shut up!" Woolly yelled. "Get out! Get off my land, you slippery...lawyer."

Angus smiled sadly and spread his hands.

"As for me – I was simply worried about you, Woolly. You *are* my father-in-law, after all. As soon as I discovered that you were standing in the way of this major development, I...well, I didn't like to think of you being...hurt. And with Alison out of the country—"

"You—"

"...I felt responsible for you. You and Nancy. All alone, with most of the town against you. All alone, in such a...*lonely* place."

"Get out!" Woolly roared.

"I can still help you, you know. I can even get you a better price for this hovel."

"This is my home!"

"Face it, Woolly, you're getting old. And I gather you said some entirely irrational things on the radio this morning. A lot of people were quite worried about your sanity. In fact, there seems to be general agreement that you should be living in the shelter of the community."

"You—"

"And that was before anyone knew that you'd burned down your own shed and mislaid your grandson..."

Woolly rushed at Angus, with his fists flailing. Angus smiled and dodged easily, and Woolly ended up punching one of the apple trees instead.

Which hurt like hell.

A dense, brownish cloud dropped over the sun and the air cooled.

Woolly stood rubbing his knuckles and watching through bitter tears as the husband of his only daughter strolled casually back to his car.

Sick Person

It was when the stream disappeared that Marco knew that, for him, the big adventure was over.

And up to then he'd been doing so well.

The stream was actually kind of comforting. It was something alive – running water glittering in the torchlight. This was probably a dowser thing, Marco had thought, trying to build himself up a bit, give himself the courage to go through with this. Dowsers had a natural affinity with water. Even claustrophobic dowsers, who were trying not to think of the tons and tons of earth and rock that were just over their heads, tons and tons of solid matter, held up by nothing in particular, that might crack and come crushing down on them at any moment.

"Oh," Rosa said.

They'd been going for maybe about fifty metres, edging along the side of the stream, which had been happily following this nice little channel in the ground no more than about ankle-deep.

But now the stream had vanished into a round hole that looked like it could even be a drainpipe.

Which obviously meant that they couldn't follow it any more.

But the torch beam, as directed by Rosa, showed that their passageway continued in another direction, up to the left.

Only it was lower. A lot lower.

In fact it was more like a rabbit hole than a tunnel.

"Oh well," Marco said, giving up with a shrug. "Worth a try."

"Oh, right." Rosa sounded surprised. "I'm glad you think so."

And she immediately got down on her hands and knees and crawled...

"Noooo!" Marco howled.

...*into the tunnel.*

"Sorry." Rosa's voice came back muffled. "What did you say?"

"I said...I was *going* to say that that was not what I meant!"

So far, he'd managed to stay on his feet, even though his neck was severely bent. As long as he was on his feet he could just about handle this situation. But hands and knees...like no way. Utterly, definitely, completely, no freaking *way*!

"...and at least it's dry," Rosa said, her voice already going dusty and distant.

"Look, just come back!"

"Sorry, can't hear you." Her voice totally falling away now.

He knew what was happening: she was getting her own back for when he'd gone down the steps into the cellar, despite her screaming at him not to do it.

Girls never forgot.

And she had the torch.

She had their only torch.

Marco was alone in the clammy total darkness. He stiffened in panic and his head crunched into the ceiling of hard-packed earth and rocks, bringing down a shower of dry dirt that got into his mouth, and he was spraying it out as he tried to shout, "Rosa!"

She didn't reply. She couldn't hear him. All he could see was a yellowy glow way, way ahead in the big rabbit hole. He started to pant.

He wouldn't find it easy getting back to the cellar in the dark, that was for sure, and he definitely, definitely, *definitely* wasn't going...down *there*. He couldn't. He even made a small attempt to get down on his hands and knees, but his knees wouldn't bend and his hands wouldn't *un*bend out of tense fists.

So he just stood there with his eyes closed and his fists clenched tight by his sides, his nails gouging into his palms, thinking, *There's no end to this.*

Or, yeah, maybe this *was* an end. *The* end. He was destined to die down here, and nobody would know. There'd be a police search, of course, but it would be just lines of cops trampling down grass for a few hours and finding nothing. And Jasper and his mates would say nothing to anybody and just carry on growing up in a town from which all the pilgrims had been driven away...while, down here, Marco and Rosa's flesh disintegrated, like on *CSI,* only slower, and their white bones would be washed downstream making little rattling noises in the dark.

"*Rosa!!!!!!!!*"

His voice rang out like a cracked alarm bell, and then there was just this terrifyingly hollow silence.

"What?" Rosa said.

"Oh God!"

The torch came on, and...there she was. She'd crawled back out of the hole and was sitting there hugging her knees as the breath exploded out of Marco.

"Never...*never* do that again!"

Rosa batted her hands together to get the dirt off. "You *have* got it bad, haven't you?"

"I'm a sick person," Marco said. "And I can't do anything about it, okay?"

He realized now that *she* was the strong one. He was sad and weak, just like Josh had always implied, and now she'd seen this dismal side of him, and if they ever got out of here he'd be ashamed to face her again. He'd be straight up to Castle Cary and on the London train, with a blanket over his head like those guys you saw on the TV news, going out of court and into a prison van for some disgusting crime.

"I just wanted to see if it led anywhere you might be able to go without panicking, that's all," Rosa said.

"Just *never* do that again, all right?"

"Anyway, it did."

"No it didn't. You're just saying that." He sat down and rubbed his head where it had banged into the ceiling.

"No, honestly, it only goes on for like, about ten seconds' crawling, and then you're in this—"

"I don't want to know! I just want to go back, okay? I'm a sad, miserable coward and you need to forget you ever knew me."

"It's just your weak point," Rosa said. "Everybody's got one, and being underground—"

"You don't have to keep reminding me! I know. There are like two hundred tons of earth and rock and stuff between us and daylight. I *know*."

"Anyway, I came out in this place where you can easily stand upright," Rosa said. "Better than here. Much better. In *that* way. It's just that..." Her voice tailed off.

"What?"

"It's just that, when you see it," Rosa said, "you might wish you were still crawling around in the dark."

Alive and Waiting

Woolly sat down at the kitchen table, and put down the white envelope he'd brought from the ruins of the shed.

In one hip pocket he found his regular pendulum, the crystal on the blue twine. In the other was his specialist *sampler* pendulum for in-depth investigations.

Woolly looked at it miserably. To think it had come to this.

The specialist pendulum was made of brass and hung on a chain; it looked like a builder's plumb line or maybe a big bullet. The top of the pendulum unscrewed and Woolly unscrewed it now, revealing the little hollow chamber inside.

He turned it upside down and shook it out: empty. Okay.

He shook it again to get rid of any dust, because all dust was the dust of *something* and carried its vibrations, no matter how weak.

It was no good, he was just putting this off. Woolly sighed and emptied out the contents of the white envelope: flecks of black and grey wood-ash from the floor of the shed. He got out his penknife and picked up some of the fragments on the tip of the blade, and then tipped them into the chamber and screwed it together again.

He'd planned to show the sampler pendulum to Marco tonight. *Like attracts like, dude*, he'd have said. *If you're looking for something, you put a sample of it inside the pendulum before you starts asking questions. Like, say you're looking for a missing cat, you'd pick one of his hairs off a cushion and put that in the pendulum, then you'd say, Is he in the garden? Is he in the house? Is he in the wood? Or maybe hold the pendulum over a large-scale map of the area and see which area it responds to strongest.*

Most times it worked. Not always, but it wasn't an exact science. You were consulting your subconscious, and maybe the subconscious was consulting your higher consciousness, and your higher consciousness was consulting...whatever was *up there.* And sometimes, of course, the message got interfered with by your emotions.

Woolly was feeling real emotional right now, after the bad scene with Angus, so he had to blank all that out. Because he knew he'd never had a more important challenge for the sampler pendulum than this.

He held it up on its chain, resting his elbow on the table. Being left-handed, he held it in his left hand.

"This fire, look," he said. "I wanner know who started it. That's what we're gonner find out, all right?"

The pendulum didn't move. Well, it was hardly going to start naming names.

But the pendulum *could* talk, and to get it talking you had to make like a detective interrogating a suspect. You had to ask the right questions in a very precise way so that there were only two possible answers: yes and no.

Woolly steadied his breathing and sat real quiet for a minute or two.

"So...this fire," he said eventually. "Was it caused deliberate?"

The pendulum didn't hesitate. It started to swing backwards and forwards.

Meaning, *Yes.* Whenever you got a new pendulum you always asked it to tell you its signal for yes – might be a circular motion, clockwise or widdershins – but this was the usual one, for Woolly – backwards and forwards.

"Was it caused by someone from the town?"

Yes. No hesitation.

"Was it personal?

Yes.

"Was it done as a warning? To scare us?"

Yes.

Woolly sat back and closed his eyes for a moment and emptied his mind and his heart of all emotion. Cancelled out all the excitement and delight of discovering, over the past two days, that there was someone who might carry on a great family tradition.

"Was it Marco?" he said. "That is, did Marco have anything – anything at all – to do with this fire?"

The pendulum didn't move.

Woolly kept his body real still and closed his mind to everything. He was dimly aware of Nancy coming into the kitchen but he didn't turn round. She must have seen what he was doing, because she kept quiet.

And then...

...very slowly, as if it had been thinking about it, contemplating all the possibilities, the pendulum began to sway from side to side.

This meant *no*.

Woolly lowered his head into his hands and realized, when it all came out in a huge whoosh, that he'd been holding his breath for well over half a minute.

"Woolly?" Nancy said.

He looked up through his hands, the brass pendulum still dangling by his wrists.

"Woolly," Nancy said. "There's a feller outside demandin' to see you. Big bloke with a beard. In a dog collar."

"What?"

"And he's terrible angry," Nancy said.

* * *

Marco wasn't aware of anything wrong at first. It was just a square room which you...wow, you could actually stand up in.

Which felt *sooo* good, particularly after half a minute (that had felt like six hours) of blanking off your mind to control your terror and taking big breaths as you crawled blindly through something like a dirty drainpipe. After that, the relief was amazing. You never realized how awesome it was just being able to stand with your back straight and have some actual space between your head and a ceiling.

Quite a lot of actual space, in fact. In the torchlight, he could see joists in the ceiling, and they were well above his head. Was this another cellar? Had they come up in another cellar.. or even under the road?

Maybe there were lorries and buses grinding along directly over his head.

Don't think about that.

Whatever, this was no ordinary cellar. In the torch beam, he saw ornate shapes like church windows carved into the stone walls, but there was no glass, only deeper, shadowy stone. Then he saw a niche with a kind of statue in it that had become worn with age. It had wings and claws, all fused together as if they'd melted, and something like a human head which was just a blob now, but it...

Well, he didn't like it.

"This is some kind of...underground chapel? Like, could we be under the church or something? Is it a...what do you call a church cellar?"

"Crypt," Rosa said. "But it's not like any crypt I've ever been in."

There was a doorway at the other end leading into blackness. There were stone flags on the floor, and some of them had markings on them. In the middle of the room was a raised section, with a flat stone on it.

And the smell in here was musty and greasy. But not *nice* greasy, like a chip shop, this was...

...*uh oh*...

This was black-candle greasy.

"Can you feel it?" Rosa said.

"Feel?"

"Something's here, with us."

There was something different about her voice. It was worried, but it was firmer. It had this *certainty* about it, and what she said made Marco whirl round, as if a cold hand had touched his shoulder.

There was nothing behind him but the drainpipe passage he'd crawled through, but he was getting a prickling, now, on the top of his head.

"I don't know what you mean," he said.

"I'm not sure I do either. But I know it's waiting for something."

"*What* is?"

"This place. This...temple. It's...like it's alive and it's waiting."

"What for?"

"It's holding its hands out. Can't you see the hands?"

"No..."

"They're smoky and they're, like, cupped and...waiting."

Marco took a step back. That scary certainty in her voice again. Something about her had definitely changed and he couldn't put his finger on it. Down here she'd become a different person.

"It thought we were bringing something," she said.

Marco had no idea what she was on about, but this was not good. No way was this good.

He directed the torch beam at the raised slab in the centre of the room. There were dark marks on it. He went closer and saw some greasy black blobs that looked like wax from a candle. He saw that shapes had been roughly drawn on the slab, smudgy, like with the tip of a finger. One shape was like a crude eye in a triangle.

This was also not good. He reached out to see if he could rub it out.

"Don't touch it!" Rosa hissed. "It might've been done in blood."

Marco backed off. "You *trying* to scare yourself or what?"

"We *need* to be scared. It thought we were bringing something, and we didn't, and so it...it has no more use for us. It hates us now. Can't you feel the hate? It's like— We've got to get out of here!"

Marco shone the torch so that Rosa showed up on the edge of the beam, and he was seriously shocked to see that she was vibrating like a wire, like she'd gone *twangggg*. But her big eyes were quite still, and she never blinked even when he turned the torch full on her.

"Rosa, are you like...have you gone psychic, or something?"

"*No!*" She turned on him, furious. "That's evil. That's disgusting."

"Huh?"

"Psychic is *totally evil!*"

"Who says?"

Now she did blink, and then she looked confused and helpless again.

"My dad." All the certainty had gone out of her voice. "My dad says it's wrong. Unholy. *Disgusting.* Can we get out of here?"

"I'm not going back into that pipe!"

"We'll go the other way, then."

She turned to the black doorway at the end of the stone room. Took a couple of steps towards it and then turned back and approached it again, and then turned back again, and...

Oh God, she was going to do it four times. The old mental Rosa was back.

Marco grabbed her hand and rushed her through the doorway.

"*Where is my daughter?*"

The invader slammed both hands flat on the table and shoved his black-bearded face to within about a centimetre of Woolly's. It was like staring into a giant Brillo pad with eyes.

Nancy hovered behind, fingering the handle of a frying pan

on the stove. Woolly knew that if this big cat went for him, Nancy was likely to clobber the beggar with the pan. It was a big, heavy pan that could hold a good half-dozen quarter-pound veggieburgers. Putting a man of the cloth in hospital was probably a fairly serious offence. And the last thing they wanted was the cops on the doorstep...

So Woolly decided not to say what he most wanted to say. "I don't *know* where your daughter is. Why would I?" He said, instead.

"Why? I'll tell you why. Because she's with *your irresponsible, maladjusted grandson.*"

"Marco?" Woolly was half out of his chair. "How d'you know that?"

"Because I saw them running away."

"*Where?*"

"In the town centre. And then they disappeared."

"Where to?"

"If I knew that I wouldn't be here talking to *you*! Now, where are they, before I—"

He looked as if he was about to heave the table over like, Woolly recalled, Jesus Christ had done in the temple at Jerusalem. Nancy had lifted the pan off the stove, and her eyes were burning. She looked like some deranged female warrior. Good thing Eleri had gone back to town, or this kitchen would be looking like the court of Boudicca, Queen of the Iceni, the day after another run-in with the Romans.

"Just...just sit down, man," Woolly said. "For your own good."

"I don't have *time* to sit down!" Blackbeard blasted. "The town's already in a state of shock over what happened to that shopkeeper. There are obviously violent individuals around, and if you think I've—"

"Shopkeeper?"

"Don't tell me *you* didn't know. You alternative types and your secret grapevine, you don't miss a thing."

"I been otherwise engaged," Woolly said, suddenly alarmed. "Who we talkin' about?"

"The heathen who runs that shop selling crystals. Don't tell me you don't know *him*. Found on the floor of his shop, with his crystals arranged over his face like the victim of some sacrificial ritual. Exactly the kind of crime likely to be committed by the pseudo-mystics who infest this town like a plague."

"Teddy?" Woolly felt the blood draining from his face. "They did this to Teddy, who wouldn't harm a fly? He's some kind of Buddhist! *Teddy?* You sure about this?"

"Of course I'm sure, I used to be a police officer."

"And he..." Woolly sank back in his chair. "He's dead?"

"No, he's not dead, as it happens. He's in hospital, unconscious, with severe head injuries. He probably *would* have been dead if my daughter hadn't found him. My daughter who, unknown to me, had formed a friendship with this man—"

"And she couldn't have a better friend than Teddy."

"He was teaching her filthy satanic symbols!"

"What *are* you on about?" Woolly stood up. "Nancy, put that flamin' pan down, you're makin' *me* nervous."

Nancy put down the pan but didn't move too far away from it. Woolly stared at the big minister.

"What satanic symbols?"

"He'd shown her how to draw a five-pointed star in the air. A pentagram."

"You mean as protection against the apparitions she'd been seeing in her bedroom? And the evil comin' from the old shop? That it?"

Blackbeard's eyes narrowed and set hard.

"Marco told me," Woolly said wearily. "And it seems to me you ain't got much of a future in the Church if you can't tell the difference between a satanic symbol and an age-old safeguard against psychic attack."

"It's evil! It's all evil! It's against God's law, and I will not tolerate a child of mine—"

"Aw, get real, man! You claims to believe in God and the devil, but you don't believe in nothin' in between. What kind of hypocrite are *you*? From what *I* can gather, that girl's been in a terrible state, scared to go to bed 'cause of what she might see. And no wonder – this town's brimful of weird stuff, always has been. And you're obviously no help at all."

"My daughter..." Blackbeard's mouth, what you could see of it, had set into a firm line. "....is psychologically disturbed. To encourage her little fantasies would be totally irresponsible. And if you think I'm going to be lectured to by a little—"

"*Right.*" Woolly stared the big bloke in the eye. "What's your name?"

"My name is David Wilcox. But if you think—"

"Cool it, Dave," Woolly said, "and you just might learn a few things."

"Like *what*?"

"Like that this town's in big trouble and these kids is in real danger. And you better decide which side you're on, man, 'fore it's too late for all of us."

Dissing God

Every so often, the underground system would divide into two, offering them different passages to choose from. This happened a couple of times and of course they had no idea which one to go for. Often the passages would just end in rock or something, and they'd have to go back and take the other one.

When they came to a junction of *three* passages, they picked the middle one and came up against a wall of earth. Then they went back and tried the one to the left, and it just got lower and lower, and Marco couldn't take it, and they had to back out.

Shining the torch into the third passage and realizing that

the beam was just not as strong as it had been, Marco knew they were in deep trouble.

He switched off the torch and sat down in the dirt.

"When I was a kid – like seven or eight – I was into Greek legends, okay? And there's one about this guy, Theseus, who has to go into this labyrinth to take out the Minotaur, which is this monster that's like a bloke with a bull's head." *Bit like your dad*, he thought.

"Is this relevant?" Rosa's voice had shrunk into something small and hopeless.

"Yeah. Because, dealing with the Minotaur is only half the problem for Theseus. He has to get out again, through this maze of underground passages in which, like, dozens of people had perished. The old white-bones-in-the-stream scenario?"

"I don't think I want to know any more," Rosa said.

"But Theseus is smart enough to have a ball of string or twine or something that he's tied to a rock at the entrance and been feeding out as he goes along. So he can follow it back when he and the Minotaur have, like, settled their differences."

"The point being that we didn't have any string," Rosa said.

"That's the point, yes."

"So we're stuffed."

"Um...yes. Probably."

"Thank you," Rosa said.

And Marco conceded that, while the story of Theseus was certainly relevant, it wasn't all that encouraging. On the other hand, it was better than throwing down the fading torch and screaming, *We're going to die!*

Which was – face it – a possibility.

They had nothing to eat down here, nothing to drink. They'd left the underground stream behind long ago. Even the possibility of finding their way back to the foul-smelling temple, where something was waiting, seemed remote.

Stuffed. Yes. *Oh God.*

"One of my granddads died," Rosa said suddenly. "He was ill for a long time, and I always thought, until then, that if you were ill you'd get better one day. But then they told me he'd died, and Dad said he'd gone to heaven. It was...very scary."

"Right," Marco said. He was thinking the story of Theseus had, on the whole, been more fun.

"My mum said I shouldn't be too upset," Rosa said, "because he was pretty old, and he'd had a good life. And so, for a long time, I thought it was only old people that died. And then a girl at school, who was like *one year older than me* didn't come back after the Christmas holidays, and—"

"Look," Marco said. "This isn't going to help. We both know that anybody can die at, like, any time, and that heaven... Well, I don't know. If the Holy Grail's a legend, then maybe heaven..."

"That's blasphemy," Rosa said.

"I'm sorry?"

"It is in our house, anyway. Blasphemy is like...dissing God."

Marco thought about this. "He's a bit of a hardliner, your dad, isn't he? You either agree with him totally, or you're the enemy."

"He can be nice sometimes."

"Yeah," Marco said, remembering Rosa's dad screaming *filthy scum* at Woolly. "Right."

"The torch battery's going, isn't it?" Rosa said. "When you last had it on it was dead weak."

"Um...yeah."

"We're going to die down here in the dark," Rosa said.

"Somebody might...come."

"You mean in about three years' time?"

At the centre of the silence that followed, he heard a thin spattering sound, like the start of a hailstorm. And it was cold. Up there, in the world, it would be a fine July evening. Down here, it was a winter's night. Permanent November. They would never again see the golden glow of Glastonbury. And, up there, Woolly was in trouble.

"I'd heard you Northerners were a bit pessimistic," Marco said after a while.

"Realistic," Rosa said. "That's the word."

They went quiet again. It was like neither of them wanted to risk the last of the battery on the third tunnel, which would probably lead to another junction of three – or maybe four – tunnels. Because this was a labyrinth, and you were not supposed to be able to find your way out. That was the whole point. In fact it was quite possible – Marco had been secretly dreading this for some time – that if they carried on they would, sooner or later, come across some bones – a skeleton grinning at them with bits of withered skin and flesh.

"I've always had feelings," Rosa said. "When I was little, I'd wake up in the middle of the night thinking there was someone with me in the bedroom. Once, I thought I saw someone standing by the wardrobe, watching me."

"Josh would say that's an only-child thing. You were lonely."

"Has it happened to you?"

"Well, er...no. I don't think so."

"There you go. Josh is stupid. Don't get me wrong, I mean, there was never anything quite as...you know...as the monk."

"You're saying you *are* psychic."

"I don't know. I never had anybody to ask."

"Because your dad always said it was wrong, even if you couldn't do anything about it?"

"In the end, I had to tell Mum," Rosa said. "It was the monk. He was just so...so strong. And, of course, she told Dad."

"Right." Marco stared into the darkness. The thin spattering sound was louder. "Still, look on the bright side," he said miserably. "At least, after we die down here, you'll be able to come back and haunt the hell out of him."

There was an almost-silence. He thought she was very quietly crying and wished, as usual, that he'd kept his smart mouth shut.

And this was when the spattering in the dark became a groaning, rumbling sound, and he grabbed the torch and switched it on just in time to see spider-cracks overhead as – *Oh God* – they widened and came apart and the ceiling came down in a choking, blinding, thundering explosion of dust and rocks.

* * *

"The *Dark Chalice*?" Dave Wilcox said. "What kind of drivel is this?"

Woolly sighed. This was taking even longer than he'd feared. It was clear this bloke was what was known as a fundamentalist Christian. He had a very narrow view of things, and if it wasn't in the Bible he didn't want to know about it.

"'Tis about greed," Woolly said. "Human greed. Let's go back to the beginning. What you got here is a holy place. The holiest place in these islands, some folks reckon. Anyway, 'twas a holy place long, long before the Christians got here. In fact, 'tis likely ole Joe 'Mathea only landed here on account of he realized Avalon was special already and a good place for his new Jesus religion to grow. Which is why he brought the boy Jesus to check it out."

"That's just a legend."

"Oh, you don't even believe *that*? A story that gives your own religion a real foothold – literally – in Britain, and you don't believe it 'cause it ain't in the Bible. Right? Well, whether the likes of you believes it or not, enough people thought Glasto was a special enough place to have the finest abbey in all Britain."

"I don't doubt *that*, obviously. However—"

"And then what happens? One king has the Abbey trashed, kills the abbot and takes all the riches for hisself. But that wasn't the end of it, look."

Woolly told him about the gold chalice. Then told him how

the gold chalice had, at some time, been replaced by something else – something more disgusting – to make it a more powerful magical tool.

"Some folks, 'tis said, kept back parts of the abbot's body, and they took the top of his head and turned it into a cup. And they took bones from his hands and made them into handles for it."

Dave Wilcox blinked. He clearly hadn't heard this bit before. Well, no big surprise there, not many people *had*. Most folks agreed that the Dark Chalice was something best not talked about, which was why Woolly hadn't even given Marco the details.

"And so they turned the abbot's head into a chalice," Woolly said. "Like the chalices you got for communion in church. The corruption of a good man's bones – a symbol of the triumph of human greed over spiritual love. And 'tis said this chalice was kept, for a long time, in its own chapel underground where 'twas used for services of dark communion – black masses, where animal and human blood was drunk instead of wine. Evil ceremonies dedicated to Satan, the Lord of This World, so he'd gratify the dark desires of them as looked after the chalice."

"What *utter* nonsense," Dave Wilcox said, making his beard jut out. But Woolly could see he was worried that there might be just a faint dusting of truth in it, somewhere.

"Wherever there's a shining light there's deep shadows," Woolly told him. "Evil do gather around the fringes of holy places, close as it can get. And soon the Dark Chalice became the black hole which sucked in the souls of all them as was hovering 'tween good and bad. I can give you names of folks in this town as went suddenly bad – sold out on their principles and made a lot o' money real fast. 'Twas always said, by them as knew, that they must've took communion from the anti-Grail. Drunk from the cup of evil."

"You can't possibly believe this." Dave Wilcox was trying to look pained, but Woolly could tell he was agitated, too.

"Yet there was periods of history," Woolly told him, "when good people – good Christians and good pagans..."

"There *are* no good pag—"

"...when they was able to contain the power of the Dark Chalice, even if they couldn't destroy something as existed in more than one world. But it would fall back into the wrong hands – maybe the hands of folk who at first didn't think it was all that evil. After all, Henry VIII *was* the king, and he *did* set up the Church of England...without which fellers like you, with a wife and kid, wouldn't be allowed to be a priest, would you?"

Dave Wilcox said nothing.

"The Dark Chalice represents the power of money over love," Woolly said. "And 'tis said anyone who has it will prosper. So, let's just say, for instance, that if a bunch of businessmen who wanted to build a big entertainment complex and put the little people out of business...if *they* had the chalice..."

"You mean Wilde-Hunt, I suppose."

"I never named no names."

"Absolute rubbish. Wilde-Hunt is a syndicate of legitimate businessmen who want to modernize this town and get rid of the web of superstition that's been holding it back for so long and all the stupid people who perpetuate it. People like *you.*"

Woolly shook his head sadly.

"And there is *no such thing as the Dark Chalice.*" The chair creaked as big Dave Wilcox stood up.

"That shop under your flat – you know what it was, don't you?" Woolly said.

"I'm not interested. All those shops are evil."

"Not this evil, even by your standards. Used to be a black magic shop. Sold satanic supplies."

Dave Wilcox went tense for a moment. It was clear he hadn't known *that.* But it didn't knock him back for long.

"Then it must be the will of God that the tenant now living over it is a priest," he said triumphantly. "And I don't see what any of this has to do with the whereabouts of my daughter."

"Nor me, yet," Woolly admitted. "But I thought if we worked together, we might—"

"Me? Work with the likes of you? Are you *mad*?"

And Woolly wondered if perhaps he *was* mad. Crazy ideas were coming at him from all angles now. For instance, if Teddy had shown this girl, Rosa, how to inscribe the pentagram, he must have realized she was in real danger from something putrid, probably coming out of the former Emporium of the Night. Something that was maybe affecting this feller Wilcox, too. Making him more angry, more wrong-headed.

And Teddy...what about Teddy? Maybe Teddy had started asking questions of his own about Roger Cromwell and his mates, and they'd decided he needed to be silenced. Leaving him for dead and making it look like a ritual killing so suspicion would fall on the pilgrims.

Oh, this went deep, all right, and it made a terrible kind of sense.

Problem was, nobody apart from people like Eleri and Orf would believe a word of it.

As for Dave Wilcox, he was already halfway out the door. He stopped and looked back contemptuously at Woolly.

"You're fooling yourself, Mr. Woolaston. You and that insane old woman in the cloak. You're caught up in a superstitious web of your own making and you've drawn in innocents like my daughter, and that...that is *despicable*."

When he'd gone, Nancy said, "Is he right? *Is* Marco with this girl?"

She'd pushed her hair back behind her ears, and her face was grey with strain.

Woolly got out his crystal pendulum.

"Is that all you can do?" Nancy wailed. "This is no time for mystical stuff. What about the police?"

"Dowsin' ain't mystical," Woolly growled. "It's a perfectly natural skill."

And he asked the pendulum if Marco was with this girl, Rosa, and the pendulum swung to and fro to say, yes, he was.

So were they somewhere in the town?

They were.

Woolly got out a street plan of Glasto and asked the pendulum to guide him to the spot where they might be found. He'd done this many times before and it had never failed. He'd once found a lost toddler this way – the kid had been accidentally shut into the garden behind the old tribunal building in High Street. He'd been recommended for a civic award for this, but Griff Daniel had told the council it would just bring bad publicity and make the police look stupid.

Right. Where are they?

The pendulum didn't move.

"What's that mean?" Nancy demanded.

Woolly gave the end of the twine a little shake – something he hadn't had to do in years – and the pendulum swung feebly a time or two.

And then went still.

"Woolly, *what's that mean?*"

"Prob'ly just means I'm a bit tired," Woolly said.

He'd gone cold inside. *Oh no, oh please...*

Nancy began to shake. "You're never too tired to get *something*. You're just not tellin' me what it means."

"Maybe I'm too emotionally involved with this, look," Woolly said.

"*What's it mean?*" Nancy shrilled, as a new shadow fell across the table.

Neither of them had heard the door open or seen who had walked in.

"If I remember the laws of dowsing," Roger Cromwell said, "it's an indication that there's no energy field around them any more. Or to put it another way…"

Nancy screamed.

"…they're both dead," Roger Cromwell said.

Family Heirloom

When Woolly had first known Roger Cromwell, he'd had no reason to think there was anything wrong with the feller. Cromwell had just looked like one of the pilgrims – long hair, bit of facial jewellery. He'd blended in easily, so nobody asked questions.

That was the problem with Glastonbury: nobody *ever* asked questions. If somebody showed up in town with an interest in magic and ancient mysteries, they were just accepted. This was a place where folks came to explore The Unknown, and if there were a few things unknown about *them*, well, that was fair enough.

And there was also, of course, this loose kind of attitude to religion in Glasto. It was, after all, a melting pot, where Christians and pagans could find a bit of common ground between the Abbey and the Tor. And that was good. They were all here and they all rubbed along: Christians, pagans, Hindus, Muslims, Greek Orthodox and...

...satanists? *Well why not?* some of the pilgrims had said, when they found out what Roger Cromwell was selling in his shop. Like, was it fair to condemn something just because it had been given a bad name over the years? It *might* have its *good side.* And who was to say what was good and what was evil? Okay, they burned black candles and drank a bit of blood...was there any *real* harm in that? Hell, no...in Glasto, anything goes.

It had worried Woolly, though, from the start. And when it came to his notice that some people who'd bought black candles and a portable altar from The Emporium of the Night had later sacrificed a cockerel near the Holy Thorn on Wearyall Hill, he'd called a special meeting at the Assembly Rooms. There'd been the usual four-hour debate, but Eleri came down on his side, and so did Orf (who, admittedly, would have agreed with Woolly if he'd suggested they should build a spaceship and launch it from the Tor) and so, in the end, did most of the others, including Sam Daniel, rebel son of Griff the mayor, Matt Banks the natural healer and Juanita the mystical bookseller.

It had been enough, anyway, to put some pressure on Coombes and the owner of the premises and get the lease cancelled and the shop closed down.

But Woolly would always remember Cromwell's final words, delivered at midnight, in a ringing cry from the Market Cross as thirteen black-clad bikers from Bristol had been riding thirteen times around the town.

You may close us down, but the night remains eternal!

And after that shop closed, nobody had been able to make a living there from that day – or night – to this.

Of course, when Roger Cromwell returned, as "spiritual adviser" to Wilde-Hunt, he looked a different man: long hair and facial ornaments all gone, nice expensive suit. A reformed character, and fellers like Griff Daniel were suddenly glad to know him. Funny how just wearing a suit and having your hair cut could make hypocrites like Griff and Coombes, the estate agent, into your best mates...especially if you were involved in a plan to clean up Glasto.

Cromwell was in his casuals: black shirt and leather trousers. The trousers alone set him apart – nobody at Woolly's end of town would wear a pair of pants made from the skin of previously living creatures.

But Woolly could almost smell the smoke on him. If he hadn't started that fire himself, he knew who had. And, worst of all, he most likely knew what had happened to Marco.

"What have you done with him?" Woolly said. "Don't mess me about, all right?"

"Me?" Cromwell's long, tanned face wore half a smile. "As I understand it, you're the one who mislaid the boy."

Oh, he was clever, this feller. Interesting, too, how his accent had got poshed-up in the time he'd been away.

"What's he saying?" Nancy clutched Woolly's arm.

"Of course, they may *not* be dead," Cromwell said. "It may be that your dowsing skills have encountered...shall we say, barriers. Not unlike the ones you yourself have used to conceal some property of mine."

He was talking about the chalice, but Woolly pretended he didn't understand.

"Where is he, Cromwell?" Trying to sound threatening but aware that his voice had gone hoarse with fear.

"All right," Cromwell said. "I'm told that he and the curate's daughter broke into a certain shop. From which they entered the network of cellars under High Street...and disappeared."

"What?"

"They're believed to have penetrated the labyrinth," said Roger Cromwell. "Which, of course many people – despite all the stories of secret tunnels under Glastonbury – believe does not exist."

"You're lying," Woolly said.

Cromwell shrugged. "If that's what you want to believe..."

"No!" Nancy shrieked. "We just wants the truth."

"You have it. My information comes from some young friends of mine, who apparently warned your grandson, in the strongest possible terms, not to enter the labyrinth. It's become blocked in places, it's unstable and is apparently so narrow that adults can't get through – which rather rules out the police or the emergency services. And, as it covers a rather large area, with many shops and houses and roads now built over it, it's virtually impossible to trace anyone from the surface."

Nancy looked at Woolly in despair. Folks sometimes talked about the legends of Glastonbury labyrinth. The Mendip Hills and Cheddar Gorge, not too far away, were honeycombed with caves and passages that went on for ever. But Woolly didn't know anyone who'd been into the labyrinth. People talked of kids being lost down there, but nobody could give you names or dates.

But it did, unfortunately, make sense. Marco had told Woolly about the old shop and the problems the girl was having. Kind of boy he was, it was quite likely he'd have taken the first opportunity to go in there and check it out. And Dave Wilcox had said Marco and this Rosa had been seen together in the town centre...and then they'd disappeared.

Probably into The Emporium of the Night.

"You're still usin' that shop, ain't you?" Woolly said. "You've still got access, you and your satanic mates."

"*Satanic mates?*" Cromwell smiled. "I'm a businessman, Woolaston. The Emporium of the Night supplied certain items for which certain people were prepared to pay good money. One doesn't have to believe in what one is selling."

"Nah, you was part of it," Woolly snapped. "You was in it up to your neck."

"Prove it." Cromwell's smile had vanished. "I'm simply a businessman with a certain knowledge of, shall we say, esoteric matters. And, of course, a particular family link with this town."

"That's rubbish, too. You got no proof you're descended from Thomas Cromwell."

"It impresses people, though – especially the ones who prefer the idea of an affluent modern town to a backward community devoted to futile dabbling. Anyway, to return to the matter of your grandson..."

"He'll come back."

"Not if he's in the labyrinth, he won't."

Nancy flashed Woolly a glance of extreme terror.

"He's bluffing," Woolly told her. And then he turned to Cromwell. "If he's in the labyrinth, there's nothing any of us can do. *If* he's in the labyrinth."

"If he's anywhere else, you would surely be able to dowse his whereabouts," Cromwell said. "And I, as it happens, am your only hope of getting him out alive...*or* dead."

"You said nobody could get in there."

"I said no *adult* could get in. However, one of my young friends happens to be an experienced potholer...who also knows how to get in – and out – of the Glastonbury labyrinth. But of course..." Cromwell's smile returned. "...if we were to go in and find these children, it would have to be done secretly. The police and emergency services would *never* allow a boy of fourteen to go down there, even if he's the only person who knows his way around."

"What you sayin', Cromwell?"

"I'm simply asking if you would like to enlist the skills

of my young friend to save the life of your grandson."

"And what would you get out of it?" Woolly said.

But, of course, he knew.

"The return of an old family heirloom."

"*No!*"

"An item of little monetary value but great *sentimental* worth to me." Cromwell's face hardened, and it was like staring into the sharp end of an axe blade. "*I want it back, Woolaston.*"

Woolly folded his arms. "No chance."

Cromwell shrugged. "Then your grandson will perish, of thirst or starvation, in pain and terror, and no one will ever know what happened to him. Because he's lost in a place that simply does not – except as a legend – exist." Cromwell smirked. "*I* certainly don't believe in it. In fact I never even came to see you, and I'm not here now."

"You evil—"

"The boy – and the girl – will simply be missing for ever. My colleague, Angus, will have lost his son and will never forgive you for failing to look after him...for allowing him to run wild in a strange town. And among *all* right-thinking people in this town, what remains of your meagre reputation will be gone for ever. Your life here will be as good as over. You're already unpopular for holding out against a project that would so improve the lives of local people and create new jobs, but being responsible for the deaths of two children...you'll be hounded out of town. Out of your beloved Glastonbury...to die alone, in exile."

Woolly turned away from Cromwell. He wasn't falling for this kind of cheap blackmail.

But with Angus already threatening to report him to the police and tell the social services he and Nancy weren't safe to be on their own up here, let alone look after a kid...

To hell with that; it was Marco that mattered. If there was any chance this boy could get Marco and this girl Rosa out of the labyrinth, how could he not go for it...

...even if it meant disclosing to Roger Cromwell the whereabouts of his *family heirloom*, the Dark Chalice?

It was only a *thing*, after all. A crude and tasteless joke assembled from bits of old bone that might have come from anywhere. There was no proof it was part of Abbot Whiting's skull.

Oh God, what was he going to do? Nancy was clinging to his arm, his dowsing arm – and her eyes were full of a hopeless pleading.

"You'll die a sad and despised old man," Cromwell said. "Having lived out your sunset years with the knowledge that your only grandson is dead...and *you* might have saved him."

A Little Stone

He started to cough. There was so much he wanted to say, but all he could do was cough.

It tasted disgusting inside his mouth, all gritty. He just coughed and coughed until his eyes watered, like he was going to cough and cough all the way to eternity and out the other side.

"You're alive," Rosa said from somewhere in the dusty, foul-smelling, foul-tasting, headachy darkness. "Oh my God, I really thought you must be dead."

She was holding the torch. It had been switched off for so long it had got some of its brightness back and he could see her face, all smudged with dirt, and there were lumps of dirt in her hair, and...

...and she looked really nice, actually. In fact, she looked totally wonderful. She was possibly the most beautiful person he'd ever seen.

Okay, they were trapped in a really small place that had become far smaller due to this great mound of rubble now blocking off the passage they'd crawled through. But somehow they were both here and somehow they were both alive.

"Don't move," Rosa said. "I don't know if it's safe to move. Can you feel your arms? Can you feel your legs?"

"Legs?" He thought about it. He clenched his toes. "Yeah. I think so. Was I, like, unconscious or something?"

"Something like that. Just...don't move."

He heard this ominous scattering sound – more bits of the ceiling starting to fall. He looked up nervously.

"How long have I been...you know?"

"Not long. Five minutes? I don't really know. Long enough for me to see that we're definitely not going to get out the way we came in."

Rosa shone the torch at the great mound of stuff. It was truly immense. It blocked the whole passage, floor to ceiling. Blocked solid. If it had come down on them, they'd have had no chance. He realized how lucky they'd been. If you could call this luck.

"We couldn't dig our way out?"

"What with?"

"Maybe we could fill our trainers with soil and keep emptying them?"

"And what would we do with the big rocks?" Rosa said. "Like, *really* big rocks. Rocks the size of...I don't know, TV sets?"

"Where?"

"There's actually one across my legs," Rosa said calmly.

"*What?*"

"No. Don't move! You can't do anything about it, I've tried. It would take like...machinery or something."

"How are we supposed to get—?"

Marco bit his tongue. Rosa was shining the torch on this immense, flat slab of rock the size of a school desk. All he could see was the rock and Rosa's top half.

This was just...awful. He didn't know what to say. It would take about three grown men to move that rock. Oh God.

"No, er...no problem," he said. "Piece of cake. They can get like...a digger or something. A JCB. That'll shift it, no problem."

"Yes," Rosa said, and he knew she didn't think there was a choc-ice's chance in hell of them getting a digger down here.

Oh God.

"I'm afraid you're going to have carry on on your own," Rosa said, in this totally matter-of-fact voice.

"I can't leave you, can I? I can't—"

"What's the alternative?"

"I don't know."

"We both know what the alternative is. It's okay. Really. I can't feel any pain or anything."

Well, Marco didn't know much about injuries, but he had a good idea that not being able to feel anything at all was a lot worse than feeling serious pain.

Oh *God.*

Rosa shone the torch past Marco at the two passages which remained unblocked – the passages which, before half the ceiling caved in on them, they'd realized they were going to have to choose between. One of them a reasonable height, the other drainpipe size.

And even the reasonable passage would lead to other passages, and those passages would open out into more passages, and soon he'd be lost again. Only this time it would be so much worse, because he'd be on his own, and Rosa would be lying somewhere he couldn't even shout to her, with her legs crushed and nothing to drink and the rest of the ceiling likely to come down any minute, and when it did she wouldn't even be able to turn her face away from the falling rocks.

"Perhaps it's best if I stay with you," he said.

"Don't be a wimp."

"I *am* a wimp. I suffer from claustrophobia. I mean, if there was some way I could be sure there was an actual way out, that would be fair enough, but there..."

"What's the matter?"

"I think I've just thought of something, but it's...I don't know. It's kind of stupid."

"What?"

Very carefully, Marco struggled into a sitting position in the settling dust and managed to reach his pocket.

"This."

The pendulum glittered in the waning torchlight. An orange fruit drop. He wished, in a way, that it *was* a fruit drop. He could have cracked it in two on a rock, and they could have had half each to get rid of the filthy taste of dry earth.

The pendulum. Early this morning, it had seemed like the best present he'd ever been given. This morning, everything had seemed so...so *inspiring*.

Now it was just a little stone on a chain. And in a truly desperate situation all that stuff seemed...silly.

"I expect your dad would think this was just some nasty pagan invention," Marco said. "And I'm like risking my immortal soul just—"

"Just go for it." Rosa snapped.

You can ask simple questions – yes-or-no questions – and get a reaction, Woolly had said. *The pendulum will change direction. But you gotter make sure you ain't helpin' him. You gotter detach your mind from the process.*

Now, obviously, he desperately wanted the pendulum to tell him that the way out of the labyrinth was through the first passage, the one he could get into by just bending his head a bit...rather than the other one which seemed to have been made as an escape route for the rats.

Mustn't let this influence the pendulum, however.

Rosa held the torch, and Marco held up the little orange stone on its string between finger and thumb, trying hard to detach his mind from the process, so that when the pendulum directed him to Passage Number One, he could assure himself this was nothing to do with his terrible fear of Passage Number Two.

He looked into the darkness of Passage Number One.

"Is this the way out?"

The pendulum began to move at once, as if it knew there wasn't much time.

It began to move anticlockwise.

Widdershins.

Nooooooooooooooooooo!

"Maybe I should try again. Like, um...best of three?"

"I don't think that's how it works, is it?"

Marco looked into the terrifyingly small opening.

He couldn't. *He couldn't.*

"Of course, it could be that neither of the passages is any good," he said. "Perhaps I should test this one, too?"

The more he looked at Passage Number Two, the smaller and tighter the opening seemed. In fact, he probably couldn't even get inside. It was a complete no-no. Still...

With Rosa watching, he went through the motions. Was *this* the way out?

The pendulum immediately went into a clockwise twirl.

"That means, er...yes, doesn't it?" Rosa said.

"Well, it...I mean..."

He hated this pendulum now and he said as much to Rosa.

He said it was a stupid idea, anyway, the whole dowsing thing. And even if it wasn't, he'd only been a dowser for one day, so, like, no *way* could he have enough experience to trust what the pendulum said.

Rosa shifted her upper body as far as she could. She closed her eyes, and he thought she was biting her lip. Was she really in some terrible pain but not telling him because she didn't want him to stay?

When she spoke again, it wasn't much more than a whisper.

"I mean...you know...it's possible someone will realize we're down here and divert all the traffic so they can dig up the main road."

"What?"

"Or get permission from the Church of England and – is it English Heritage? – to take a JCB to the Abbey ruins. Demolish them all so they can get down to us."

"Stop it," Marco said.

"Of course, they'll probably have to fill in a lot of forms first, and that probably takes weeks while a lot of committees consider them, so..."

Rosa sighed again.

Marco closed his eyes and gritted his teeth.

Rat Food

Woolly carried on threading a new piece of twine into the little loop on the end of his pendulum. His fingers felt numb, and so did his brain.

"Don't waste time," Roger Cromwell said. "The council's planning committee and all the officials will be here soon to inspect our site."

"Why would I care about that?" Woolly muttered.

Cromwell smiled. "Meanwhile, in the labyrinth, there are a hundred ways a child can die."

"You're sick," Woolly shouted. "Barterin' the life of a young boy, just to get your hands on some'ing that should stay buried for ever."

"And will be buried again," Cromwell said. "Never fear."

Woolly thought he knew what Cromwell meant. It had always been rumoured that, in the old days, the Dark Chalice had been kept in a deep and secret temple under the town – perhaps even under the Abbey itself.

The greatest evil was often to be found in the shadows around something holy.

So what was Cromwell's plan? To put the Dark Chalice under the foundations of Avalon World...or return it to some black chapel under the Abbey, where its strengthened negative vibes would create poisoned arteries around the sacred heart of Glastonbury. Altering the whole psychic vibration of the holiest earth in England. Turning it bad.

Woolly's own heart seemed to freeze in his chest. He couldn't let this happen. He had to play along with Cromwell and...think of something.

He must be able to think of *something*.

He wondered how much Angus knew about Cromwell's secret motives. But then, Angus didn't believe in anything outside the world of legal issues and finance. He'd been quite happy to use the boy to help his clients get what they wanted, and if you told him Cromwell's motives were satanic, he'd just laugh. It was all fairy stories to Angus. Wilde-Hunt were important clients of his legal firm, and he wouldn't be able to get his head around the idea that Cromwell was just as loony as he thought Woolly and Nancy were.

So *was* Marco down there? The pendulum had indicated that, unfortunately, he probably was.

If Woolly went to the police about this, they'd never believe him. It'd be pointless trying to explain what was behind the campaign to blacken his name – they'd just laugh in his face, say he was mad. They'd listen, instead, to Angus, who would already have told the social services about how his in-laws had lost their marbles and weren't safe to be left on their own in a lonely cottage in the hills.

Woolly felt the weight of the pendulum on its new twine – three times as long as the old one. He found a pencil and rolled the twine around it, so that it could operate at different lengths, as it would need to do if he was going to locate the burial place of...

He tried to shut his mind against thoughts of what lay buried out there and what he would soon be guilty of exposing.

He would be the one who'd released the evil into the town.

How would he ever live with that?

On the day he'd shut Marco in the cupboard in his bedroom, Josh had told him that claustrophobia was like a flashback to when you were born and you were being pushed up the birth canal or whatever it was called.

Yeah. Sure. Except in this documentary he'd once seen on TV, about a baby being born, the birth canal had seemed all slippery and slimy.

It had not been cold and spiky with buried rocks.

This place was bone dry, apart from the sweat that was all

over his forehead and dripping down into his eyes.

Alone, in this stifling, lumpy tube, Marco was in agony.

His head was aching and his chest felt like his lungs were bursting. But he knew that if he gave in to the panic and started trying to roll and flail around in a place so horrifyingly tight he'd just go insane.

He'd die insane.

All he could do was keep on inching forward, while every part of him was screaming: *Go back, go back.*

And, like...

...like, what if it went on for miles? What if, deep underground, beyond all help, the rat passage became even narrower and he got stuck with his head in a hole that was too tight to take his shoulders?

What if it came to a dead end and the earth had collapsed behind him, leaving him trapped in something like a stone coffin, where he would slowly suffocate?

And so he'd become rat food. One day they would find his pathetic bones all bunched up and twisted...

These were the very worst moments of his life. If he'd been any kind of true pilgrim, he'd have been able to summon up that fifth wavelength thing that had happened to him on the Tor...and he would leave his body. Leave his body wedged in the tunnel and go walking on the Tor in the soft, fresh air – birds singing, the grass springy under his trainers.

But the so-called fifth wavelength had probably been just some brain-chemical thing, a hallucination – that's what Josh would say.

But what was so wrong with that? He prayed for a hallucination. Anything to take him out of this, even if it was just an illusion. *"Please,"* he whispered, his mouth like a sandpit in August and his voice all parched. *"Please..."*

Whispering to God. Or to anything. If he could reach his pendulum, he'd probably ask it if he was ever going to see daylight again. Only this time he'd influence it to say yes, so he'd at least have a tiny bit of hope right up to the end.

Could be you're asking a part of yourself you didn't know existed, Woolly had said. *I reckon what you're really asking is your higher self. The part of you that's connected to something bigger and deeper.*

Yeah, whatever. It made no difference, anyway, as the pendulum was back in his pocket and his hands were out in front of him, one holding the torch, which was now issuing no more light than you got from a luminous clock face, and he couldn't even bend his elbows, as he squirmed along like a dried-up caterpillar, thinking about Rosa now. Hoping she'd just fall asleep in the dark and have nice dreams.

No chance.

What he wished – and the old Marco would've been as embarrassed as hell to admit this to Josh – was that he'd had the courage to kiss her goodbye or something.

It was no good, he had to stop. His fingernails were all broken and painful and his elbows were red raw. He didn't even think he could inch his way back, just didn't have the strength. The pendulum had lied. It was just a stone on a chain, and he had no higher self. He was the pits.

This was when the torch went out.

He started to cry, and he closed his eyes in anguish and disgust at himself and let go of the dead torch.

The torch fell.

He expected it would just go *clunk* on the earth underneath his hand, but it didn't. It was several seconds before he heard it land, with a distant, muffled splash. At the same time he felt new air on his face, and his breathing was echoing back at him from some vast invisible space.

And now he *really* went into a panic.

When you couldn't move, or even feel your legs, when you couldn't see anything...and when all you could hear was the scurrying of the rats and the occasional spattering of earth and stones falling from the low and unstable ceiling to the lumpy floor... When you were totally and utterly helpless, there weren't many things you could do four times.

Rosa giggled faintly through her tears.

As the alternative was thinking about how soon she would die, she was thinking about what Marco, in the absence of his know-all friend Josh, had identified as Obsessive Compulsive Disorder.

The need to do things four times. The need to check, check, check.

Like, why *four* times? How had she chosen that particular number as her personal safeguard, her way of preventing something tragically horrible happening to Mum or Dad or her?

All the years of doing things four times and repeatedly going back and checking that she actually *had* done them... it was like Marco had said, everything was taking four times as long as it took everyone else. And because she spent so much time feeling anxious, she didn't have time just to think and feel and just be alive. *She'd been wasting three quarters of her life.*

And now, when it was too late, she *did* have time, too much of it. Now she had time to be alive, and there was...no life to be had.

Nothing to do.

Nothing to see but darkness.

Nothing to hear but the kind of spattering, crumbling noises that suggested the end was not too far off.

Nothing to feel but goosebumps trickling up both her arms, responding to the creeping sense that, here in the cold, musty-smelling blackness, far beneath the surface of the earth, imprisoned by the huge rock, she...

...was not, in fact, alone.

There was a...

...a *nearness.*

The cold was suddenly intense. Rosa hugged herself tightly through her thin clothes.

And felt that this was not a normal cold. She felt light-headed, and her breathing, like the air, seemed to have gone thin. It was like only half of her was here, but she wasn't sure where the other half had gone, as she became aware of something forming out of the dark hollows at the bottom of the rock that was holding her down. A cloudy, mournfully-grey shape, hovering and vibrating.

A shape she knew.

Only this time his cowl was thrown back and she could see his eyes, and they were white and gassy.

Untold Wealth

Bizarrely, he could hear dogs.

Far above him, he could hear them circling and barking and snarling. They sounded like they were in some kind of frenzy.

He couldn't look up because half of him was hanging in space.

"Hey, you lot," someone shouted. "Back off! What have I taught you about hunting?"

There was the sound of splintering wood and then light came down, great vertical shafts of it, and it was so painful at first that Marco had to shut his eyes.

The dogs barked happily.

Marco tried to say something and produced a croak.

"Leave it, you dumb mutts!" the man shouted. "Come on...home!"

"*No!*" Marco howled.

"Stone me!" the man said. And there was some more wrenching and splintering, and more shattering light. "Where the hell did you come from?"

"I don't know," Marco moaned.

"Okay..." The man's voice was closer, but still a long way above Marco. "Listen, don't move. Don't move an inch, you hear me, or you're dead in the water, and I ain't kidding. I'm going to get some help. Just...do *not* move, all right?"

Now there was some light in here, Marco could see exactly why it would not be wise to move, except backwards.

Half of him – both arms and his chest – was out of the narrow passage and hanging over a deep stone shaft. Far below, he could see the glimmer of water.

It was some kind of well, and another push forward in the dark would have sent him tumbling down into certain death.

"Right," Cromwell said. "Let's not waste any more time. My colleagues at Wilde-Hunt will be here soon, and then the council's planning committee – drooling over the prospect of our champagne reception in the marquee."

Woolly sniffed in disgust.

"It's just to reassure the councillors," Cromwell said, "that the future of Glastonbury will be champagne rather than..." he sneered, "carrot juice."

They were in Woolly's sloping field, with the cottage below them and the Tor to their right. The sky was a deep grey, which made the green grass luridly bright. Woolly unslung a canvas bag from his shoulder and took out the little velvet pouch containing his pendulum.

Two kids had appeared. They must have been waiting outside. One was a bulky red-haired boy and the other was taller, with dark eyes and a bit of a sulky expression. Cromwell had introduced him as Jasper, the potholer who was going to rescue Marco, if Woolly cooperated.

Jasper smirked. Woolly had seen him around town and didn't like the look of him. Today, he had that sense of *smoke* about him.

And Woolly was outnumbered now. Nancy hadn't argued when he'd suggested she should stay at the cottage.

He held up the pendulum, with most of its twine wound round the pencil.

"*Iron*," he whispered.

"You watch what Woolly does, Jasper," Cromwell said. "It's a useful art, dowsing."

"But it only works if you uses it for good," Woolly said.

Cromwell smiled. "What *is* good? Good for you? Good for me? You're a fool, Woolly. You're the finest dowser in Somerset – you could be making a fortune finding water and minerals. You could work all over the world, finding oilfields."

"And what real good would I be doin'?" Woolly said. "Helpin' rich companies get richer."

"Listen to him, Jasper...and learn why Glastonbury is still in the Dark Ages. He's wasted his life believing in ephemera... like the Holy Grail, something that exists only in dreams. He's a dreamer."

"And I'm not the only one," Woolly muttered bitterly.

"Which is why this town stagnates in the past. There's so much natural energy here, but it's undercrued, fuelling pointless dreams when it could be making money – serving the force which *truly* powers this world."

Woolly eyed him over the pendulum. "You talkin' 'bout Satan, by any chance?"

"That's a meaningless term. I'm talking about doing what we *want* to do. Taking our pleasures. Gratifying our desires. If Jasper wants a new computer and a pile of computer games, why should he wait when he can have them now?"

Woolly looked at Jasper. Jasper grinned. Woolly began to see how the boy had been seduced by Cromwell's promises – promises that always came true, in the short-term, if you committed to evil. If you believed that this world was all there was, and you were entitled to take from it what you could get.

"What you hanging round here for?" Woolly said to Jasper. "Why don't you get down that labyrinth and get Marco out and this girl, too?"

Jasper looked at Woolly out of blank, cold eyes.

"Why should I?" he said.

God help us, Woolly thought.

"The quicker you find what I want," Cromwell said, "the sooner Jasper will go down. If you fail...well, I expect you've heard the stories about the labyrinth taking sacrifices."

Woolly turned away from both of them, snatching a breath. He'd have to go through with this.

All right...*Iron.* With one hand, he lifted the pencil holding the pendulum on the requisite length of twine to find iron and held the other hand out in front of him, one finger pointing.

He set the pendulum swinging, and waited for a moment, and then began to turn slowly, his arm out, the finger pointing like a weather vane on a church tower. Extending his force field, his aura, in front of him, searching for another force field, the static aura of a lump of iron.

All the time, Woolly was watching the pendulum as it swung on its twine. His finger was pointing, he guessed, in a north-easterly direction when the pendulum began to change to a circular motion, clockwise.

Woolly nodded and walked slowly off in that direction, with Cromwell and Jasper following. The further he walked, the faster the pendulum spun, and when it began to slow again, he stopped.

From his pocket, he took a wooden peg and a ball of string. He pushed the peg into the ground and tied the end of the string to it and walked to where he'd left his canvas bag, unravelling the string as he went. He took out another peg and pushed it in close to the bag and tied the string to it.

Then he walked off for a few yards at a right-angle, set the pendulum swinging and did his pointer thing with the finger of the other hand, once again following the signal when the pendulum began to twirl. When he reached the string, he stopped and bent down. Took out his penknife and used it to scrape away the grass and the surface soil.

Aha...

Holding up the horseshoe, he couldn't conceal the satisfaction he always experienced when the dowsing worked.

"Iron," he said.

Stage one.

"Remarkable," Cromwell said. "What's next?"

"Copper," Woolly said. "And then silver."

"Hmm. Each mineral increasing in value, leading us closer to the chalice."

Woolly nodded. It had been the only way he could think to do it at the time, laying a trail of metals in different directions, confusing the issue. For any other dowser who might be hired to find the filthy thing. Because, of course, the dark chalice wasn't made of metal. The original gold chalice had been replaced with a thing of bone. They'd soon get fed up with finding odd metallic objects of little value and think they were on the wrong track. Only Woolly would know.

"And what's the final one?" Cromwell asked.

"Gold." The cheapest gold ring he could buy at the time.

"Ha! Turning base metal into gold. Alchemy. How appropriate. The chalice has proven alchemical properties. In the reign of Elizabeth I, the psychic Edward Kelley, associate of the royal magician Dr John Dee, came to Glastonbury and – it is said – found, in the ruins of the Abbey, some powder and a scroll of instructions for turning base metal into gold – powder from the Philosopher's Stone."

"Notorious liar, that Kelley, far as I remember," Woolly said.

"My understanding is that he found the powder in the Dark Chalice. In the brainpan of the executed abbot."

"Rubbish."

"On the contrary, it makes perfect sense. I expect *you* think of alchemy in terms of turning the human spirit into light, but I see it in its original sense: generating wealth. It's said that Kelley was able to use the powder to create a massive amount of gold."

"Money," Woolly said. "Can't you think no further than that?"

"Money is the lifeblood of this world, Woolly. Henry VIII and my ancestor found untold wealth in Glastonbury—"

"Oh, ar! By plundering the Abbey and killing a harmless old bloke who liked to help the poor!"

"Henry knew what he wanted and he took it. He wanted a new queen and the Church wouldn't agree, so he destroyed the Church and created a new one. Even our belligerent friend Wilcox owes his job to Henry VIII – a man who took what he wanted from the world." Cromwell put his face close to Woolly's. "*As could you.*"

Woolly reeled back. Cromwell's breath smelled strange, faintly sweet.

"Think about it, Woolly," he said. "At Avalon World, you could do displays of dowsing for the tourists. We'd pay you well..."

"I never charges for it," Woolly said. "'Tis a gift."

"Then you should use it to make money. And we could put other, more lucrative work your way. More work, for far more money, than you've ever had in your life. You could soon be a rich man, Woolly. Have you never thought about that?"

"Me...rich? Oh, sure..."

"Look at your cottage. It's old and decrepit. Think of the repairs it's going to need. Think of your wife – I bet you haven't even got an automatic washing machine, have you? Or central heating. And neither of you are getting any younger. You'll soon be old...and cold."

"Old and c—?"

Woolly's normal reaction would be to take a swing at the beggar, show him how old and cold he was. But he was thinking, no...maybe he'd go along with this, let Cromwell think he really was clapped out. If he thought Woolly was no threat, he'd be less careful what he said, more likely to show his hand.

"Angus says he...he's going to bring the social services in," Woolly said, a bit tremulous. "He can't do that, can he?"

"Angus knows precisely what the law will allow him to do, and he'll do it," Cromwell said.

"Can't nobody stop him?"

"He's a *lawyer*," Cromwell said. "However...people with *money* can tell the social services to keep out of their lives.

People with money can look after themselves. Money can make you free."

"You reckon?" Woolly said.

Roger Cromwell's smile was like acid. His eyes were gleaming softly, like orbs of gold.

Above him, the sky had darkened.

A Dark Sun

The smell of grass was almost certainly the best smell in the world. Marco lay in it, and the dogs – there must have been twenty of them – were sniffing all around him and one was licking his face all over. He didn't care; the dogs had found him. The dogs had saved him.

The man hauled up the rope ladder, its metal rungs clanking on the stone rim of the well. Marco remembered how, when he was a little kid, he'd always wanted a rope ladder – although, living in a block of flats, there wouldn't have been a lot of use for one – and now he'd climbed up this one without even noticing it. All the time he'd been staring up at the sky, and he still was. It was a grey and ominous kind of sky, but a sky was a sky, and he'd thought he'd never see one again.

The man stood over him. He was middle aged – maybe thirty-five-ish – with either a half-grown beard or an aversion to shaving every day. He had long, tangled hair and he wore denims and canvas shoes. Marco thought maybe he'd seen him before.

"Don't tell me," the bloke said, with his head on one side. "Your dad's called David Blaine and he's taught you everything he knows."

"Huh?"

"Or how else did you manage to get down a well that's been boarded up for half a century?"

"I didn't," Marco said. "I came out of...out of the labyrinth."

Marco remembered where he'd seen this guy before. It was just after he and Dad had arrived in Glastonbury, and Woolly and Eleri had been trying to warn the pilgrims about the bad vibes. He'd been there with a couple of his dogs, and both of them had howled eerily as if they alone had understood every word Eleri was saying.

They were in a field, with trees and some cows at one end. The only building you could see looked like some big mansion, about half a mile away.

"*Listen*," Marco said, fear overcoming his sense of relief. "Problem is...my friend – she's still stuck down there."

"What?" The guy heaved a couple of the dogs away. "Towser, get off! Say that again, pal."

"The ceiling came down on us, and this massive rock fell across her legs, and she can't move."

"Sh...*sugar*. You don't do stuff by halves, do you? What's your name?"

"Marco. I'm staying with my granddad. Woolly?"

"Woolly! You're *Woolly's* grandson? Alison's kid? Stone me! I used to fancy—" He coughed. "Okay, this friend. Who is she?"

"She's called Rosa. Wilcox."

"The new curate's daughter? How far in is she?"

"I don't know. It took me ages to get through the tunnel. It's, like, really narrow."

"How'd you get into the labyrinth, then?"

Marco told him about The Emporium of the Night and its cellar. And he told him – because, frankly, he *deserved* to be grassed up – about Jasper and his mates.

"Why am I not surprised?" the bloke said. He got out a mobile phone and stabbed out 999. "Fire brigade and ambulance, I reckon."

"There's something evil about it," Marco said. "I'm not making this up. I don't know how else to describe it. There was like a temple?"

The bloke nodded. "I've heard that, too." He gave their location to the emergency services, then he called another number. "Diane, can you get over here? We got a problem. Field by the old well." He paused and listened. "Yeah, I know, but this is more important, look." He clicked off, grinned at Marco. "Sam Daniel, my name. These are my dogs."

"They look like hunting hounds or something."

"Used to be. Used to be my late father-in-law's pack. Lord Pennard. Only he didn't know, when he was alive, that he was gonner be my father-in-law. Old devil's prob'ly spinning in his grave faster than Woolly's pendulum."

"Why?"

"I, er, used to be the bane of his life. Friend of the foxes. Hunt saboteur. Did it for years. We laid false trails and stuff to send the hounds in the wrong direction. Old Pennard thought I should be lynched. Which is why it gave me great pleasure, when his daughter and me got married, to domesticate these fellers and teach them the error of their ways. Now...gotter think how we can get this girl out. Are her legs...?"

"She said she couldn't feel them."

"Hell." Sam drew in a whistling breath. "That ain't good at all, pal."

"I could try and go back—"

"Forget it! No, we gotter wait for the fire brigade... paramedics. Even if they gotter dig their way in."

An old Land Rover came rattling across the field, then, and a woman got out. She was, well, on the plump side. Wore a lemon yellow T-shirt the size of a duvet cover with a big red heart on it.

"Sam, what are you *doing*? We've got to get ready for the demo! We're going to be frightfully late!"

Sam put up both his hands. "This guy was down the well, Diane – got in through the labyrinth."

"Gosh, does that actually exist?" She talked like the Queen.

"And there's a girl still down there, apparently. Trapped. Seems she...can't feel her legs, Diane. Rescue guys are on their way."

"Oh." The woman went still.

"They got in through Cromwell's old black magic shop," Sam said. "Well, got pushed in, accordin' to this feller, by young Jasper Coombes and Shane Davey and a couple of their mates. What do you reckon to that?"

"They said Woolly was a traitor," Marco said.

"This is Woolly's grandson." Sam looked at Diane and raised an eyebrow. "Don't sound like they got banged up by accident, do it? Might be a good day for certain people to be puttin' a bit of pressure on Woolly?"

"And after what happened to poor Teddy..." Diane said.

"Rosa thinks—" Marco shut up. The idea of Rosa's dad attacking this Teddy for showing her how to draw a pentagram now seemed slightly silly.

Diane turned to Marco. "Where's Woolly now?"

"I don't—" Marco shook his head. "I don't *know*. I think...I think they've done something to him. Like that Teddy...somebody killed him, didn't they?"

"Teddy's not dead," Diane said. "I've just spoken to the hospital in Taunton. But it's touch and go, apparently, he was ever so badly beaten up." She looked at Sam. "I...I don't think I like any of this. It's all a bit too coincidental."

"Supposed to be a protest demo over Avalon World in an hour or so," Sam told Marco. "We were gonner wait for the council after they came off the site and make our views known."

"You're against it?"

"Course we're against it. Look, you wanner wait for the emergency services, Diane? And somebody needs to tell the girl's parents – Wilcox, the curate?"

She nodded. "What about getting the cave-rescue people from Cheddar..."

"It's no good!" Marco wailed. "Adults can't get into the labyrinth any more. It's all too narrow."

"They'll find a way." Sam looked at Diane. He didn't look in the least hopeful. "How about I go with Marco back to Woolly's place? See what's goin' down. Be quickest to go across the fields, look. You can walk okay, Marco?"

"Sure. But what about Rosa?"

"Diane'll do everything she can."

Sam patted Diane's arm and strode away towards a field gate, beyond which the Tor sprouted, almost black against the luminous grey sky. Sam opened the gate and all the dogs surged through. Marco looked up at the sky. It was getting darker.

Over the church tower on the Tor the sky was almost black. To Marco, it was like there was a ball of black behind the Tor that was radiating outwards, like a dirty sun.

Child Sacrifices

Woolly picked up the old silver half-crown. He'd found it just as easily as he'd found the copper penny.

And it was making Roger Cromwell excited.

"Now the gold," he said. "And then...*the chalice.*" He gazed up towards the Tor. "Just look at that sky – the day is preparing itself for the moment of revelation."

"' Tis just the Blight," Woolly said gruffly. "Building up for a storm. "'Tis normal."

But he knew that this kind of darkness in the middle of a summer afternoon was not *that* normal, even in Glastonbury. They were at the top of the ridge, opposite the Tor, and it was like heavy curtains were being drawn across the day, the way people used to draw their curtains when a funeral procession was coming past.

Jasper Coombes and the kid called Shane had lost interest in the dowsing and were wandering around, kicking tussocks of grass. They were probably responsible for the holes in Woolly's fields – scrabbling around at night to try and find where the Dark Chalice was buried. *No* chance.

And it was disgusting, using kids to do your dirty work. They thought it was a game, never realized how tainted their souls were becoming, until it was too late. Woolly was aware again of something about Jasper and Shane, the way their mouths twisted and their eyes gleamed slyly when they looked at you.

With kids like this around, Woolly thought, it was important that there should also be kids like Marco.

He just had to save Marco.

Woolly was getting real desperate now, and confused. He couldn't do it, he couldn't expose the world to the evil of the Dark Chalice, but how could he *not* do it if it was the only way to save Marco?

"My whole life's been leading to this." Cromwell moistened his lips with his tongue. "I've been obsessed with the chalice since I was a child. It wasn't like the Grail, it was *real* – there to be rediscovered, whenever it was needed."

It was clear he thought he had Woolly now, like a fish on a hook. Scaring him with all that stuff about getting old and how money could save him. And Woolly was letting him go on thinking that, because it was making him indiscreet. As they walked to the top of the ridge, Cromwell was revealing his plans.

"Over the years, I made contact with several powerful groups all over the world who were interested in locating the chalice."

He would mean the *black lodges* – the hidden societies studying the darkest forms of magic. Most people thought they didn't exist, but the Glastonbury pilgrims knew they did because they'd often turned up here. Many of their members must have been Cromwell's regular customers at The Emporium of the Night.

"It was they, in fact, who put up the money to open The Emporium of the Night," Cromwell said. "Scholars of the Unseen from Europe, America, Africa...the Far East. Some of them have great personal wealth. So you see..." He gripped Woolly's arm, and the muscle was suddenly paralysed like it had been plunged into a deep freeze. "When you and your airy-fairy friends had my business closed down...you offended more people than you could know."

Woolly went rigid. Their little rag bag of pilgrims against some great worldwide, dark consortium.

"My customers have been doing specific rituals to help me," Roger Cromwell said. "To empower me."

He tightened his grip on Woolly's arm. *Empowered.* You could believe it. It was as if the nearness of the chalice was pumping dark fuel into Cromwell. His eyes were like molten metal and there was a sheen, like oil, on his long, predatory face. Next to him, Woolly felt very feeble. Small and old and helpless.

Cromwell smiled at him, almost kindly.

"You've been on the wrong side for too long, Woolly. The side of the losers. You're a Glastonbury man, born and bred, but you were led astray by incomers and their stupid dreams of this patch of countryside as some kind of Garden of Eden."

It has been! Woolly yelled inside. *And it could be again.*

He looked at Cromwell. He wanted to drag his arm away and run like hell, but there was a kind of hypnotic, cold fire in Cromwell's eyes. Something working through him, something that used people, fed on their lust for wealth and influence.

"My customers were not at all happy at having their supplier shut down," Cromwell said. "I was soon directed to the group of businessmen that would become Wilde-Hunt. Property developers, entrepreneurs."

"And do they know...the power they're serving?"

"Does it matter?" Roger Cromwell sniffed with scorn. "They don't care anyway. They're businessmen. Their god is money."

"The root of all evil," Woolly said.

Funny how you suddenly realized the element of truth in a tired, old phrase.

"It's surprising who serves my cause without realizing it." Cromwell laughed. "Take the curate who lives over the shop. He thinks all his aggression is directed against the powers of evil – people like you."

410

"What about the girl?" Woolly said. "His daughter. She seems to have had an instinct that something wasn't right, even if her ole man didn't notice."

"And the stupid child went to Teddy for help." Almost gently, Cromwell let go of Woolly's arm. "Whereupon, the poor sucker came to see me. He wanted to know what the girl had seen through the shop window in the hallway. I didn't know what he meant at the time – but it seems young Jasper here was playing with candles."

Jasper looked up, grinning.

"I arranged to meet Teddy last night and talk it over," Cromwell said. "But Teddy wouldn't listen to reason. So I'm afraid we had to have him...warned. A couple of my associates came up through the cellar and were waiting for him this morning when he opened his shop. We couldn't have him shooting his mouth off – not today, with the radio people in town and the council due. You do understand, don't you, Woolly?"

"Oh, I understand, all right."

"Same with the girl. A persistent child. Unfortunately, she was the one who found Teddy, so the police would have had to talk to her. And children are so volatile – she'd have come out with all the background. They wouldn't have believed her, of course, but they might just have checked out The Emporium. So...I'm afraid she had to be...got out of the way. And, unfortunately, your grandson was with her."

Woolly couldn't believe what he was hearing...although he knew Cromwell would deny having said any of it.

"A dangerous place, the labyrinth," Cromwell said. "With a history of taking its own child sacrifices."

He looked up at the sound of a car engine. Over a hedge, Woolly saw two Range Rovers winding their way up Well House Lane. In a field below, on the other side of the ridge, he saw that a marquee had been erected. Cars were parked on the grass, and a few people in dark suits were moving around with cases and clipboards.

Wilde-Hunt people. He thought he could see Angus, standing with his hands behind his back and his briefcase at his feet.

"Time to find the gold, Woolly," Cromwell said softly. "I want to get the chalice out of here and into the temple before the council leave. Perhaps we can collect your grandson, too...if we're in time."

He and Jasper exchanged smiles that were full of venom.

And suddenly Woolly saw it all.

He was thinking how, during World War II, the first Watchers of Avalon had focused on the Tor, using its ancient energies against the Nazis. It was well known that Nazi leaders were obsessed with the occult and were directing bad vibes at Britain, to prepare the way for an invasion. So the British mystics had reactivated the Tor as a great psychic power station, bringing the energy of the old gods and King Arthur together with the forces of Jesus and the Holy Grail, to erect psychic barriers around Britain and keep the Nazis out.

And it had, after all, worked. Well...*something* had worked. No invasion of Britain had ever taken place, anyway. And

Eleri had been right – they needed to get the *new* Watchers of Avalon together again.

Too late now, though.

If only they'd realized that Cromwell and his associates were planning something similar to the Watchers' wartime exercise, but with a destructive purpose. When the anti-Grail, the Dark Chalice, had been unearthed it would be taken – probably by the potholing Jasper – into the stone chamber under the town, to become, once again, the centrepiece of its altar...

...so that, from tonight, Cromwell's customers all over the country could focus their satanically enhanced will power on the chalice with a single purpose – to influence the council to accept the Avalon World proposal and thus destroy Glasto's little shops and break up its mystical community.

To kill the dream.

To suck the light out of the town.

The Dust of Dreams

"What's up with the dogs?" Sam Daniel said. "Ain't never seen them like this before."

The pack of dogs had gone very quiet and subdued, all bunched together, keeping close to Sam. Some of them were whimpering.

Glastonbury Tor was up ahead of them now, and it looked huge and forbidding, this great, moody silhouette, and the only light left in the sky was like a halo around it. The Tor seemed to have different moods, according to different times of day and changes in the weather, and Marco reckoned its mood at this moment was...well, black.

"I'll be honest, I don't like this, pal," Sam Daniel said.

Some distance below them was a stretch of woodland and, in a field on the other side of it, a big tent had been put up, and you could see people moving about amid cars and Land Rovers and people carriers. It was so dark now that some of the vehicles had their lights on, Marco noticed.

"Is that the council?"

"Ar. My ole man'll be down there, too," Sam said. "Bein' as he's the mayor."

Marco remembered the old guy with the ratty beard, in the tweed suit. Griff *Daniel*. Of course. But the mayor was...

"*Not* one of the good guys," Sam said, as if he'd picked up on Marco's thoughts. "Bit of a crook, my ole man. We never got on too well. Course he pretends it's all sweetness and light between us, now I'm married to the Lady of the Manor."

Marco couldn't quite get his head round this. "That big mansion we saw...?"

"Bowermead Hall. That's hers. Hate the place, personally, but Diane feels it's her responsibility to keep it going, now her dad's gone. And when Wilde-Hunt came along one day and offered to buy it off us and turn it into a luxury hotel as part of their scheme...well, even *I* was determined to hold on to it after that."

Sam peered down, in a hostile kind of way, at the gathering in the field below them.

"But when Wilde-Hunt announced their plans, my ole man and his mates was right behind them. Conveniently forgetting what kind of shop Cromwell used to run."

"So you reckon the council will say yes to Avalon World?"

"Bound to, now, 'specially after that stuff on the radio this morning. They'll force Woolly to sell his land—"

Marco was shocked. "The council can do that?"

"It's called Compulsory Purchase, Marco. Councils can do a lot of stuff like that. Poor ole Woolly." Sam patted one of his dogs. "Poor ole Glasto."

Marco wondered if this Compulsory Purchase thing was what Jasper had meant when he suggested something had been done to Woolly, but feared it was something even worse. In the distance, he saw what he thought was the roof of Woolly and Nancy's cottage. No sign of life down there, not even Merlin.

"If I know Woolly, he'll be down there with the demo," Sam said. "Orf and a few of the guys have put a bit of a last-minute protest together, with banners and stuff. They'll be there now. We were supposed to join them, me and Diane."

"Can we go and see if Woolly's down there?"

"*I'd* better not go too close," Sam said. "I'll get accused of setting the dogs on them. You could run down there, though."

"Thanks, Sam." Marco started down the hill then turned back, feeling there was something else he ought to say. "I mean, thanks for, like, saving my life."

"Oh Gawd." Sam rolled his eyes. "Bring on the flamin' violins. Go on...I'll go and check out Woolly's place, make sure there's nobody there."

"Okay."

Marco felt the springy grass under his trainers and

remembered just how bad it had been in the labyrinth. Then he ran down the hill through the fading light, far too fast, to smother a new wave of anxiety about Rosa.

Orf was standing outside a five-barred wooden field gate. He was carrying a placard that read: SAVE THE SPYRYT OF GLASTO!!! With him were a bunch of people including tho big guy with the didgeridoo and the waitress with the multiple lip rings from The Cosmic Carrot.

On the other side of the gate were two policemen, whose job seemed to be to keep Orf and his friends well away from the council and the MP and all the official guys.

"Woolly?" Orf said to Marco. "Nah, we was wondering where he was, too, actually, son. Woolly's the main man. We need him."

Marco peered over the gate, between the policemen. There was no sign of Woolly on that side, either. Or Nancy. Or Fleri. No sign of anybody he recognized, among the councillors and the people with clipboards and briefcases – except for Sam's old man, Griff Daniel, who was looking kind of self-important in a suit of dark tweed. Most of them wore suits, and one guy, some distance away, even looked a bit like Dad. Weird. Must be the light. It *was* getting ominously dim now – was that a distant crunch of thunder? Maybe Griff Daniel had heard it too, because he stepped forward into the headlights of a big black people carrier and clapped his hands.

"Right then! If my meteologic...if what I knows about the

weather's correct, we're in for a bit of a downpour, so let's get this sorted quick, eh? We've all seen the plans for Avalon World. All we gotter do now is decide if this site's right for a development this big. So I'll introduce you first of all to a gentleman we all know – a local man who's acting as special adviser to Wilde-Hunt. Ladies and gentlemen – Mr. Mervyn Coombes!"

This smooth, salesman-looking guy with a moustache and shiny, gelled hair stepped into the headlights and started telling the councillors what a perfect location this was for the most exciting tourism project ever planned for Somerset. He wiped a hand quickly across the green horizon to show that there were no properties in the area likely to be affected. Nobody would even *see* it until they were almost there, Mr. Coombes said.

Marco noticed how he brushed his arm past Woolly's little cottage as if it wasn't there. Marco was furious. He wanted to shout out, *Don't listen to him!* but he saw one of the policemen looking at him and kept quiet.

"Well," Griff Daniel said when Mr. Coombes had finished. "Far as I'm concerned, this is all just a formality and the chance to have a few free drinks, ha, ha, ha. But let's all stand back for a minute and imagine how great it's gonner look when it's finished – this huge building, with nice stone claddin' and lots o' fountains and stuff, that's gonner tell visitors about our history like it *really* is, with none of this ole rubbish about magic and healin' your aura and all that malarkey, and nobody with rings through their noses like prize bulls!"

A few people in suits were going *ho ho* and nodding and patting each other on the back. Orf looked miserable, and the chain that connected his ear to his nose hung limp. The woman from The Cosmic Carrot shouted out, "You old fascist!" and one of the policemen on the gate growled, "*Watch it, you,*" with some menace.

And the sky, at this moment, was the colour of industrial smoke.

"Right, then," Griff Daniel said. "If nobody else—"

"One moment. If I might just..."

A woman had stepped into the lights. Like most of the others, she had on a dark business suit, and her black hair was pinned up tight to her head. She wore a pale orange silk scarf, which she flicked over her shoulder.

"And you are, Madam?" Griff Daniel said.

"I am...Dr. Cadwallader, formerly Professor of Celtic Studies at the University of Wales, and I think that, before a decision is made..."

Marco gasped. It couldn't be.

But it *totally was.*

"I think, before a decision is made," Eleri said softly, "we should remind ourselves of a few things."

She was actually some kind of distinguished professor? *Eleri?* With the Egyptian headband and the doomy dreams?

"I came to Glastonbury," Eleri said, "after many years studying the ancient history and the mysteries of these islands. For I knew there was only one place where I could come close to the truth."

Thunder. This time it was the real thing, rolling in like a transcontinental lorry. "Make it quick," muttered Griff Daniel.

"I saw a very ordinary little town – run-down, some would say. Perhaps even a little scruffy. Some ancient buildings, but not many left. And its abbey in ruins – hidden away behind small shops."

Griff Daniels cackled. "Be hidden away behind *big* shops when we gets rid o' the rubbish."

"But I soon realized," Eleri said, "that the beauty of Glastonbury – the essence of Avalon – is what one does *not* see. There is a most remarkable mystery here. As the great Dion Fortune said, it is indeed a gateway to the Unseen."

"Piffle," Griff Daniel said.

"A place which, by its very modesty, inspires dreams. Its *modesty* – note that word. For the doors to the great mystery are small doors, with warped timbers and rusting hinges – not plate glass doors which open automatically when money has been paid."

"Trouble with your sort," said Griff, "you want everythin' for nothin'."

Eleri swung round at him, a forefinger pointed. "*Not* for nothing. The way to the light – to the Holy Grail – is often through suffering and hardship. It cannot be bought. It is a journey that takes years, not a day trip. And Avalon World will not even be *that*. It will reduce over two thousand years of history and mystery and magic to a couple of easily forgotten hours...leaving in its wake broken hearts and a heap of scattered ashes...the dust of dreams."

Marco thought the rain had started, then he realized Eleri's face was awash with tears. It must have taken a lot of courage to come out here and face up to the enemy without her cloak and her Egyptian headdress. To go back to being what she used to be, in the hope that it might impress the council and the MP and all the nobs.

He looked at the faces of the people watching her, mainly men but a few women. Some of them looked faintly sneery, some of them looked bored, most of them just looked...blank.

Marco found he was having to blink back his own tears. He looked at Eleri and he thought of Rosa, who might be dead – might have died alone, in the dark – and he couldn't stand any of it any more. He turned away and slipped past Orf and the pathetic protesters and ran away across the field and up the side of a small hill, as if the black and rolling sky was after him.

"Nooooo!!!!"

Marco stopped, up against a high thorn hedge.

A great wail had risen up from behind it.

"I can't do it! I been goin' along with you just to find out where you're comin' from, and now I've worked it out you can get stuffed, far as I'm concerned."

Woolly.

"If I was twenty years younger, look, I'd beat the livin' daylights out of you and take this boy back to that cellar and force him down that hole and not let him out till he had Marco and the girl with him."

Behind the hedge, Marco froze.

"But unfortunately," said a low and lazy voice, half-familiar, "you're *not* twenty years younger, and I don't have time to listen to your fantasies. You've found the iron and the copper, the silver and now this gold ring. I think we're here, at the spot. You alone know how deep it is and I don't want a sacred relic damaged."

"Sacred relic?" Woolly's voice full of outrage. "*Sacred relic?*"

"And you can take it that Jasper will not be going back to that cellar until I see you standing there with the late abbot's brainpan, intact, in your hands. And then perhaps we'll go back together to the entrance of the labyrinth."

It was Roger Cromwell. And somehow Marco knew – and this was like having a ball of cold lead in your stomach – that when Woolly had found the *sacred relic* they would *not* be going back.

He looked along the hedge. It was two or three metres high and it went on for ever, with no sign of a gate anywhere.

"I'll be the Judas Iscariot of Glastonbury!" Woolly howled. "You think I can live with that?"

"Oh, *that's* not a problem," Roger Cromwell said. "Or at least, Judas Iscariot didn't find it a problem."

"He hanged hisself!" Woolly said, and his voice was faint with dismay.

"Precisely. And, as you see, there's no shortage of suitable trees."

"*You—*"

"It's not a bad idea, actually. My friends Mr. Coombes and Mr. Daniel say you've been a traitor to your roots for years – making the wrong kind of friends. And now...now your useful life is as good as over, anyway. Would you like Jasper to run down and fetch you a rope?"

Marco heard Jasper laughing.

They were just mocking Woolly. Playing with him. Marco felt this huge rage building up in his chest like a bonfire. He looked at the thorny hedge – there was a part that seemed a bit thinner than the rest. He remembered the Holy Thorn of Glastonbury. Thorns in this area weren't necessarily nasty.

"*Dig*," Cromwell said.

Marco heard a sob and then the clangy sound of a spade being thrown down onto hard ground and Woolly's voice, scared but determined.

"*Dig it up yourself, you scumbag!*"

There was a moment's silence, then the short, thick, cruel sound of a stabbing blow, followed by a small, defeated noise – *uhhh*.

And in his head Marco saw Woolly sinking slowly to his knees and...

...and, as lightning turned the sky white, he forced himself, in ripping, wrenching agony, through the angry thorns of the glistening hedge.

The Unearthing

It was like the whole world had gone into negative.

Marco's other grandparents, Dad's mum and dad, had a collection of old family photos, black and white, and when you held the negatives up to the light, they looked like this, with the sky dark and faces dark, but people's eyes sometimes eerily white.

Scary, the first time he'd seen those negatives. He'd probably been about four. All the family photos had been of people who were now dead, and he'd thought that this must be what happened when you died – you went into negative.

It had given him awful nightmares; night after night, he'd wake up terrified.

He'd forgotten about that.

Until now.

He thought maybe it was telling him something. About Roger Cromwell and Jasper Coombes.

But he already knew, didn't he? They really *were* negatives. When he stumbled into the field, thorny hedge-tendrils still tearing his clothes and twanging behind him, neither of them moved.

Cromwell's eyes were like stones.

Woolly was the only one in motion, backing up against a tree, holding his stomach where Cromwell had hit him. He looked at Marco and his eyes widened. He started to smile and then stopped, as if he couldn't be really sure that this *was* Marco.

There was this unearthly silence, as all this uncertainty flickered rapidly, like moths, across Woolly's face.

Marco stood there, his hands wet and ripped and smarting. His cheeks and his forehead felt like they were on fire. The hedge hadn't been all that thin, after all, but when he'd found this out it was too late. Now, he saw black blood all over his hands and felt it dripping down his chin. Lightning came again and, in the flash, he saw a glitter of fear in Jasper's eyes and figured he probably looked like...who was that guy in *Macbeth* whose ghost appeared at the dinner table, all dripping blood?

He saw the spade lying in the grass and wondered how quickly he could grab it. A spade was a weapon.

He reached for it.

As a powerful arm came round his neck from behind and wrenched his head back.

"*Hippy-trash,*" Shane whispered in his ear.

"Good boy," Cromwell said. "Hold him." He turned to Woolly. "Looks like a change of plan, Woolaston."

"You...you all right, dude?" Woolly called out.

"Urfff," Marco said, Shane's knuckles boring into the flesh under his chin.

Jasper picked up the spade. It was an old spade, its blade worn sharp. Marco struggled as Jasper advanced on him with the blade out, keen and shiny.

"How'd you get out?" Jasper hissed. "There's no way out of the labyrinth. *There's no way out.*"

"Ummmf," Marco said.

"Let the child speak, Shane." Cromwell came over, with a swishing of his leather pants, and looked down at Marco. "How *did* you get out?"

Shane eased the pressure on Marco's throat. Marco glared up into Cromwell's hard eyes.

"I don't talk to people who call me a child," he said. "*Oooof!*"

With his free hand, Shane had knuckle-punched him in the small of the back. It felt like he'd been stabbed. At the same time, Jasper held the spade to his throat. Through his tear-filled eyes, he saw Woolly rushing forward, then Cromwell grabbing Woolly, hurling him onto the grass.

"Don't be foolish, Woolaston. It doesn't matter how he got

out...he's ours now, and I shall allow Jasper to hurt him unless you deliver to us what we want. You have five seconds to decide and then Jasper will begin. *One...two...*"

"Don't do it, Woolly!" Marco yelled before Shane squeezed his windpipe into silence.

"*Three...*" Cromwell took the spade from Jasper and held it out to Woolly, who was painfully picking himself up, cowering away from the spade, like he was being offered a rope to hang himself. Marco's head was filled with the sound of Woolly crying out, just a few minutes ago, *I'll be the Judas Iscariot of Glastonbury! You think I can live with that?*

"*Four...*" Cromwell glanced at Jasper. Jasper smiled.

Woolly hesitated, looked despairingly across at Marco and then held out a hand for the spade.

"No," Marco howled. "Tell him to stuff it up his—"

"*Five,*" Cromwell said softly, and Jasper hit Marco in the left eye.

Marco's head shot back, and so did his right elbow. He heard an unexpected but satisfying grunt of pain from behind him and he managed to struggle free, backing away towards the hedge, his left eye closed.

"No," he said. "You can't. Woolly, you *can't*! *I'll* do it." He looked at Roger Cromwell. "*I'll* dig up the Dark Chalice for you."

Woolly tried to grab the spade but Cromwell held it above his head. With the spade brandished like an axe and the Tor soaring behind him, he looked like some deranged warrior from the Dark Ages.

"Yes," he said. *"Out of the mouths of babes and sucklings..."*

"Marco," Woolly said urgently. "Listen to me, dude. You mustn't go near it. I'm an ole bloke, I don't have that much to lose. You dig that thing up, you'll be corrupted like these two. You'll be set on the wrong path. Your soul will go black."

"All right," he said to Cromwell. "You win. I'll do it. I'll dig it up for you now, look. Just let the boy go. Let him get away before that thing comes up. Just do that for me, and I'll do whatever you want."

Cromwell thought about the offer, a long finger to his lips. Behind him, light from somewhere silvered the tower on the Tor.

"No," he said. "The child's right. He *should* do it." He held out the spade to Marco.

Marco strode between Jasper and Shane and took the spade. It was heavier than he'd expected and he nearly dropped it, and Shane sniggered.

"Marco..." Woolly had his hands held out, imploring. "Just put the spade down. They want to sacrifice your innocence. That would invest the moment – the moment of *the unearthing* – with even more power, do you know what I'm saying? Put the spade down, dude."

They were in a circle now, around a patch of field big enough to build a shed on. Marco looked up at Woolly, unsure where to put the spade in.

Woolly shut his eyes, obviously didn't want to tell him.

Marco put down the spade and took out his pendulum.

"Well, *well...*" Cromwell said.

The orange pendulum looked murky grey, like it didn't want to work.

Marco held it at chest height in his left hand, instinctively holding out his right hand, palm downwards, over the grass. He began to pace the patch of field, in a slow decreasing circle.

Where is it?

"Marco, no—" Woolly's eyes were open and full of anguish.

But in Marco's world, there was a hollow silence. The gathering of councillors and nobs was only a few minutes' walk away, and yet he couldn't hear them. He couldn't hear anything. Even the birds had stopped singing. In a great, yawning kind of way, it was just as quiet as it had been down in the labyrinth.

He knew he had to do this. The unearthing of the Dark Chalice – he had to take the responsibility for that away from Woolly. He wasn't quite sure why; maybe something to do with the age difference. Woolly would never have the strength to recover from this.

"Look," Cromwell said.

And Marco saw that the pendulum had begun to go round in circles. Anticlockwise. Widdershins.

Negative. The only way it could possibly react to the Dark Chalice.

"Stop there." Cromwell held out the spade to Marco. "Now *dig*."

* * *

When Marco stabbed the spade into the grass, Woolly moaned like it had gone into his foot. Marco drove the spade hard into the ground and took out the first chunk of earth. As he lifted it, he glanced up at the Tor, which seemed closer, its tower haloed, now, in a startling, ethereal, greenish light.

He took out three more spade loads of earth. The blade was very sharp, and the ground yielded easily. The soil seemed to spring onto the spade, as if what lay beneath couldn't wait to be uncovered, and it was surprising how soon he had a hole.

"*Stop!*" Woolly pleaded. "You don't know what you're lettin' out. Just give it to me. Give it to me and get the hell out of here, Marco...*please...*"

"Nobody goes anywhere," Roger Cromwell said, excitement pumping up his voice.

And Marco couldn't stop, anyway. He was locked into a rhythm and his own strength amazed him. Shovelful after shovelful came out of the hole, faster and faster, it seemed, and the mound of earth next to it was already higher than his knees.

Then, in the blackness of the hole, a spark leaped up as the spade clanged against a stone. It was quite a big stone, and he had to lift it out separately.

"Excellent," Roger Cromwell kneeled down with a creak of leather to peer at it. "Contains quartz crystals." He looked at Woolly. "Part of a protective screen for the chalice?"

"Ar...to protect us and the earth from *it*," Woolly said in disgust.

By the time Marco had uncovered three more stones, he

was feeling a weird kind of thrill, a vibration coming up through the soles of his trainers.

And then he hit...plastic?

Black plastic. In fact it looked like...

He leaned into the hole and gripped it in both hands and it suddenly came out in an explosion of soil and clay and there was a sudden blinding flash of lightning that turned everything white, except...the plastic.

He saw pain in Woolly's eyes, but at least he wouldn't be Judas Iscariot, the traitor.

Cromwell screamed in fury. "You put *my chalice* in a *bin liner!*"

"Too good for it, really," Woolly murmured, "but I didn't have much time, look."

It was like this big anticlimax. A bin liner. All five of them stood in a circle looking down at the black plastic bundle, its neck bound with white electrical tape.

"All right," Cromwell said, "open it, Marco."

"*No, don't touch it!*" Woolly made a dive for the bag, but Cromwell seized him from behind and held him back. Woolly struggled and hacked back at Cromwell's legs, but his trainers only skidded down the leather. "Don't make him *do* this. I'll do anything, Cromwell, I'll — "

"We can't stop him, Woolly. He *wants* to do it. He's desperate to get at it. He wants it more than anything because he knows it will bring him *everything*: money...worldy success..."

Marco heard this like it was from a great distance. He was

looking up into the unnatural sky, and that seemed no distance at all because the sky was something that was happening inside his head.

He was dimly aware of being on his knees in the dirt, his fingers scrabbling frantically, what was left of his nails ripping holes in the greasy plastic.

And then something happened, and he saw the Tor as he'd never seen it before.

Wild Hunt

It became, for a moment, transparent, as if it was made of glass.

And yet, no...not glass, something finer than glass. Something like steam. Vaporous, that was the word. He had the impression of something bubbling from the bottom, like chemicals heated in one of those crystal flasks in some old-style laboratory.

And then it went cloudy. The church on top was still a church, still stone, but the pear-shaped hill beneath it was like the inside of one of those glass ornaments you shook and it filled up with powdery snow.

Only this wasn't glass and it wasn't snow and the whole thing only lasted for an instant, and it left Marco shivering and electric, as if whatever had been shaken up inside the Tor was now inside *him*. For just an instant, he was aglow with it. It was like the fifth waveband. Except there was no illusion of floating, just something rising up through his feet, up his spine and into his head, and then...

...then it was gone, and the sombre sky was falling back around him like a dark dust sheet, and he was just...

...just a kid holding up a black plastic bin liner with a...

uuuugh!

...with *the remains of someone's head in it*!

Horrified, he let the bin sack drop back into the hole, and he slid back into the mud, away from it, as Roger Cromwell and Jasper Coombes both turned on him.

When Jasper pushed him, he went over like a cardboard cut-out and just lay there.

All the angry strength that had kept him digging like a demon had drained out of him now, and he felt weak and sapped and empty with relief, and he just lay there in the mud behind the hole, limp, confused, and only dimly aware that something was happening.

It was a sound in the air. At first, that was all it was. Lonely and doleful, like funeral bells, the kind of sound that you weren't sure whether it was something in your ears...until it grew louder and then it was everywhere, as if the sky itself had become taut, like the matt black fabric that was stretched across stereo speakers.

Marco sat up.

And he saw, in a channel of white light under the sooty sky, the hounds coming down from the Tor.

At first, he thought he must be the only one seeing this, because it was like some ancient black-and-white movie with flecks at the corners of the screen. And the picture kept breaking up and coming back, like when you lost the signal on a mobile phone.

That was probably him. He was losing the signal. Too much had happened to him, too quickly, and he was losing it.

It was then that he heard Woolly drawing in his breath.

"What have we done?" Woolly whispered, and Marco wanted to tell him, *You haven't done anything, Woolly, you're one of the good guys, you—*

A thin cry came out of Jasper Coombes. Jasper was on his feet, backing away, his hands out in front of his face, his fingers like claws, kind of *get away, get away...*

Roger Cromwell was standing on the edge of the hole. Marco couldn't see his face, but he wasn't moving. It was like he was frozen to the field.

"See what you've done, Cromwell," Woolly croaked. "See what you've brought down on us." His voice was faint and faraway, as if there was no air to carry it.

"It's an illusion," Cromwell said, but his voice was thin. "It's a phantasm. Jasper, Shane...it won't—"

"'Tis the Wild Hunt," Woolly said. "'Tis *old Wild Hunt!*"

"No. *Nooo!*" Jasper was panting in panic, and the sky sang with the wild, hollow whooping of the hounds. But Marco was sure – he didn't know why – that no one else, no one in the town or in any of the hundreds of places where you could see the Tor, no one who was not on this spot, would be aware of it happening.

"'Tis coming," Woolly cried. "'Tis coming for us. My *God...*"

It was in the distance yet, but Woolly was right: it *was* coming...coming, coming, coming...white eyes and the jagged teeth exposed, riding the thunder across the sky. Down from the sacred hill of the ancients, out of the Land of the Dead...in a dead straight line.

As he scrambled to his feet, Marco found he was grinning like he'd gone insane. "Woolly," he said, "Woolly, it's only..."

He bit off the rest, seeing that Roger Cromwell was very seriously shocked and trying to hide it, and Jasper was blatantly petrified, and Shane...he could just make out Shane in the distance, running and tripping and stumbling towards the gate on the other side of the field. Thunder crashed and split the sky directly overhead, and Marco stood up and felt this shining ripple of animal energy, *sooo* close, now.

Marco smiled.

"You wanted to know how I got out of the labyrinth? *He* brought me out!"

"*Gwyn ap Nudd?*" Woolly reeled back. "For God's sake, Marco—"

"The Lord of the Dead." Marco raised both his arms into

the electric, swirling sky. "He saved me. He brought me out of the labyrinth!"

"Marco..." Woolly breathed. "Oh God, no. You can't be...you can't be *dead.*"

A cry broke in Jasper's throat.

Marco spun round to face him, feeling blood running down his face where one of the cuts from the hedge must have opened up again.

"And now he's coming for *your* soul, Jasper. His hellhounds will tear out your throat and rip your filthy soul from your—"

Jasper screamed and ran through the hole in the hedge that Marco had made, and Marco was so angry he ran after him, as the sky exploded and the rain began, with massive drops that landed like daggers. Marco held up his arms to them in glee, and in his head he heard: *Sam Daniel, my name. These are my dogs.*

"*Yesss!*" Marco howled and burst through the hedge.

Down on the Wilde-Hunt site, the rain had driven the councillors and the MP and the tourist office officials into the big marquee.

It was all done up inside to look like some fancy reception room. It was lit by a chandelier powered by a generator, which you could hear grumbling somewhere like an old lawnmower. But the biggest noise was the rain slamming down on the canvas, and Marco – standing in the entrance, getting his breath back – saw that some of the suits were looking a bit nervous as they sipped their champagne, glancing up at the roof as if it might come bellying in under the weight of the rain.

"All right, everybody!"

Mr. Coombes, the estate agent, Jasper's dad, was standing in the middle of the marquee in front of a big, round table with a white tablecloth holding all these open bottles of champagne and trays of smoked-salmon-type nibbles and four big chocolate gateaus and heaped bowls of strawberries and jugs of cream.

There was an expensive-looking scale model of a big, low stone-covered building surrounded by what looked like a park with plastic trees and plastic fountains. There was also what seemed to be a car park, which was twice the size of the building and the parkland put together. On the edge of it all, like somebody had remembered it at the last minute, was a model of the Tor.

Welcome to Avalon World.

"On behalf of Wilde-Hunt," Mr. Coombes said, "I'd like to offer you all a little modest refreshment and thank you all, once again, for coming. I must, of course, first apologize for our Glastonbury weather which is – ha ha – a little unpredictable. But I suppose that's all part of the, er, so-called *magic* of the place that brings in so many thousands of visitors."

Griff Daniel made a scornful noise.

"The magic that will now, thanks to Wilde-Hunt Developments," said Mr. Coomes, "be contained safely under one roof...so that the people of Glastonbury can at last realize the full tourist potential of our history without any of the, er, unseemly and detrimental side effects, which have been such a regrettable feature of the town for so long. Now, if I may—"

"*No!*"

Jasper Coombes had burst out of the crowd.

A woman screamed.

Jasper looked like...well, like somebody who had come through a hedge, pursued by the Hounds of Hell. His hair was full of leaves and stuff, and there was a red cut across his forehead. His eyes were staring – not staring at anything, just *staring*. He was scattering bits of mud and twigs, and people were looking annoyed and shrinking away from him.

"Jasper," Mr. Coombes hissed. "Not *now...*"

"Dad, you've gotta..."

"Jasper!"

"Please...you've gotta...you've gotta stop it!"

"Don't be stupid, Jasper. Get out of here at once."

"It's evil, Dad!" Jasper clutched at the white tablecloth, leaving these huge black handprints. "The Wild Hunt! It's all *evil!*"

Mr. Coombes put on this lavish smile. "My son is, er, my son is..."

"It's coming to get us. We're going to die!" Jasper sobbed. "*I'm going to die!*"

A lot of people drew a lot of breath.

"Going to die and lose my soul to hell!" Jasper whirled on the crowd, his face all distorted and sheened with sweat. "You'll *all* die! You hear me? You're all going to *die!*"

"Don't be so *utterly stupid,*" Mr. Coombes snapped. "I can't, for the life of me, imagine what—"

"Wilde-Hunt..." Jasper had his hands clawed, and he was shaking them. "Wilde-Hunt are into the occult just like everybody else, only they're stirring up...satanic forces...stuff they can't handle! Stuff *nobody* can handle! I'm serious. You can all stand there drinking your fizz and pretending you don't know what's happening out there, but it's—"

"Get out!" Mr. Coombes pushed Jasper away. "I'll deal with you later. Get *out* of here."

"You don't understand!" Jasper screamed. "I *can't!*"

And when Mr. Coombes tried to grab him, he spun round, stumbled and snatched at the tablecloth.

"I'm not! I'm not going back *out there!*" Jasper ran into the crowd, dragging the tablecloth and everything on it after him. "I *don't want to die!*"

Bottles upturned and rolled over, champagne flowing and hissing. Cream was slurping in the air, strawberries jumping out of their dishes and the chocolate gateau smeared all over the cloth. And women were screaming and sober-suited councillors coming out with words you didn't expect from civic leaders, and people started tumbling towards the exit flap...and somebody must have dragged out a wire because the chandelier started flickering, *off-on, off-on*, and then went out.

Marco caught a brief glimpse of the expensive model of Avalon World, on the floor, splattered into pieces.

And then it was all screaming, clattering chaos, with the raging rain thudding like bullets on the canvas.

And, at some point, Marco, standing just inside the doorway flap, felt a very familiar face come very close to his, smelled a very familiar aftershave and heard a very familiar voice in his ear.

"*This is all down to you, isn't it?*" Dad's voice snarled. "*This disaster – probably the ruination of all our plans – has your name written all over it, Marco.*"

The Watchers...

*H*ad it been Dad? He didn't know.

    Glastonbury played strange tricks on you.

The lights had gone out in the marquee, and there'd been a lot of confusion, everybody swearing and screaming and trying to get out of there. And Marco was getting so used to hearing voices in his head that...he just didn't know.

Yeah, okay, he'd seen a bloke earlier who looked like Dad, but surely if that had been him he'd have hung around. Wouldn't he?

In the end, nobody had hung around.

By the time the rain had stopped and the light had returned

– this amazing electric blue, with the Tor basking in it and looking totally harmless – all the vehicles had gone, and the marquee stood drooping in the middle of the field, looking like it really didn't belong here and could never belong here in a million years.

Just like Avalon World.

That evening, the central committee of the Watchers of Avalon met – for the first time in years, apparently – at Bowermead Hall.

Marco had been a bit nervous, hadn't been sure what to expect. Maybe sinister masked figures sitting around a long table with silver candlesticks. In fact, he was amazed he'd even been invited.

However, although Bowermead Hall had looked ominously vast from the outside, the Watchers of Avalon were meeting in an airy white-walled room full of squashy furniture and beanbags and a white grand piano. The only candles were those big, chunky, coloured ones that smelled of berries and vanilla, and there were books all over the place and crazy pictures painted by people like Nancy.

A bit like Woolly's kitchen, really, only about ten times as big.

"Gosh, yes, *quite* a panic, really," Sam's wife, Diane was saying. "We were jolly lucky, I suppose. Mustn't be caught on the hop like *that* again."

Marco wasn't sure what she meant, but the others seemed to know, especially the women, Nancy and Eleri.

Diane had rung the hospital in Taunton again. It seemed that Teddy had come round and was talking to the police, though Marco reckoned he wouldn't be able to finger his attackers. He suspected they would have been wearing balaclavas. Just a feeling.

The feeling in this room, however, was generally optimistic...in a guarded kind of way.

"*My* feeling," Eleri said, "is that the council will turn down the plan...*this* time. Mud always sticks, and rumours about Wilde-Hunt and dark occultism...well, they might not *believe* it, but they won't want to risk it. They cannot be associated with anything like that. Even Griff Daniel was strutting around saying he'd been misled."

Apparently, a local cameraman had been hired by Wilde-Hunt to record the event for promotional purposes, and had captured the whole disaster on a video, which he'd lost no time in selling to the local TV news. So now most of the region had heard Jasper sobbing about *the evil out there*.

Sam Daniel nodded. "Course if *we'd* accused Wilde-Hunt of bein' satanic we'd have been sued for every penny we got. But nobody's gonner sue a boy of fourteen – especially when his dad's Wilde-Hunt's frontman in town. Brilliant, that was, Woolly."

"All down to Marco," Woolly said. "When we seen...what we seen...well, I was too scared to move. But he was just totally unfazed. Amazing."

Marco didn't think it was *that* amazing that he hadn't been scared of the hounds, seeing as he'd been walking across the fields with them only half an hour or so earlier, but he didn't say anything.

Earlier, Woolly had said there were some things he and Marco had to discuss. Family things.

"And where is the Dark Chalice now, Woolly?" Eleri said.

"Safe, I trust."

She was still wearing her professor's kit, which didn't look right. She was obviously a different person now from when she'd been a university lecturer, and it just looked odd. Even here at Bowermead Hall.

Woolly shifted uncomfortably on his beanbag in the corner by the piano.

"You're right," Eleri said. "Better not to tell us. As long as it's safe."

"Safe as I could make it in the time, Eleri, man," Woolly said. "Just in case Cromwell comes back to try and dig it up for himself."

"Anyone know where *he* is?" Sam Daniel said.

"Don't seem to be around town. When the kid, Jasper, lost his cool, Cromwell...well, when I turned round he'd gone. Likely he realized there was something happenin' here as he couldn't handle. Like a warning from the ancient spirit of Avalon. But he *will* be back."

"And when he returns," Eleri said, "he won't be alone."

"You had a dream about it?" Woolly asked. "Bit of a vision?"

"I merely know..." Eleri's voice went hollow, and it sounded particularly weird coming from someone dressed like a professor. "...that we must reactivate the old shrines and power points. We must make this town glow from within, with a great incandescence – protective light, against the looming dark. The Goddess warns us, she who is Isis, Ceridwen, Mary. She who holds the Grail. Who knows where Arthur sleeps, where lies the sword Excalibur, where the moon and the—"

"So you're sayin' 'tis not over yet," Woolly said.

"Correct," Eleri said. "It's *far* from over."

Deep in the house somewhere, a bell clanged.

"That's the front door," Diane said. "I'll let them in."

When they'd told Marco about her, he hadn't believed it. He'd *wanted* to believe it, but he was thinking they were lying to him, not wanting to upset him – the way parents were inclined to say the guinea pig had gone back to live with his brothers and sisters in a guinea-pig colony, when in fact...

So he'd been tense about it. Fearing what he *hadn't* been told.

She'd arrived with her big, bearded dad, who strode into Bowermead like he was raiding the joint, and also her mother, who Marco hadn't seen before. She looked a bit like Rosa – big eyes. Diane, who seemed kind of scatty and all-over-the-place but had, he noticed, very *watchful* eyes, suggested Rosa and Marco might like to go into the kitchen, get themselves a couple of Cokes from the fridge.

Meaning the Watchers of Avalon wanted to talk to Mr. Wilcox.

* * *

The kitchen turned out to be the size of Woolly's entire cottage, and you could have parked a Mini in the fridge. Marco sat on a tall stool and just stared at her, standing there in front of him.

Standing in front of him.

Like on both legs.

No crutches, no bandages. No whatever they called a Zimmer frame for kids.

Okay, maybe she was a little pale. He was probably pale, too. Big deal.

"I don't understand," he said. "You were trapped. Your legs had gone dead. *You couldn't feel your legs!*"

She shrugged. "And then...somehow, I could. I could feel them again. And I just...I just slid them out from under the rock and rubbed them for a while and then I just went through the little passage, calling out the whole way, because it was dark, and Diane heard me, and..."

She shrugged again.

"So that was it?" Marco said.

"Yeah."

Marco said, "Tell me something. Do I *look* like some kind of stupid, wide-eyed complete...innocent?"

"I try not to judge people by appearances," Rosa said.

She was wearing a black skirt and a skimpy cotton top. She looked older, somehow. He felt very aware, maybe for the first time, of what he must look like, with the three strips of Elastoplast Nancy had slapped over the cuts on his face made by the thorns. And he was sure he must smell of this disgusting herbal ointment she'd spread like butter all over him.

"That's that, then," he said.

He felt empty. Lonely. Offended, somehow.

Sometimes you just got things wrong – especially about people. It was clear that something had changed and he and Rosa had nothing much to say to one another. He looked out of the window at a stretch of lawn where a peacock was taking an evening stroll.

"*What?*" Rosa said suddenly.

"Huh?"

"What are you thinking?"

He swallowed some ice-cold Coke before answering. He couldn't look at her.

"Well, I was just wondering if...maybe you'd lied to me about not being able to feel your legs. Just to, like, make me go off on my own. Just to...get rid of me."

"Why would I?"

"Because, um, I was beginning to annoy you. Being a wimp and claustrophobic and stuff."

There was a silence.

Rosa climbed onto the stool next to his. "I really *couldn't* feel my legs. My legs were dead."

"So what happened in between when you couldn't feel your legs and when you could? What were you doing?"

"Talking to somebody."

Marco thought about her dad. "You mean like...God?"

"Not...exactly. This was someone I used to be, you know,

terrified of. But this time I couldn't get away. Couldn't even *turn* away. I couldn't...do anything...but listen."

"We're talking about the monk?"

"Mmm."

"You *talked* to him?"

"I, like... You find there's a way of talking to someone where you don't actually...talk. You just go really still inside, and you suddenly know what they're saying. I don't think I'd...ever been that still before. Inside. You know what I mean?"

Marco wondered if he really did know.

"His name was Richard," Rosa said. "I think."

"The monk."

"Whatever," Rosa said.

This didn't sound like the monk who'd stitched up Abbot Whiting by planting the chalice and then sold his soul totally to evil. But then why would it be?

"And what were you talking about?"

"That's the weird thing," Rosa said. "I don't remember. I just remember feeling incredibly...you know, relaxed. And he was talking to me, very softly. Almost a whisper. And then, a bit later, when he'd gone, I found I could move my legs, and I just...eased them out from under the stone."

Marco didn't know what to say. He seemed to remember that the abbot's first name had been Richard, but he wasn't entirely sure.

"Cool," he said.

* * *

What they did next was entirely legit.

The way Marco saw it, it was a fundamental educational tool. In fact, most of the essential data he'd gathered about the workings of the adult world had been gathered this way.

Diane had even left the door open a crack, so all they had to do was keep extremely quiet as they squatted on the mat outside.

Sounded like the atmosphere in there, to put it mildly, was heated.

"Look at you!" Rosa's dad was raging. "All of you! You're supposed to be...well, *some* of you are supposed to be responsible people with a certain stature in this community! All I'm saying is, how can you *possibly* expect someone like *me* to swallow this blasphemous rubbish? I'm a *Man of God*."

"And, unfortunately, also a bit of a pompous git," Woolly said.

There was the sound of a big man leaping out of a chair.

"Siddown, Dave," Sam Daniel said. "One thing the clergy in Glasto gotter learn, look, is to be a bit flexible."

"You mean to *accept paganism!*"

Diane said, "Mr. Wilcox, this is absolutely nothing to do with paganism or Christianity. It's the way she is. Your daughter is a *sensitive*. Look, I've had a good, long chat with Rosa, and it's clear that she has some of the same problems I had at her age. I say problems, because at that age they certainly *are*...especially if one's father preaches a brand of Christianity which is somewhat...narrow."

"In other words," Eleri said, "Rosa is a natural psychic and you've been suppressing it."

"That's nonsense! And *you*...as an educated woman...you expect me to sit here and accept the idea of having a daughter who...who *sees things that aren't there*?"

"The alternative, Mr. Wilcox, is to have a daughter with severe and worsening psychological problems. *Because* she's been brought up with the belief that anything psychic is wicked, her mind has set up its own screening mechanism. As soon as she begins to experience something other-wordly, it kicks in and forces her to go back and repeat the action she was doing when the feeling came over her. She does this four times, at the end of which the feeling has gone away. Do you understand what I'm talking about? OCD, Mr. Wilcox. Obsessive Compulsive Disorder is her subconscious defence mechanism against becoming someone she's afraid her own father would not want anywhere near him."

"Bottom line is you're messing up her mind, man," Woolly said. "Your own daughter. 'Tis mental cruelty."

Mr. Wilcox said nothing, but Marco could hear him breathing like a steam train in an old movie.

Eleri said, "The situation became acute when you brought Rosa to Glastonbury, which has a far higher...shall we say, psychic vibration...than anywhere else in these islands. Her life became intolerable. Especially living in a building which had become a psychic battleground between two opposing forces – the sanctity of the Abbey ruins and the foulness which lingered in the labyrinth and found an outlet through The Emporium of the Night."

"It's *all* foulness to me," Mr. Wilcox said.

"You have so much to learn," Eleri told him.

Diane said, "Rosa's just come through a crisis, in more ways than one. She was placed in a situation she couldn't escape from. Trapped in the labyrinth, she was forced to slow down her vibrations and...let something in. Something which, in the darkness of the labyrinth, brought healing and, in the end, freedom. Without it, I truly think she'd be dead."

There was a very long silence. Marco and Rosa looked at one another. Rosa looked a bit apprehensive, like she was wondering what she'd become.

Marco remembered the things she'd seemed to see in the underground temple. Things he *hadn't* seen, like the smoky cupped hands, waiting to receive something – probably the Dark Chalice. He wondered what else she might have seen over the years if her mind hadn't given her Obsessive Compulsive Disorder to divert her attention from these... visions.

It was hard to imagine which was worse: having OCD or being psychic.

She was going to need help. Maybe Eleri...

"What are we to do?" Rosa's dad's voice. And this time there was a wobble under it. "What can I do?"

Marco reckoned the reverend had been crying, but he didn't say anything about that to Rosa, now or later.

A voice he didn't recognize, probably Rosa's mum, said, "I think we all have a lot to learn."

* * *

Later, when it was going dark and everybody came out, chatting and stuff, ready to go home, Marco stood on the edge of a lawn the size of an airport, looking up at the Tor.

The Tor looked blue and misty and, frankly, a bit smug.

"All right, pal?" Sam Daniel had wandered over.

"Yeah. Cool."

"Must feel a bit strange for you – a London kid."

"Can't believe I've only been here a couple of days," Marco said. "It seems like...half my life."

"Ar, when things start happening in Glasto, they create their own time frame."

"What's that mean?"

"No idea, pal. Eleri said it."

"Ah. Right."

"Bonkers that woman."

"You reckon?"

"No."

They both looked at the Tor. It had changed colour, was kind of mauve now.

"Anyway, thanks Sam," Marco said.

Sam groaned. "For Gawd's sake, all I did was pull you out the well. I mean, I wasn't gonner leave you down there, was I? Though I might just throw you back in if you thank me one more time."

"No, I meant...you know...the thing with the dogs?"

"What?"

"Driving the dogs down from the Tor, during the thunderstorm? Totally scaring the pants off Cromwell and

Jasper? Particularly Jasper. Luckily, I realized it must be you, so I was cool with it. So, like, I really laid it on for Jasper – like I was part of it. Like I was a big mate of Gwyn ap Nudd, Celtic Lord of the Dead. And he's like, *wooooh...aaaggh...keep away from me*! It was...just...sooooo brilliant!"

"I'm sure *you* know what you're on about, Marco," Sam said. "But the fact is, my hounds are absolutely scared stiff of thunder."

"Huh?"

The Tor seemed to shiver in the mist.

Or maybe it was Marco.

"The whole time that storm was on," Sam said, "they were all cowering under the shed. Every one of them."

Marco went totally cold. "Wh...?"

"Sounded like a nice idea, mind," Sam said.

...of Avalon

That night, Woolly came up to Marco's room.

Marco was at the window, with the light off. There was a soft glow over the Tor which might have been starlight. Whatever, it somehow lit the room.

The orange pendulum lay on the window sill, curled up in its chain.

Marvin, the little stuffed rabbit, lay at the bottom of the bed, and Woolly picked him up.

"Had him all your life, eh?"

"Kind of a sentimental thing," Marco mumbled, a bit embarrassed. "I'm not sure why. I can't even remember who gave him to me."

"Your mother, I expect," Woolly said.

"Possibly."

"At least, it was your mother we sent him to."

Marco turned away from the window. "What?"

"By the time you was born, Alison wasn't speaking to us, look. But we wanted to give you something, our only grandchild, and we hoped she'd pass it on." Woolly held Marvin up. "Nancy made him."

Marco felt close to tears.

"If you unstitch him up the back," Woolly said, "you'll find a tiny little pebble amongst all the stuffing. A Glasto pebble, from the Tor. Idea being that maybe the pebble, one day, would...you know..."

"Find its way back," Marco whispered, all choked up.

And now he was remembering the first time he'd seen the Tor, from Dad's car – that feeling that he'd seen it before...*if only in dreams.*

When he was little, Marvin the rabbit had been on his pillow, every night.

Oh, wow...

"We always hoped Alison might bring you herself, one day," Woolly said. "I never thought that when you finally turned it up, it'd be with..."

"My dad."

Woolly said nothing. He sat down on the bed.

"My dad's in with Wilde-Hunt, isn't he?" Marco said. He'd been avoiding even asking himself this particular question, but suddenly it seemed easier to talk about. "That's why he brought me, right?"

"He wanted a reason to come and see us," Woolly said quietly. "Maybe find out how to persuade us to sell our land. And maybe..."

"...maybe to use me as a spy."

"It's possible. I'm sorry about this, dude."

Marco looked out of the window. The sky over the Tor seemed to be full of complicated star patterns.

"What's going to happen now, Woolly?"

"Well, looks like your dad's gone back to London. When your mother comes home from the States, he'll probably have some explaining to do. But I expect he'll have his story all worked out."

"He's a lawyer."

"Exactly," Woolly said.

Marco would consider the implications of all this...maybe tomorrow.

"So I can stay here..."

"For a few weeks, anyway, I reckon," Woolly said.

A few weeks.

He'd only been here a few days, and it was like...like all the important things in his life had happened in those few days.

He picked up the pendulum. It seemed to be glowing with an inner light of its own.

And in Glasto...

He looked out at the Tor.

In Glasto, a few weeks could be like...for ever.

The End...

...or is it?

Could Rosa really be in contact with an alternative father figure? Is this, in fact, Abbot Richard Whiting, executed on the Tor in 1539? And what will Dave Wilcox make of *that*?

What, meanwhile, will the analytical Josh make of Glastonbury and the art of dowsing, when circumstances compel him to spend a week with Marco at Woolly's?

How will Marco react to the discovery of his dad's role with Wilde-Hunt? And which side will his mother be on when she returns from America to find out that her son is living with her estranged parents and halfway to being *one of them*?

And did you *really* think the Dark Chalice was as simple as a jug cobbled together from old bones?

If you thought things couldn't get any worse, think again – Marco's next encounter with the ancient spirits of Glastonbury is coming soon...

Acknowledgements

If you don't live near Glastonbury and didn't know already, it is, of course, a real place. And the Tor is just as magical. And they *do* say that Joe 'Mathea came here with the Holy Grail.

In fact there are lots of other fascinating legends on The Isle of Avalon that Marco may well encounter.

Don't go looking for the Dark Chalice, however. Only Marco and Woolly and their friends (and enemies) know about that. It's safer that way.

Anyway, several people helped me with crucial background information, so thanks go to...

Geoffrey Ashe, author of *King Arthur's Avalon* and *Mythology of the British Isles*; Paul Devereux, who's written loads of books about mysterious happenings; Steve Wakefield, who runs a bookshop in Glastonbury High Street, just far enough from the former Emporium of the Night to feel safe after dark; and Jamie Munro-Nann, who sold us some crystals from a shop in the Glastonbury Experience Arcade which, as he showed us, backs on to the Abbey just like...another shop.

Oh, and there's Geraldine Richards, who knows all kinds of curious things. And, of course Richard Bartholomew, Ced Jackson, Helen Lamb and John Moss from the British Society of Dowsers in Malvern.

And thanks for brilliant edits to Megan Larkin and my wife, The Cat.

Thom Madley